# THE SERPENT BEARER

## KARA FORD

Printed in the United States of America
First Edition

Published by Kara Ford
www.karafordmusic.com

Editor: Sarah Collingwood
www.sarahac36.wordpress.com

Proofreading: Bryony Leah
www.bryonyleah.com

Cover Design: Hylton Mayne
hmayne4@gmail.com

Interior Formatting: Champagne Book Design
www.champagnebookdesign.com

For a more immersive experience, check out Kara's original soundtrack for *The Serpent Bearer* at www.karafordmusic.com, where you'll find music written for specific scenes and characters!

*Dedicated to first responders, health-care workers, and anybody who has struggled during the 2020 pandemic. Your light shines bright for all to see.*

*Finally, this book is dedicated to my mom, dad, and brother; the best serpent bearers I know.*

*Love you guys.*

# PART I

*"God, grant me the serenity to accept the things I cannot change,*
*The courage to change the things I can,*
*And the wisdom to know the difference."*

—Reinhold Neibuhr

One

*September*

Danica Torres's legs burned. *Damn, how much did I eat out this summer?* Every stride felt like fire shooting up her calves.

The unusual scorching heat for a Californian September evening only added to her discomfort as she panted around USC's Soni McAlister field.

"Hurry it up, girls!" Coach Winston's low voice bellowed from across the track.

Dani's muscles clenched tighter, sweat dripping down her forehead as Haley, the lacrosse team captain, jogged up beside her. "Is the bet still on?" Haley smirked, her brown ponytail bouncing behind her.

"Shut up," Dani huffed between breaths. Always one to revel in Dani's misery, Haley had of course bet that the team wouldn't touch their lacrosse sticks until October. She *loved* competition as much as Dani, and Dani supposed it was why they were such good friends. "Winston can't keep it up for much longer," Dani panted. "Look at us—we're dying."

"You mean *you're* dying." Haley laughed and ran ahead as Dani's pace slowed.

Dani ignored her friend's jab. Everyone knew Dani had been the one most out of shape since practices resumed weeks ago, though she didn't want to admit it.

Winston, the new head coach, had been handing their asses to them for nearly a month. It wasn't as if Dani and the team hadn't been warned—the ex-Florida lacrosse coach's drill-sergeant reputation preceded her across the National Collegiate Athletics Association—but Dani thought they'd at least have moved on from strenuous, non-stop conditioning by now.

Such a stupid, naïve thought.

So far, Haley was winning the bet. Coach Winston had drilled the team nonstop with suicides, weight lifting, laps around campus, and other Olympian feats—and not a single lacrosse stick had been touched.

It took all the pride Dani could muster to not collapse when she finally passed Winston and the other four men and women assistant coaches at the end of the track. She bent over pathetically as she tried to catch her breath, her arms and legs drenched with sweat and her heart pounding a mile a minute.

"Seven minutes, thirty seconds, Torres," Winston murmured, her tall, athletic figure towering over Dani. She shook her head, wisps of blond hair loosening from her ponytail and framing her stern face. "That's high school pacing! We've been conditioning for over a month now. You need to be under seven fifteen by the end of next week."

The other girls squatting in the grass a few yards away turned their heads uncomfortably, and Dani's face burned red. As if losing a bet against Haley wasn't already bad enough! But even without Winston's comments, Dani knew she looked pitiful. She was hands-over-head exhausted and out of breath like someone who hadn't run in years. The freshmen were probably thinking she had no business wielding a full scholarship on USC's reputable women's lacrosse team.

Winston spun on her heel and addressed the rest of the girls with a sharp tone while the other coaches looked on. "All right, ladies. Don't be late tomorrow. At 4:30 sharp, I'll be splitting you off into groups for more conditioning and ladder drills. You need to work on your footwork."

Haley shot Dani a satisfied smirk as the rest of the team dispersed, but Dani's mind wasn't on their wager. *You need to work on your footwork.* The phrase nagged at a memory Dani kept locked away somewhere deep inside her; a memory that ignited a fuse of rage, guilt, and shame.

And then a familiar voice echoed in her head: *Failure after failure after failure…*

Images threatened to coalesce: the pitch-black darkness of that night, the bloodstained plaid shirt, and the glow of a car's headlights. And then the sounds: the raspy breathing, the sound of a distant siren, the bloodcurdling scream in the distance…

She started to sway and bit her tongue, the sharp pain bringing her focus back to the clean-cut grass of the lacrosse field.

"Damn, girl. You are *really* out of shape." Haley crossed Dani's line of sight with a puzzled expression. "You okay? You look like you're gonna pass out."

Dani blinked and glanced around the now vacant track, the fading daylight causing long shadows to spill across the field. The coaches and the rest of the girls were already midway back to the locker room.

"Yeah, I…don't know what happened. I think I just got a little sick." Dani scratched her cheek. Everything had been going fine until now. A small relapse was nothing, right?

Still, her heartbeat raced, and her senses were hyper-alert as if she was back in that dark, terrible memory.

*Just keep breathing. You're fine. Suck it up.*

Dani was quick to change the topic. "Don't get so smug with yourself about the bet. You're not gonna win!"

Haley slanted her thin eyebrows and blew a loose strand of hair out of her face. "I mean, there's still time to back out if you want to. October's almost here, and you know I'm gonna win." She winked, and Dani snorted with an aggressive roll of her eyes.

The two of them picked up their water bottles and lacrosse sticks and headed across the darkening track toward the locker room. A few underclassmen guys were sitting on the bleachers as the two of them approached. The same three guys had been coming to their practices at least twice a week since school started, ogling the girls during their drills. She could feel their eyes latch onto her as Dani and Haley passed the bleachers.

"…looked like she almost fainted."

The snickers that erupted halted Dani in her tracks. The stab of despair and shame and loneliness in that moment came from that same dark place she'd almost fallen into a few minutes ago—a place she'd told herself she'd never go back to, because it was a long-forgotten thing of the past.

Those ignorant douchebags had no right to take her back there.

She clenched her fists, that familiar defense mechanism of fury flooding her insides, but a soft tug on her arm cooled her emotions.

"Just ignore those assholes," Haley whispered. It was a few more seconds before Dani finally swallowed her emotions and resumed her route to the locker room, Haley pulling her along.

*Calm down, Dani. Just keep breathing.*

*Breathe.*

Their taunting grins drilled into the back of her skull during each step she took, and she was thankful Haley was there to keep her moving.

Dani glanced at her smartwatch as they entered the locker room. 6:20 p.m. *Shit.* She still had a ton of reading to do for sociology, but her body groaned for a deep, relaxing sleep after another grueling lacrosse practice.

Too bad she hadn't majored in something simple, like a normal person. A year and a half from now, she would finally receive a BA in Health Promotion and Disease Prevention. But even after graduation, her life would be chained down for another four years of med school— if she got in.

But of course she would get in. She had to.

She promised.

And it was a promise she couldn't break.

*The fresh pine tree scent of the forest filled Dani's nostrils as she leaned out the window of her dad's red pickup. They were coasting down a long, winding dirt road toward the outskirts of Helena, Montana. The edge of a small creek*

*peeked out of the shadows as they came closer to her parents' large two-story house.*

*Dani would have enjoyed the scenery in any other scenario, but right now, she was struggling to hold back her anger. Her dad was purposely driving in the wrong direction.*

*"…you'll just have to tell them you aren't coming. You need to work on your footwork," Francisco Torres's gravelly voice scolded from the driver's seat with the hint of a Spanish accent.*

*"I practiced a ton yesterday! I'm sick of you chauffeuring me around like a guarded princess."*

*"You still need more practice," he scolded. "More scouts are coming to the Helena tournament in a few weeks…" The truck picked up speed as it continued driving down the road away from the theater, away from her date, Ethan, who would soon be wondering why she ditched.*

*Her anger trickled into a boiling pit of rage in her stomach.*

*Then she smelled it. The metallic smell of blood dripping from her hands. A plaid, wrinkled shirt soaked in red. She couldn't remember what color the shirt was originally…*

*And she heard it. The constricted sound of someone gasping for breath. A bloodcurdling scream in the distance spiked the hairs on the back of her neck.*

*The cold, foggy night air rattled her bones—*

Dani's body stirred from a cool breeze of air bathing her skin. She jerked awake, breath labored, heart racing, and frantically scanned her surroundings—a familiar plush couch, the coffee table and TV that made up a small living room… She was in her townhouse apartment.

She stiffened as a wetness dripped down her hands, and her eyes crept down with horror. It was only sweat.

*Just breathe. You're fine. Calm down.*

*Breathe.*

She tried to relax as her mind slowly put the pieces back together. She recollected biking home after practice, eating a quick bowl of ramen, and falling asleep on the couch, too exhausted to move.

It was just a nightmare.

Just a damn nightmare.

No sooner had Dani's heart slowed to a normal pace than her stomach lurched. *No, no, no. I can't be having nightmares again.*

Cold air still tickled her skin, and Dani turned around

apprehensively to see one of her roommates, Emma, carefully closing the front door behind her, a bag of groceries in one hand.

"Oh, sorry, did I wake you?" The Salvadoran brushed back her long, dark hair before setting the grocery bag on the countertop. "We were out of a few things, so I thought I'd run by Target after class…"

Still reeling from her nightmare, Dani took a deep breath and tried her best to respond in a relaxed tone. "It's okay. I needed to be woken up anyways. I forgot I needed to shower." She stood abruptly and grabbed her backpack and duffle bag by the couch. Even as she tried to keep her face stoic, the terrible, haunting images followed her all the way up the stairs and into her room.

*It was only a bad dream. Just a single, harmless bad dream.*

*Get over yourself.*

*September*

D ANI'S SLEEP-CRUSTED EYES JOLTED OPEN TO THE INCESSANT blare of her alarm clock. She slammed her fist on the snooze button with a yawn, squinting in the morning light seeping through her window. She had never slept so well in her life.

And no nightmares.

She blinked happily at the poster montage of anime characters smiling at her from the wall on her left side. Her eyes drifted beside it to the huge board of lacrosse memorabilia: medals, pennants from top lacrosse college teams across the nation, pictures from her time playing with the Helena Lacrosse Club… The scrap board was a daily reminder of all the countless hours of training it took to land her a scholarship, and her goal of leading the team to a PAC-12 championship.

This was the year; Dani could feel it in her bones. The NCAA ranked USC women's lacrosse as seventh this year—the highest they'd been in a long time.

She sat up and stretched, her eyes halting on the textbooks laying on her bedside table. She slumped backward with a groan.

Of course she forgot to finish her homework.

*Well, shit. Junior year is starting off just great, five weeks in.*

Hopefully, there would be time to catch up on the readings later.

Her hands darted to her phone on her desk, and three messages from her mom flashed across the screen. Dani had forgotten to call her last night.

*Double shit.* That was also something she'd worry about later.

She slipped out of bed and sifted through her closet. After pulling on a cute yellow dress and white Vans, she jotted on some mascara and performed a final assessment in her closet mirror.

The dress shaped her slim 5'9" figure nicely. All of those hard lacrosse workouts had been worth something, at least. Her arms were a little thicker now due to all the weight lifting Winston had them doing, and her core was flatter than it had been last season.

She shrugged and stuffed some track clothes into her duffle bag, grabbed her backpack, and said goodbye to a shirtless Channing Tatum poster by her window.

Carolyn trudged out of the bathroom, nearly running into Dani in the hallway. "Morning," her roommate yawned, her green eyes sagging underneath a mess of frazzled red hair. She wore the same loose cat T-shirt and sweatpants she always did for bed, taking care to hide her heavy midsection.

"Were you studying late again? School has barely started!" Dani exclaimed with a smile.

Carolyn's lip curved, but her eyes remained half-closed. "Says the one who never studies."

Dani rolled her eyes. "Whatever. I wouldn't want you to fail your pop quiz on the third week of school."

Carolyn's tight features loosened into a smile. "Hey, it happens sometimes!" She waved a hand and brushed past Dani down the hall.

A flicker of a moment passed where Dani contemplated telling her about the flashback and the nightmare; Carolyn was the only person besides Dani's parents who knew about her past. But that would only lead to Dani explaining that she had stopped taking her medication, and Carolyn would most likely be appalled…

Dani bit her lip. No, there was no reason to worry Carolyn. Yesterday was the first flashback she'd had in a long time, and she had slept fine last night anyway! For all Dani knew, things were still okay…

She scratched her cheek and headed down the stairs, eager for some breakfast.

Alisha must have gotten home late because her psychology books and backpack were sprawled out on the coffee table.

Dani entered the kitchen, where Emma stooped lazily against the counter, pouring coffee grinds in her bright blue PJs. She looked up and grinned, displaying a set of perfect, white teeth.

"Oh, hey." Her brown eyes widened as she scanned Dani's figure. "Cute dress!"

"Thanks. That's what I was going for." Dani beamed, Emma's compliment shoving the memory of yesterday's flashback further away in her mind. She snagged a box of frosted flakes from the cabinet, then a bowl and spoon, before plopping into a chair at the kitchen table.

Emma joined her with a cup of freshly brewed coffee a minute later and offered a shy smile, her eyes shining. "So, Chase from my social sciences class invited me to a frat bowling party next Saturday night, but I don't want to go alone. Think you'd want to join?"

The corner of Dani's mouth perked up. "Ahh, making moves already, huh?" She dug into her frosted flakes, contemplating Emma's invitation. In truth, Dani hadn't been to a frat party since freshman year, and there was a good reason for that. But maybe it had been long enough…

She grinned as she met Emma's hopeful eyes. "I think Winston is having us do a scrimmage that day, but if it doesn't go too late, that sounds awesome."

Relief washed over Emma's face as she sipped her coffee. "Awesome! I'm really not great at these things—parties. And no, I'm not making any *moves*."

Dani cracked a lopsided smile as she chewed her cereal. "We'll see about that," she said with a wink. Emma was blatantly unaware of how frequently she turned the heads of more than a few guys. Long, dark hair framed her brown Salvadoran cheeks, complemented by dark lashes, full lips, and a friendly gaze. The fact that she was bilingual gave her extra points; people were usually surprised to learn that Spanish was her first language when her English held no trace of an accent. Dani herself understood a bit of Spanish thanks to her dad, but couldn't really speak it.

Emma shook her head. "Chase is just a friend. Calm down." She failed to hide the blush crawling up her cheeks, though, as she raised her mug to her lips.

After breakfast fifteen minutes later, Dani wheeled her weathered mountain bike across the living room from the back porch, stepping through the front door to meet a blinding, warm sun. Such was typical weather in Southern California, she'd come to learn.

She hopped on her bike and sped along 23rd St., turned right onto Hoover, and continued down past the small shops that made up the Village just north of campus. Students rode beside her on motorized skateboards, bikes, and scooters, cutting into the street and irritating drivers as she navigated around cars blocking the bike lane.

Los Angeles was definitely a change from her quiet hometown on the outskirts of Helena, Montana. It had taken Dani a while to get used to the bustle of traffic and crowded sidewalks; all of her neighbors in Helena had been few and far apart. While Los Angeles had an exciting, energetic atmosphere, she sometimes missed the peaceful, colorful landscapes of her hometown.

USC was only a few blocks away from downtown, which meant it sat smack dab in a higher crime area. Dani's mom had freaked during freshman year when they saw the graffiti, bars on shop windows, and a few alleys of homeless tents. Luckily, Dani had so far survived two years without a scratch in this polluted, dense hub of people.

Dani biked through USC's north gate and swerved around the steady trickle of students, admiring the campus's rich scenery like she did every day. Marble fountains scattered the major intersection pathways, and the redbrick buildings provided a nice backdrop against the small grass fields and red and gold flowers. Students swung in hammocks between trees and sprawled on the grass—something Dani never seemed to have the time to do amid her busy schedule.

She pulled her bike in front of the Dornsife building and hiked up the steps to her first class of the day—writing. The room was full when she entered, but her designated chair was vacant as usual beside Dakota, a well-dressed sophomore with curly hair and dark skin. He pushed back his glasses and offered a timid smile as Dani plopped down beside him, discarding her duffle bag and backpack by her ankles.

"Good morning, folks," Dr. Nichols greeted, strolling to the front of the room. He was a thin man in his forties, looking sharp as always with his burgundy blazer and dark pants. "I hope you're ready for an exciting week." Nichols opened a binder on his podium and raked the class with his whiskey eyes. "Anyone ever heard of this guy named Shakespeare?"

A few lame chuckles erupted.

Nichols grinned. "I see we have some people familiar with the guy…"

Dani sat through the professor's monotonous lecture, bouncing her leg impatiently as she stared through the window at the bustling students outside. Taking a boring G.E. this late in her schooling probably wasn't the best idea…

As her focus waned, yesterday's haunting flashback images flooded her mind, leaving a sour taste in her mouth. Lacrosse practice had been going on for three weeks now, so why were there suddenly triggers? It had been two over months since she'd stopped taking her meds—

She blinked as a hand darted in front of her face. Dakota was waving at her. "Dani? We're supposed to partner up and choose a Shakespeare play to analyze."

Nichols was probably the only professor on campus who made his students partner up and sit in the same seats every week like high school kids.

Dani rubbed her eyes and forced a smile. "Okay. Which play do you want to do? *Hamlet? King Leer? The Merchant of Venice?*"

"Uh, I was thinking *Julius Caesar.*" Dakota flipped open his laptop. "One second while I pull it up…"

Dani smiled. "No need. *'Cowards die many times before their deaths; The valiant never taste of death but once. Of all the wonders that I yet have heard, It seems to me most strange that men should fear; Seeing that death, a necessary end, Will come when it will come.'*" She stroked a pencil carving on her desk. "Shakespeare uses a lot of elegant chiasmus, like when he turns Brutus's phrase around to call upon 'bad strokes,' yadda yadda. There you go."

Dakota's jaw dropped as he stared at his laptop. "Holy shit. That was verbatim."

Dani shrugged. "Everyone studied *Julius Caesar* in high school—it's nothing new."

He scratched his dark arms. "That's…still impressive. I've never remembered any Shakespeare passages *that* well."

Dani shrugged. Shakespeare was nothing. Dakota would be *really* impressed to hear her recall all the masses for each element's isotope on the periodic table or see her write out a proof of Einstein's theory of relativity by memory.

The thing was, everyone thought having a near-perfect memory was a wonderful, amazing ability. But they didn't think of the drawbacks. They didn't know how bad it could really be; how having such a *great*, enviable gift could cause you so much pain; how it could make you relive your worst memories in excruciatingly accurate detail…

She and Dakota whizzed through their assignment, deciding to kill time by analyzing two more plays before Nichols finally dismissed them. Dani bolted out of class, hopped on her bike, and rode past the Tommy Trojan statue to the food court for her quick lunch break. The tight half-hour gap between classes was the only time she had to eat until dinner after lacrosse practice.

She trudged into the long, winding queue for Panda Express and tapped her foot impatiently, glancing around for an open table.

A familiar handsome face caught her eye. Dustin Mottley, her mentor for med school, sat in his scrubs at a corner booth picking at a salad.

The sight of the fourth-year med student drew a grin from her lips. *What is he doing here?*

After winding her way through the queue and finally paying for her entrée, Dani tossed her hair over her shoulder and strutted over to Dustin's table with her lunch. "Is this seat taken?" she asked with a smirk, sliding into the booth across from him before he could answer.

His head shot up, eyebrows arching, before recognition dawned on his face. His lips teased upward. "Hey! How's it going? It's been a while." His tousled brown bangs were gelled up as usual, but he'd let a bit of stubble grow along his jawline since she last saw him for their first mentor meeting this past summer. And of course, he still had the same piercing blue eyes and lazy, crooked smile.

"I'm good. What are you doing on campus? Isn't Keck downtown?" She opened her Styrofoam box and frowned as the orange chicken slid through her weak chopsticks grip. She failed two more times before giving up and resorting to her fork.

Dustin watched her amusedly. "Yeah, I actually don't start till 2:00 on Thursdays for my current clerkship. I came by campus to say hi to Dr. Turner."

"Ah, gotcha."

Dr. Turner was one of Dani's pre-med professors; the same person who had recommended Dustin as a mentor when she mentioned she'd be applying to med school. Turner taught several courses in the same pre-med sequence, so Dani was taking him again this semester for organic chemistry.

A group of girls at the next table burst out laughing at something, earning them a glare from Dani as she raised her voice for Dustin. "How are your studies going?"

He took a sip of his soda before responding. "Everything's good. A ton of research, shadowing, and patient trials. But I got into USC's anesthesiologist residency program for this summer."

Dani's brows rose. "Oh, wow, that's awesome!"

"Yeah, I was thrilled when I found out." His lips tugged upward as he stabbed a tomato with his fork and popped it into his mouth. "How's junior year going for you? Or are you shitting on everything as usual?"

She rolled her eyes. "Wow, your motivating mentor-ness is *glowing*. I think I'm gonna tear up." She reached a hand to her cheek and brushed away imaginary tears. "Well, sorry to be a huge disappointment—I kind of *am* shitting on everything as usual. But hey, at least I got one assignment done this week."

Dustin snorted, the crooked smile spilling across his lips. He leaned on his elbows and pointed his fork at her. "Come on. You're acting like you're not spending a ton of money, which—oh, right. You're not. You're a special snowflake with a lacrosse scholarship." He rested his fork on his salad bowl and folded his arms. "But your undergrad program is practically over. You have to start studying for your MCAT if you haven't already. You'll have to take it in May if you want to go to med school the fall after your senior year."

Her gaze fell to her lap. "I know, but between my lacrosse practices, classes, and trying to have a social life, it's kind of hard to keep up with it all."

His eyes rolled. "Bullshit. I did all the same classes, was on the basketball team, *and* fed the homeless, so no excuses for you."

She threw back her head and almost choked on her orange chicken. "Yeah, right. You totally did not feed the homeless."

"But the point is, I could have found time if I wanted." His brows wiggled as he took another bite of his salad.

"Sure." She stuffed rice into her mouth and mumbled between chews, "So you're telling me you won't be dating, like, three girls this year? Since you're so focused? Mm-hmm, got it."

He flashed a smug grin. "Actually, this year, I'm not. Nothing—not even *dating*, believe it or not—can get in the way of med school graduation. Besides, it was *four* girls last year, not three," he corrected, flexing.

She was about to give him a snarky reply when her phone started buzzing. "One sec." She glanced at the screen and wrinkled her mouth. *Mom.* "Sorry, I gotta take this. I forgot to call my mom last night."

He nodded and continued prodding his salad.

Dani dropped her fork and pressed her brand-new iPhone to her ear. "Hey, sorry I forgot to call you. Got caught up with some things." Like falling asleep.

"Dani, why didn't you respond to my messages yesterday?" Angelina Torres's light southern accent blared in Dani's ear. Growing up, Dani's friends had wondered why she didn't accumulate a strange accent from her parents, considering her dad had his own tinge of Spanish accent. Maybe Helena had forced her to sound more like the locals.

Dustin looked up from his salad with a raised eyebrow. Dani shrugged at him, rolling her eyes before responding to her mom in a hushed tone.

"I know, I know. I'm sorry."

"It's okay." An aggravated sigh punctured the line. "Are you keeping up with your classes? You know your scholarship depends on your good grades." Dani could imagine her mom's hazel eyes tightening, her hand darting to her hip.

Dani pinched her nose and folded her legs up sideways onto the booth. "Mom, I already told you, you don't need to worry." Her grades had never been spectacular, but it wasn't as if she was a bad student. She just got easily distracted. Besides, this year she had Dustin to help her stay on track—she *needed* to get into med school.

Her mom's voice relaxed slightly. "Okay, good. How are you doing otherwise? Need more medication?"

The words sunk into Dani's stomach like a burning coal. She swallowed and sat up slowly, flickers of her dream creeping into her consciousness. Glancing at Dustin, she mouthed "sorry" and got up from the table. The laughter of the neighboring group of girls and the bustling noise of the cafeteria faded away as Dani pushed through the entrance's giant glass door and into a hallway.

"No, but I can order them myself anyways," she said, scratching her cheek. The solidifying images from the previous night's nightmare threatened to upheave her orange chicken. "I'm fine, haven't had any problems." Everything *had* been fine, up until yesterday.

"You're sure? I can call a counselor in that area if you need one. Dr. Salvador mentioned a few people he knew. Let me know if I should—"

"Mom, I'm fine!" Dani protested, continuing down the hallway so the students in the cafeteria, especially Dustin, couldn't see her sudden distress through the glass wall. "I promise, I haven't had any episodes."

"Okay…" There was a deafening beat of silence. Dani didn't know if her mom believed her or not. "On another note, now that you're twenty-one, don't get distracted with parties. You don't need to get into any more trouble."

Dani knew what her mom was referring to specifically, but she never dared to bring up the details if she could avoid it. And neither did Dani, for that matter. That was a time neither of them wanted to revisit.

She bit her tongue to help shut down the sickening flashes of those awful memories.

Her eyelids blinked back the images as she deflected to what her mom had said before that. *"Don't get distracted with parties."* Dani smiled guiltily as she remembered the bowling party next Saturday. She was tired of her mom imposing rules on her all the time. Dani wasn't the girl she was three years ago; she could enjoy herself once in a while, and that didn't mean she'd be getting into *trouble.*

"Sure, Mom."

Another deafening beat of silence. "Don't forget to call me next time." Her sign-off sounded empty, leaving Dani with a tight pain in her chest.

She hung up the phone just as Dustin pushed through the glass door into the hallway, his laptop bag on one shoulder. He'd slung her backpack over his other shoulder, and his hand gripped her unfinished Panda Express box. She had forgotten how tall he was—it was a few months since she'd last met with him. At 6'1", it was no wonder he'd played on USC's basketball team during his undergrad years. Even though Dani was taller than the average girl, Dustin still made her feel small.

"Thought you might want these," Dustin said, holding out her barely-eaten lunch and backpack.

"Thanks." She pocketed her phone and took both items from him, slinging the backpack over her shoulder.

He gestured with his thumb at the door. "I've gotta head to Keck." His eyes raked over her. "Everything okay?"

She curled her hair behind an ear as her other hand tightened on the Styrofoam box. "Yeah, just annoying family stuff as usual." She hoped he would buy it.

"Sure," he murmured after a moment's hesitation. "If you need anything or want to ever just chat…you have my number. Otherwise, I'll check back in with you in a few weeks to go over MCAT prep."

She gave a small nod.

"Fight on." He smiled briefly, displaying the two fingers in the school's V-for-victory salute before exiting through the hallway glass doors opposite the cafeteria.

Dani watched him go and sighed in frustration, her gut jostling with something bitter.

For a brief moment, she thought he had seen through her, catching a glimpse of her hidden self.

But he had no idea.

He hadn't the slightest idea about her problems. He didn't know that she had been on meds for three years. That she had refused to take her medication once before, during freshman year. That consequently, the lacrosse field had haunted her with a swirling vortex of turmoil and grief. That she had cried desperately into her pillow for weeks, waking Carolyn from her sleep in their underclassmen dorm room. He didn't know that just last night, a bad dream had rekindled the haunting images of those painful nights three years ago.

But he didn't need to know those things.

*September*

FOR SOME LUDICROUS REASON THAT ESCAPED DANI, LACROSSE practice was becoming a sort of entertainment show for the three underclassmen guys. They sat on the bleachers, smirking, watching Dani and the girls during their warm-ups.

"Don't they have anything better to do?" Hannah sniped. She flipped her long braid over a shoulder as she ran through Winston's ladder drill.

"Of course not, 'cause underclassmen waste all their time trying to pick up girls," Haley replied.

Winston whistled from the sideline, swinging a huge bag of balls to the ground as she joined the other four chatting coaches. "All right, girls, grab your sticks and a ball and line up at midfield. Pickett and Ramirez, grab your sticks and faceguards and head to the goalpost."

Dani grinned conspiratorially at Haley as they trotted to pick up their sticks from the sidelines. "Well, damn. I actually won a bet against you? We're touching our sticks and it's not even October!"

Haley rolled her eyes. "Sure, sure. Got lucky this time though. I'll pay up after practice."

After retrieving their sticks and collecting balls from the bag, Dani, Haley, and twelve of the girls lined up at midfield. Arianna and Olivia faced them from in front of the goal with their own sticks.

Winston marched alongside the other coaches in between the goal and midfield, her beady eyes darting back and forth among the girls. "We're doing Rapid Fire. Anyone to score gets to sit out on suicides. If Pickett or Ramirez block more than five, they get to sit out."

The girls cheered, raising their rackets and whooping.

"You first, Pickett. Ready…" Winston retreated to the side and waited while Arianna tugged her faceguard securely into place and posed in a defensive position in front of the goal, twirling her stick from side to side.

Winston blew her whistle, and Hannah ran up first, feigning left and shooting right. Arianna blocked it easily.

Next was Taylor—blocked.

Isabel—just wide of the goalpost.

Dani watched Arianna dance across the goal, impressed at the ease with which she blocked left and right, high and low. A memory crept to the forefront of her mind, slipping her back into Montana…

Dani blinked, and Soni McAlister Field peeled away, replaced by a wide field of grass and tall lodgepole trees.

She was sixteen, standing on the field in her family's large back yard beside a large cart of balls, her lacrosse stick in hand. Her palms were slick with sweat, and her arms were strained.

Jeremy, her twenty-three-year-old brother, grinned at her from across the crease by the goalpost, twirling his stick cockily. His dirty-blond hair shone in the daylight, and his hazel eyes twinkled on a round face that matched Dani's.

"Let's go, Dani. Hit me with your best!" He shifted his weight from foot to foot, ready to pounce like a lion onto its prey.

Dani grinned back; it was just like old times with him. She was glad for his final return home from New York after his college graduation.

She scooped a ball from the cart, took a deep breath, and flung it with all her might.

Jeremy caught the ball with a flick of his wrist, tossing it aside.

"You've gotta do better than that," he teased. "Don't let your feet give away your shot."

She slung another ball, and he batted it away with a lazy flick of his wrist.

His dumb grin infuriated her. "I can't believe the Montana High School Lacrosse League chose you as their MVP. You're so sloppy," he mocked.

"Shut up, you asshole," she spurted. Before he had time to think, Dani scooped another ball and aimed it above his head.

He spun his stick up and blocked that one too.

Dani shot ball after ball in masterful throws, but Jeremy didn't let one fly into the goal. He just danced back and forth, that big smile on his face beaming at her from across the yard. His laughter echoed in her mind, fading, until images of her sunny back yard morphed into a dark, cold night…

She strained to breathe, whimpering as her body shook—and then sunlight flooded her eyes.

The lacrosse pitch. Her teammates and coaches. Winston.

They all blurred back into clarity. She was in Los Angeles, not Montana. And it was Arianna who stared back at her from across the field, not her brother.

A sharp pang dug into the pit of her stomach, and her hands trembled. Her entire body felt weak as the dark memory crept its way out of the depths of her mind.

"Dani? You're holding us up," someone urged behind her.

She shook her head to clear it of the haunting images and backed out of the line of girls, hiding her shaking hands behind her back. Her words came out hoarse. "You guys go on ahead. I can't do this."

*Breathe. Just breathe. Suck it up. You're fine.*

Winston called from the edge of the crease. "Torres, what the hell? Hurry up and shoot!"

Dani remained motionless, failing to control her rapid heart rate as the pain in her stomach worsened. The confused girls' faces began to blur…

*No, no, no. Twice in two weeks?*

Winston jogged to her, waving to another coach to continue the drill. She placed a hand on Dani's back and led her to the sideline.

"What happened, Torres? I thought you knew the point of Rapid Fire is to fire *rapidly*." Her dark eyebrows narrowed at Dani, and she put a beefy hand on her hip.

Dani swallowed, the pain in her stomach subsiding a bit. She glanced at her teammates' successive shots at Olivia, who had taken the place of Arianna, and her stomach lurched again. "Coach, I'm sorry… I don't think I can do this. I think I need a break…"

Winston's eyebrows shot up, her tan face aghast. "You're funny, Torres. Unless you're feeling sick, you'll take a break from my team when you want to lose your scholarship."

Dani shook her head and rubbed her eyes. "It's just that…I keep seeing…"

"Keep seeing what?" The humor had vanished from Winston's tone, and her hand fell from her hip.

Dani wracked her brain for a plausible answer. Of all the things that came to mind, each of them ended with her having to explain the flashbacks, which would only plunge Dani back into that inescapable darkness.

She scratched her cheek and sucked in a breath. "Never mind. Could we just do something other than Rapid Fire?"

Winston raised a skeptical brow. "I'll change it up if it's bothering you so much, but you're gonna owe me an extra suicide for interrupting the drill."

Dani nodded, and Winston blew her whistle and sorted the girls into groups of three for conditioning stations.

As her group rotated from squats, sit-ups, and bench jumps, Dani tried to clear her head of the turmoil threatening to unleash again. The strain of conditioning helped to suppress her emotions, but it wasn't enough.

When she stepped up to the track to run their daily mile, she was eager, happy almost, to put her body through the agonizing physical pain she usually loathed.

Because it blocked out the emotional pain.

*Just keep breathing, dammit. You're fine.*

Dani's mile time was faster by thirteen seconds. She had never loved physical exhaustion so much in her life.

Winston gave the team a "generous" ten minutes to relax before lining up Dani and the few girls who hadn't scored against Arianna for their suicides. Dani practically walked through the drill, her body begging for rest as each stride stretched the limits of her endurance. The other girls soon finished and gathered up their belongings, leaving Dani to run her extra suicide punishment alone.

After her last excruciating trek across the field, she finally relaxed her hands on her hips, panting like a dog while her muscles screamed in agony.

But physical pain was okay. She needed it.

Funny how she was the last one off the field *again*. She gazed across the desolate, darkening track. Apparently, Dani's lone suicide had taken longer than she thought. Her isolation brought a stab of sadness, widening a small fissure that had dug its way into her heart.

*Shut up, Dani. Stop feeling so sorry for yourself. You're fine.*

She snagged her lacrosse stick and water bottle at the edge of the track and made her way toward the locker room—and glimpsed their faces on the bleachers. In her worries, she had forgotten about the worst part of lacrosse practice: passing by the Three Bastards, as Haley called them. Sure enough, they were still there, sitting in the half-dark, smirking at her.

Why the hell were they still here? They'd had their fun with their usual gawking during practice. Didn't they have lives?

Dani pulled her iPhone out of her pocket and tried to focus on her newsfeed, counting down the steps that led her to the open, inviting locker room door.

"…looked like she almost passed out again. Damn, Peter, sure you want a flimsy chick like that?" They thought they were being quiet, but Dani made out their words loud and clear.

She turned her head as the sandy-haired guy—Peter, she assumed—smirked at the dude who had just spoken. "I bet that smokeshow isn't so flimsy under the bed covers." They chuckled and flashed cocky grins in her direction.

Dani's eyes narrowed. They had no right to tease her about her trauma. They could tease her about her looks or whatever other stupid things guys talked about, but anything that poked fun about her triggers crossed the line.

"Hey…" Peter called to her as she passed the bleachers. "Wait up, I wanted to ask you something."

She spun and walked the few extra steps to the bleachers. From where they sat high up, she had to crane her neck to make eye contact with the sandy-haired guy. She was absolutely tired of this shit. On top of that, her limbs were sore, her lungs ached, and all she wanted was a bowl of ramen and a hot shower. Something snapped inside her.

"Go to hell," she spat.

Peter's grin fell. "What?"

Her anger boiled over in a frightening rush. "I said, go to hell, you piece of shit!" She whipped her new iPhone into a powerful throw at Peter, but her exhaustion rocked her off-balance. Her phone ricocheted off the bleacher step a row down from them and landed with a crunch on the concrete below.

Peter eyed her with a mixture of bewilderment and amusement as his buddies erupted into laughter. She didn't know what to think of it.

"Damn, Peter! I didn't know your boo was so feisty!"

Dani ducked under the bleachers, her throat clenched tight with emotion as she picked up her phone. Puffy eyes stared back at her from the smashed screen.

*Thanks for my $800 indestructible phone, Apple.*

"So what are you wearing tomorrow night?" Dani asked Carolyn a few days later as they walked up their apartment driveway after an evening appointment at the Apple Store. Dani cradled her new—correction, *second new*—iPhone tightly as if it would break any moment. The innovative, expensive phone had just been released a few days ago, but Dani didn't see any hurt in upgrading as well as getting a new number to rid all of those scam callers. Too bad she hadn't thought to save her contacts through iCloud.

Thank God for Facebook.

"I never said I was going to the frat party!" Carolyn protested as she swung her keys around her finger.

Dani scoffed. "Uh, yeah you are. How else are you going to get a guy?"

Carolyn's cheeks turned the same color as her hair. Dani chuckled and hoisted her backpack up her shoulder as she pulled open the front door.

"I already told Emma you're coming anyways."

"You what!"

Dani gave a devilish grin as she followed a disgusted Carolyn through the kitchen. Both of them halted when they caught sight of Alisha sitting at the coffee table in the living room. She was poring over a textbook, her pencil scribbling in her notebook.

"What are you doing home on a Friday night?" Dani teased, crossing the room to stand in front of her while Carolyn busied herself in the kitchen.

Alisha shrugged, flipping a lock of her shoulder-length dark curly hair to reveal dark eye shadow. She propped up a ripped jean leg, exposing her belly button from underneath a blue crop top shirt. "I was planning on going to the Irish bar on Figueroa, but Noemi bailed. Something about a doctor's appointment she forgot," she muttered.

"That's a bummer. Maybe it's time you made some new friends." Dani didn't usually make an effort to be so conversational with Alisha, but anticipation for the bowling party had put her in a good mood. After all the physical and emotional hell she'd been through in the past two weeks, she was ready to enjoy herself.

Apparently, the good mood wasn't mutual. Alisha lowered her long, thin eyebrows as if Dani's genuine attempt at small talk appalled her. "I don't care to be surrounded by annoying people all the time." Her gaze returned to her textbook, and she slumped back on the couch in disgust. "I really don't see the point in history. Why would anyone care about some guy who died two hundred years ago?"

"Psh, I ask the same question all the time," Dani murmured.

Alisha rolled her eyes and turned back to her studies, her curly dark curtain of hair covering her face again.

Dani smirked, then pivoted to head up the stairs behind Carolyn. Plopping her backpack on her bed, she fished some pajamas out of her closet and slung a towel over her shoulder.

As she walked into the hall, she spotted Carolyn sprawled on her bed with her laptop in front of her, typing away. Dani shook her head and tucked her hands on her hips.

"Still studying?"

Carolyn turned. "Huh? Oh, no. I'm just finishing up some research for one of my classes since *someone* is forcing me to give up weekend homework time in favor of a party."

Dani's eyes rolled. "Uh-huh. I'm sure your assignment isn't even due till, like, December." She leaned on the doorframe. "What are you researching anyways?"

Carolyn sat up with a smile. "Well, since you're so curious…check this out. I came across this article from June." She tossed some printed articles from the *LA Times* in front of her on the bed.

Curiosity piqued, Dani entered the room and sat on the bed, picking up the first paper.

Homelessness jumps 12% in L.A. County and 16% in the city; officials 'stunned'

Dani skimmed through the story and looked back at Carolyn quizzically. "Okay…"

Carolyn's lips pursed. "I'm researching capitalism's effects on the increasing the wage gap. In my opinion, capitalism has constructed a sort of *Hunger Games* mindset. It's like this mentality that there's an 'us versus them,' and success and wealth are the focus instead of healthy livelihoods and people's well-being."

Dani wrinkled her mouth, her mind drifting to the countless hours she'd spent training for a lacrosse scholarship and a PAC-12 championship. She supposed her mental health hadn't been the best because of all the relentless training…but wasn't there a price for everything?

She scratched her cheek. "Success and wealth are the reward of hard work, though. People shouldn't just be handed everything. Government aid gives some people an excuse to slack off and is ultimately a drain on everyone else's tax dollars."

Carolyn shook her frazzled red head. "Mmm, I disagree. Just because people aren't successful doesn't mean they don't work hard; sometimes life just deals people unlucky hands. In heated competition—like sports, for example—the loser doesn't get any praise, regardless if there was a high amount of points scored. Capitalism is great, but somehow we've evolved into this society that feeds upon people's failures instead of recognizing their strengths and encouraging them to get up and keep fighting." She rubbed her arm, her eyes distant.

Dani's throat tightened, and she bit her lip, looking away as vivid imagery flooded her vision: her dad's contempt-ridden face as he berated her with dark eyes and clenched fists… The Soni McAlister bathroom stall she had shut herself into during her freshman year as the flashbacks consumed her… Dustin's skeptical blue eyes in the cafeteria hallway as she reassured him she was okay.

*Failure after failure after failure…*

Carolyn's voice was soft. "I'm not saying capitalism should be abolished… I just wish there was a better balance between the rich and the poor, like, if more people actually cared for one another and stopped trying to come up with excuses to not help out others less fortunate." She took a breath and shook her head. "I can't understand how we live in a country full of good-willed, intellectual people who seem to be blind to those suffering right outside their windows…"

Dani tried to swallow but found herself struggling against a growing lump in her throat. "Yeah," she choked.

*Four*

*September*

I T WAS THE FIRST TIME DANI HAD BEEN THANKFUL FOR A RARE BOUT of rain in sunny California.

Hair and clothes damp, she sat squeezed between her rowdy teammates at Wahlburgers on Saturday afternoon, smiling as she dug into her burger.

A small fortune of bad weather had cancelled their lacrosse scrimmage, and though all of the girls had been ecstatic for the rare break from practice, Dani had needed it most. The break was a blessing considering the rise in triggers lately.

Arianna leaned across the table at Dani as the girls laughed beside them, sharing dirty secrets. "Did you actually throw your phone at Peter?" she asked in a soft tone, curling a lock of dark hair.

Dani blinked and set her burger down, searching her memory. "What?"

Arianna's eyes darted around the table at the other chatting girls before latching back onto Dani. "Zoey told me earlier she saw you throw your phone at him when she was leaving the locker room that one day."

"Oh, yeah, I did." Dani's eyes rolled, and she dipped a fry in ketchup. "He is such a dick."

Arianna gave a small nod and leaned close, maintaining a low tone. "I haven't told many people, but he asked me out last year, and I said no. I think he was stalking me at practice."

"Damn!" Dani whispered with widened eyes. She toyed with the straw in her drink. "I didn't know he asked you out."

Arianna scoffed, her dark lashes fluttering as she leaned back slightly. "Yeah, he was a complete asshole about it when I refused, saying he's a really cool guy, blah blah…"

"Confirmed douchebag. You just gotta ignore them."

Arianna's eyes hardened, and her jaw went tight. "That's the thing. I've heard he can be abrasive and obsessive and that his parents are rich and have connections at the school. Just be careful."

Dani's mind raced back to the hungry, amused expression in Peter's eyes when she threw her phone at him. Whoever this douche was, she only hated him more.

She pursed her lips. "Thanks, I'll keep that in mind. I don't plan on throwing my phone at him again, if that's what you're implying. Apple would love me for cashing in on a third phone in a week."

Arianna's mouth twisted into a wide smile, and she folded her arms on the table. "Damn, I wish I could've seen you confront him."

Dani flicked a loose strand of dirty-blonde hair out of her face. "Eh, it was super sloppy work on my end. Haley would've kicked my ass for my pathetic aim." She brightened, remembering she'd see Haley at the frat party tonight. Her loser boyfriend was a friend of one of the members, and she had left immediately after practice to accompany him as he helped with party logistics.

Finished with her own fries, Dani eyed the two remaining fries on Arianna's plate. She darted a hand to steal one, but Arianna swatted her away with lightning speed.

"Goalie here, remember?" She laughed at Dani's pout before stuffing it into her mouth with savage cruelty.

Isabel ceased her chatter with Hannah and swiveled beside Dani.

"Hey, Dani, you're good at bio, right? Can you help me with something while we're here?"

Dani swallowed another bite from her burger and set it down. "Sure."

Isabel returned a dimpled smile and set her empty plate on the vacant table adjacent to them. "Awesome!" She dug into her backpack at her feet and pulled out a notebook, flipped through it, then rotated it in between them toward Dani. "I was solving for the reaction rate of a thigh of frozen chicken to defrost in a refrigerator at 3.6 degrees Celsius, but there's no way an internal drop of 6 degrees per day is right."

Dani frowned at Isabel's scribbled equations. "Your temperature coefficient is wrong for the formula. You put 'one hundred' instead of 'ten' for the numerator here." She pointed on the notebook as Isabel twirled a dark strand of hair.

"Oh, dang, nice catch!"

Dani gave a mechanical shrug and returned to her burger as Isabel pulled out a pencil and frantically erased her mistake.

Olivia snorted from the other side of the table. "Dani's a genius. Remember how she showed up Winston that one time during film in August and strategized how to outmaneuver Ohio's full press? Winston freaked when Dani also pointed out Ohio only pressed our team twice in the past two years."

The other girls shared giggles at the memory.

"Yeah, how did you even remember that, Dani?" Lisa teased. "I can't even remember our record against Ohio, let alone how many times they pressed us!"

Everyone flashed impressed smiles in Dani's direction.

She flushed, reveling in their praise, before mumbling with a mouthful of burger, "Thank you, thank you. Tips appreciated."

They broke into laughter, grinning from ear to ear.

Dani rode her bike home as fast as she could in the rain, winded and soaked by the time she finally reached the safety of her apartment. She stowed her bike in the back yard and trotted up the stairs, pausing as Emma gawked at her from the bathroom, an eyeliner brush in her hand.

"Girl, your hair!"

Dani snorted and waved a hand. "It's fine."

Emma turned back to the mirror and shook her head as she finished applying her makeup. The pretty Salvadoran wore a simple bright green blouse with matching stud earrings, blue denim, and heels. Her long dark hair drooped in light curls, framing her slim waist.

"Chase is gonna love you." Dani whistled.

Emma fumbled with her lipstick as her cheeks heated. "You think so? I wanted to wear something suggestive but not scandalous, you know?"

Before Dani could respond, Carolyn popped out of her room to join the conversation, and Dani stifled a snicker. Emma's outfit *did* look scandalous in comparison to Carolyn's. The redhead wore baggy jeans and a brown sweatshirt with a "California" logo on the front, her frazzled red hair messy as ever.

Dani's mouth curved as she scanned Carolyn up and down. "Shit. You trying to pick up men, Carolyn, or trash on the freeway?"

Carolyn put her hands on her wide hips. "Not all men are turned on by glittering jewelry and glamorous dresses, Dani. What matters is underneath."

Emma and Dani shared a blank glance for a beat before they both exploded with laughter.

Carolyn blanched, and her freckled cheeks scrunched. "You know what I meant! Personality is what matters. Not…that."

Dani bent forward while Emma held onto the sink for support, both failing to restrain their amusement. Carolyn huffed out a breath and trudged down the stairs, leaving them to drown in their laughter.

When they finally recovered, Dani retreated to her room to change out of her wet lacrosse clothes. She shrugged on some tight blue jeans that showed her curves and a blue button-up dress shirt, with cute boots and a raincoat to complement.

Fifteen minutes later, the three of them ducked out of the rain to the best of their abilities and piled into Carolyn's battered-down Toyota Camry.

Emma poked her head from behind Dani's passenger seat as they drove along the wet streets into downtown. "So apparently, the frat has the entire place booked until 2:00 a.m." Both Carolyn and Dani gave her shocked looks, and she just shrugged. "They have a lot of funding from rich parents, mostly. Chase said they are mostly athletes and student body leaders. Not really my type of frat."

Carolyn frowned as she turned into the crowded lot of Lucky Strike Bowling. Dani glanced out the window at a group of students laughing as they ran through the rain into the building. Bad weather didn't appear to deter college kids from anything.

After finally parking at a meter on the main street, the three of them trekked through the storm, up the lot, and pushed through the double doors of Lucky Strike Bowling.

All three of them gave a double take.

It was packed.

Music blared over a crowded dance floor at the end of the alley, and bowling lanes to the right were bustling with students. People lounged on small couches and hovered around tabletops, laughing and bouncing to the music while others bowled or picked at appetizers. To the left, leathered couches, neon suspended lighting, and velvet dining booths made for a lavish scene. As if the alley's contemporary décor wasn't already vibrant enough, streamers had been hung from the ceiling, and balloons floated everywhere. To top it off, a huge banner above the shoe rental read, "Welcome back, PSK!"

Emma wasn't wrong—Lucky Strike was the perfect place for a wealthy frat.

What a great use for rich parents' money.

"Hey," someone called to their immediate right. The three roommates turned to see a skinny guy with long brown hair standing next to a fold up table. On the table were a checklist, a small poster with upcoming frat events, and a basket of buttons with phrases like "Phi Sigma Kappa Alum" and "Beat UCLA!"

"This is a private party," the guy noted. Dani supposed it had something to do with them being at a dude party. And the fact that they weren't dudes.

"We're with Chase Coleman," Emma said cheerily.

The bouncer raised an eyebrow, unconvinced. "Nice try. Everyone knows Chase."

The cheer on Emma's face evaporated. She raised her head and darted her eyes around the crowd, searching. Then a warm smile crept to her cheeks. "Chase!" She waved at a pale boy with wavy dark hair, dressed in khaki shorts and a polo with PSK's Greek letters.

The guy named Chase glanced up, and when he saw Emma, his mouth stretched into a mile-wide grin. "Emma! I'm so glad you made it!" he exclaimed as he made his way over to them. He swept Emma into a huge hug, disregarding Dani and Carolyn as if they were no more interesting than the "Beat UCLA!" button on the bouncer's shirt.

"Hey, Jake, they're with me," Chase assured the bouncer.

Jake's hard expression loosened, and he nodded.

Chase offered a hand to him, and he grasped it in a bro-shake. "Thanks, man. I owe you one." He turned to face Dani and Carolyn and shot them a judgmental look as if unsure they would fit in with the crowd. Then the skepticism dropped from his face and he flashed his wide grin again. "Welcome to our back-to-school party! Lane 23 is open if you guys want to join?"

Carolyn opened her mouth to respond, but Dani nudged her, shutting her down. "You two go ahead. We're gonna browse around a bit."

Emma raised an eyebrow in hesitation, but Dani made a shooing motion with her hands. Emma took that as approval and let Chase lead her into the crowd.

Dani blew a strand of hair out of her face. "Well, we won't see her for the rest of the year."

Carolyn nodded, her nervous eyes drifting over the raucous crowd. "At least he seems like a nice guy."

Dani shifted her weight and stared longingly after Emma, something like jealousy twinging in her gut. She swallowed away the bothersome feeling and scanned the sea of students. A healthy mix of athletic guys and girls flooded the alley, as could be expected with a frat party.

Why had that asshole, Jake, been so difficult with Dani's crew when he'd let all of these other girls past him?

She continued searching the crowd and finally spotted Haley standing by a tabletop a ways down across from the dining area. Haley caught sight of her at the same time.

"Dani!" she shouted, waving her over.

Dani dragged Carolyn along behind her as she weaved in between people chatting and dancing to the booming music.

"About time you showed up!" Haley said as they approached. The two other girls at her table eyed Dani suspiciously, and it put her on edge.

She tried her best to ignore them and gave her friend a once-over, gaping at Haley's tight black dress and high heels. "Damn, Haley!"

Haley laughed and tossed her long brown curls, shimmying in her dress. "That's what Mitch said. He went to get more booze from Blake. There's plenty if you want some." She smiled playfully. Clearly, bowling wasn't on her mind. On the lacrosse field, Haley was a fierce, strong-headed leader. Off the field, however, she was something else entirely.

"I thought frats weren't allowed to have alcohol at events for the first few weeks of school," Dani speculated in a safe volume. Carolyn shifted awkwardly beside her.

One of the girls at the table shot Haley a skeptical look, but Haley waved her off. "She's a close friend, Nicole. Trust me." She turned back to Dani. "Nobody really follows those rules; we just keep it on the down-low. What's a party without a few drinks anyways? The school is so overly strict sometimes."

Dani raised an eyebrow and then relaxed. Figured. Why would she be so naïve as to think college kids wouldn't bring alcohol? But these people were definitely another kind of stupid, smuggling it into a business venue. Dani was sure the frat could suffer serious consequences if they were found out.

"Try the watermelon margarita—it's bomb," Haley encouraged, holding up a regular Coca-Cola can. When Dani wrinkled her brow in confusion, Haley smiled slyly. "Blake is some kind of manufacturer. He makes cans with soda logos but puts booze in them. Coca-Cola is for the watermelon margarita—premixed—Dr. Pepper for Modelo, Sprite for Bud Light… Pretty clever, huh?"

The only thing Dani knew about Blake was that he was a friend of Haley's boyfriend, Mitch, who Dani thought was a lazy scumbag. So Blake probably was too.

She glanced at Haley, hesitant. The offering of alcohol brought back a dark tremor of déjà vu. It had been a long time since she'd had a drink, and she wasn't too thrilled now about taking one manufactured by a sketchy friend of a sketchy guy from a sketchy frat. Plus, she knew giving in to alcohol would piss off her mom to hell and back.

If she found out.

*Screw it. It's about time I enjoyed myself. I already decided I can't keep living in fear.*

"Two margaritas please," Dani told Haley, to Carolyn's shock.

As Haley grinned, that condescending voice reverberated in Dani's mind: *Failure after failure…*

"I think I'll pass on this one," Carolyn declined.

"Come on—just try it," Dani urged. "We're here to have fun! It's not like we're underage anyways."

Carolyn stepped backward as if appalled Dani would say something so ridiculous. She looked between Dani and the other girls for a long moment, probably weighing her options. At last, she nodded, defeated.

Haley nodded and gestured to the other girl, Nicole, who walked through the crowd and returned a minute later with two ice cold "Coca-Cola's."

As the next few hours rolled by, Dani felt the alcohol working her fast. The drink was amazing, blotting out the anxiety that had been building inside her chest over the past two weeks: the idiots murmuring perverted remarks during lacrosse practices, the stress of balancing loads of homework, her mom's worried call…

And the horrible, sickening flashbacks.

Dani scratched her cheek and took another swig. Haley and Carolyn's faces blurred a little bit, and Dani teetered. She grabbed Haley's arm to steady herself.

She thought she had only had a few drinks but couldn't remember. Wasn't she good at remembering things? Whatever she was drinking, it was strong.

But she liked it.

She relished in the numbness and power it gave her, the buzz circulating through her veins. It tasted salty and sweet and burned her throat, and she was enjoying it.

*Failure after…* The voice faded farther away with every sip.

She made her way over to where a DJ was blasting Bruno Mars's "24K Magic" in the center of the alley. As she walked between the dancing bodies, she noticed a tall boy with messy dark hair and a strong build watching her with a curious gleam in his eye. She was vaguely conscious of her hips swaying widely as she strolled by him. When she blinked, he stood in front of her with a mischievous smile painted across his thin lips.

"Who's your date?" His voice boomed over the pulse of the music, and he took a pull from his Sprite can—Bud Light, if she remembered correctly. Or was it Modelo?

"Hmm?" She tilted her head and licked her lips.

"To get you into the party."

"Why do you assume a date got me in? I could've had a friend." She gave a teasing, lopsided smile.

He curled his lips and wiped his bangs out of his face. "So you're saying you didn't come with a date?"

Dani took another drag of her sweet, sour booze, and a relaxing hum gushed through her veins. "Why does it matter?"

He stepped closer and brushed a stray hair off her cheek. Her skin squirmed at his touch. "Just sayin'. There's no way a pretty girl like yourself just waltzed in here without a guy attached."

She rolled her eyes and batted her lashes with a small laugh. "Thanks for the flattery."

He grinned. "I'm Tanner. Wide receiver on the football team, if it interests you."

"Oh, wow. Is that supposed to impress me?" Dani folded an arm beneath the elbow of her drink hand and shifted her hips. She knew the effect her body had on guys—they'd been ogling her ever since she could remember. The alcohol was commanding her to use her body now; to let it do what it was made to do.

A voice nagged in her memory: "*This is what I mean when I say you go around being irresponsible! Partying all the time, going out with boys…*"

She shoved the thought away. "I'm Dani. Starting midfielder on the lacrosse team, if it interests you."

Tanner's chuckle was deep and consuming, and it sent shivers up her spine. He wasn't bad-looking with his dreamy brown eyes, charming smile, and sharp jawline.

He wiped his hair out of his eyes again with a nonchalance that suggested he knew Dani was checking him out. "That's pretty dope," he murmured, reaching up to brush the long bangs out of his eyes. "What year are you?"

"I'm a junior."

His eyes twinkled. "Yeah? Me too. Sounds like we have at least two things in common." He cocked an eyebrow. "We should hang some-time. You can tell me all about your killer lacrosse skills."

Dani quirked her mouth suggestively. "Hmm, tempting…"

A familiar glimpse of red hair caught her eye, and she glanced past him to see Carolyn beyond the dance floor. She was seemingly enjoy-ing herself next to a high-top table, chatting away to a tall, handsome guy with curly hair who appeared to have no interest in what she was saying.

Both Dani and Carolyn were sure going all-in tonight, hot damn.

Dani chuckled. "If you'll excuse me, I gotta rescue my roomie." *From herself.* She gave Tanner a flirtatious smile and pushed past him toward Carolyn.

Dani paused to stabilize herself on a dancer as a wave of light-headedness rocked her backward. The girl pushed Dani off her, and Dani managed to walk straight, albeit slowly, during the last few yards toward her friend.

Carolyn's hands moved animatedly, and her eyelids fluttered. She brushed her frazzled hair over a shoulder, tossing back her Coca-Cola. The girl was definitely wasted.

"I had to go buy this gift for my little brother, and I forgot he was allergic to chalk wit—did I say chalk wit?" A laugh sputtered from her chattering mouth. "I meant choc-oo…late! So I went back to the store and got him gummy worms instead. You'd like him… You should come visit my family in Arizona!"

The guy she was with scanned his surroundings, probably search-ing for an escape.

When Carolyn placed her can on the table and teetered, he grabbed her arm, steadying her. "I think you should sit down."

Dani stepped in front of him and grasped Carolyn's other arm. "Thank you, Mr. Right. I'll take her from here," she slurred.

The guy scowled, but when she turned to glare at him, his hard look morphed into intrigue. His eyes swept Dani's figure top-to-bottom.

"I said back off," she ordered, her tone dripping with scorn now. His face contorted into a scowl, and he finally released Carolyn before meandering away from them.

*Damn, the pretentiousness of the guys at this party…*

Carolyn grabbed her can off the table, while Dani snagged Carolyn's handbag off the floor. Then Dani shuffled her friend down a set of stairs to a vacant bowling lane booth. At this point, more people appeared to be mingling on the dance floor than bowling.

"Dani, what are you *doing*? I didn't get a kiss goodbye!" Carolyn yelled.

"Dammit, Carolyn!" Dani exclaimed. "You got his attention. I just think you're not in the best state to make any m—"

"Shut the hell up!" Carolyn bellowed as she plopped on the couch. She gulped another sip of her margarita, sloshing it on herself in the process.

Dani cracked a smile. "You're jacked."

Carolyn guffawed and tipped backward onto the couch.

A loud, cheery group of people meandered past them, drawing Dani's gaze from her wasted friend. Emma tagged behind the group, smiling beside Chase. Her eyes widened when she saw Dani and Carolyn, and she tapped Chase on the shoulder. He nodded, and she skirted around the students, slipping onto the cushion next to her roommates.

"Are you guys okay?" she asked with a small laugh.

"Yeah, we're managing. How is Chase treating you?" Dani squinted at Chase, who continued down the alley with the group, laughing beside another guy.

Emma's brown cheeks flushed a dark red, her eyes dancing. "He's been really nice, introducing me to all his friends on the baseball team. He doesn't drink either, and he's really easy to talk to. I think we're going to meet again tomorrow." She glowed and covered her face.

"That's great," Dani murmured with a toss of her hair. She nodded at Carolyn. "I think we're gonna head out soon."

"Shit, we're leaving?" Carolyn drawled, sitting up straight. "Why?"

Emma giggled as Carolyn burped. "That's a good idea. It's probably a sign things are pretty bad if Carolyn, of all people, is swearing." She looked over at her group, which had stopped to bowl a few aisles down. "I think I'm going to stay a little longer and bowl with Chase, if that's okay?"

Dani tilted her head. "Actually, if you're staying sober, you can take Carolyn's car, and we'll Uber home." She reached into Carolyn's handbag and pulled out a keying. Emma shot her a skeptical look as Dani tossed her the keys.

"We're fine." Dani waved her hand. "Make good decisions, yadda yadda."

Emma bit her lip. "Well, if you're sure. Just be careful." She stood and moved to rejoin the group, now crowded around a nearby lane.

It took Dani a moment to spot Chase's dark wavy hair in the crowd; his medium height made it easy for the tall athletes to block him out. She watched him pick up a bowling ball and scour his eyes around the lanes for Emma. His face lit up when he spied her returning. Dani's heart sunk as he wrapped his arm around Emma's waist and she huddled into him.

Why couldn't Dani have someone care that much about her?

She glanced at the hammered roommate sprawled next to her and chuckled. *Well, someone besides you, Carolyn.*

Dani stood and was just about to help Carolyn to her feet when sandy hair caught her eye near the end of the alley. She peered down at the group of guys bowling a few lanes over and zeroed in on Sandy Hair. It was that dumb asshole from their lacrosse practice. Paul. Patrick? No—Peter.

His muscles flexed under his PSK shirt as he picked up a bowling ball. Sauntering to the lane, the bleacher douchebag swung his arm back and heaved the ball toward the pins. It was a promising throw, but it spun right into the gutter at the very last second.

Dani tossed her head back in flippant laughter.

Without a second thought, she abandoned Carolyn and strutted over to his lane, watching him pick up another ball and prepare to roll again.

"Well, your bowling skills are the *shit*, aren't they?" she jeered from behind the onlookers. A few people turned around—the bleacher douchebag Peter among them.

"Who the hell are you?" one of the guys spat as she shoved past a few guys and planted herself in front of Peter.

"Peter's bitch," she drawled.

"Oh shiiit," one of the guys on the couch cooed.

He hesitated for an instant as his hungry eyes soaked her in. Then a greasy, feral smile spread across his face. "Oh, hey, babe. What took you so long?"

"I know. My bad." She traced a finger seductively along his chin.

He relaxed his grip on the bowling ball and hooked a tentative hand around her waist. When she didn't resist, he leaned forward and brushed his lips against her ear, his breath hot against her neck.

"Damn, girl, you're getting me all worked up." He set the bowling ball back in the feeder and worked a rough hand up her midsection, breathing her in. "Mmm, sweet and salty smells good on you."

She feigned a sigh and curled at his touch. When a low grumble escaped his throat at her display, she dragged her hand to his neck and brought her mouth an inch from his.

"Listen, asshole," she whispered. "You can keep your fantasies to yourself, 'cause you're never gonna get anywhere with me."

His smile dissolved, and his hold on her loosened.

"So keep your whoring, ugly-ass face away from me and all the other lacrosse girls," she finished. She spun out of his arms and began marching toward Carolyn, who was helplessly slumped over her seat, smiling dumbly.

Several of the guys in Peter's crew "oohed". Out of the corner of her eye, Dani saw him gape at her, eyes narrowed. His face contorted, and he yelled, "Just lost your golden opportunity at some of this!" He grabbed his crotch and yanked it.

Dani whipped back around, staggering. Finding her balance, she closed the distance in three huge steps and kicked him right where he had grabbed. It was clumsy, but it was enough.

He crumpled to his knees, both hands on his crotch. "What the hell, bitch!" he squealed. His frat friends didn't so much as get up from their seats to help him; instead, they burst into laughter.

Dani didn't waste a second and staggered back to Carolyn, pulling her up off the couch. "Us bitches gotta go."

Carolyn teetered as Dani tugged her up the steps to the main floor, shoving confused students out of their way.

"Hear that, guys? Us bitches gotta GO!" Carolyn echoed into the throng around them. A few people shot her confused looks while others raised their drinks and whooped.

*Five*

**T**HE HAMMERING IN DANI'S SKULL WAS UNBEARABLE.

Her eyes squinted against the burning morning sun flooding through her window. She groaned as black spots filled her vision, yearning to sink through her mattress into oblivion.

"Hey, girl." Emma's soothing voice greeted Dani's limp form. Dani pulled back the covers to see Emma set a plate of crackers, sliced bananas, and a water glass on her bedside table. The Salvadoran gazed down at her with pity. "You look terrible."

Dani closed her eyes and stretched her arms above her head. "I feel worse."

"Well, on the plus side, it looks like you made it through the night without puking!"

A blur of memories rushed through Dani's mind: the rowdy cheers of a group of athletic guys, the sway of her hips as she strolled across the dance floor, a lot of alcohol…

Dani moaned and closed her eyes as nausea bubbled in her stomach.

Emma's light footsteps retreated to the door. "I'm gonna make a quick run to the store and grab you and Carolyn some more fruit."

Dani's eyes shot open. Carolyn! Hopefully, she was faring better than Dani, but if her vomit on the way home last night was any indication, it was probably wishful thinking.

Emma put a hand on Dani's doorknob. "I hope Alisha is here later to check on you guys, 'cause I'm leaving around 1:00 p.m."

Laughter burst from Dani's chest, which did nothing to help the pounding in her skull. "Well, Carolyn and I will both be dead by nightfall if you're putting our lives in the hands of Alisha."

Emma chuckled. "Yeah, probably not the best idea."

"Where are you going on a Sunday anyways?"

"Uh…" Emma shifted her weight, her cheeks flushing. "Chase and I have a date."

Dani rolled over, sighing. "The bastard."

"So…yeah. I'll let you get some sleep. If you need anything before 1:00, just holler!"

The sound of Dani's door closing signaled Emma had left her alone to wither in her bed. She lay in pain for a few minutes, her pounding headache making it impossible to think clearly. Dani closed her eyes, pleading for the pain to end, to succumb to a deep sleep…

Dani dreamed of a dark, cold night. Liquor swirled on her tongue as she danced and laughed with a brown-haired girl in a plaid shirt. Her vision blurred as she danced to the blaring music, blocking out her dad's reprimanding words, her rationale slithering away with every drink…

*Failure after failure…*

She woke again sometime later, still haggard but feeling well enough to snack on the fruit Emma had left her. The only company she had was the characters from One Piece, Attack on Titan, and her other favorite anime shows on her wall poster. And, of course, Channing Tatum in his glorious state as usual.

The house was quiet save for the small moans coming from Carolyn's room.

Guess she wasn't faring better.

Dani silently thanked the universe she had a hangover on a Sunday and not during the week. Winston would have her ass running extra miles if she missed practice. Unfortunately, she still had an assignment due tomorrow for organic chemistry. Dr. Turner wasn't one to let things slide.

When the thundering gong in Dani's head had eased to a lull a few hours later, she dragged her lifeless body out of bed. She drew her backpack off the floor and pulled out her textbook to begin Turner's assignment.

After rereading the same passage for ten minutes, her headache decided it would resume its relentless pounding in her ears. That deep voice crept back into her head, yelling incessantly, *"Why don't you ever listen? Failure after failure after failure… You never learn!"*

She coiled on the covers as that dark night threatened to swallow her. *Damp grass seeped through her jeans. Fogginess clouded her vision, but it was not the wooziness from the alcohol. Blood filled her nostrils; the bitter chill of the night rattled her bones…*

*And above all else, that choked wheezing echoed in her ears…*

Dani dipped her chin between her knees as the nausea made her head swim. The marks of that night were still raving inside her, clawing eagerly to escape past the walls she had built.

Her head snapped up as the bang of the front door closing planted her back in the present.

Was Alisha home? Eager for a distraction, Dani slid her textbook to the side of her bed and located her slippers by the closet. She snuggled her feet into them, opened her door, and skirted downstairs in her pajamas.

Alisha wasn't alone. Another small girl trailed behind her, and both of them paused when they caught sight of Dani poking her head out of the stairwell.

"Hey!" Dani stepped into the kitchen, her face lighting up.

"Hey, Dani." Alisha raised a long, thin eyebrow, suspicion oozing. She inclined her head to her friend. "This is Noemi."

Noemi brushed aside long dark hair to reveal slanted eyes and a warm smile on her round face. She wore a cute flannel shirt and tight, ripped jeans, not unlike Alisha's attire next to her. Ultimately, Noemi's sunny, welcoming presence was a stark contrast to Alisha's dim, indifferent one.

She offered a hand, her fingernails brimming with bright orange polish. "Nice to meet you." Her voice was light, with a faint accent Dani couldn't place.

Dani shook it, returning the smile. "Nice to meet you too." She grasped her elbow and shifted her feet. "So…what's your favorite anime? Do you like *Castlevania*?"

Noemi's eyes dimmed, and her lips pressed tight. "I don't watch anime," she responded flatly.

Dani's brow wrinkled. "You don't?"

A timid smile stretched across Noemi's plush lips, and she put a hand on her hips. "No… And in case you're also wondering, no, I'm not a bad driver, and no, I won't tutor you in math either."

Dani deflated, her face reddening. "Uh… Shit. I'm sorry, I wasn't thinking…" She bit her lip. How could she have been so stupid? It must have been the damn hangover.

Alisha remained neutral as always, but Dani suspected she wasn't particularly thrilled at Dani's first impression. Dani yearned to be back under her covers, hidden away from the world with her writhing headache.

Noemi's mouth perked, and she shrugged off Dani's misstep with a laugh. "It's fine. Don't worry about it. You're not the first."

The tension eased from Dani's shoulders. Her mouth twisted into a small smile, and she scratched her cheek as a sticky silence followed. She bit her lip, turning to Alisha.

"You missed the frat party last night."

Alisha shrugged. "I ended up chilling here. Too tired when I got home." Her eyes raked over Dani's pale face, messy hair, and wrinkled pajamas. "You look like shit. Had fun?"

In a flash, blurred memories of the previous night resurfaced: a crowd of woozy students dancing on the bowling floor, messy dark hair complementing a charming smile, and the squeal of a guy grabbing his balls. She clutched her sides as nausea stirred in her stomach again.

"You should sleep," Alisha said with a finality that ended the conversation. She nodded to Noemi and led her up the stairs to her room. The click of the bedroom door shutting behind them confirmed Dani was once again alone with her thoughts.

So much for that distraction.

Suddenly hungry again, Dani rummaged in the kitchen cupboards for a box of Cheez-Its, flinching as her mind rewound her racist comment and Noemi's disappointed expression.

She headed back upstairs and flipped through her textbook, munching on a handful of Cheez-Its. Her phone pinged on the bedside table, startling her. She wiped her hand on her pajamas before grabbing it and sinking into the pillows.

It was an unknown caller. **Hey, it's Dustin. This is your new number, yeah?**

Her lip curved upward as she thought of a response. **Uh, I think you have the wrong number.** She pressed send and immediately followed up with: **Jk jk! It's me.**

He replied an instant later. **Damn you had me all freaked out xD Anyway, I heard some girl on the lacrosse team kicked an underclassman's ass at a frat party. Just taking a wild guess it was you?**

*He already heard about that?*

She cracked a smile and texted back: **It was more of a balls-kicking than ass-kicking, but yep.**

Dani wound a finger in a strand of hair, flicking her eyes back and forth from her hair to her phone. It was a few more seconds before he answered.

**Shit Dani. School just started! You trying to jack up junior year already?**

Her lips wrapped into a sly grin, and she sent him an emoji of a middle finger.

No response.

She read his text again and bit her lip. Maybe he was being serious. It was difficult to tell with Dustin sometimes.

She sighed and flopped onto her stomach. Her headache started pounding hard again, and that familiar sinking feeling in her gut returned with it, bringing pictures of a foggy night and a blood-drenched plaid shirt.

Damn alcohol.

*Six*



**O**RDINARILY, DANI LOOKED FORWARD TO HER LAST MONDAY class, Organic Chemistry 306. Today, though, she dreaded the class. Of all her classmates, Dr. Turner seemed to take pride in her, even see something in her, which was reason enough to make her feel guilty for not completing her reading last night.

She only hoped Turner didn't embarrass her in front of the class.

To her relief, Turner pulled down a projection screen. "All right, folks, I thought I'd give you med school aspirers some inspiration for today. Dr. Stanton will be doing the lecture for today while I answer some emails. Stanton has a lengthy albeit well-earned title: M.D. in Radiology and Ph.D. in Public Health and expert consultant to the Center for Disease Control and Prevention."

Dani slouched forward in her chair, fixing her gaze on the screen as Dr. Stanton, a middle-aged stout man with glasses, stood in front of a lectern. His lengthy white coat evoked authority as he presented medical research to an auditorium packed with people. He spoke with the confidence and air of a person who was fully driven and passionate about what he did. When the audience asked questions, he answered them with humor, personality, and a friendly smile.

Dani recalled all the men scientists she'd been lectured by in the past two years and imagined a woman taking their place for a change. In that moment, Dani saw herself standing in front of the lectern as Dr. Stanton, presenting life-saving research and medical practices. Although she loved lacrosse, science was where she wanted to make her living. She had always harbored a profound interest in the way things worked in the world.

Now, besides a PAC-12 championship, her promise was the only other thing driving her forward.

And she could get there. She was smart.

Smarter than most people, thanks to her eidetic memory.

*But are you really that smart? Look at all the dumb, shameful mistakes you've made. Are you so naïve to think you've moved past them?* The sinister thought sent a tremor through her limbs. She squeezed the wooden edge of her desk, and her knee bounced anxiously.

When Dr. Stanton's presentation finally ended, she slung her backpack over her shoulder with a sigh of relief and followed the trickle of students exiting the classroom. As she passed by Turner's desk, his low voice stopped her in her tracks.

"Miss Torres, one second."

She paused and turned to face him, biting her lip as the last students continued by.

He folded his large black hands across the arms of his chair and looked up at her with a calm curiosity. "It's good to see you're back in another one of my classes. I wondered if our talk last year about the rigorous demands of med school scared you into another major." A gleam shone in his warm eyes. "Has Dustin been of any help to you?"

She nodded. "Yes, he has. A lot."

Turner beamed, rocking back in his chair and steepling his hands. "I'm glad. You have a lot of potential. Keep working hard, and I'm sure you'll get into med school without any problems. You'll do extremely well beyond it for that matter."

She forced a smile, the guilt from her missed assignment settling uncomfortably in her stomach. "Thank you, Professor." She paused and shifted her weight, wondering if she should attempt to carry out the conversation. "I really enjoyed the lecture today—not that your other lectures have been any less enjoyable—"

He tossed back his bald head, and a deep laugh boomed from his gut. "Although unnecessary, I appreciate such an innocent, fashionable attempt to compliment my class." She bit her lip in embarrassment, and his eyes crinkled. "Forgive me. My humor is stark at times."

He stood and gestured his arm to the door. He was a large, robust man, and though he towered over Dani with intimidating height, his smile was friendly. "My door is always open should you need anything, Miss Torres."

Dani zoomed on her bike around a sea of students, seething at her mindless actions this past weekend. Turner's words of encouragement were a sharp reminder she had to stay focused on med school, not go out partying when she had assignments to complete.

And the alcohol—what had she been thinking?

*Failure after failure after failure…*

She scratched her cheek and clenched her handlebars tightly, forcing the voice away. As she approached Soni McAlister field, she spotted Winston through the fence, setting up cones in a triangular fashion on the field. Dani skidded her bike to a stop as her pulse intensified and a memory absorbed her senses.

Then she was falling, falling down a dark hole, her body flailing in a desperate attempt to escape…

*An eighteen-year-old Dani zigzagged around cones set in a large triangle across her family's lacrosse field, her arms slick with perspiration.*

*Franc Torres sat on the porch bench, digging into a plate of lasagna while scrutinizing Dani's every move with a hard gaze. Although he was a tall, intimidating man when standing, he looked just as menacing seated. Her brother and mom were inside, also eating lasagna at the dinner table, while Dani continued to practice, running back and forth, back and forth.*

*The warm August sun cast shadows over the lawn as she bolted across the grass, her long dirty-blonde ponytail whipping in the wind behind her.*

*She pivoted and spun inside the crease her dad had drawn in front of the goal, shooting the ball into the net.*

*"Can I eat now?" she shouted to her dad from across the field.*

*"A few more back-handed hooks, minus your alligator arms. Hurry up—the food is getting cold," he ordered in a light Spanish accent, his black mustache collecting red sauce as he took another bite.*

*Dani's stomach rumbled as she watched Franc wipe his mouth with a napkin. Her arms were stiff from practicing for the past three hours, and her calves ached from her constant pivoting and shooting.*

*She threw down her lacrosse stick in a huff and marched toward the back porch.*

*Her dad pointed a greasy finger at her. "Get back down there. Now!"*

*"I'm hungry!" she snarled, stomping up the porch steps in defiance.*

*"Danica Evelyn Torres. Get. Back. Down. There. You're not done until I say you're done." His stern tone gushed with authority, and he leaned forward, setting his fork on the plate.*

*She halted on the landing in front of the back door, a challenge in her eyes. She contemplated if she could slip past him, steal a plate of food, and dart into her safe spot in the forest before he could stop her.*

*Franc placed his food on the ottoman in front of him and slowly stood, his slim, menacing figure towering over her. Her mom appeared behind the screen door and gave Dani a worried look that said, "Listen to him before he takes it out on all of us."*

*A dangerous anger bubbled in the pit of Dani's stomach, but it was only Jeremy's helpless shrug through the kitchen window that convinced her to retreat to the field.*

*But that anger continued to fester, boiling…and the bloodcurdling scream reverberated in her mind. She felt the damp grass beneath her knees as she stared shocked at her blood-drenched hands. She saw the life spilling out of the body lying in front of her knees.*

*And then came the guilt. The nauseating, unbearable, horrid guilt…*

Dani clutched at her stomach, blinking, and she was suddenly back in front of Soni McAlister Field, staring at the small orange cones through the gate.

*Not again. No, no, no, no.*

*It's fine. You're fine. Stop acting like a little girl.*

She swallowed, pedaled slowly to the bike rack, and locked her bike, trying to dismiss the horrible images that kept teasing her conscious. Even as she headed through the Recreation Center to the locker room, changed, and joined the girls walking toward the pitch, the bloodcurdling scream echoed in her mind and raised the hair on the back of her neck.

Haley's smiling face didn't dull the numbing sensation in her hands and feet; didn't keep her fists from clenching and unclenching. Nausea hovered in the shallow depths of her stomach as she approached the cones on the field.

Then she remembered something that drew her mind away from the impending darkness. Dani glanced over at the bleachers.

They were free of any onlookers.

And just like that, the nauseating sensation subsided, receding back into that forsaken place.

She forgot what had been worrying her and smiled.

**September**

DUSTIN PARKED HIS CAR IN FRONT OF THE SMALL REDBRICK house in Culver City. He had just finished a two-hour shadowing of a knee replacement surgery, and that had been *after* the previous five hours he'd spent at Keck for clerkship schooling. The only thing he needed now was a long, relaxing lounge in a hot tub.

He walked up to the front porch, opened the door, and was greeted by Max, his family's large golden retriever.

"Hey, Max. How you doin', boy?" He dropped his laptop bag on the plush chair next to the door and kneeled to pet the dog. "You ready for a run?"

Max jumped up and down, slopping drool everywhere, then trotted over to where the leash sat on the kitchen table.

As tired as he was, Dustin couldn't help but grin. "Just let me change, and we'll go out." He stood and stretched his stiff arms above his head, a deep whoosh of air expelling from his lungs.

The small pile of mail by the door slot caught his eye, and he squatted to shift through the envelopes. Bills, bills, more bills. He really had no basis for exhaustion; his mom had been the one working non-stop to cover their payments for the past few months. He wished summer would come faster so he could start his residency and earn some additional income.

Sighing, he headed into his bedroom and stripped out of his scrubs, shrugging on a pair of running shorts and Nike sneakers. Shirtless, he grabbed his AirPods off his dresser and scrolled through his Spotify playlists, searching for some good running tunes.

The squeak of the front door opening perked his head, and his neighbor's familiar voice drifted through the living room.

"Hello? Dustin?"

He walked down the hallway, Max trailing close behind, as Bettie poked her curly white hair through the door. The elderly woman stretched her bright pink lips into a warm smile when he approached.

"I thought I saw your car drive up."

Dustin smiled at his neighbor. She was looking less and less frail these days, her posture straight, her pale blue eyes beaming. She had a fresh floral smell to her that reminded him of lilies. He supposed it was fitting considering her house looked as if someone had vomited floral decorations all over the furniture.

He shoved his hands into his pockets. "Thanks for watching Mel again. Long hours today."

Bettie nodded, waving a hand. "Of course. You know I love the company." She opened the door further to reveal his nine-year-old sister, a backpack slung over one shoulder. Her long brown hair was tied back in a ponytail, revealing the permanent smirk on her small, round face.

His lip curved. "Hey, twerp. How was school?"

Mel hiked her backpack higher, blowing the stray flyaways out of her face. "Boring as usual. And why do you never wear a shirt? Have some decency for the rest of us!" She brushed past him into the living room, her large brown eyes brightening when Max greeted her with a bark. "Hey, boy! How are you doing?" She giggled as Max pranced around her and licked her arm.

Dustin returned his attention to Bettie, who combed her eyes along his bare chest and running shorts. "Are you going out?"

He ran a hand through his tousled hair, glancing at Mel and Max playing behind him. "Yeah, I'm just taking Max for a run, but Mel can ride her bike alongside."

Bettie's pale blue eyes sparkled through her aged face. "Oh, that's nice! Is your mom still working?"

"Yeah, she's been working later shifts these days. She rarely gets home before I do." His mom was the one who loved taking Max out, but since June, she'd had to put in more hours at the hospital to keep up with the bills, her student loans, and car payments. That meant he had to walk Max and watch over his little sister when she wasn't at school or softball practice.

Bettie rubbed Max behind the ears. "Well, I'm sure she's glad she has you to help out with Mel."

He dipped a shoulder and rubbed his neck. "You are more of a help than me these days."

Bettie tossed her hand in the air. "Anytime. Mel is a delight." She smiled and retreated through the door as Dustin closed it behind her.

He turned to see Mel coming back from her room, planting her hands on her hips. "Are we gonna have something good for dinner tonight?"

"I'm too tired to make dinner. Heat yourself a Hot Pocket later." He walked over to the couch where Max was squatting patiently and hooked his collar to the leash. Max barked and tugged him to the door.

Dustin nodded to his sister as he fought Max's pull on the leash. "We still have to take Max out. Grab your bike."

Mel groaned, her head falling backward. She spun on her heel and stomped to the garage, leaving Dustin to lead Max out the front door. A minute later, she met him in the front yard with her bike, a blue helmet covering her small head. Max sprung to action at the sight of her and yanked Dustin forward on their route, Mel following close behind.

He led Max and his sister out of their neighborhood and down Venice Boulevard, along his usual loop. The fading sun cast an orange-purple glow on the small shops to their right as Dustin's feet pounded along the pavement, keeping up with Max's fast trot.

Culver City was a nice quiet town compared to Los Angeles's

sketchy neighborhoods on the east side. Couples and other dog-walkers waved and offered friendly smiles as they passed, reminding him subtly of a time when the neighbors had waved as he rode his bike along the winding streets of the Pacific Palisades. But that was a time long ago, when his parents were together. Things were easier then; carefree. He didn't realize how much he'd taken for granted until they split years ago and his life was flipped upside down.

And his dad had ruined everything this past summer… A mixture of longing and fury swirled in Dustin's gut at the very thought of Derek Mottley.

He inhaled the warm autumn air, his blaring music helping to drown out the worries that had been pounding his head for the past few months. There were so many times he had wanted to pull out his hair this semester. The constant grind of his clinical studies only added to his mountain of stress.

As much as his body begged for rest after his long shifts, running was the one thing that relieved the tension in his mind. Every strenuous stride and pained exhale shifted his focus to the satiating rush of oxygen through his body.

Mel pulled up beside him along the sidewalk as they rounded St. Cecilia church. Her ponytail blew behind her in the light breeze, her mouth moving.

Dustin held up his phone and paused Lizzo's "Juice." "What?"

Her eyes rolled underneath her long lashes. "I *said*, when are you gonna get a real job?"

"Why do you say that?"

She raised an eyebrow. "'Cause you always boast about how much money you're gonna make, but you haven't brought it home yet."

"Hmm, I guess you're right." He contemplated his answer as they crossed the street toward Sony Studios. "Why don't *you* get a job?"

"I'm sure many people would love to hire a sweet, responsible girl like me." She whipped her ponytail over her shoulder and batted her dark lashes. "The age thing, though, it might be a problem."

A smirk tugged Dustin's lips. This kid was way too facetious. Just like him.

"After I graduate this spring, I'll be in a residency, which means I can start getting paid."

She cocked her head. "But what if you don't graduate?"

Dustin sniggered at her absurd question as they rounded a corner, long shadows from an adjacent building blocking the dying sun. "You think I'll fail all my classes? That rarely happens for students who get accepted into a residency. And besides, I have a *stellar* academic record." *Don't jinx yourself. Graduation is still seven months away, yet you're barely making it through day after day, stressing over your life like a damn dramatist.*

Mel rolled her eyes again and clicked her tongue.

Dustin wiped his sweaty brow with a forearm and raised his phone to scroll through Spotify. "Now, quit asking questions before I get a headache."

*October*

"ALL RIGHT, GIRLS, REGULAR WARM-UPS," HALEY ORDERED AS Dani and her teammates exited the locker room on a warm October evening. Winston was nowhere to be seen, and they assumed she was running late, although it was rare. The four other women coaches usually didn't show up until after their warm-ups, but they might as well have not existed while Winston was in charge.

The girls set their sticks and water bottles at the end of the field and began jogging down the track in their usual mile.

As Dani rounded her first lap, she spotted Winston walking toward the track from a door to the rec building. A stout bald man in a red USC polo and khaki pants followed her.

"Torres!" she called. "Over here, please."

Dani jogged off the track and over to Winston's side, placing her hands on her hips. "What is it, Coach?"

Winston's almond eyes tightened, her mouth pursing. She gestured to the man standing next to her. "This is the athletics director, Sean Dellery. He was just speaking to me about an incident involving you and another student last weekend. Sound familiar?"

Dani bit her tongue, the antics of last Saturday night rushing back to her. "Oh… Yes."

Dellery scratched his beard and focused his gaze on her. "Miss Torres, Peter Harrison sent in a report a few days ago that accused you of aggravation and physical assault at a frat party last weekend. Is this accurate, to the best of your recollection?"

Winston crossed her thick arms and shot a dangerous, accusing stare at Dani.

Dani swallowed. *Peter. That dick!* "Yes, sir, I acted out of character."

Dellery's lips curled into a frown. "This kind of behavior will not be tolerated, especially at any school-associated event. Mr. Harrison said you also threw a cell phone at him a few weeks ago?"

Dani rubbed her arm, her stomach coiling. "Yes, but it didn't hit him. I threw it because he and two other guys were making shrewd comments at me."

Winston's eyebrow shot up. She unfolded an arm and rubbed her temple. "Next time something like that happens, come to me, and I'll take care of it. You know better, Torres."

Dellery scratched his beard again. "Yes. Had you reported that sooner, we could have settled any issues, but now it looks like you have committed aggravation on two occasions. Several students have confirmed both incidents as witnesses." He paused, and his chest fell in a deep sigh. "Unfortunately, I will have to suspend you from lacrosse until further notice. You will also be put on academic probation."

Dani's stomach plummeted. A million thoughts flew through her head as her brain tried to process Dellery's words. *This can't be happening! I'll kill Peter. How long is "until further notice"? What will my parents say? What will Haley and the girls say? What if my suspension sabotages our chances in the PAC-12 tournament?*

She staggered back. "What? I don't understand… Am I…losing my scholarship?" Her eyes darted between Dellery and Winston, hoping Winston would come to her aid.

But the coach remained silent, her tan face drawn, eyes hardened.

Dellery's level stare didn't waver. "Your scholarship will remain intact, but you must retain a GPA above 3.0 if you hope to keep it."

"Sir, I—" Dani stuttered, choking on her words. She turned to Winston in disbelief, but her coach made no indication of sympathy.

Dellery shook his bald head slowly. "This is the best option we have to work with if you want to retain your scholarship. If you keep your grades up and stay out of trouble, however, you should be able to resume in the spring."

Dani squeezed her eyes closed in disbelief. How could she be suspended? This had to be influenced by Peter's dad, like Arianna had warned. Dani wanted to kick herself for her stupidity. She'd played right into Peter's hand, giving him what he wanted. Why did she have to give in to alcohol? And gotten drunk at that? *Stupid, stupid!*

*Failure after failure after failure…* The haunting words echoed in her mind, a dark reminder of the troubled girl lurking just beyond the shadows of her past.

But it wasn't all bad. She still had her scholarship and would be able to return in the spring—should she refrain from kicking anyone else's balls, that is.

Maybe this was what she needed. Maybe this was her chance to get back on track with med school. And maybe time away from lacrosse would finally put a stop to those…unsolicited memories.

This was actually a good thing, she decided. Peter had done her a favor.

Dani expelled a breath she didn't know she'd been holding. "Okay," she concluded.

Winston gritted her teeth and stepped forward. "I expect better from you, Torres. Get your grades up and do whatever you have to do to get back on the field." Her disappointed eyes sank Dani's esteem. "And when you're back, I expect you to be in shape."

Dani hopped off her bike at her apartment's driveway after a long ride home, her head still reeling in disbelief of her predicament. She wheeled her bike through the front door to find Carolyn sitting at the kitchen table, twirling a fork in a bowl of ramen.

Carolyn's green eyes widened, and she sat upright, clinking her fork on her bowl. "Dani! Why are you home so early?"

Dani wrinkled her mouth and brushed a loose strand of hair behind an ear. "I'm… suspended from lacrosse," she admitted with a shameful half-smile.

The crease in Carolyn's brow deepened, and she wove a hand through the red hair tangling past her shoulders. "What? How'd that happen? That's terrible news!"

Dani sucked in a breath as she dipped her head. "It's bad, but not terrible. That douchebag Peter ratted me out after I kicked his balls last weekend." She wheeled her bike past the kitchen table and leaned it against the wall by the bar window. "My scholarship is still intact; I just need to keep my grades up until I'm off academic probation. If all goes well, I should be able to play in the spring."

"I don't understand…" Carolyn leaned forward on her elbows, brow wrinkled. "Why aren't you more upset?"

Dani hesitated, her teeth grazing her bottom lip. She still hadn't told Carolyn about the multiple times she'd nearly blacked out at lacrosse practice.

Swallowing, Dani shrugged her backpack onto the floor and sank into a chair across the table from her roommate. "These past few weeks have been…not the best. I kind of needed a break from lacrosse."

Carolyn shifted in her seat and tilted her head. "What do you mean? Is Winston that bad?"

Dani tapped a nail on the table, contemplating various answers, but none of them ended well in her mind. Her stomach churned with a brewing storm.

"No."

One second. Five seconds. Ten seconds. Carolyn waited patiently as Dani lowered her head and scratched her cheek. "I've been having flashbacks again."

Now she had done it.

Carolyn's jaw dropped, and she stared at Dani in horror. "Oh my gosh. Why is that happening? You were fine for the past two seasons!"

Dani averted her eyes, digging her nails into a chip in the table's wood surface.

"Dani…answer me honestly." Carolyn paused, the silent moment dripping with tension. "Have you been taking your medication?"

A long breath escaped Dani before she met Carolyn's eyes and shook her head.

Carolyn folded her hands. "Why didn't you tell me?" she asked in a level tone, and Dani could see the hurt in her eyes.

Dani glanced down, the horrors of freshman year all too clear in her mind: the long hours locked away in her dorm room, her frequent escapes to campus bathroom stalls to cry when a small thing triggered her emotions, the nightmares...

She sucked in a deep breath. "Sorry. I didn't want you to worry." She bit her lip and wound a strand of dirty-blonde hair around a finger. "It feels like I'm going through freshman year all over again," she said quietly.

She had tried to go that first year without medication, telling her mom the distraction provided by a new school and friends would be enough. But she was wrong. Carolyn had been the one to comfort her during those first few weeks of freshman year after hearing Dani cry late into the night. In all her generous glory, Carolyn had declined attending campus events and group study sessions in favor of being by Dani's side. Before long, the timid, awkward redhead Dani had met on move-in day soon became a friend for life.

To this day, Carolyn was the only person besides Dani's parents who knew about the flashbacks.

Carolyn's bright green eyes remained locked on Dani, concern tinging the edges of her voice. "When did you stop taking the meds? And why? You knew what would happen."

Dani's sea of emotions surged against the floodgates of her core. Her fingers clenched the edge of her seat as she struggled to suppress the grief. "Because I'm sick of medication messing with my life. I'm sick of it numbing my emotions and convincing me I can't have a normal life without it. It's always been a guilty reminder of what I did, of how weak I am." She rubbed her arms and tried to keep her voice steady. "It's time I moved on with my life and stopped cowering in fear for once."

Her jaw gritted as her heart thundered through her chest. She closed her eyes and forced air into her lungs, grabbing a hold of her wavering voice. "I stopped taking the meds this summer. In July. It's been three years now since...you know...and I figured I should be okay after so much time. And I was. Everything seemed fine for the first few weeks after I stopped taking them. But then lacrosse practices started, and the flashbacks came back."

Carolyn blinked slowly. "I'm…so sorry, Dani. Did you…did you consider taking your meds again? Since your flashbacks returned?"

Dani shifted her legs under the table and glanced at her lap. "No. It's just a weird withdrawal phase—it'll pass eventually. I just need to suck it up. And I've managed to avoid the worst of it. Anyways, lacrosse was the main thing that triggered them, and now I'm suspended."

Carolyn's freckled nose scrunched. "Sucking it up is a terrible idea."

Dani sat back in her chair, folding her arms. "Well, thanks for your support. I suppose I should just stay on meds for the rest of my life because I can't handle a few episodes?"

Carolyn's lips spilled into a frown. "Girl, if there's anyone with a fighting spirit, it's you. After what you've been through, I'm positive of that." She paused and rubbed a chubby cheek before resting her eyes on Dani once more. "But…I don't know. I think you should at least talk to a therapist and find another way around this. Suddenly backing off the meds without any professional assistance could do some serious damage to you."

Dani twiddled her thumbs as her last therapist visit flooded her memory. In an assessment, Dr. Salvador had prodded her emotions and brain activity to the point where one of her most excruciating flashbacks had been triggered. He came to the grim conclusion her eidetic memory enhanced the severity of the flashbacks and meds were the only way to ease her pain.

"But…" Carolyn went on, snapping Dani's eyes back up to meet her roommate's. "Just remember, I'm always here for you, Dani. Don't forget that," she said with a warm tug of her lips.

Her roommate's reassurance gave Dani a bit of hope. She managed a half-smile. "Thanks, Carolyn. But please don't tell my mom. She would freak like always. I don't need her adding extra stress to my life."

Carolyn scowled. She pursed her lips in contemplation before leaning back and sighing. "Fine, but only if you promise to never hide anything from me again. You can go on a tantrum and complain all you want about it, I don't care."

The snort that came out of Dani rivaled Alisha's. "Yes, Mother."

*October*

A FEW WEEKS LATER, DANI LOUNGED WITH CAROLYN ON A weathered red couch at the Village, their laptops and notebooks scattered between them.

It was a sultry October evening. Normally, she'd be at lacrosse practice at this time, but since she'd been suspended, Dani had ample time in her day. When she wasn't completing schoolwork or studying for the MCAT with Carolyn, she was running miles around campus to keep in shape.

And she still had extra time to watch anime in the evenings.

But the best part of her suspension was that she hadn't had any flashbacks or nightmares since September, and she could thank Peter for it. Peter and his rich dad could think they'd won their little feud and celebrate in their belief of her demise, but in truth, *Dani* had won.

Finished with her op-ed analysis for English class, Dani pulled out some papers for physics and scribbled some formulas in her notebook.

She supposed she was getting used to this idea of "study sessions," especially with Carolyn as an encouraging companion. Well, Dani's version of studying didn't involve re-reading things since she easily remembered things the first time. It just meant she'd be using her eidetic memory to zoom through assignments and jump ahead on essays and projects due at the end of the semester.

A few minutes into her English assignment, her phone pinged, and she dropped her pencil. She picked up to see a Messenger request from a "Tanner Stevens."

**Hey, how's it going?**

The face in his profile picture looked familiar. Tanner… Oh! It was the cute football guy from the frat party—he had found her on Facebook. She remembered the mesmerizing gaze of his brown eyes, the attractive spill of his bangs across his face, his firm jawline and charming smile… A small thrill went through her at the thought of him being interested enough to seek her out on social media. She couldn't contain the smile that spread across her face.

Unfortunately, dating around right now would only distract her from her studies. Her GPA couldn't afford to slip if she wanted to keep her scholarship, and med school also depended on her good grades. Her mind jumped back to her conversation with Dr. Turner and the vision of herself standing at the CDC doctor's lectern. She wouldn't taint that vision if she could help it.

Slipping her phone into her jean shorts pocket, she sighed and glanced over at Carolyn. The redhead clicked her tongue happily, her highlighter whizzing through her textbook.

Dani tsked. "I keep looking at you and seeing that party animal at Lucky Strike. You were quite the opposite of bashful with that one guy."

Carolyn ceased her tongue-clicking and lost grip of her highlighter. It rolled off her textbook and onto the ground, and she bent clumsily to pick it up, blushing. "Oh no. Was it Kyle Walker? What did I say?"

Dani blanched. "Uh, nothing crazy. Why? You like him? I thought that was just the alcohol speaking…"

Carolyn smiled and found sudden interest in folding a page in her textbook. "I like him a little." Her green eyes twinkled when they latched with Dani's. "He's on the baseball team, and he's so cute! Are you sure I didn't say anything I'll regret?"

Dani thought back to that night and remembered Carolyn's babbling. "You were just going on about your cousin or something. I'm sure it was very interesting; he looked engaged," she fibbed. She left out the fact he had eyed Dani's body with an appreciative jaw drop. Carolyn's hopeful heart was too precious to crush.

Carolyn rubbed her eyes and moaned. "Oh my gosh, I'm such an idiot. I told you to never let me drink! Something wild always happens."

Dani snickered, brushing her hair behind an ear. "Well, that was the first time I've seen you drunk, and I have to say, I really like the wasted Carolyn. Aside from the vomiting part."

"Don't count on seeing that version of me anymore." Carolyn leaned her chin on a fist and peered at Dani curiously. "What about you though? Anyone catch your eye at the party? Or have you been seeing anyone at all for that matter?"

Dani wrinkled her mouth. "Not really." She didn't want to get excited over Tanner, so he was best left tucked away.

She hadn't had that much experience with dating if she was honest with herself. Her dad had bombarded her free time in high school with lacrosse drilling and scared away any guy who was brave enough to come to her house. And her college dating life hadn't been that much more successful; lacrosse workouts and the laborious workload of pre-med classes had consumed her social hours.

Dani sighed before her lips twisted into a smile. "The closest I was to a guy's dick lately was when I kicked Peter's balls."

Carolyn chuckled as she rolled up the sleeves of her *Doctor Who* sweatshirt. "Oh, yeah, I wish I was sober enough to remember that!" She straightened with a devilish grin. "But what about your mentor—that grad student in med school? You guys have been meeting over the summer, right?"

Dani's shoulders perked in amusement. "Dustin? No, he's not my type."

Carolyn punched her shoulder. "Yeah, right! From what you've said, he's *so* your type. Hilarious, sarcastic, smart, tall...*and* gorgeous."

"I never said any of that! You're just making up things." She couldn't help but smile at Carolyn despite herself. "He's like five years older. And I don't think of him like that. He's just a friend."

"Uh-huh, sure." Carolyn winked.

*Ten*

*October*

Dustin's eyes crinkled in disdain at Dani as he sipped his Americano and set it back on the patio table. "I hate Dulce's coffee. Why'd we have to meet here?"

The faint smell of smoke from the Getty fire wafted on the breeze between them at their meeting spot in the Village. Dani supposed she was used to California's crazy fire season by now, but the familiar huge, smoky cloud in the distance was no less daunting after two years.

Dani rolled her eyes as she took a drink of her iced caramel Frappuccino. *Who doesn't like Dulce's coffee?* "All coffee tastes the same. And why'd you get some if you hate it so much?"

"To see if my mind changed about Dulce. It hasn't."

She gave him her best glower. "You know there's a Starbucks right there?" She hitched a thumb over her shoulder.

"You know there's a booger right *there?*" He pointed to his nose, staring at a spot above Dani's lip.

"What?" She swiped at her face, her cheeks heating.

A devilish grin spread across his mouth, and he tossed back his head with a sharp laugh. "I'm just messing with you."

Dani leaned over the table and socked his arm. "You ass! What the hell!"

He chuckled as he swirled his drink. "It's too easy with you."

Her eyes narrowed, more annoyed than amused. She only put up with his jabs and cringey, cheesy jokes because he was her mentor.

Dustin winked and took a second sip of his coffee before setting his cup down with another disgusted twist of his lips.

She smiled despite herself. *Ha, that's what you get.*

He pointed to the list of classes on one of the papers in between them, directing her attention back to her course planning. "It's gonna be a challenge, but you should take at least twenty units in the spring to help you prepare for your MCAT. I'd suggest one non-HP course, two core HPs, and then two HP electives. You still have some more bio courses, and human physiology… What's cool is that Turner also teaches Theoretical Principles of Health Behavior, so you could take him again. He really is a genius."

Dani skimmed over the sheet absentmindedly, taking in a fraction of what he said as her thoughts drifted. She needed to take twenty units next semester? With lacrosse season in full swing? There went all of her free hours.

Dustin drawled on. "Also, you'll need to get some shadowing experience. My mom said one of the hospitals downtown is offering an introductory nursing program during winter break. I think you should do it."

She dropped her head into her hands. "Well, shit. All my lacrosse games are in the spring. I'm gonna die before my twenty-second birthday."

He snorted. "That's your fault for doing pre-med and sports simultaneously."

Dani lifted her head and scowled at her mentor. "Excuse *me,* Mr. I-Can-Do-Sports-And-Med-School-And-No-One-Else-Can."

He placed a hand over his heart and pressed his brows together. "It's a difficult feat only for those willing to make the utmost sacrifices."

"And you think I can't?" Dani scoffed, folding her arms. She was prepared to do whatever it took to get into med school, even if it meant losing sleep and attending more of Carolyn's little study sessions. To hell with Dani if she was going to come all this way just to crash and burn right before the finish line.

His shoulder lifted in a shrug, and his lips twisted into a guilty smile. "It's none of my business how you spend your time, but maybe next semester, you should use it to study for the MCAT instead of hitting up frat parties."

*Burnnn.*

She took a long sip of her coffee, glaring at him. "Well, it just so happens that outside my *one* rambunctious party night, I *have* been studying for the MCAT. Not that it matters anyways considering you'd just find some other thing to pester me for."

He didn't need to know she'd only just started studying for the MCAT since she was suspended from lacrosse. Let him think she was making sacrifices.

He raised an eyebrow and scratched the stubble on his cheek. "Yeah? Good. Keep at it. There's still a lot of time between now and next summer."

"You still don't believe me," she grumbled.

His patronization annoyed her. Plenty of people lectured her all the time; she didn't need to add Dustin to the list. Nor did she need another reminder of all the bad decisions she'd made. She had plenty of those. "I may not be as perfect as *you*, with your impeccable focus and star-student status, but that doesn't mean I'm an automatic failure."

He stared at her with bewilderment, taken aback. "I never said you're a failure." His tone softened as he ran a hand through his hair. "And I'm definitely not perfect." A silent, heavy moment passed between them before he expelled a deep breath and leaned forward on his elbows. "I'm just saying, I know the load from pre-med sucks, but I don't want it to be harder for you than it is. I had friends forced to retake classes, and it put them into an extra year of schooling. And that's a shit-ton of wasted money." He raked his hand through his tousled hair. "And grad school is another kind of hell. It's been enough work without me even playing basketball or going to parties and other stuff. What's worse is that med school only amplifies the stress you feel from whatever else is going on in your life…" He rubbed his palms together, his blue eyes distant.

Dani traced the table's warm metal, her fingers looping around the circular design. She was all too familiar with the feelings of stress and anxiety. If there was anything she'd learned over her two brief years in college, it was how easy it was to screw everything up. School was hard, but add life on top of that, and it was like you suddenly had a huge weight on your shoulders while you teetered on the rim of success and failure.

Maybe she shouldn't blame Dustin for berating her when he only wanted what was best for her. But she couldn't help wondering if he'd never had an outlet for his own stress, like lacrosse had been for Dani.

No longer interested in course planning, Dani drained the rest of her Frappuccino and stood to toss it into a nearby trash can. She lifted a shoulder, gesturing for him to follow, as she picked up her backpack and walked around the tables toward the cafe's gated exit.

"Dani, what the hell?" He scrambled to pick up the papers she had left on the table, then slung his laptop bag over his shoulder and dumped his coffee in the trash behind her. "Hungry already?" he asked, catching up to her. She was headed past the fountain in the Village center toward Kobunga, the Korean Barbecue restaurant.

He handed her the course lists, and she stuffed them into her backpack without making an effort to stack them neatly in a folder.

"No." She stopped by one of the cornhole boards that was set up in the walkway in front of Kobunga and dropped her backpack.

"What are you doing?"

"You're so full of questions." She gathered the bean bags that were laying on the wooden board and tossed the red ones at him. He caught them and stared at her, baffled. Her hip sagged as she tossed a blue bag in the air. "But if you must now, I'm teaching you how to retain your sanity." She folded her arms and nodded at the board opposite them, several yards away. "You're first."

"I don't h—"

She rolled her eyes. "Yes, you do have time. Shut up and throw."

His brow scrunched before he dropped his laptop bag and stepped next to her, focusing his gaze on the distant board. He tossed the first bag, but it landed way far left of the target.

"Damn," he exhaled, his mouth slanting downward.

Dani laughed and tossed another bag lazily above her head. "What are you whining about? You're a natural!" She playfully shoved him to the side and squinted at the board. Her throw landed at the bottom of the board. "And…one point."

He shook his head as he tossed. His bag landed precariously on the edge, only to be knocked off by Dani's next throw. He missed his next two tosses, while another one of Dani's landed on the board, and her last one went through the hole.

He raised an eyebrow at her, and she grinned. "See?" she teased. "You can study and still have time to get your ass kicked in a game of cornhole. It's called *fun.*"

Dustin snorted, and the two of them headed toward the opposite board to collect their bags. They went back and forth a few more times, a smug grin stretching Dani's mouth as she cancelled out any points he managed to land. She laughed through his curses as she beat him round after round.

She eyed him curiously, scanning his tall, athletic form as he stepped forward to take his next shot. A warm breeze rippled his messy hair and the folds in his shirt, outlining a hard stomach. Eyes continuing upward, Dani was acutely aware of how his finely trimmed stubble accentuated his dark lashes and bright blue eyes…

"Dustin?" she asked, brushing a strand of hair behind her ear.

"What?" he huffed, his eyes still trained on the board.

"What made you want to pursue med school?"

His eyebrow arched, and he straightened slowly, rubbing an arm along his forehead. "I'm doing it because…my mom inspired me to. She'd come home from work telling stories about saving people's lives." He licked his lips, his gaze fixing on the bag in his hand. "I guess I wanted to be like her—someone who could make a difference. Do some good in this world. Take others' pain away."

Dani scratched her cheek, shoving away the haunting memories swimming behind her lids. "Sounds like a pretty solid reason." To be honest, it was a really poetic, selfless reason.

He tossed his bag, landing it on the front of the board. "What about you?" He turned to face her, tugging the front of his shirt to air it out.

She contemplated her answer. "I…want to save lives. I…" *You what? Are you really going to tell him about your promise? About your past?* Dani shrugged. "The world needs more doctors." *Didn't think so.*

He tilted his head, and the corner of his mouth tugged upward. "Yeah. The world does need more doctors."

She turned, threw a bag, and missed. "You must really be excited for graduation."

His tone lightened. "I guess so, yeah. Eight years of schooling gone just like that... I'll never disrespect a doctor again, that's for sure."

She nodded and cursed under her breath as she missed another throw. "I'm super jealous. I'm not looking forward to another four years."

"Yeah, it sucks, but it'll all be worth it." He averted his eyes as his Adam's apple bobbed. "I just need to start working and help out my mom. It's been pretty hard the past few months..." He seemed to drift away in thought for a few seconds.

Dani tightened her lips, studying his deep blue eyes and relaxed posture. She hadn't imagined Dustin to be so...family oriented. It seemed so contrary to the sarcastic, joking personality she was used to, and it puzzled her.

He seemed...different from other guys. Maybe underneath his good looks and facetious jabs, he was just an easygoing, goal-oriented guy who sucked at cornhole.

Carolyn's words echoed in her head from last week, and Dani tugged her eyes away from Dustin, cursing herself. *What am I doing?* She squeezed the bean bag, her thumb tracing the stitching along the sides. "I know you think I haven't been taking my studies seriously, but I am. It's just been hard to find time to do the homework. But I've been doing a lot better lately since...I don't know." She bristled and scratched her cheek. She had almost spilled the beans about being suspended from lacrosse. But for some reason, she wanted to tell him suddenly, and not just about her suspension, but everything—the flashbacks, the full truth about her motivation to get into med school, why her dad wouldn't talk to her...

But as she considered the idea of telling him, the horrid creature stirred in her gut, and she swallowed down bile with difficulty.

*It's too much. It would wreck me.*

Dustin's eyes danced as he leaned to aim his next shot. "I know this game was supposed to teach me about retaining my sanity, so thank you for that. But allow *me* to teach *you* something, if I may." A smile crept onto his lips, and he turned to focus on his target. "Never start something unless you have the guts to accept the results, no matter how much uglier they might turn out than you expected." His next bean bag flew into the hole with surprising grace.

Dani scrunched her face, drawing her brows at him. Lucky shot. He had beaten her this round.

But the next few rounds, he landed bag after bag on the board, and the one time she matched him, he went ahead with a holer and stole the points.

The tables had turned. He scored fifteen straight points, shutting her down and sealing his win.

He grinned at her as she crossed her arms and sulked in defeat. He strutted to the opposite board, picked up a bag, and tossed it into the air.

"Basketball player." His arms arced in an overhead throw, and the bag sunk clean through the hole at Dani's feet.

Dani stiffened, eyes narrowing in disbelief at his perfect form. In the heat of their competition, she had forgotten he played basketball. Her cheeks flared as she realized he had let her lead this whole time. He had planned to show her up in the end all along! *What a scheming, aggravating piece of—*

"Learned your lesson in discipline yet? Or do I have to *school* you again?" He tossed another bag in the air, mocking her with a wicked crooked smile.

This time when she rolled her eyes, it was in the slowest, most agonizing fashion she could manage.

"WANT TO WATCH *CASTLEVANIA*?" DANI ASKED CAROLYN hopefully as she scrolled through Netflix. They were plopped on the couch with their feet propped up in matching bright-colored pajama pants, a large bowl of hot, buttered popcorn sitting between them.

It was Halloween. Alisha and Emma had gone out to a party down the street that had been advertised all over campus. Both Dani and Carolyn had decided to pass in favor of a movie night at the apartment.

They both needed a break from partying for a while.

"Nice try, but it's not gonna work." Carolyn crunched on a handful of popcorn. "Let's try something Disney."

Dani stuck out her tongue and trekked to the bookshelf beneath the TV, scrolling through the DVD's before shoving *Mulan* into the DVD player.

When the doorbell rang a quarter into the movie, they looked at each other.

"I got the first few," Carolyn offered as Dani paused the movie. She rushed to the door, grabbed the bowl of candy on the counter, and greeted the kids with an excited, "Happy Halloween!" She dashed back to the couch a minute later, not missing a beat.

On the fourth doorbell ring, Carolyn didn't budge, instead raising a suggestive eyebrow at Dani.

"Fine, I'll go," Dani huffed, pressing pause. She marched to the kitchen, grabbed the candy bowl, and opened the door.

"Trick-or-treat!" Two little kids held up their jack-o-lantern buckets with wide smiles. The boy wore a skeleton costume, and the girl was dressed as Elsa from *Frozen*.

*Love that movie. I'll make Carolyn watch it after* Mulan.

A smile escaped her lips. They were pretty cute. "I love your costumes!" She dropped a handful of lollipops, Starbursts, and chocolate into each of their buckets. "Here you go. Happy Halloween!"

The two kids turned around and ran back to their parents waiting on the sidewalk. "What do you say?" their mom ushered with a hand on her hip.

"Thank you!" they yelled back with harmonious giggles.

The parents waved at her with warm smiles, triggering a sinking feeling in Dani's gut. It was a moment before she remembered to wave back, thoughts of her own parents clouding out the jubilant night.

It was years since her family had done anything remotely fun together. The happiest time with them recently was when they came to her lacrosse matches at USC, but even then, her dad had glared at her from the sidelines, berating her afterward for her missed shots. Every conversation with them always ended with heated words and finger-jabbing, and she was glad for the distance college put between them.

All her parents were good for was reprimanding her for every little thing, making sure she didn't mess anything up.

*Too late for that.* She wondered what they would say if she told them she had been suspended from lacrosse for beating up a guy while she was intoxicated. Maybe their scolding was justified.

Maybe she'd only ever be that little, shameful girl cowering in the dark…

"You coming back anytime soon?" Carolyn called from the living room, snapping Dani out of her thoughts.

She shook her head and closed the front door, rejoining Carolyn on the couch. "I'm surprised we've had so many trick-or-treaters in this college neighborhood," she muttered as Carolyn pressed play.

"What?" Carolyn asked, her lazy eyes trained on the TV. "Ooh, this is the best part!"

Mulan had just come home after defeating Shan Yu, expecting her father to reprimand her for her dishonor on their family. Instead, her father brushed aside her sword offering and hugged her, claiming *her* as his greatest honor. The swell of music as father and daughter embraced filled Dani's heart with a painful longing.

An image of Francisco Torres shimmered to the forefront of her mind. His brown face was hard-pressed, frowning in judgment. She couldn't even picture him smiling or laughing.

*But you can't blame him, can you? His fury and disappointment in you are justified.*

The credits rolled across the screen as Carolyn reached for the remote with a cheerful smile. "What do you want to watch next? And you'd better not say '*Castlevania.*'"

Dani hid her face as she brushed away the small tear that trickled down her cheek. "You choose," she murmured as she tried to swallow the lump in her throat. Carolyn's eyebrows drew upward as Dani stood from the couch. "Actually…I think I'm gonna check out early."

Carolyn set down the remote and pursed her lips. "Are you okay?"

Dani turned so Carolyn's compassionate eyes wouldn't tip her emotions over the edge. "Yeah, yeah, I'm good. I think I'm just movie-d out is all." She headed toward the stairs before Carolyn could object. "Happy Halloween," she muttered over her shoulder.

She trudged upstairs to the confines of her room and stuffed her face into the pillows, choking back a sob. She didn't want Carolyn to see her like this—she might overreact and pressure her to take her meds or call Dani's mom.

Dani didn't want her to worry. She could get through this. She was fine.

Rolling over on her bed, she wracked her brain for someone else she could talk to. Someone who might humor her and make her feel good about herself.

She sat up, sniffing, and pulled out her phone. A small smile crept onto her face as she scrolled through her messages and found the thread she was looking for.

**Hey**, she sent.

*November*

DUSTIN RUBBED HIS EYES, TRYING TO KEEP AWAKE LATE INTO the evening. He focused back on his laptop video of an anesthesiologist handling a tracheostomy tube. After a few minutes, he paused the video, threw his arms back in a stretch, and walked across his bedroom to open the window. A chilly night breeze cooled his face as he leaned on the windowsill.

November had brought with it a drop in temperature and clouds for the first few weeks, allowing the exhausted California firemen to finally put an end to the fires. The change in cleaner, breathable air was subtle, as Los Angeles was engulfed in a huge cloud of pollution anyway.

He turned and tripped over his guitar stand. "Shit!" He caught the guitar before it toppled over and stood it upright in its place by the window. A burn crept up his throat as he gazed at the finely furnished wood, thoughts of his dad surfacing.

Why did he even have the damn thing out still? Fist clenching, he jerked open his closet door and found the guitar case he kept stowed away in the corner. He dragged it out and placed the guitar inside before shoving the case back into the closet. Rubbing his eyes, he fought against the knot twisting in his chest, trying to shove away the nagging memories.

The loud squeak of the front door opening jerked him out of his head.

"Mom's home!" Mel yelled, her light feet prancing past his door, down the hallway.

*Dammit, I thought you were asleep.*

Dustin pinched his nose and opened his door. He meandered down the hall to see his mom lift Mel up in a sweeping hug, Max barking as he circled them.

Rachel was a relatively tall woman with a confident gait and wide smile, but tonight, her gait was weak, her smile strained. She closed weary eyes and kissed the top of Mel's head as the girl clung to her blue scrubs. After a minute, she lowered Mel to the floor and brushed back her daughter's long brown hair.

Dustin stepped forward to give Rachel a kiss on the cheek. "Hi, Mom. How was work?" He petted Max before lifting his gaze back to her.

Rachel's lips tightened, and she brushed a flyaway that had escaped her tight bun of brown hair. She peered at Dustin with heavy eyes, and he noted the dark bags sagging beneath her lids. "It was a tough day," she replied with a sigh, walking into the kitchen. She pulled out a pitcher of orange juice from the refrigerator and poured herself a glass. "We had more ER visits than usual. There was a high number of pneumonia cases, and the nurses were low on staff, so I was running back and forth between many patients."

She chugged the entire glass of orange juice and wiped her mouth. Her weary gaze fell to Mel's bright face. "Did you do your homework?"

Mel rubbed her wrists. "Most of it, but Dustin said I could play on his iPad after 8:00."

Dustin turned and scowled at her. "I did not, you ass! I said you could play on it *after* you finished all of your homework."

Rachel frowned at him. "Dustin, *language*."

"Well, maybe you shouldn't have given the iPad to me in the first place," Mel shot back at Dustin, tossing her chin up.

He shook his head, and she responded with a punch to his arm.

Rachel folded her arms. "Stop it, you two. I don't have time for this. Mel, you're supposed to be in bed anyway. It's a school night."

Mel's shoulders sagged.

Rachel pursed her red lips and planted firm hands on her hips. "Go to your room, *now*."

With a pout, she dragged her feet to her room and yelled sarcastically, "Thanks, Dustin!" before slamming the door.

After a moment, Rachel unfolded her arms and slumped on a barstool. "Dustin, this can't keep happening. You know she needs to be in bed by 9:00 with all of her homework finished."

Frustration rose, pressing on his own exhaustion. "I'm doing my best, Mom, but I'm more concerned with graduating from med school at the moment." He rubbed his neck. "Bettie is picking her up from school, and I'm making dinner for her most nights. I'm sorry if I forget to check her homework once in a while."

His mom patted the barstool next to hers, and he sat down with chagrin. She smoothed the sleeve of his shirt and plucked a hair from his shoulder, her long lashes blinking slowly. "His attorney called me today."

Dustin stiffened, any lingering agitation dissolving. "What did he say?"

Rachel's chest rose as she locked eyes with him, her high cheekbones drained of color. "The trial didn't go well. He's not leaving jail anytime soon."

A weight plunged in his stomach, and his head dropped into his hands. In the corner of the living room, Max whimpered as if sensing Dustin's turmoil.

"Mom, what are we going to do?" he asked finally, slowly raising his head.

She didn't immediately answer, turning her head and flashing a half-smile at Max. "We're not going to worry about it, Dustin. We'll get through this like we have been. Without him."

*November*

"**W**OW, EVEN ON THE FIRST DATE YOU CAN'T WAIT FOR THE guy to get his food before you start digging in? I'm offended." Tanner plopped his personal pizza in front of Dani at the small table. He was dressed in his football practice gear: a tight spandex shirt that framed his hard pectorals, running shorts, and long black socks with Nike shoes.

Dani scoffed as she dropped her slice of pepperoni pizza on the tray, chewing. "Who said this was a date?" She wiped her hands on a napkin before combing her hair back into a ponytail. "You were just super hungry, and, conveniently, I was too. It would have been rude to decline your invitation to Blaze Pizza considering I was free after your practice." She didn't add the fact she was freer than a bird because of her lacrosse suspension. It wasn't something she was particularly proud of.

A charming smile spilled across his face, and he whipped his dark hair out of his eyes. "Uh-huh. So all that texting between us this past week wasn't a prologue for a date?"

"Nope." She licked the grease from her fingers, her tongue burning.

"That hurts." He whipped his dark bangs out of his eyes, a charming smirk spilling across his lips. "I guess I gotta up my game. It only took you a month to respond to my message. I was afraid you'd shot me down."

Dani rolled her eyes. "Don't flatter yourself. I never said I wanted to start anything with you."

A fire brewed in his brown eyes, and Dani found herself studying the soft curve of his mouth, the hard line of his jaw, and his tan, clean-shaven cheeks. Dani had told herself he was just someone she could talk to, heeding her promise to herself that she wouldn't do anything rash to distract her from her studies.

But…maybe a little flirting wouldn't hurt anything.

"So what are you studying?" Tanner took a huge bite of his pizza and struggled to pull it away as cheese stretched from his mouth.

Dani snickered as he fumbled to sever the cheese with his fingers. "I'm in pre-med. Health Promotion and Disease Prevention." She bit into her slice and struggled to pull her mouth away just as he did.

"Damn! You're going for a hard-ass major? I dig it." He set down his pizza and sipped his soda. "I honestly had no idea what to major in considering I came here just for football. I went with psychology—it's definitely way more laid-back compared to *pre-med.*" He took another huge bite, and an olive rolled off the slice and into his lap.

Dani giggled and covered her mouth, trying to prevent her food from spilling out. "You lost an olive there."

He peered down and picked it up off of his lap before popping it into his mouth without a second thought.

"Ew, isn't that your sweaty workout shirt?" She scrunched her face in disapproval.

"Yeah, that bother you?" He whipped his hair out of his eyes again. She wondered why he didn't just cut it if it was in the way all the time.

"Uh, yes!"

He grinned mischievously. "Then I guess it'd bother you if I did this." He picked an olive off his slice, dragged it along his shirt, and tossed it at her chest. It bounced off her skin and fell to the floor.

"Wowww. So mature." She whipped out the napkin on her lap and prissily wiped the spot on her chest, but her smile deceived her. Damn, it was so easy to flirt with him. Were guys always this fun?

"So when's your next football game?" Dani asked, tilting her head with a playful perk of her lips.

Finished with his first slice, Tanner started digging into the second. "Saturday," he dished with a mouthful of pizza. "You should come! I need to grow my fan base beyond my parents."

Dani grinned. "They come to your games?"

"Only once in a while. They're from Colorado, but they come down every now and then. And they send me a ton of embarrassing mail on game day."

Her stomach sank, and her tone softened. "They send you fan mail?"

He chuckled, and another olive fell onto his lap. "Yeah, the bastards. It's full of 'love and kisses' and all that dumb shit."

Dani tore bits of her crust into small pieces and piled them onto her plate. "They sound…fun. And supportive."

He shrugged as his cheek bulged with food. After he swallowed, he leaned lazily on an elbow. "Just annoying, mostly. How's lacrosse going for you?"

She bit her lip. "Eh, it's all right." If he knew the team was practicing right now, she'd have to explain why she wasn't there. And that would lead to a not-so-good first impression. "Our new coach made it clear she will break all the limbs in our bodies if we don't make it to the PAC-12 championship this year."

His dark eyebrows wiggled. "Mmm, spicy. I like dominant women. Is she single?"

Dani's fingers stopped tearing the crust as she stared a stoic face at Tanner. Then she tossed her head back and burst into laughter. The couple at the table nearest them turned their heads and raised skeptical eyebrows.

Dani brushed back tears from her eyes and met his dumb smirk. "That was…a stupid, unexpected comment."

He cocked his head, and his bangs fell back into his face, but his smirk didn't budge. "I'll take making you laugh as progress. And I have plenty more stupid comments."

She rolled her eyes again as she took another bite of pizza.

He chuckled, leaning back in his chair and stretching out his muscular arms. "Where do you live?"

Dani swallowed and sipped her soda before responding. "By the Village on 23rd."

Tanner raised an eyebrow. "Yeah? I'm right across the street at Trojan Hall." He glanced at his remaining two slices. "Wanna walk back? I'm full."

She eyed her own two slices with disdain and shrugged. "Sure."

Dani tossed their trash into the wastebin as he boxed their leftover pizza. Then she followed him through the exit and into the chilly evening air. She folded her arms and pulled her sweater tight, wishing she'd worn something thicker.

"You good?" he asked, lifting a brow. "This is barely even cold!"

She nodded, biting her lip as the autumn breeze whipped her cheeks. "Aren't *you* cold? You're in shorts and a T-shirt!"

He snorted, the streetlights illuminating the smooth planes of his face as he gazed at the sidewalk. "California weather is nothing. I stripped to my boxers and jumped into a freezing lake in Colorado one time. *That's* cold."

Dani lifted her hood and yanked on the drawstrings. "That sounds idiotic. And it's not like I'm not used to cold weather—I'm from Montana. But I still freeze just like any other human."

"Bro, you look like an Arctic bum." He tugged her hood over her eyes, and she giggled, pushing his arm away.

"Leave my freezing Arctic bum self alone!"

His low, throaty chuckle warmed her bones. Their sides brushed, and she sucked in a breath as tingles shot up her spine. *Whoa, what is happening to me?*

The remaining few blocks sent her pulse into a frenzy, and though she tried to concentrate on their small talk, she failed, her mind instead concentrating on the proximity of his body to hers.

Tanner stopped in front of the large Trojan Hall building that housed upperclassmen. "Wanna check out my dorm?"

Dani hesitated and twisted a lock of hair. She still had some pre-med assignments to complete…

He nodded toward the door. "Come on—I'll show you around." Before she could protest, he placed a hand on the small of her back and led her up the steps to the entrance.

*Failure after failure…*

The voice echoed in her mind as she followed him up the staircase to the second floor and down a long hallway. He paused in front of a door and fed a key into the lock.

"Well, shit. I didn't expect to get a girl into my dorm on the first date."

"Still think this is a date, huh?" she scoffed, stepping inside.

The layout was a smaller version of the first floor of her townhouse apartment. The bar and small kitchen were on the left, a tiny wooden dining table on the right, and a TV, plush couch, and sitting chair made for a cozy living room across the way. Cologne hung heavily in the air, although for Dani, it was a preferable smell to the reek of a few football hunks' body stench.

"Nice place. I don't know why, but I was expecting a ton of trash and clothes to be thrown everywhere," she teased as he shut the door behind her.

"Then you won't be disappointed. Our rooms are just that." Tanner walked into the living room and tossed his backpack beside the couch.

Dani followed him into the room, laughing, and folded her arms. "Of course. Why would I assume a frat-going, sweaty football player would have a clean place?"

"Hey, guys can be clean. Sometimes." He smiled and combed a hand through his dark hair. "I like your wit." He raked his brown eyes up and down her figure. "And your curves. Damn, you're beautiful."

She gazed at him curiously. Guys had told her she was beautiful before, but coming from him, it felt different. Genuine. Warmth gushed through her core.

"You think so?"

He stepped closer, his broad frame sparking an electric tension between them. He was close enough that she could smell the pizza on his breath. "Yes. You're breathtaking, Danica."

She bit her lip to cover her smile, then forced a frown. "I told you I don't like that name."

"Hmm, how about 'D'?"

Dani's cheeks heated. "Mmm, I'd have to think about it."

His breathy chuckle tickled her cheek as he grinned, flashing perfect white teeth. "So, you don't like your full name, you don't like olives thrown down your shirt... What *do* you like?"

"Lots of things." Her mouth curved as she peered into his brown, sultry eyes. His fiery gaze made her feel embarrassingly naked, like he was scouring her soul and could see the parts she tried to keep locked away. But he didn't turn from her in revulsion; he just continued staring at her, his lips pulling into a teasing smile—

She cringed at the situation she had created for herself. What was she doing? She told herself she wouldn't involve herself with anyone, but Tanner… It was incredibly difficult to resist the magnetic pull he had on her. He was gorgeous and had made her smile more in the past few hours than she had in the past several years, let alone months. The warm feeling he gave her seemed to fill a gaping hole in her chest, and she wanted more of it; to soak it in and confirm that it was real.

He wet his lips. "My roommate is out, by the way." When he touched the soft of her back, she wasn't prepared for the jolt of tingles that shot up her spine. He brushed a thumb under the hem of her shirt, and she writhed, arching her back. Her heart raced, and she was very much aware of his warm breath on her face; of the proximity of his lips to hers and the heat of his body against her skin. It made her sigh in a pathetic plea.

"Like that?" he teased. His thumb traced small circles at her back, then trailed around to the front of her hip bone and traced more circles there, forcing a gasp from her. He lowered his gaze to her mouth, and she found herself doing the same, focusing on the thin curve of his lips. "It seems you like it a lot. Would you say this is a date now, D?"

At the sound of her nickname on his lips, butterflies fluttered through her chest. *Gahhh, why do I like him so much? End this now, Dani, before it gets worse! Think about your scholarship!*

She paused as a war raged between her mind and her heart. She couldn't do this—shouldn't—because she had to stay focused on school. Tanner would only ruin things, distract her from her studies, and risk bringing her grades down. Risk losing her scholarship and, more importantly, her chances at med school. She was about to give her mom a reason to be angry with her!

But Tanner felt so *right*. When she was with him, all of her worries—lacrosse, Peter, med school, her parents—melted away. With him, she felt good enough. She deserved this; needed this.

Was it so bad to want to be loved? Wasn't love worth the risk of everything else?

His sultry brown eyes bore into hers, searching for any hint of approval. "You didn't answer my question," he purred.

"Hmm?" she asked breathily. She couldn't even remember his question.

She wanted him—wanted to explore more of this warm feeling that filled a void that had been empty for so long. She angled her face upward, her heart pounding in her ears.

In response, he crushed his mouth to hers and kissed her in long, fiery strokes. His hands seized her hips and tugged her against him as if the narrow gap between their bodies was painstakingly far.

Her body exploded with arousal, and she found herself returning every kiss he gave, eager for him to consume her. A primitive part of her took over, and her hands took on a life of their own, creeping under his shirt, up his sweaty chest and back down again, and tracing the hard ridges of his abs.

She wondered if her electrified response showed her lack of experience, but whether Tanner recognized her desperation or not, it didn't seem to deter him. He pulled away from her lips to plant kisses along her neck, his hot breath igniting goosebumps over her skin.

In a moment, his lips were aggressively back on hers, and his hands were sliding down her stomach, her sides, her thighs. When he squeezed her butt, Dani gasped as fire jolted her core, and a giggle forced its way to her lips.

"What?" he murmured against her ear, his breathing heavy.

Her mouth stretched into a smile. "It's just…no one has touched me like this before."

He drew back and arched a long eyebrow, his bangs falling into his face again. "What kind of shit guys have you been with?" One of his hands drifted under her shirt and began to dip beneath her jeans, but even as her pulse quickened and her body screamed for more, she grabbed his wrist.

"Uh, on the first date?" she exclaimed with a scowl.

Tanner's mouth slanted into a smug grin. "Oh, so you've decided it's a date finally?" When Dani's expression didn't budge, he retreated his hand, disappointment washing his features. "My bad. Guess I got a little carried away there… We can stop if you want."

As he pulled away, the weight of Dani's predicament came back to hit her full in the face.

*Failure after failure after failure…*

*But I want this. I need this. He gives me so much.* She shook away the condescending voice and flashed a cunning smile. Her arms flew around his neck, and she twisted her fingers through his silky hair. "I didn't say *stop*, now, did I?"

*Fourteen*

*November*

H ALEY PULLED UP TO THE CURB IN A BLACK, SHINY BMW ON Black Friday morning, blaring her horn as Dani came down the front steps of her apartment. Dani hopped in the passenger side, dragging her purse around her shoulder before slamming the door behind her.

Haley shook her head as Dani fumbled with her seatbelt. "Slept well? It's only, like, one o'clock!" She thrust the car in gear and sped down the street. "We'll be lucky if there's anything left at this point."

Dani's mouth slanted. "It's good to see you too. And you know I'm not an early riser!" She turned her head to stare out the window at the traffic-heavy street. "I doubt we'll find parking. Why didn't we just take the subway? Downtown's only a few stops."

Haley flicked a long-nailed hand in dismissal. "You want us to carry our huge bags through the swarm of Black Friday shoppers on the metro? I've been mugged before. Not fun."

"Oh, true." Dani shot her a quizzical look. "Dang, Captain Haley Burslow, mugged? How did that happen?"

Haley snorted. "I wasn't paying attention. Had my earbuds in, and we were packed like sardines on the subway." Her long lashes fluttered, her eyes rolling back. "I had to change my credit cards and everything! Muggers suck."

As expected, the Bloc's parking garage was at capacity, so after circling the streets a few times in search of an open meter, Haley resorted to parking in a supervised lot a few blocks away from the shopping district.

Haley stepped out of the car after Dani and scowled. "Dang. Why does it feel like downtown is ten degrees hotter than SC?" She shrugged off her leather jacket and tossed it in the driver's seat, revealing a blue plaid shirt.

Her shirt triggered something in Dani's memory, stirring that familiar sick feeling she'd gotten months ago on the lacrosse field. She scratched her cheek and forced it away as they walked down the sidewalk.

"How is lacrosse?" she asked with a curious smile.

Haley pulled her long brown hair into a ponytail, wrinkling her mouth. "Winston's a hard-ass as usual. And she seems super upset you're not there to run through plays with us. You're kind of messing everything up with your suspension."

Dani smiled, swiveling her head to glance for oncoming cars as they crossed the street. "I'm kinda liking suspension. I get to hang out with Tanner a lot."

"Oh, yeah, you have to tell me all about him!" A devilish smirk spread across Haley's face, and she shoved Dani's shoulder. "Damn, girl. Never had a boyfriend and you end up going for the hottest commodity on the football team. That's like being limited to veggies all your life and then suddenly getting a huge, searing, hot rib-eye steak delivered on your doorstep. Must be nice." She shot Dani a wink.

Dani's cheeks flushed. She and Tanner had been dating for about a month now, and things were going really well. She'd met him almost every day after his football practice, assuring Carolyn she wouldn't stay out too late. Unfortunately, today, Tanner was in Texas for a football game and wouldn't be home until later that night.

Haley was a great substitute though. It had been practically two months since Dani last saw her friend at lacrosse practice, and she hadn't realized how much she missed Haley's company.

When Dani pulled open the door to Uniqlo, Haley skirted past her into the sea of people flooding the tiny outlet store. She took a blue lacy bra off a rack and held it in front of her matching plaid shirt.

"Blue's not bad on me, huh? Think Mitch will like it?"

"I don't think Mitch will care what color you're wearing," Dani replied stiffly. She didn't care for Mitch. It was funny that he and Haley had lasted for three years now considering Haley always flashed flirtatious smiles at any cute guy who walked past her.

Haley traced the seam of the bra, a wicked grin spilling across her face. "Dope. I'm getting it."

After some more browsing, the two of them eventually made it to one of two long checkout lines, Haley with at least seven items in tow, and Dani with a few shirts. Their line moved agonizingly slow, and a few of the customers ahead of them shifted their feet impatiently or folded their arms.

"I'm sorry, do you think you could recheck the price on that? The advertisement online said $30.45." An older lady with curly white hair stood in front of the checkout counter, showing something to the cashier.

The girl gave a plastic smile. "No problem, ma'am, but the tag says $65.50, so I just need to check with my manager."

"What the hell, lady, you're holding up the line!" a skinny man with thick eyebrows spat when the cashier left the counter to find a manager.

The lady turned around to face the man. She had a straight posture, shining pale blue eyes, and bright pink lipstick. "Pardon me, sir. I drove all the way from Culver City to buy discounted shoes that were only sold in this store, so I hope you'll excuse me if I make sure I get that discount." Her face was relaxed as if she was used to dealing with rude men all the time.

The man shifted his weight, frowning, as the cashier returned to the counter with a manager, and they took another few minutes to sort out the issue.

"Ugh, this is taking forever," Haley murmured.

"Tell me about it," Dani agreed.

When the lady was finally checked out, she gathered her discounted shoes and strolled toward the exit. As she passed, Haley whispered a little too loudly, "Some people think they're so entitled, putting themselves first at the expense of everyone else."

Dani nodded. Although she didn't mean harm to the old lady, Dani was tired of waiting for so long. The lady turned toward them and opened her mouth, then smiled and continued out of the crowded store.

After finally checking out, they browsed a few other stores and bought some ice cream. Haley nudged Dani's shoulder as they exited the duplex, raising her phone.

"Hey, is it okay if Mitch meets us at the Pool Table Penthouse a few blocks away? He just got off his shift."

Dani shrugged. "Yeah, sure. That sounds fun."

*Hell no, it doesn't.*

A half hour later, Mitch met them waiting inside the crowded Penthouse for an empty pool table. He was a tall guy with half of his head shaved in the popular style, brown bangs hanging over one eye. Although he was seven years older than Dani and Haley, he walked with the cocky strut of a teenager.

"Hey, babe," Mitch said with a low growl, ignoring Dani and pulling his girlfriend in for a deep kiss. "Hope you haven't been waiting long." He wore a light gray polo shirt, 'The Gap Factory' stitched across the front in small letters, but he smiled with the pride of someone who worked for Bill Gates.

Haley unwound her brown hair from her ponytail and combed it over a shoulder with a smile. "We've only been here, like, twenty minutes. They said it could be up to an hour's wait. It *is* Black Friday, you know."

"I'm fine with waiting however long it takes, as long as I have you to keep me company." He drew a hand along Haley's thigh, making her giggle.

Dani forced bile down her throat and turned away. They were always embarrassingly gross on their PDA. She supposed she could take an Uber if she really wanted, but Haley would probably get all pouty if she tried to leave.

"Table six for Haley!" a voice called over the intercom as if in answer to Dani's prayers.

Mitch turned to Haley as Dani collected their Uniqlo bags and began heading toward the corner table. "Got some cash, babe? I'll order drinks," he offered.

Turning her head from their view, Dani rolled her eyes. Of course he would get the drinks—with *Haley's* money. How generous. He always mooched off her, and when Dani pointed it out, Haley always waved her away with a condescending laugh. *"You'd understand if you'd been in love,"* she jeered, and the comment had jolted Dani. Since then, she'd dropped the subject.

Dani and the couple played a few rounds of nine-ball and cutthroat. Haley was a natural, kicking both Mitch's and Dani's asses, so when Dani finally won a game, she threw her hands in the air in victory. "Uh-huh, who's the boss now!" Dani strutted around the table and flexed her arms.

Haley rolled her eyes as she walked to the mug of beer on the small table nearby, her and Mitch's glasses in her hands. "Lucky shooting. Have a drink, Dani!"

"You're just trying to ignore the fact that I *won!*" Dani danced around her and twerked in front of Mitch, drawing a heated glare from Haley.

"Seriously, have a beer." Haley held out the glass with a stiff arm.

Dani stopped her victory dance and shook her head, the memory of her last hangover surfacing. "Nah, I'm good. Last time, it hit me pretty hard." Alcohol only risked triggering all of the dark images she'd tried to suppress for so long. She wasn't about to go down that road again.

Haley shrugged. "Your loss." She refilled Mitch's glass and walked it over to him. He grinned and grabbed her butt, prompting her to set down their glasses and proceed into a hasty make-out session. When Dani tore her eyes away and pulled the balls out of their pockets, Mitch swung Haley onto the pool table, blocking out any opportunity for Dani to play a solo game.

They'd both had at least three or four drinks by now, and their PDA was escalating by the minute.

Dani groaned and turned away, gazing around at the other billiard players. Many of them were couples, she realized. Her heart lurched, an image of Tanner's warm brown eyes filling her vision. If he was here, he'd make her feel special and kiss her like Mitch was kissing Haley—if not as disgustingly.

While glancing over the crowd of people, she noticed a heavyset, middle-aged man with thickly built arms leaning over a pool table. He missed an easy shot. One of the other middle-aged skinny guys at his table laughed and leaned down for his turn, only to be chagrined when the cue ball soared into the pocket for a scratch.

"Hey, think we could take those guys?" Dani suggested to Haley in a provocative tone. The lacrosse captain had her legs locked around Mitch's hips and was dipping her hands somewhere Dani didn't want to know.

"Hmm?" she murmured against Mitch's lips. "Oh, what? Who?" She pulled away from Mitch and glanced to where Dani indicated with her head.

The thickly built man was leaning over his table again, aiming intently at the seven ball with the cue ball. When he shot, the seven ball danced around the edge of the pocket, then rolled out.

"Dammit!" he bellowed.

Haley laughed. "Hell yeah. Three on three! Who's up for a friendly game? Losers pay up?"

"Yesss," Mitch slurred. "I could use the extra cash. Chubby looks like he needs some competition, huh, babe?"

Haley smiled conspiratorially and strutted over to the men's table. Dani smirked and folded her arms, satisfied at having successfully disrupted her friend's make-out session.

After a moment of the lacrosse captain's smooth talking, Haley motioned for Mitch and Dani to join her. As Dani approached the men, they eyed their opponents lazily. Chubby chugged back his mug of beer and plopped it on the small table before eyeing them with a sly curve of his mouth.

"Just don't give him a reason to leave us dead in a ditch somewhere," Dani muttered in Haley's ear. These guys seemed less menacing from further away.

Haley bristled as an amused laugh escaped her. The musty smell of beer wafted into Dani's nose. "Don't worry, girl. I know you're not used to winning, but you have me here." She winked.

Sure enough, Chubby's team was no match for Haley during their game of eight-ball. She shot in ball after ball and was winning single-handedly—even more impressive due to her tipsiness. Dani and Mitch shot in maybe three balls combined, but Haley didn't give Chubby's team a chance to compete, slamming in three, four, five balls in a row.

After she sunk the eight ball, she teetered away from the table and held out her hand with a smug smile. "I think that's a win, boys. Thirty bucks for each of us, please."

Chubby growled and strutted over to a chair where he'd left his jacket. He dug into the pocket and pulled some bills out of his wallet, slapping them onto Haley's outstretched hand. The other two men followed suit and piled their cash on top.

Haley's mouth perked. She handed Dani's cut to her and tilted her head toward the door. "Let's bounce. Mitch wants to run to the liquor store." After picking up her shopping bags and latching Mitch's arm around her hip, she led her boyfriend through the crowd, not waiting for Dani.

Dani walked around the table to pick up her own shopping bag. When she turned to leave, Chubby stepped up to her, blocking her path.

"I had a hundred in my wallet. Hand it over," he snarled, his breath reeking of liquor.

Dani looked up at him, brows drawn. "I don't know what you're talking about."

His beady eyes narrowed, and he gritted his teeth. "Like shit you don't. My jacket's been left unattended with my wallet inside. Give me the damn bill back."

She wracked her brain. Haley had been shooting for most of the game and standing by Dani's side when it wasn't her turn, but Mitch… he had wandered around the table.

"I told you, I don't know what you're talking about. I didn't take it. Do you think I'd still be here if I had?" Her voice came out emphatic, but her heart started racing.

Chubby sized her up and folded his burly arms. "The brunette said the game was your idea."

"Yeah, but I didn't steal from you!" She pivoted around him, but he grabbed her wrist. Her eyes widened when he lifted a badge from his pocket.

The hot stench of beer coated her face as he spoke. "Hand it over."

"What—?" Dani's eyes widened. This asshole was a *cop*? And was he threatening her with arrest? For a hundred-dollar bill she didn't even steal?

"Dom," one of the other guys muttered, stepping close, "you

should take it easy. You had a lot to drink. Those other two kids were probably the ones who stole from you. And it's just a hundred, not a grand."

The thickly built guy called Dom kept his angry eyes trained on Dani. "This girl's trouble, I can tell." He gestured with his open hand again. "Hand it over unless you want to be arrested."

"You're insane." She wrenched her hand away and bolted past him, but the third guy grabbed her. Dom stomped over, twisted her arms back, and slapped a pair of handcuffs on her, wrenching her shopping bag to the ground in the process.

"Dom," the second guy warned again with a frown as he picked up Dani's bag, "this is a bit much."

"You're not gonna say anything about me drinking," Dom muttered to his partner. He marched Dani outside while she flailed and cursed, the other pool players peering at them curiously. When Dani stepped on the pavement outside, she glanced up and down the dimly lit sidewalk. Haley and Mitch were nowhere in sight.

Dani's gut clenched. Haley must've known what Mitch had done, which was why they hadn't bothered to wait for Dani and fled into the night. Was Haley really that irresponsible? She was the damn lacrosse captain!

As the weight of Dani's predicament sank on her, frustration and anger were overpowered by betrayal and abandonment, and she succumbed to a stabbing rush of hurt.

Not even her best friend was on her side. It was as if the world had turned its back on her. Her parents hated her, she'd almost lost her scholarship, and now her best friend had turned on her. Nobody wanted her, cared what happened to her, or spared her a second glance. Not even any of the ogling pool players had the decency to step in and stop a drunk cop from arresting an innocent girl.

She stopped flailing as her swirling emotions overwhelmed the will to fight.

Dom took the opportunity to tighten the cuffs until they pinched her skin. He nodded to the third officer. "Call a patrol car, Fred."

He pulled Dani in front of him, and she winced as the cuffs dug into her wrists. "Isn't that a bit tight? Can you loosen them? I'm not even fighting anymore." She tried to keep her voice steady as her walls threatened to crumble. "Please?"

Chubby sneered at her, his breath blowing a hot stench of beer in her face. "Not until you learn a bit of respect for your officers."

Light footsteps approached from behind, and for an instant, Dani thought Haley had returned for her. When the officer turned, a glimpse of white hair and bright pink lipstick struck down any ounce of hope she retained.

Dani's face flushed. *As if this night couldn't get any worse, now I get to be humiliated in front of her? She must think karma finally caught up to me after Haley and I berated her for holding up the line at Uniqlo.*

*Stop sprucing yourself up, Dani. This is a fitting image of you, broken and shackled in handcuffs. It's exactly what you deserve.*

The old lady's eyes narrowed as she neared, tugging the numerous shopping bags on her shoulder. She looked fit and spirited for her age, having walked these few blocks from the mall with all those bags. When she scanned Dani's face, her expression became calm, stoic.

"Officer." She had the same confident demeanor she'd shown to that rude guy in Uniqlo.

Dom swiveled around to her, a frown tugging his parched lips.

The old woman pursed her mouth. "The young lady asked you to loosen the cuffs. They are clearly hurting her."

Dom grunted and turned away. "This isn't of your concern, ma'am."

Her tone hardened. "I would suggest loosening her cuffs, sir, if you want to earn the respect you just demanded from her. She doesn't appear to be all that menacing."

He shot a glare at the lady before reaching down to loosen the cuffs with the smallest possible margin, but it was enough to unpinch Dani's skin from the metal.

Dani stretched her wrists as the pain slowly subsided. She stretched her head to look at the old lady, but the woman had already stepped into a silver Volkswagen that was parked by the curb in front of the Penthouse. As she drove away, Dani stood there, shrunken and helpless, a swarm of guilt and self-loathing gushing through her stomach.

*November*

"I NEED SEVEN HUNDRED DOLLARS, MOM. TONIGHT. PLEASE." DANI clutched her phone to her ear while she stood in the marble holding room, officers and attendants bustling around her.

Seven hundred bucks was a steep price for a hundred-dollar theft she didn't even commit; she suspected the hothead cop had reported some bullshit exaggeration about her putting up a fight. She *had* resisted arrest, but it wasn't that much of a fight.

"Why? Are you okay?" The alarm in her mom's voice was sharp enough to drill a hole in Dani's skull.

Dani had promised herself she wouldn't cry in front of the officers as she rode in the patrol car all the way to the downtown precinct. So far, she'd kept her promise, but now, the tight lump in her throat was close to bursting.

The burn of forcing back tears made it hard to speak. "Yes, I'm fine. I just… got arrested."

Angelina Torres's silence on the other end of the line was deafening. *Failure after failure after failure…*

"What happened?" The alarm in her mom's voice had vanished, replaced by a stern, low tone.

Dani chose her words carefully. "It's nothing. I just was out with some friends playing billiards. I was making good choices and didn't drink—"

"Out with it, Dani. What did you do?" Dani could imagine her mom's long eyebrows drawn in a blazing gaze, impatience seething through her ears.

She sucked in a breath. "I…I'm in for petty theft—"

Her mom's voice blared through the line. "You *stole something*?"

"It wasn't my fault!" Dani defended, squeezing the phone. "It was my friend's dumb boyfriend. He was the one who—"

"Danica Evelyn Torres! I cannot *believe* this." Dani could see her mom pacing furiously, her back hunched as she whirled back and forth. "You already have a DUI on your record, and now this?"

Dani's stomach clenched at the mention of her DUI. Why did her mom have to bring that up?

"You are heading down a dangerous path," Angelina continued, her tone ice-cold. "You're close to throwing away your college career, not to mention your life! Do you not care about anything we've worked so hard for you to have?"

Dani sucked in a breath as she stared at the marble floor. *They* worked so hard for *her?* What was her mom talking about? Dani's whole college experience was something *Dani* had worked for, shed blood and tears for in the late hours of the day practicing lacrosse in her family's back yard. *She* had gotten herself to USC through her own merit, while her parents had yelled and shoved her from the sidelines, warping her love for lacrosse into a sick, demeaning boot camp.

*"Don't let people control you…"* The words reeled through her mind.

Her mom's scolding buzzed beneath Dani's thoughts. "…can only hope that you make better friends and better decisions that steer you clear of this dark place you're heading." She took a breath. "I'll send you the money, but this is the last time."

*This is the first time you've had to bail me out from jail, Mom. Are you expecting me to get arrested again?*

Dani barely managed to keep the angry tears from spilling down her face as she whispered, "Thank you," and hung up the phone.

Her mom didn't even see her; couldn't understand that she was already toeing the line of a lonely, dark place that was only getting darker by the moment. Even without her flashbacks, she felt that dark hole stretching wide, threatening to swallow her whole. One more push, and she would fall helplessly into oblivion while the world bustled on around her, ignorant to her demise.

Once the funds were transferred into her account, she paid the fine to the attendant and shuffled out of the precinct doors with her purse and shopping bags—now only a painful reminder of her friend's betrayal. She pulled her phone out of her purse and dialed Tanner's number with trembling hands. He was most likely home from his flight this late into the evening.

He answered on the first ring. "D! I've been thinking about you all day."

She sniffed back her emotions before answering. "Hi. I… Can you pick me up? I don't really want to call an Uber…"

When he showed up at the precinct doors half an hour later, she couldn't hold back her tears a second longer, and they cascaded down her face, smearing her makeup. She ran into his arms, and he claimed her in a huge hug, squeezing her tight as she bawled into his chest.

Dani cuddled with Tanner on his couch an hour later, her legs draped over his lap. "Thank you for picking me up," she whispered, winding her finger around his long dark bangs. "You were the first person I wanted to see."

She had cried into his arms at the precinct for a while before she managed to climb into his car, asking if she could stay with him. She wasn't ready to face her roommates and explain she'd just been arrested courtesy of her best friend's boyfriend.

"Of course." Tanner stroked her cheek as his brown eyes bore into her. "I'm here for you." He kissed the top of her head, shooting a warmth down her spine.

Her cheeks were now dry, and her body had finally ceased its shaking as she lay with him on the couch. He seemed to absorb Dani's pain, easing the tension in her limbs and wrestling the weight from her shoulders. She didn't know what she'd do without him.

Although better than she was an hour ago, Dani was still reeling from the deep wound where her friend had stabbed her in the back. She had turned her phone off after messages from Haley piled up on her screen; the captain hadn't even texted her until hours later. Thankfully, Dani's lacrosse suspension meant she wouldn't have to see Haley in person unless she ran into her somewhere on campus. Dani didn't know if she'd hit her teammate or cry if she saw Haley's face.

Maybe she'd do both.

She eyed the bag of Uniqlo clothes she had discarded at the end of Tanner's couch. She didn't even want them anymore.

"I don't know what I would do without you." Dani unraveled her finger from his hair and shifted on his lap. "My parents have been…so misunderstanding and controlling for the longest time, and I feel like you're one of the few people I have left who cares for me."

The door to his dorm opened, and in strutted a broad-shouldered guy with messy brown hair—Tanner's roommate from the football team.

"Hey, Wes," Tanner called. "Dani is here."

Wesley nodded and dropped the grocery bag he was holding on the kitchen table. Noticing them curled on the couch, he gawked. "I walk into the middle of something?" A devilish smirk spread across his mouth, and he took a few steps toward them. "Don't let me get in the way—carry on. But damn, you're right, man. She is a hot one."

Tanner's hold on Dani tightened, and he shot a glare at his roommate. "Back off, Wes. Not the time."

A warm rush oozed through Dani's core in response to Tanner's protective words. No one had made her feel so valuable before.

That gaping hole in her back from Haley seemed to shrink a little bit more.

His roommate raised an eyebrow, then put his hands up and backed away. "Whatever, man. I'll be in my room."

When Wesley's large figure had disappeared down the hallway, Tanner turned his face back to Dani's. "Sorry about that. He can be a dick sometimes."

Her lip curled. "It's okay. I'm kinda used to people dicking around by now." She paused. "I guess I've always had low expectations for relationships 'cause my own parents think I'm trash." *And maybe they're right.* "When you said on our first date that your parents gave you fan mail for your football games, I was super jealous. When my parents came to my lacrosse matches, it was like they expected me to be the best player, and any bad performance I gave was more reason for them to put me down."

He rubbed her shoulder with his thumb. "Damn. I'm sorry. Well, when I come to your first home match, I promise I'm gonna be your biggest cheerleader. I'll wear the damn skirt and everything."

Dani smiled and nuzzled her head into his neck.

But then Tanner's chest rose and fell with a labor she hadn't notice before. "So… my parents actually thought I was trash, too."

Dani lifted her head and met his troubled brown eyes.

He pursed his lips before going on. "They were super controlling, always gave me strict rules, curfews, and monitored my phone activity in high school. For some reason, they thought I didn't give a shit about college, and to be honest, I stopped caring about what they wanted from me. They yelled at me and my friends when we smoked weed and did regular teenager stuff that didn't hold up to their standards. I was a joke to them, a complete waste to society. So instead of concentrating on school, I focused on football and got into college on my own terms. Eventually, they stopped hounding me and let me live my own life. Now, they respect me and shower me with gifts as if we never fought in the first place."

"Really?" Dani's eyes widened.

"Yeah." He dragged a finger along her arm, drawing goose bumps. "Anyways, I guess the moral of the story is: Don't let people control you, D. You're in college, building a foundation for the rest of your life and figuring yourself out in the process. You should make your own choices without having to worry about what others are going to think, and your parents should support you through that process. It's not fair of them to give you so much negativity. It's your life, and if you end up making decisions they don't agree with, so be it." He turned his head and blew his bangs out of his face.

Dani looked down and bit her lip. "You're right. My dad always told me that lacrosse was my only ticket to college. Like, he never even asked me what *I* wanted and didn't believe I was capable of anything else. And my mom too. She always acts like I'm gonna screw everything up if she doesn't have her eye on me."

Tanner smiled and held her chin up. "Don't let them control you like that."

*"Don't let people control you…"* The words tugged at something in the depths of her memory.

She swallowed. Tanner was right: Dani was letting her parents walk all over her again, just like they had for most of her life.

Tanner brushed his bangs out of his face. "And I promise, I will never control you in that way. Or do anything to make you feel abandoned like they did."

She gave him a warm smile and kissed him.

He pulled away after a few moments and sat up straight. "Listen, I know it's only been, like, a month since we started hanging out, but being with you just feels so right. I really like you." Cupping her cheek, he focused his dark brown eyes on her. "Dani, will you be my girlfriend?"

Sixteen

*December*

"ARE THOSE NEW EARRINGS?" DANI ASKED EMMA, LEANING over Carolyn in the crowded restaurant's lobby booth.

Emma struck a pose with her hands underneath her chin, her brown skin flushing. "Yeah, Chase got them for me!" She turned her head to showcase the long silver hoop earrings, matching her black and silver dress.

All of them had dressed up for their end-of-semester celebration dinner at the sushi restaurant downtown. Dani flaunted a modest orange dress with a wide neckline and leather boots, while Carolyn wore jeans and a loose flannel shirt, not having even bothered to tame her messy red hair.

Alisha had even decided to "play dress up," as she called it; her bare pale shoulders peeked over a plain black blouse and tight jeans.

"Well, they look great on you." Dani beamed, folding her hands into her lap.

Alisha snorted on Emma's left, brushing aside her dark curls to reveal her heavy-shadowed lids. "How are those any different than what you always wear?"

Emma tsked. "I don't *always* wear hoops, but these have my initials, in case you didn't notice." She pointed to the faint engraving on the earrings.

Alisha rolled her heavily shadowed eyes. "Whatever. They all look the same to me."

Dani laughed at her roommate's candidness. Even Alisha couldn't ruin her good mood. Dani had a boyfriend, and she wouldn't have to worry about her arraignment for a while. The courts had scheduled her initial arraignment during finals week, but luckily, they had accepted to postpone to a future date notifiable by mail in the coming weeks. The holidays were expected to delay it even more.

Furthermore, she had passed all of her classes with solid grades. She was thankful for all of the study time with Carolyn; her organic chemistry and physics classes received As, and her sociology, history, and biology classes averaged out to Bs. Considering how poorly she had been doing at the beginning of the semester, Dani was quite proud of herself. Now, she could finally relax during her long-awaited holiday break.

Her phone buzzed on her lap, and she looked down to see her mom calling. She nudged Carolyn, pointing at her phone. Carolyn nodded, and Dani walked through the oak door to the chilly courtyard outside, bringing the iPhone to her ear.

"Hey, Mom," Dani answered, shuffling through the line of people waiting outside to be seated.

"How were your finals, honey?" she asked hesitantly.

"They were good. I didn't flunk!" Dani joked, her voice perking up several pitches.

"Good. You'd better keep your grades up considering how you've been acting lately."

Evidently, her mom didn't share Dani's enthusiasm. Dani thought she'd be happy for her, proud that Dani had done well in school and proven to be a good student. But her mom still thought of her as a failure.

And just like that, Dani's happiness dissipated.

Her voice dropped to its normal octave. "I told you, Mom, what happened with the arrest at the billiards place…it wasn't my fault."

Angelina's tone was low, condescending. "Even if it wasn't, you need to find better friends."

Dani's fingers squeezed her phone as she swallowed her mom's words. Dani hadn't talked to her mom since the incident, and since then, she'd worked hard to heal the wound of Haley's betrayal, Carolyn's disappointment at her arrest, and her own dipping self-esteem. But now, her mom was sinking a knife back into that wound, pushing it deeper with every word. If it wasn't for Tanner, Dani didn't know if she could handle another of her mom's painful blows.

Thinking of Tanner reminded her of their conversation a few weeks ago and how he had told Dani to not let her parents bring her down. Dani should be proud of who she was now and the decisions she made and not sulk about the dumb things her parents berated her for.

A familiar boiling from within seared her throat before it reached her lips. "Dammit, Mom! This is my life! Stop acting like I don't have any control over it!" A few people in the courtyard turned their heads her way, alarm brimming their features, but Dani didn't care.

Her mom let out an exasperated breath on the other end of the line. "Evidently, you don't have control over it when you need your parents to bail you out of jail!" Dani thought she heard something close to a sob, but she wasn't sure. "Since your arrest, your father has been… more uptight than usual. I keep trying to get him to drive us down to Yellowstone so we can get some fresh air, but he won't leave Helena…" She drifted off.

A small part of Dani remembered the ending scene from *Mulan*, of Mulan's father embracing his daughter. She exhaled a shaky breath as a pang of guilt jolted her fury.

Dani shook away the guilt. No—she was supposed to be the opposite of weak and docile. *Remember what Tanner said. Making you feel sorry for them is how they rein you in.*

Dani's grip on the phone tightened again. "I wish you'd stop worrying about Dad. He makes you both miserable!"

"You know it's not that simple, Dani," Angelina scowled, and Dani could imagine her dark, thin eyebrows drawing down. "He's been more quiet lately, but it's because he's been holding a lot in. On Thanksgiving, he burst out at me and started throwing things, and eventually, he just left the house and cooled his temper walking off down the road. It took me a while to find him…"

Dani deflated as that damn guilty pang nudged her again. Her dad had always been temperamental—he had blamed it on his mom dying from leukemia when he was so young—and these last three years had incrementally worsened his mood. Still, it wasn't fair of him to take his pain out on everyone else. Dani and her mom didn't deserve to have their lives revolve around her dad, folding and shifting to *his* needs.

"And how is lacrosse going?" Angelina asked, thankfully changing the subject.

"Fine," Dani lied. If her mom knew she had been suspended, that would be the end of her.

"Great!" Her mom's bright tone blared into Dani's ear. Her parents getting excited about Dani's lacrosse games was nothing new; it was the one thing they seemed to care about. "Make sure you're in good shape for the PAC-12 Conference. You know that USC is ranked seventh this year…"

Dani wrinkled her nose. "I will." If her parents found out she'd been suspended, they'd fly out to LA in a heartbeat and monitor her every move to make sure she kept in line.

She curled her hair behind an ear. "Oh, I'm going to stay in LA for Christmas—it's for a two-week nursing program at Dignity Health Hospital." She hoped her quick change of topic didn't draw suspicion from her mom.

"That's nice." Her mom's tone wasn't as enthused as earlier. Dani for the life of her could not understand why her mom was not more supportive of her schooling. Med school was what she was investing her life in, not lacrosse! "I've got to go, Dani," her mom noted. "We'll talk later. Goodbye, honey."

"Bye, Mom."

Dani turned back toward the restaurant and saw Carolyn waving her over by the door. The other two roommates were apparently already seated. Dani followed Carolyn through a long hallway, dodging servers with drinks and appetizers, until they came upon Emma and Alisha's table.

Dani slipped into the booth next to Carolyn just as a waitress approached them with a tray and began dispersing drinks among them.

"I ordered root beer for you. I didn't think you'd want anything strong," Carolyn whispered, leaning close. "We already looked over the menu, but you can take your time."

Dani smiled. "Thanks. And root beer is perfect."

The waitress flashed them a grin as she snagged the drinks tray along her hip. "I'll give you some more time so your friend can look over the menu."

When the waitress had left, Emma folded her arms and looked across the table at Dani, her bracelets clinking as she fluttered her bright brown eyes. "How are your parents?"

Dani picked up a menu and gazed over the appetizers. "They're good as usual," she answered while scratching her cheek. "Have you all reached out to your parents since finals?"

Emma and Carolyn nodded, but Alisha shifted uncomfortably in her seat. Dani recalled a phone call argument barreling through Alisha's door last night. Could the argument have been with her parents?

As if Alisha realized what everyone was thinking, she piped up. "My parents don't want me to go out anymore. They think I spend too much money on shit. Well, cheers to that!" She raised her mug of beer in a salute and took a long swig.

The other three exchanged awkward glances as Alisha set the mug back down with a toss of her short, curly hair. This was the most vocal Alisha had been about her personal life since Dani had met her, and yet she'd exposed more than Dani had with her roommates. Other than with Carolyn, that is.

A guilty pang nudged the pit of Dani's stomach, and she had to bite her lip to settle the disturbance.

Emma took a sip of her lemonade and rubbed her arm. "Sooo, you want to split an order of California rolls, Dani?"

Alisha's lips twitched to the side, and Dani tore her eyes away, her heart sinking. Maybe that was why Alisha always kept quiet: sometimes, it seemed as if no one cared at all.

***December***

"Is this what I think it is?" Mel's face lit up as she tore off the wrapping paper of a medium-size box. She pulled off the cover and gasped. "It is!" She pulled out a pair of white-checkered shoes and danced on her toes.

Both Dustin and his mom shot awed, disbelieving looks at Bettie sitting in the rocking chair in the corner of their living room. Her pale blue eyes twinkled as she beamed at Mel's reaction.

Mel dropped the shoes and bolted into her arms. "Thank you, Bettie! This is the best gift *ever!*"

Bettie laughed as she wrapped an arm around the little girl. "Aw, sweetie, I'm glad you like it."

Mel had been raving for months about the shoes ever since she saw a popular Netflix show last summer. She'd begged Rachel for them, but the shoes had been designed exclusively for the show, and Rachel deemed them too expensive, to Mel's disappointment.

"How…?" Rachel's expression was somewhere between grateful and appalled, probably because she hadn't wanted Bettie to spend so much money on them.

Bettie's mouth quirked as Mel plopped on the carpet and began tugging her prized shoes onto her feet. "Oh, I have my ways." She winked conspiratorially. "I saw online that a Uniqlo downtown was selling them for half-price on Black Friday, so I made it my mission to buy them for her."

Rachel's jaw dropped. "Bettie, you didn't have to go out of your way!"

The old lady's pink lips stretched into a smile, and she waved her hand. "Oh, honey, it was worth it to see Mel light up. It wasn't an easy feat arguing for that discount either!"

Dustin couldn't believe the magnanimity of the woman. She had done more than enough to make Christmas special for the Mottleys, showering them with gifts and offering to host a large dinner at her house. He supposed it was partially to do with his dad's absence this Christmas.

As Dustin scanned their vibrant faces and took in the striking Christmas tree he had set up by the window, he found it hard to swallow. It just wasn't the same without his dad. Derek Mottley had always made an effort to stop by their house on Christmas despite Rachel's protests. Not having him here, smiling his big, crooked smile and unloading his truck of gifts for the three of them, left a gaping hole in Dustin's chest.

But that hole was quickly filled with revulsion. This Christmas, Derek was rotting in a jail cell for sexual assault. All of his assets had been ripped from him, including the finances Rachel, Dustin, and Mel had lived on for so long. The lack of gifts and spending on Rachel's part this year, unfortunately, was a harsh reminder of how much they'd depended on him, whether Rachel liked to admit it or not.

Dustin gritted his teeth as he opened a trash bag and began scooping up the wrapping paper scattered across the floor, trying to ignore the nagging pain in his throat. He watched Mel trek around the living room in her new shoes, doing little poses for Bettie and his mom.

Mel knew he was in jail because of sexual assault, but neither his crime nor his absence seemed to have any effect on her, thankfully. She had been just two years old when Derek confessed to Rachel he'd cheated and Rachel had whisked Dustin and Mel away from him. Mel only knew him from the few times a month he joined them for dinner or softball games and holidays, so Dustin wasn't sure if she missed him as much as he did. It was harder for Dustin at eighteen when his parents had separated.

Still, how could Derek abandon them both? How could he choose personal pleasure over family?

"Aren't they super cool, Mom?" Mel asked with big brown, joyful eyes, holding up her shoe.

"They're gorgeous, baby. Bettie sure knows how to make a fashion statement on you!" Rachel's eyes danced, more so than past Christmases, as she collected the china Bettie had gifted her and passed Dustin toward the kitchen.

A few seconds later, Dustin felt a squeeze on his shoulder from behind. "Smile, honey. It's Christmas!" his mom urged.

Dustin stood from the floor and tightened the trash bag, turning to face her. "Am I the only one who is torn over him not being here?" he growled in a low voice.

The brightness faded from his mom's eyes. She glanced at Mel, who giggled as Bettie chatted with her, before turning back to Dustin. "I know it's hard to accept he's not the man you think he is, honey. I had the same problem myself." She brought her hand to his cheek and brushed her thumb underneath his eye. "I hate seeing you so down. Can you please just enjoy today? For Mel?"

The mention of his sister made his shoulders tense. "Did he even stop to think how his actions would affect Mel? How they would affect us?" He shook his head. "I can't believe it. I always thought he had tried to be a better guy. Even after he cheated."

Rachel pulled her hand away and expelled a breath. "I was with that man for twenty-one years before we separated. When he admitted he'd cheated, I warred with myself. A part of me didn't believe it and wanted to think he was still a good man because he'd been honest with me. But that reasoning fell flat against the need to keep my kids safe. To keep them around honest, loyal people." She stepped away and returned to the couch, the bright smile that lit up her face minutes ago returning as she rejoined Mel and Bettie.

Dustin spun on his heel and tugged the trash bag through the back door slider before his emotions could show. His mom wasn't upset her children had been stripped of a father in their life; if anything, she seemed happier Derek was locked away. It had taken Dustin a few years to convince her to allow his dad to be closer to them and for her to accept him into a small part of their lives.

But now, Dustin reeled as his mind battled with an image of the loving dad he'd grown to love and the monstrous sexual abuser rotting in jail. If his father was in fact such a monster, his mom was right in wanting to cut ties with him. Dustin knew Derek had never been a wise man when paired with alcohol and women, but this? How could he stoop so low? Maybe his father really was a cruel, selfish, sick bastard. How could he do something so senseless; so despicable? How could he risk his family's well-being for such a disgusting, horrific act? It made no sense.

As much as Dustin wanted to believe Derek Mottley was a good person, a family man, his absence this year was a stabbing revelation of the man he really was.

Dustin slung the trash bag into the large bin on the side yard before turning back to the house. When he entered the living room through the slider, Mel was cross-legged on the floor, flipping through Netflix with the remote.

"It's okay, honey. I'm sure Bettie would rather chat with us than watch a show right now," Rachel ushered.

"Nonsense, Rachel, it's fine. Don't ruin the girl's fun." Bettie's eyes crinkled happily as she watched Mel jump up in excitement.

"Found it! The main character wears the same shoes, see?" Mel lifted a foot as if she hadn't already shown Bettie a thousand times.

Dustin couldn't help the smile that tugged at his lips as he leaned against the slider door, arms crossed.

His mom was right. Mel's happiness was too precious to be crushed by his turmoil over their dad. Dustin would be happy today, for his sister. As he stared at Mel's spirited, pudgy face, he promised himself he would be the rock for her that his father hadn't been, no matter what happened. Dustin would protect her and make her understand what it meant to be loved; to truly sacrifice your needs for someone else's.

And celebrating Christmas in a place absent of their father's haunting memories would be a good way to start.

Taking a step forward, he clapped his hands, and Mel, Bettie, and Rachel tilted their heads up from where they sat, faces curious. "You guys want to go to Santa Monica?"

Bettie shrugged, and Rachel turned to Mel, whose eyes grew to the size of tennis balls. "Yes!" she shrieked.

Dustin smiled his first genuine smile all day. *Finally, some time away from this sick place.*

*January*

DANI'S EYES FLUTTERED OPEN AT THE TICKLING SENSATION OF soft fingers tracing her bare midsection. Tanner's arm was wrapped around her, and she smiled at the feel of his body curled with hers.

She had been thrilled when he said he'd be staying at USC over Christmas break, and she had begun hanging out with him more often, to the point where, eventually, she couldn't hide it from her roommates any longer. Although Carolyn nagged her about how he was too much of a distraction, touting Dani's commitment to keeping her grades up for med school, Dani dismissed her concern.

Tanner made her happy, and he was the main reason she hadn't been sucked helplessly into the dark abyss that had been threatening her the past few months.

Dani leaned her head back into the crook of his neck.

"Awake, hmm?" His hand drifted up her stomach to tuck a loose strand of hair behind her ear.

"Barely." She yawned. "I could use some waking up."

That was all he needed to roll himself on top of her and trap her between his elbows. She took in the sight of his washboard abs—eye candy she'd become used to in the past two months. She took pleasure in watching his sultry eyes roam over her stomach and the black-laced bra she'd bought especially for him.

This was all still too good to be true. She had to be dreaming. Tanner had made her happier in the past few months than she'd felt in three years, and she kept pinching herself to remind her it was real.

"I'm still wondering when you'll let me take this damn thing off," he said, digging his arm underneath her back and tugging at her bra clasp playfully.

"Still no patience, huh?" she teased, smiling scandalously.

The truth was that she hadn't fully given herself to Tanner because she hadn't been completely honest with him about her past. Could she tell him though? How would he take it? A small part of her feared he'd break off their relationship. Regardless, she knew Tanner had found it increasingly difficult to hold back the past few nights they'd slept together, and she was finding it increasingly difficult too.

That deep, painful feeling in her gut started to claw at her.

*Failure after failure…*

Dani squeezed her eyes tight, trying to block out the thought. Why did it still haunt her wherever she went? She couldn't let it control her life all the time.

Screw it.

Dani ran her hands along his firm biceps, then down his pectorals and along his six-pack, feeling his muscles tense. A soft moan escaped the back of his throat, and he roughly lowered his lips to hers.

She reached her hand behind her back, found the clasp he had been fumbling with, and unhooked it. Sucking in a breath, she pulled down her straps, exposing her breasts to him.

He pulled away and drank in the sight of her, his eyes brimming with desire. His palms roamed freely as he nuzzled his head in the crook of her neck, and she writhed underneath him. One of his hands crept along her thigh and tucked her leg around his hip. She swung the other leg in place and gazed up at him, her heart pounding a mile a minute.

His soft chuckle tickled her cheek before he whispered, "Who's the eager one now?" He squeezed her hips and moved against her, sending spasms through her core.

Pausing, Tanner brought his hand down to her panties and started to tug them off. She opened her eyes between heavy breaths, watching his steady hands.

Then fear for what was about to happen lurched like a cobra in the pit of her stomach.

She wasn't ready to do this. What was she doing?

Dani unclenched her legs from his hips and pulled up her panties with frantic hands.

Tanner paused, and he jerked a disapproving eyebrow at her clumsy motions. "What are you doing?"

Her brain raced for an excuse, but all of them seemed utterly pathetic. "I can't do this," she squeaked.

A chuckle escaped his lips. "Sure, you can."

When she tried to sit up, he lightly pushed her back on the bed with a quirk of his mouth. An icy chill crept up her flesh as he buried his face against her neck.

"Tanner, stop," she protested.

"Your squabbling is only turning me on more, D," he whispered in her ear with a chuckle. "Come on, you were totally egging me on. And you've weaseled out enough times already."

"No—get off." She tried to push him off her, but his hands seized her wrists and held her in place. Her heart seized in her chest as she found herself trapped underneath him.

"Shit, Dani. Calm down." Frustration and lust oozed from his brown eyes, no longer the silky comfort she'd ingrained in her memory.

She continued fighting against his restraint, and he slapped her.

The shock of his force froze her. Her throat constricted as sheer terror overtook her body.

"It's okay, I got you. Just relax. You wanted this, remember?" he murmured.

She hardly registered his words. Her body was immobile, lifeless. Her arms stopped flailing and fell limp, bolted next to her head by his hands.

He released her wrists. "There you go, babe. It's all right. I got you." His hand trailed down to her panties again.

Her heart hammered against her chest as his hands dipped lower. *No, no, no, no. I'm not ready!*

A vibrating buzz beside them made them both jump. Dani turned her head to see her phone rumbling on the bedside table. Life instantly rushed back into her body, and she sprang out from under Tanner's startled form to grab her phone.

It was Dustin.

"Hello?" Her voice was weak, raspy, as she pulled her panties up with trembling hands.

His tenor voice warmed her core. "Hey, Dani? I'm on my way. I texted you that I'm coming early, but you didn't respond. I was planning on dropping off my little sister on the way to the program, if that's okay?"

Dani wracked her memory. *What was today?*

It hit her like a hammer whacking a bell. The volunteer program.

She glanced at the clock on the bedside table. 11:10 a.m. The program didn't start until 12:30, but Dustin was already on his way? He was on his way! Trepidation swept through her limbs, then relief as her mind registered an escape.

"Oh, sorry! Yeah, I'll be ready."

"Cool. See you in a bit."

Dani lowered her phone and peeled her eyes to the floor, standing stiff as a board as her heart jackhammered through her chest.

Tanner raised an eyebrow, sitting back on his haunches. "What is it?"

Snapping back into focus, she jerked her eyes to his. "I have to go. I'm late for something." A numbness in her cheek gave way to a throbbing pain as she moved to grab her bra off the mattress. Her shaking hands fumbled with the clasp, and it took her several tries to attach it.

A snort escaped Tanner's flared nostrils. "Where the hell do you have to go during Christmas break?" His eyes prowled her as she stumbled to her duffle bag to pull on a set of clothes.

"It's for my med school application." Her jeans and shirt on, she went into his bathroom and threw her toiletries into her duffle bag. She shuffled back into his room and collected the clothes along the floor she had shed the night before.

"Since when did you have to worry about school stuff when we were together?" His tone was heated, his once mesmerizing gaze now flushed and annoyed.

She struggled to swallow as she took in his angry, disappointed state. It was her fault. She had effectively cock-blocked him several times now.

She fought not to curl into herself as a swirl of emotions bubbled to the surface. Her brain warred with the fear of disappointing Tanner, the fear of his hands slapping her into submission, and the fear of losing her own happiness if she denied him.

Dani scratched her cheek as she answered him. "It's not just school stuff—it's med school stuff. I've always been serious about that."

The exasperation didn't leave his face as she gave him a quick kiss on the cheek and dashed out of his dorm with her duffle bag, her hair disheveled and shirt askew.

She ran down the single block to her apartment as fast as she could, putting her lacrosse conditioning to the test. As she bolted down the sidewalk, the previous scene replayed nonstop in her mind, nauseating her stomach: Tanner's menacing expression as he pinned her to the bed, the sting of his slap throbbing her cheek, her limbs locking beneath his powerful figure...

But then that condescending voice tore through her like a harpoon. *You did this to yourself. You gave him the green light, then you denied him. What the hell were you thinking?*

Guilt flooded through her bones, nausea building with every stride. She deserved Tanner's frustration for being so weak. He had waited such a long time!

When she crossed Hoover Street, she spotted a gray Honda Accord parked by the curb in front of her driveway.

*Dustin's already here!* An odd sense of safety flooded her at the sight of his car idling in front of her apartment, washing away the fearsome images flickering in her head. But whatever security she felt was quickly replaced by shame. What would her excuse for not being home be? There was no way she could sneak past him. She only hoped the paranoia of what had just transpired was hidden from her face as she circled by Dustin's car window.

When he glanced up, she raised her index finger. "One sec, sorry!" she called before darting up her apartment steps, through the kitchen and up the stairs.

Once in her room, she tossed her bag onto the bed and changed into a green blouse and slacks. She ran a brush through her hair, quickly traced on some mascara, and dashed back downstairs, brushing past a confused Emma in the kitchen.

She hopped down the porch steps and skidded to a stop in front of his car. Her breath was labored by the time she plopped into the passenger seat, shutting his car door behind her.

"Sorry I'm late," she panted. "I went to Target and lost track of time."

He arched a brow. "With a duffle bag?"

Blood rushed to her face. *Idiot.* Her embarrassment was immediately replaced by a guilty lurch in her stomach as the images of Tanner resurfaced.

Dustin's mouth curved in a half-smile as he shifted the car into gear. "Relax. I'm just teasing." The humor dissipated from his gaze. "You okay?"

She realized how she must look: frazzled, winded, flustered… Her head turned away before she mustered in a calm tone, "Yeah…I'm fine."

He glanced at her outfit and smirked. "And you know it's a volunteer program, not a job interview."

Dani scanned his casual T-shirt and jeans and bit her lip.

"Anyways," he added, "thanks for letting me drop off my little sister, Mel." He nodded behind him.

Dani followed his gesture, turning toward the back seat. A little girl with a round face, big brown eyes, and long lashes peered at her disinterestedly from the back seat. Her brown hair was stretched back in a ponytail, and she wore in a T-shirt and shorts complete with long socks, kneepads, and cleats.

"Oh, hi! I didn't even notice you," Dani greeted with a friendly smile.

The girl flashed a quick upward tug of her lips and returned her gaze to the window, disinterested.

Dani turned back to Dustin. "I'm totally fine with going early." She tried to block out what happened earlier prior to Dustin calling about coming early. But Tanner's disappointed expression resurfaced, and her stomach coiled with guilt.

"Great. The softball field is just around the corner. She of course had to join a team that practiced across town." He rolled his eyes as he pulled the car around and drove onto Hoover Street.

"Only 'cause all the teams in Culver City are lame. Down here, they play more competitively," Mel defended.

He covered the side of his mouth. "Ignore her 'cause she can be a pain in the ass."

Mel scoffed, and Dani laughed.

"Mom said you're not supposed to swear," Mel accused.

Dustin rolled his eyes. "'Ass' isn't a swear word. It's just a vulgar term."

"You know that every time you swear, God gets angry," Mel went on. "One day, He's not going to be able to hold all of His anger any longer, and we're all going to pay the price."

Dani bristled in her seat and glanced at Dustin. He just shrugged and waved off his sister's comment.

"Did you have a good Christmas?" he asked Dani as he pulled the car to a stop at an intersection.

"Yeah. Two of my roommates went home for break, but Emma and I managed to cook a ham and had a chill time." *Before we went and cuddled with our boyfriends.*

Memories of Tanner's kisses made her cheeks flush, until his fiery eyes clouded her vision…

*She continued fighting against his restraint, and he slapped her. The shock of his force froze her. Her throat constricted as sheer terror overtook her body…*

Dani scratched her cheek and swallowed a brick down her throat. "What about you? Did your family do anything special?"

"Yeah, we went to Santa Monica. It was pretty low-key," Dustin answered in a level tone, his face stoic.

"I still don't forgive you for eating all of my ice cream, you jerk," Mel snarled.

"I only had a small bite when you abandoned it to go to the restroom," he shot back.

"Yeah, right! It was almost completely gone when I came back. If Dad was there, he'd've kicked your butt."

Dani giggled. Their adorable banter reminded her of a funny memory, replaced by a murky stirring in her gut a moment later. Her hand crept up to scratch her cheek, shoving away the memory.

When Dustin pulled up next to a large park, Mel leapt out of the car and fetched a gear bag from the trunk before running off. Dani watched her brown ponytail flop behind her small figure before saying, "You two are so cute. I hope you realize how precious she is."

He gave her a lazy smile and responded, "Yeah, I know. She's fun to tease."

Dani cocked her head. "What is 'Mel' short for?"

"Melody."

"That's such a pretty name!" Dani beamed.

Dustin's lips teased upward. "She hates it—thinks it's a princess name, like Ariel's daughter in *The Little Mermaid 2*. What's funny is, she's the one who named Max after Eric's dog in the first place."

Dani laughed. "Sounds like me when I was younger. I hated 'Danica,' so I went by 'Dani' with an 'N-I,' though my friends always teased me that it sounded like the guy name 'Danny,' with an 'N-N-Y.'"

He shook his head, rubbing his neck. "I think guy names for girls are cool. It gives the impression that you don't put up with shit."

"Maybe." After a few silent seconds, she asked, "Your dad wasn't with you on Christmas?"

His eyes softened and remained focused on the road. "No…he couldn't make it."

Dani sensed there was more he wasn't telling her, but then again, she wasn't exactly gushing to tell him everything about her own life, so she let it go.

"Any other fun Christmas break plans?" she prodded.

"Not really," he answered in a dull tone.

When he didn't go on, she returned her gaze to her window, watching the cars whiz by and trying to forget the images of her tussle with Tanner. After a moment, Dustin turned up the volume on his radio, and the soft thrum of U2's "Beautiful Day" struck down any further chance of conversation between them.

When they arrived at the hospital twenty minutes later, Dustin led her to the front desk and asked the attendant about the nurse program. The lady gave them directions to a back room where the other participants were gathering.

There was a group of about fifteen undergraduate medical students, a few of whom Dani recognized from her pre-med classes. Dani and Dustin signed their names on a clipboard upon entering and mingled for a while before two doctors in white coats entered around 12:40 p.m.

"Hello, everyone! Welcome to Dignity Health Hospital's Nursing Apprentice Program," said one of the doctors, a middle-aged blonde woman with high cheekbones and a friendly gaze. "My name is Doctor Felix, and this is my associate, Dr. Gregson." She gestured to the older, brown-skinned man with a balding head.

"Nice to meet you all," Dr. Gregson greeted. "We are all delighted to have you here today, and we hope the next two weeks will be an encouraging introduction to what you may encounter after your medical studies."

After the doctors' introduction, the students fastened on masks and latex gloves before splitting into two groups and shadowing their respective doctors. Dustin and Dani followed Dr. Felix as she walked them through medical rooms and explained various tools and operating machines.

"Make sure you all do well in your biology classes because you'll be using that knowledge more than you'll be comfortable with," she said with a wink.

Dustin nudged Dani, and she punched him back, a smirk spilling across her face.

"We are treating a patient with Parkinson's disease and trying a system of regenerative treatments that would restore the dopamine levels in his brain…" Dr. Felix went on.

Dustin leaned down to murmur in Dani's ear. "To elaborate, levodopa treatment for PD patients results in—"

"I know, I know." She waved him off. "Erratic plasma levels of levodopa can result in significant motor fluctuations and involuntary movements that develop in the form of dyskinesia. I learned it in class last year."

He leaned away and drew his brows, but Dani just shrugged.

As they continued through their day, Dustin pointed out things Dr. Felix didn't mention, explaining operating rooms and tools in greater detail thanks to his four years of med school practices. Dani normally might've had a harder time keeping focus on Dr. Felix's snail-pace tour, but Dustin's engaging presence kept Dani attentive, curious, and amused at the same time. It was like having her own personal tour guide who also monitored her discipline when she forgot to monitor it herself.

She was elated when the group finally dispersed at 5:00 that evening. Although she still had another thirteen days to go in the program, she was one step closer to putting a check mark on "world experience" for her med school application. One step closer to standing in front of the lectern as Dr. Stanton had in her organic chemistry video. And one step closer to fulfilling her promise.

"That was super interesting," she said as Dustin backed his Honda out of the parking spot after the group had dispersed. "Thank you for suggesting the program, and especially for coming with me when you didn't have to."

"No problem, I needed to make sure you didn't skip out." His mouth quirked into that familiar crooked smile. "Just kidding. I thought it'd be helpful if I came, and besides, I have nothing else to do for the next two weeks anyways."

"Well, you were definitely not helpful," she teased, her tone dripping with sarcasm.

A disgruntled snort was his only reply.

*Nineteen*

*January*

USTIN TURNED UP THE RADIO AS HE DROVE DANI HOME AFTER the last day of the nursing program. He couldn't believe how fast the past two weeks had flown by. Now winter break was almost over, he found himself wishing he had more time to relax before his clerkship resumed.

He stole a glance at Dani. Her eyes were distant as she leaned on the armrest, staring out the car window. She had surprised him with her incredibly detailed biology statements during the program. As far as he could tell, she was smarter than she had let on or she had messed with him by reading through lines from a textbook the night before each session.

Regardless, if either was true, he was puzzled as to why her grades had slacked last semester.

When "Angela" by The Lumineers flooded the car speakers, his hands tightened on the steering wheel. It had been one of his dad's favorite songs to sing. Dustin's memory was flooded by Derek's handsome face and dancing brown eyes as he strummed his guitar, his warm baritone voice ringing in the air as Dustin and his mom huddled around a beach bonfire.

The serene family picture wrenched Dustin's gut. His fingers changed the dial, shutting out the song and images of his dad.

Dani swiveled her head, shooting him a frown. "Hey, that was a good song! Can you go back?"

Dustin wrinkled his mouth. "Sorry. Sure." He turned the dial, and the familiar guitar strums reverberated throughout the car again.

A small dimple dented Dani's left cheek as her fingers drummed on the armrest in time with the beat. "Is this The Lumineers? It sounds like them."

"Yeah." Dustin's lips lifted slightly as she hummed along with the melody, but his amusement washed away as his thoughts drifted to his dad again.

"You okay?"

Dani's hazel eyes brimmed with curiosity when he turned to her. He bit his lip and returned his gaze to the road. "My dad loved this song. He used to strum his guitar and sing it to me and my mom all the time before Mel was born."

"Did…something happen? I remember you said he wasn't with you on Christmas."

Dustin was silent as he pulled to a stop at an intersection and watched the cars whiz by. When the last chords of "Angela" faded out a few seconds later, he turned down the volume and met Dani's eyes.

"Uh… my dad has been in jail for seven months…" He paused, searching her expression. Her face remained calm, neutral. Dustin dropped his gaze and let out a rough exhale. "He…committed sexual assault. My mom separated from him years ago after he cheated, so he has always been a poor role model to begin with…" He rubbed his neck. *What the hell am I doing? She didn't need to know that.*

Dani traced the seam of her seat, tightening her lips. "My dad hasn't been the best father figure either." She scratched her cheek in hesitation. "People like that, they only tear families apart. And as many chances as you give them…it's useless, 'cause people don't change."

The helplessness in her voice echoed that of his mom's, and it swept his mind to the arguments he'd had with her to try to keep his dad in the family. Despite the man's past mistakes, he'd mostly been a good person.

He pursed his lips, and he found himself defending his dad in the same way he had against his mom. "I don't know if that's completely true… Sometimes, given enough time, people do change. If you just give up on them, they don't have any motivation to be better."

Dani narrowed her eyes at him, her chest rising. "So the liars and the thieves and criminals should just be given chance after chance? Because somewhere deep down, they're good people? Where do you draw the line?" Her eyes became glassy as she stared at him with sudden fury. Then she released a sharp breath and glanced down, her tone softening. "Sorry. I didn't mean that your dad…was like any of those people." She fixed her gaze on a couple pushing a stroller across the street.

The signal turned green, and Dustin gassed the car forward, the happy family disappearing from view. His stomach lurched, and he forced a half-smile. "No, it's okay. My dad is all of those things. He's also a disgusting, lying piece of shit. For the longest time, I believed he had changed, but I guess he didn't."

When he glanced over and caught Dani's eyes tearing up again, he wanted to cling to any fading hope for his dad. God, he didn't know what he'd do if she started crying!

"But," he continued, inhaling deeply, "as hard as it was for others to see sometimes, he did some good things. He tried to be there for Mel and me even after my mom separated from him. Everything was fine up until he committed sexual assault."

Her watery eyes stayed fixed through the passenger window. "So why do you think people can change if your dad didn't?"

Dustin licked his lips, pondering her question. "I don't know. Maybe a small part of me has always been hopelessly optimistic and still thinks he can change… When I was growing up, I only saw the good in him, and I wanted a dad in my life, though my mom kept pushing him away." He sighed. "It seems wrong to want what's best for a leeching, sex-offending bastard like my dad…but maybe, despite all the bad shit, it still doesn't hurt to hope."

Dani met his gaze briefly before looking out the window again, her face somber.

His face flushed, and he turned away. "I'm sorry. I don't know why I told you all that. It was stupid."

She gazed back at him and offered a half-hearted smile, the small dimple returning. Her voice came out weary. "No, no, it wasn't stupid." She paused. "It was…an interesting perspective. I'm glad you told me, and I think…it's nice that you believe in him."

Dustin continued driving in silence, listening to Dani's strained breaths before turning up the radio volume again, hoping the cheery music would soothe her. She stared out the window with pensive eyes. She looked so…fragile. He yearned to know what was troubling her, but it wasn't his place.

As the radio music washed through his ears, he found himself replaying their conversation.

What had Dustin just said? That someone as vile as his dad, a sexual abuser and disloyal husband, could deserve forgiveness? It sounded pathetic the more he thought about it, but who was Dustin to weigh one's journey of redemption?

When he finally pulled up to the curb in front of Dani's townhouse apartment driveway, she hopped out of the car and faced him with a small smile.

"Guess I'll see you at our next mentor session, Professor Mottley?"

He snorted before he returned her smile. "Yeah, whatever, weirdo."

Her lips tugged upward as she closed the door, and he watched her saunter up the path to her apartment and disappear within.

He swerved the car around to Hoover St., releasing a breath he didn't realize he'd been holding.

Dustin shot hoops at West Hollywood Park, practicing jump shots and layups in a tank top and USC shorts. It was a warm Sunday afternoon in mid-January, the day before classes resumed, and it would be a few months before he had any spare time to shoot around again. It was crazy to think the next time he'd shoot a basketball, he'd be done with med school.

The hum of a black Lexus pulling up in the lot by the court made Dustin turn. Out hopped Jessie, sporting red shorts, a black tank top, and a wide grin. He nodded at Dustin as he sauntered along the sidewalk to the court.

"What's up, man? How've you been?"

Dustin smiled and armed the basketball, walking to meet the tall, dark man halfway.

Other than the shallow trim of a beard running up his jaw, Jessie Turner looked more or less the same since Dustin saw him a few months ago. His almond eyes shone with confidence, and he flashed his familiar wicked grin. He was every bit the younger version of his father, who was also Dustin's former professor.

Dustin slapped Jessie's hand and pulled him into a hug. "I'm good. Just drowning in med school as usual."

Jessie shook his head, smirking. "Damn, can you hurry up and graduate so we can hit up that cruise?" He swaggered back a step and eyed the nearest hoop. "Man, it's been months since I've picked up a basketball. Thanks for the call."

Dustin nodded. "Yeah, just like we're back in school, bro." He dribbled and shot a fadeaway, but the ball bounced in and out of the rim.

Jessie sprung into the air, caught the rebound, and dunked it. "Man, why do you still suck at jumpers?" He dribbled the ball around to the corner and shot up a swish. "What else is going on besides med school?"

Dustin lifted his tank top to wipe his sweaty brow. "Eh, not much. I'm mentoring a pre-med student at SC though. We just finished up a two-week volunteer program at Dignity Health Hospital."

"Yeah?" Jessie kicked the ball up into his hands. "So that's why it took you so long to call me up during your break!" He smirked as he threw up a shot. "I hope you're getting paid. That's a lot of time out of your way for a *free* service."

The ball rebounded back to Dustin, and he snagged it out of the air. "It's not that bad. Dani's pretty cool." His thoughts drifted to his and Dani's jibes during the volunteer program, and their talk about his dad on the last drive home.

"Is he as cool as me though?"

Dustin's lip curled as he armed the ball. "Dani's a girl. And she's at SC on a full-ride lacrosse scholarship. So, yeah, I'd say she's cooler than you. You only got a half-ride."

Jessie tossed his head back and laughed. "I thought you weren't picking up girls this year."

Dustin grabbed the ball and dribbled it, shaking his head. "I'm not. She's my mentee."

"All right, bro." Jessie's grin dripped with mockery.

Dustin shook his head as he dribbled to the three-point line. He couldn't deny Dani was cute, and she was definitely talented in more ways than one, but she was a bit immature. Besides, if he were really interested in dating during med school, he wouldn't have broken it off with Lila. It was bad enough seeing her on occasion during their clerkships.

"So how is the writing going?" Dustin mused as he eyed the hoop, shaking his head of his ex. "Anything interesting lately?"

Jessie picked up a ball that had rolled to his feet from the other end of the court. He tossed it to the kid who came to retrieve it. "Actually, yeah. Did you hear about that respiratory virus going around in China at the end of December?"

"Yeah." Dustin threw up a shot, but it bounced off the rim again.

Jessie snatched the ball and threw it back at him. "A few of us at The Times have been digging deeper into it, and it turns out the virus is worse than China let on. They were covering up a huge outbreak in Wuhan, and it looks like it's been spreading like crazy in the meantime."

"Shit." Dustin dribbled around and shot again. Swish this time. His lips twisted into a smug smile.

Jessie shook his head, smirking. He grabbed the ball and juked around Dustin, crouching into a low dribble. "Yeah. This virus is looking pretty bad, man. I'd hold off on traveling right now."

"Good to know. I was actually planning on going to Wuhan this summer. I've got some Chinese relatives… Hope they're doing okay." Dustin placed his hands on his hips.

Jessie held the ball and drew his eyebrows up. Then he threw back his head and guffawed. "Man, your ass is so white, the day you show me Asian relatives is the day I shit gold." He chucked the ball at Dustin.

Dustin dodged the throw before displaying a cool and collective scratch of his nose with his middle finger.

*January*

**Dinner tonight?**

Dani waited two full minutes, but Tanner didn't respond. With a long, painful breath, she pocketed her phone and hopped on her bike, wheeling it down the campus path.

It was the first day back after winter break, which meant Dani should've been amped up about returning to lacrosse practice, but her relationship concerns blotted out everything else; the intervals between Tanner's texts were getting longer and longer. His last text a few days ago stated that he had been busy, but Dani had a gut-wrenching feeling he was still upset with her for leaving him pre-coitus that morning during winter break.

That guilty pang twisted her stomach as she recalled his frustrated, pained face when she'd pecked him on the cheek and left in a hurry.

She'd take it all back if she could—it was her fault for being such a coward. But so far he hadn't acknowledged her apologies, let alone texted more than a few words to her in his responses. Maybe she could squeeze in time to catch him at one of his practices this week...

A chilly January breeze whipped at Dani's face as she kicked her bike into higher speed and weaved through the scattered trickle of students. Although the Californian sun was still as bright as ever, it was setting earlier now, and most of the trees on campus had shed their leaves. Less people were sprawled on the grass in between the redbrick buildings compared to last semester, and most of the chairs outside of the cafeteria were vacant as students gathered indoors to stay out of the chill.

Once she rounded the Tommy Trojan statue, the perimeter of Soni McAlister field came into view, and her spirits soared. Her high GPA had convinced the athletic director to allow her to return in the spring, after she presented an apology letter to Peter. There was just one more caveat: She would have to miss the team's first away game on February 2nd.

But it was all worth it. She had missed lacrosse, the thrill of competition, and the roar of the crowd in the bleachers. She was even looking forward to the agonizing burn of her calves after practice.

But as the lacrosse field came into view at the end of the redbrick walkway, that sinking feeling returned to her stomach. *God, please don't let me have any more flashbacks.*

She pulled her bike up to the rack, locked it, then swung her duffle bag and backpack over her shoulder and trekked up the recreation center's large concrete steps.

Most of the team was already in the locker room when Dani entered.

"Dani!"

"Hey! Our star player is back!"

Dani beamed as the girls greeted her with bright smiles, whoops, and back pats. She had missed them all so much. Well, all except one.

Haley looked up from where she stood beside her locker, which was right next to Dani's. Dani's fist clenched against her duffle bag strap, and she lowered her gaze as she made her way down the aisle.

"Hey, Dani, it's good to see you!" Haley grinned as she tugged on her practice shirt.

Dani avoided eye contact while she dropped her bags and fiddled with her locker combo. "The feeling isn't mutual." She opened her locker and shimmied out of her jeans in silence.

Haley's grin dropped, and she turned back to her own locker, brushing a hair out of her eyes. "I'm…sorry you feel that way. You know I apologized, like, thirty times, right?"

Dani dug into her duffle bag and pulled out her shorts without responding. She had seen Haley's texts and ignored them. They hadn't talked since the events of Black Friday, which were still as painful for Dani as if they'd happened yesterday.

"Come on, Dani. We're teammates! You can't be like this on the field."

Dani snorted as she shrugged off her sweater and T-shirt. "On the field, no. Off the field is another story." After pulling her practice shirt over her head, she stuffed her duffle bag into the locker, slammed the door closed, and strutted out of the room with her lacrosse stick in hand.

As soon as she stepped onto the sunny field, her revulsion toward Haley was swallowed by the pound of her heart beating through her ears. She took a deep breath.

*Breathe. It's just another lacrosse practice.*

Winston's hard-edged yell from the edge of the field snapped her from her fears. "Let's go, girls! Two laps!" Her pouty face swam with content as Dani broke into a jog toward the coaches gathered on the sideline, who beamed when she approached.

"Torres, it's great to have you back!" Winston patted Dani on the back and offered a dull smile. "We'll see pretty soon if you've been keeping in shape."

Dani's lips tugged upward, and she dropped her stick and water bottle by the track before falling into pace behind the other girls.

With every familiar, burning stride, the throb behind her ears faded further away. It was a good thing she had run around campus after class during her suspension, because she was able to complete the entire two laps without collapsing.

During their water break, Haley sauntered up to her with a perk of her red lips. "So I noticed Peter and his gang stopped coming to our practices. That piece of shit should—"

"We're off the field, Haley. I'm not talking to you," Dani

interjected, and the brightness in Haley's eyes dropped. Before she could say anything else, Dani turned to the timid freshman walking past them. "Hey, Zoey, excited for your first match as a Trojan?"

Zoey turned, eyes wide. "Huh? Oh, yeah. I can't wait!"

Dani grinned and led Zoey back onto the field, leaving Haley to herself. Normally, Dani would feel bad about abandoning someone so abruptly and rudely, but Haley needed a taste of her own medicine.

Winston lined up the girls for drills and ran through some plays. Dani sprinted across the field and passed to her teammates, including Haley, cooperating as a teammate should. But aside from drills, Dani did her best to avoid any interaction with the captain for the entire practice.

It was only halfway through Dani's bike ride home that she realized she had made it through a practice without any flashbacks.

At least there was one thing she could be happy about.

*Twenty-One*

*January*

DANI LIFTED A LEG OVER HER BIKE AFTER LACROSSE PRACTICE A week later, her muscles straining after another exhaustive practice.

Haley had given up trying to talk with her. Maybe she was finally starting to understand how Dani had felt when Haley abandoned her on Black Friday. It was now evident to their teammates that Dani and Haley weren't on good terms. Despite their concerns, however, Dani refused to feel any guilt for shunning the captain.

The thought tightened her stomach, and she tried to distract herself by focusing on the fact she'd endured a week free of flashbacks.

As she rode past USC's pressroom across from Soni McAlister field, a small group of students standing in front of the giant news screen caught her eye.

*That's weird.* Normally, the pressroom didn't attract that many bystanders, especially this late. Dani slowed her pedaling and turned her bike around, rolling it closer to the giant glass windows.

CNN was displayed on the giant screen, and Dani's eyes went to the headline: FIRST CONFIRMED CORONAVIRUS CASE IN UNITED STATES.

Dani narrowed her eyes and walked her bike to the entryway so she could hear what the commentator was saying.

"The United States is among several countries to now have confirmed cases outside China's mainland, including Japan, South Korea, and Thailand, according to the World Health Organization. The United States' first confirmed case has been reported in Washington State, where a man in his thirties developed symptoms after returning from a trip to Wuhan.

"Despite health experts' warnings, the president has expressed optimism in the United States' efforts in containing the virus. Take a listen…"

The screen showed a clip from a White House press briefing earlier that day, the president standing at the podium.

The murmurs of the crowd of students washed over her:

"I thought China had it under control?"

"The president said it's contained."

"I heard the Chinese guy who discovered the virus was detained."

"Is it super contagious?"

"Damn, Anderson Cooper needs some good hair dye."

Dani straightened and backed her bike away from the door. She recalled Carolyn mentioning something about the virus surfacing in China earlier that month, but that was the last she'd heard about it.

Viruses circulated every few years. This seemed like a lot of hype over nothing.

She wheeled her bike around and pedaled down the path, leaving the gathering crowd of students to continue their mindless TV ogling.

The chilly wind whipped her ponytail behind her as she rode past the bookstore and Tommy Trojan statue, and she found herself scanning the few students she passed for a familiar face with long, dark bangs. She'd texted Tanner before practice to remind him of her upcoming lacrosse match in February. It was easier to tell herself that he was just busy with football practice in classes, although she felt a sinking ache in her heart that the growing distance between them was too substantial to ignore. A stubborn part of her still clung to the hope that he would attend her first home lacrosse match—one of the first promises he'd given her.

She also couldn't forget his other promise, the one where he said he'd never abandon her.

When she finally pulled her bike up her apartment's driveway, she walked through the door to find Emma and Carolyn eating spaghetti at the kitchen table.

"Hey, guys. How were classes?" Dani asked as she rolled her bike through the kitchen toward the back porch.

"Pretty good," Emma answered, dropping her fork on her plate. The large hoop earrings Chase had given her swung from her ears as she glanced up at Dani. "My calculus teacher is starting to get on my nerves though. He just reads through what we read in our textbooks the week before! I'm considering switching classes." She nodded her head to the stove as Dani trekked back across the living room. "Want some spaghetti? We made extra."

"Yeah, thanks!" Dani beamed, dropping her backpack by the kitchen table. She grabbed a fork and plate from the cupboard and scooped up a good chunk of spaghetti from the pot.

"Oh, Dani, there's mail for you," Carolyn piped. "I put it on the counter."

Dani glanced at the letter at the end of the sink and narrowed her eyes. A letter? Her parents never wrote to her…

She placed her bowl on the counter and picked up the envelope, her stomach sinking as she read the return address: "Los Angeles Superior Court."

Of course. Why would Dani dare to hope any written correspondence would contain good news?

She ripped open the envelope and scanned the letter. It detailed the date of her postponed arraignment, settled for the first Thursday of February. She had almost forgotten about her arrest; it had been weeks since she'd postponed her arraignment. The courts weren't kidding when they warned her to expect significant delays.

She swallowed against a rising burn in her throat and folded the letter, stuffing it into her backpack.

Haley deserved every bit of shunning Dani gave her. Dani was paying the ultimate price for Mitch's crime.

Carolyn shifted in her seat as Dani brought her plate to the opposite end of the oval table, planting herself beside Emma. "So, uh…are you gonna tell them you're innocent?" Carolyn asked with a wrinkle of her lips.

Dani twirled her fork in the noodles before answering. "Haley and Mitch deserve what's coming for them."

On Dani's right, Emma curled her hair behind an ear. "Hopefully, your mom will finally get off your case."

Dani snorted as she stabbed a meatball. "My mom will never get off my case even if the heavens open up and every court in Los Angeles rules in my favor."

Carolyn scratched her nose. "But why doesn't she understand it wasn't your fault? That cop was just being callous. He was drinking too! It's too bad 'cause most police aren't like that. You were dealt a really unlucky hand…"

Dani rolled her eyes. "I told you, my mom will never believe I was 'dealt an unlucky hand.' She's convinced I'm a dirty, cheating piece of trash. No matter what I say or do, she's made her mind up about me. It's why I didn't bother telling her I'm suspended from lacrosse."

Carolyn glanced down, brushing a strand of red hair out of her face. "That's not fair to you. Both of those incidents were…set up against you. I think your mom should at least be more understanding and hear your side of the story."

A haughty smirk spilled across Dani's face. "That'll be the day I sprout wings and turn into a unicorn. I can't win with her."

The two roommates were quiet as Dani shoved her noodles across her plate and chewed in silence. It was no use having this conversation again. She'd told them countless times her parents were incorrigible people, and the evidence was plain as daylight. Why was Tanner the only one who understood that?

Emma broke the tension. "So you guys saw the news today?"

"Oh, the coronavirus?" Carolyn mumbled through a mouthful of food. "Yeah, but it's in Washington, so I'm not that worried."

"Yeah, seems like the news is only trying to scare people." Dani shrugged, twirling the noodles with her fork and stuffing them into her mouth.

Emma threw up her manicured hands in exasperation. "Guys, I read in one of my history classes that the last time something spread this fast was the 1918 Spanish Flu. And that was before we had planes and ten times less the world population we have now!"

"Hmm, true," Carolyn pondered, pushing the noodles around her plate. "Imagine how quickly it'd spread if someone in LA got it and used the subway… We'd be dead in weeks!" Her green eyes widened as she lifted a hand to her cheek.

"Exactly." Emma nodded, curling her dark hair behind an ear. "Hopefully, they knock this thing out soon."

Carolyn burst out laughing at something on her phone. Several students walking out of the cafeteria shot Dani and Carolyn puzzled looks when they walked by their table, but Carolyn's laughter didn't cease.

"What's up?" Dani asked with a mouth full of burger.

It was odd to see anyone so jubilant following the tragic death of the basketball legend Kobe Bryant last weekend. The school and city had been eerily quiet for the past few days, any news of the coronavirus or politics drowned out by memoirs and loving tributes to the sports icon.

Carolyn's bubbliness, however, was a stark contrast to that reality.

"Oh, wow, you have to see this!" Carolyn turned her phone around to show Dani a clip of an SNL skit that had aired last week.

Dani raised the volume and watched celebrity guest host Adam Driver portray an annoyed science teacher. A grin spilled across her lips. "Nice. Adam's such a good actor."

Carolyn nodded. "He totally is. Have you seen *Marriage Story?* There's this scene where he totally breaks down…"

Dani took another bite of her burger, her focus drifting behind Carolyn. Dani's chewing paused when she noticed Alisha and her friend Noemi enter the courtyard around a corner.

Dani considered waving to them right before two boys blocked her view. They were close enough for Dani to hear the taller guy say with a chuckle, "Looks like some of the Chinese got through the POTUS's immigration ban."

The guys snickered as they passed Noemi. Her face fell, and a weight dropped in Dani's gut.

As quick as a fox, Alisha whirled and yelled at the tall boy who had commented. "Looks like USC is still admitting racist assholes like yourselves. She's not even Chinese—she's *Filipino!*"

Carolyn rotated in her seat to see the source of the commotion. Students who were walking by or sitting at nearby tables also turned their heads, and any surrounding chatter died instantly.

The tall guy turned to face her, lips tightened and eyebrows drawn down. Clearly, he hadn't expected such an angry retort from a small girl such as Alisha, but she pressed on, her body poised like a lion inching toward its prey.

"You dicks think you're hilarious, you dumb pieces of shit."

The tall one gave her the finger before he and his sidekick turned away.

Undeterred, Alisha flipped double middle fingers at their backs before turning to Noemi, who was holding her arm with glassy eyes. Alisha muttered, "Forget the cafeteria; let's eat at one of the food trucks." She ushered Noemi back in the direction they came, disappearing from view around a corner.

"Holy shit," Dani whispered when Carolyn turned slowly back around, her face ghost-white.

Dani lay in her room two days later, furiously typing away on her laptop for one of Dr. Turner's assignments. The squeak of the front door drifted upstairs, and Emma's surprised greeting met Dani's ears.

"Hey, Alisha!"

Dani jerked her head up. She shut her laptop and crept downstairs in her sweats and T-shirt, the carpet muffling her bare feet. Alisha had her back to Dani from where she stood in the living room in front of Emma.

"Is everything okay?" Emma asked Alisha, closing a textbook she had been reading and setting it on the coffee table.

Alisha folded her arms, her back arching. "Not really. Noemi isn't doing too hot. She's gotten a few racist comments since COVID hit."

A dumbbell dropped in Dani's stomach as she recalled her own racially motivated comment about anime toward Noemi in September. It appeared Dani had only added to the pile of racism Noemi had to deal with lately.

Dani sucked in a breath before stepping down from the last stair and clasping her hands, fully in view. "Carolyn and I were eating outside the cafeteria on Monday," she said softly.

Alisha spun, her dark curly hair swishing to reveal her startled expression.

"We saw what happened," Dani continued, "and I thought it was awesome how you stuck up for her." *Like that old lady stuck up for me when that cop wouldn't loosen the cuffs…*

Dani grimaced at the memory, remembering the red glow of the lady's taillights disappearing from view as Dani stared back, flabbergasted and struck with guilt.

Alisha's face remained neutral, dark shadows looming under her eyes, her curly hair ratted in places. "That wasn't the first time she's been attacked. When we were out at Santa Monica last weekend, a few times, people walked by her with weird looks or made other Chinese comments. She's been stressed with a lot of school stuff too, so Monday was sort of the tipping point."

No wonder Alisha was so heated when she'd reprimanded that guy. Noemi had endured enough already.

Emma glanced at the floor and fiddled with the bracelets around her wrist. "I'm really sorry that happened to her. I'm glad you were there to support her. I can't say I'd have been brave enough to do the same."

Alisha's mouth bent up slightly on one side then went neutral again. "Well, you can thank our president for all the racist shit that's happening. I've never once heard him attempt to show empathy with people of color; he only spews hate and divisiveness and blames China for everything."

Emma blanched as Alisha turned and brushed past Dani up the stairs. "I'm going to bed. See you all in the morning."

Emma's gaze drifted to Dani, her brows drawn and jaw slacked.

Dani bit her lip. "Before this week, I've never seen her behave so… passionately," she said quietly.

"Me neither." Emma curled her bangs behind an ear. "She's right. Although I hate to get into politics, we should be focusing on the health and well-being of ourselves instead of blaming China for everything. Although the president has given a lot of aid to health-care workers with the hospital ships and ventilators, stirring up hostility just undermines all of that." She shook her head and exhaled a sharp breath. "Whatever happens, I really hope this whole situation doesn't get worse than it already is."

Dani nodded mechanically.

*February*

"READY FOR TODAY?" HALEY APPEARED NEXT TO DANI AS they ran around the track, warming up for their first home game.

"Yep." Dani quickened her stride to run ahead of her.

"Dammit, what is your problem?" Haley raced to catch up with her. "I keep telling you I didn't mean for you to get arrested! Mitch didn't want to wait for you outside, and when I asked, he said he'd stolen from that guy's wallet. I didn't know what to do, I wasn't thinking clearly, so I left with him thinking you were right behind. I didn't think anything would happen to—"

"Save your breath, Haley. Your energy is better directed at kicking Michigan's ass," Dani huffed.

Haley had left Dani that night for her dumb criminal boyfriend, and the fact they were still together made Dani sick. She could care less about Haley's sorry-ass apology.

Speeding up again, she left Haley behind and tried to keep her mind focused on the game. Haley had no business ruining Dani's mood right before the match she had been anticipating for months.

She peered at the slowly crowding bleachers as she rounded the track and spotted Carolyn, Emma with Chase, and even Alisha squished in one of the front rows, true to their word. Emma hoisted a giant sign that had Dani's number "14" and "Go Dani!!" painted in sparkling red and gold. Dani rolled her eyes, feeling the heat rush to her cheeks as she ran by.

She scanned the rest of the bleachers in search of broad shoulders and dark, messy hair, but her spirits dipped the longer she searched. Tanner had promised he would be there, and Dani still believed he would come. Even as his absence from the bleachers chipped at her heart, she tried to brush it off. He would come later.

Dani shook her head. *I can't worry about petty distractions today.*

Her eyes flitted over the green jerseys on the opposite end of the field. Today, the Trojans were playing against ninth-ranked Michigan. Dani had woken up with the excited rush of adrenaline spilling through her veins like she always did on the morning of lacrosse games. To her delight, even her mom had said she and her dad had organized a small gathering at one of the bars in downtown Helena to kick off her opening match.

She had told her mom she was feeling terribly sick last week when the team flew to New York and would therefore be missing the first game. In actuality, Dani had watched the game, healthy and full of Trojan spirit, with Carolyn and Emma on their widescreen TV. It was a close, nerve-wracking match, but USC beat Hofstra 9–8.

By noon, the bleachers had filled to capacity. Winston ushered the girls to the sideline along with the other coaches for a final huddle before the match. "One, two, three..." she prompted.

"Fight on!" the girls finished before dispersing.

The beating sun had Dani drenched with sweat by the time she positioned herself at midfield, Taylor preparing for the face-off against a tall, fierce-looking girl with beefy arms and a scrunched glare.

Dani clutched her stick tightly, her heart pumping a steady rhythm in her chest. This was it. This is what she looked forward to most every year. The adrenaline pulsing through her veins, the fiery competition, the roar of the Trojan fans propelling her forward—this is what made all the hard times worth it.

This is what she was good at.

The referee placed the ball and blew the whistle, signaling the start of the match. Taylor body-checked the other girl and wrestled her before scooping up the ball and flinging it to Olivia. Olivia ducked out of the way of a Michigan midfielder and ran down the field, spotting Dani open in the corner across the way. She chucked it over a midfielder's head with a quick fling of her stick. Swiping the ball from the air, Dani took two long strides and juked around a defender, her eyes on the goal. When the goalie braced for her shot, Dani hurled the ball to Taylor at the last moment, catching the goalie off-balance. Taylor caught her pass gracefully before slamming it into the goal with a giant leap.

The sea of red and gold on one side of the bleachers erupted into cheers, but it wasn't long before Michigan scored and silenced their hooting. For the next few minutes, both teams fought viciously for the lead. Dani boosted their score with two more assists and a goal on a new play Winston had designed, giving the Trojans a 6–5 lead by the end of the first half.

The second half started just as exciting, and each team continued to alternate scoring, battling to the death. By the third quarter, the Trojans were behind 6–8, when the tall girl's long arms intercepted Zoey's pass for the third time. The defender dwarfed her in comparison.

"Dammit, Zoey!" Winston yelled from the sideline. "Stop passing ahead when 24 is in front of you! Pass it back around her!"

Zoey dipped her head briefly as she ran down the field after the tall girl.

Dani shook her head, pursing her lips. Zoey was new to the team, but there was no excuse for her careless passing. They wouldn't last long in the season with rookie mistakes.

In the fourth quarter, Arianna found a rhythm as goalie, blocking four back-to-back shots that kept Michigan at their score of 8. After a few press plays, the Trojans finally managed to even the score with six minutes left in the quarter.

Dani knocked the ball out of a shorter girl's stick and scooped it up. Seeing a gap in front of her, she sprinted ahead, outrunning one of the defenders. Isabel raised her stick in the opposite corner of the field, but she apparently didn't see the Michigan midfielder running up behind her.

One defender side-stepped into Dani's route as she approached the crease. Dani juked left and threw her stick around, trying to score over the girl's shoulder, but the defender stood her ground. They collided painfully, Dani toppling onto the girl as the ball flew easily into the goalie's outstretched stick.

The referee nearest them whistled. "Personal foul on Red 14! Slashing!"

The Trojan crowd booed, and Dani fumed from the ground, rolling onto her knees. She tore off her facemask. "What! I was shooting—that wasn't slashing!"

The referee's face remained stoic as he raised an arm. "Two-minute suspension for Red 14. Possession goes to Green."

"You've got to be kidding me," Dani growled.

"Torres!" Winston shouted from the sideline. "Stop complaining and get your ass off the field!"

After a few seething moments, Dani reluctantly complied, catching a sly smile from the girl who had knocked her down. Dani sneered as she tugged off her facemask on her way to the penalty box.

Her foot bounced as she watched the next two minutes in agony from the sidelines. There were only three minutes left in the match, the score still tied 8–8. She tried to ignore the sting in her chest for not being able to help her team under pressure. As midfielder, she was a critical player who was permitted to defend as well as attack.

Michigan had the ball, and it was their ten against the Trojans' nine players, Dani's suspension making the balance uneven. Three of their attackers passed around two of the Trojan defenders until one of them whipped the ball at the goal. Dani's knuckles whitened on the bench as Arianna's stick shot out. When she deflected the ball in a fantastic block, Dani let out a breath she didn't realize she was holding. Haley scooped up the ball and passed it far ahead to Olivia. Dani's eyes trailed Olivia, her heart racing as her teammate flicked the ball past a defender to Isabel. In one swift motion, Isabel swept the ball past the goalie's foot into the goal.

Dani and the Trojan crowd sprung to their feet in applause, just as the referee approached.

"Your two-minute suspension is over," he notified.

Snatching her facemask off the bench, Dani sprung back onto the field, reigniting some applause from the bleachers.

It was 9–8, but there were still one and a half minutes of play. Anything could happen.

The midfielder who had knocked Dani down trotted the field to pick up the ball. Dani bounced on her heels, eyeing her fiercely when she got in position. As soon as the ref blew his whistle, Dani bolted forward. The girl flashed a smug smile before flinging the ball over Dani's head to another midfielder. Olivia rushed up to the receiving girl and stick-checked her, and the ball popped out of the midfielder's net. Olivia scooped it up, feinted sideways from an attacker, and chucked it to Haley.

Dani glanced at the clock: Thirty seconds left. They'd better score quickly.

She sprinted ahead down the field and waved her stick, signaling she was open. Haley saw her but continued running straight ahead as if she hadn't.

*The girl had better keep our fight out of this. I'm gonna kill her if she doesn't pass to me.*

Haley crossed midfield, juked a defender, and hurled a no-look pass to Dani who was waiting for her in the opposite corner, her stick ready. In one fluid motion, Dani whacked the airborne ball like a hockey player, and it soared into the net over the baffled goalie's shoulder.

The horn blared, ending the match, and the next few moments seemed frozen in time.

The bleachers exploded into a rumble of cheers, high-fives, and feet stamping as Trojan fans celebrated the team's second victory. Dani threw her stick down in triumph, running to jump into her teammates' outstretched arms.

Haley ran up to her with a wide grin. "Where the hell did you learn to shoot like that!" she shouted over the cheers of their teammates.

Dani couldn't help but smile and join in the girls' jumping and whooping. Winston beamed the brightest of them all, her usual callous expression replaced by an exuberant smile. She slapped Dani on the back as she yelled, "Glad to have you back, girl!"

Dani turned her head to the bleachers to see her roommates screaming and waving the sign with her name on it. Her heart warmed at the sight of their excited faces, and she grinned before searching the rambunctious crowd further. Her stomach clenched as she realized Tanner hadn't made it after all.

But over on the right side, standing next to the bleachers, a tall, familiar figure caught her eye. A huge smile was painted on Dustin's face as he waved his fist in the air, cheering wildly. Beside him stood Mel in a dirty uniform, gawking at the rowdy fans.

Dani's heart lifted, and she grinned at Dustin, the pain of Tanner's absence temporarily subsiding.

In that moment, it felt as if her team had won the PAC-12 and were champions, although there was still plenty of season left. Their team was phenomenal this year, and she had no doubt they could go all the way.

This was one of the reasons she did lacrosse: all of her worries seemed to vanish with the excitement of competition. In high school, the cheers of the crowd and high-fives of her teammates had washed away her frustration with her parents at home. And now, with every smiling face that congratulated her on the team's win, the swirling vortex of emotions that had haunted her the past few months faded further and further away.

She was back where she belonged.

Haley scrambled atop the pub's barstool, peering down at the crowd of giddy faces. Strands of brown hair had wound their way out of her ponytail, and a wild grin danced across her lips. She raised her glass of beer in an awkward salute. "Cheers to my amazing teammates, who kicked *ass* today!"

Dani whooped along with the girls and the rest of the college students who raised their drinks along with the team captain.

"And cheers to continuing our undefeated streak to the PAC-12 champion—shiiit." Haley tottered and spilled some beer on her lacrosse jersey. She shoved a hand onto the shoulder of the guy who stood closest to her. He smiled as she swung her messy brown hair along his face and straightened on the barstool. "What the hell was I even saying?"

"Who cares? Have another beer!" someone shouted, and the crowd cheered as the bartender turned up the tunes, drowning out the rest of Haley's speech. The guy in front of her lifted her down from the barstool, and she slumped into his arms, gazing up at him with a flirtatious grin.

"Haley being Haley, as usual," Hannah yelled over the roar of the crowd, although she stood right beside Dani.

Dani smirked as Haley said something to the guy and flicked her hand across her boob. After the familiar adrenaline rush of competition and today's victory, it had been hard for Dani to stay mad at Haley.

"Do you think Mitch even cares?" she asked.

Hannah laughed and held her martini above a train of students ducking around them. "Mitch does the same. Olivia saw him get cozy with other girls at her sorority the other week. It's so pathetic how guys always throw a fit when their girlfriends catch other dudes' attention, but when someone flirts with the guy, it's totally fine." She took a swig of her drink, and her tone dropped a level. "I'm sure Haley just does it to make up for lost time with him. I think it's been even harder for her since you stopped talking her, to be honest. You were the one she always went to, aside from Mitch."

Dani bit her lip, watching the captain saunter to another group of smiling guys. Her stomach twisted as she watched Haley laugh and run a hand along the chest of an eager-looking senior. On the surface, Haley looked happy; playful. But Dani could see now it was the outward display of someone who was hurting inside, longing to be comforted.

Perhaps Haley was just lonely, and Dani had been wrong to treat her so harshly. Haley had only wanted to please Mitch, and it had unfortunately forced her to choose between her boyfriend and her friend.

What if Dani had to choose between Tanner and Haley? Would she have acted the same?

"Why don't you get a drink?" Hannah asked, drawing Dani's attention back to her teammate's friendly stare. Hannah perked her lips and swirled her glass. "You did make, like, five assists and scored an awesome game-ending goal. Come on—it's on me."

Dani shook her head. "I'm good, thanks. There's plenty of—" She cut off as her pocket vibrated. She dug a hand into her shorts, her pulse racing, but her spirits fell when she scanned the caller ID.

Her mouth pulled into a frown as she turned to Hannah. "Sorry, I forgot to call my mom after the match." She skirted through the crowd and stepped through the glass doors onto Figueroa Street's darkened sidewalk. Her bare arms shivered in the evening chill as she raised the phone to her ear.

"Sorry, Mom. The team and I went out to a bar, and I—"

"Dani!" Angelina blared. "What did I tell you about drinking!"

Dani squeezed her eyes and took a few steps down the path around a laughing group of students. "I didn't have any drinks, Mom. Calm down."

"You need to stop acting so irresponsibly," she lectured for the hundredth time.

Dani rolled her eyes. If she had a dollar for every time she rolled her eyes while talking to her mom, she wouldn't need her scholarship.

"Whatever. Did you guys watch the game?"

"Yes, it was a great game! Except for the part when you got fouled out."

*Of course she would note that.* Dani gritted her teeth and leaned against the pub's brick wall. "That ref pissed me off. He didn't know what he was calling."

Her mom's sigh made Dani's lip twitch. "It looked like you argued with him. That attitude of yours only escalates things."

Dani shoved off the wall and paced up the sidewalk, taming her rising anger before she spoke. "Did…Dad watch?"

A few silent seconds ticked by. "Your dad only stayed for half of it."

*Failure after failure after failure…*

Dani's face fell. He hadn't even seen her make that buzzer-beater goal? Was it too much to ask that he watch one full game?

She recalled her dad's condescending demeanor and all those years he had berated her for her imperfect lacrosse skills. Her moment of self-pity vanished. Apparently, it was too much to ask from him. He would always be disappointed in her.

The subdued anger bubbled again in the pit of her stomach. She was tired of her Dad's shit. This had been going on way too long.

"Why the hell can't he sit through a single game and support his daughter?" she growled.

"He did, Dani. It was just too much for him after so lo—"

"Yeah, well, he isn't the only one having to deal with shit!" Dani yelled. "We've all been trying to cope, and his selfishness isn't making it any better!"

"Dani…please don't be angry with him." It was as if Dani was once again that high-school girl crying in her room late at night, and her mom was attempting a therapy session.

When Dani didn't respond, Angelina said, "Are you taking your meds? You need to—"

"Oh my god, Mom, the meds aren't the problem!" Dani hung up and shoved the phone into her pocket. Her head fell into her hands as her mind waged war between anger at her parents and herself.

After a few minutes, Hannah's voice drifted from the pub entrance. "Hey, girl. Everything okay?"

Dani lifted her eyes and responded softly, "Yeah, fine." She trekked to Hannah's side and pushed open the glass doors. "Let's get back to the party."

Hannah followed her as she shuffled through the crowd and joined Lisa and Arianna, who were sharing laughs by the bar.

"Dani, there you are! The star of the night!" Arianna raised her glass, and Lisa and Hannah did the same.

Dani feigned a smile as they tossed back their drinks. *Star of what? My own parents won't even watch my games.* That damn self-pity started to rise again, and Dani struggled to swallow against a burning lump in her throat.

While her teammates chatted and giggled beside her, she grabbed her phone from her pocket and scrolled through her messages. It took her a second to find Tanner's name before she typed out a text.

**You missed my buzzer-beater goal today. You should come over to 901 Bar and Grill on Fig and celebrate with us!**

After a few seconds, her phone buzzed, to her surprise. She raised the device, heart racing, and her breath hitched.

It was him.

**Ah, shit I forgot about your game!! You're such a beast. Sorry, can't come tonight.**

Dani bit her lip, but hope still flooded her veins at the fact that he had responded so quickly. She quickly texted a reply. **Want to go out tomorrow? I'm free!**

**Uh… I'm busy.**

Her heart crashed to the ground. He was never busy on Sundays. **Whatcha up to? Maybe I can join :)**

One, two minutes passed. No response.

When her phone finally buzzed, she read his message with eager eyes and nearly crumbled.

**I think we should take a break.**

She stared at those seven words for what seemed like an eternity, shocked and devoid of breath, before she typed a reply with trembling fingers. **What's wrong? Talk to me. I want you to be happy :'(**

His next message came two minutes later. **Sorry Dani.**

The phone slipped from her grasp as a sea of grief threatened to drown her. She scooped it up off the dirty, alcohol-swept floor and began pushing her way to the exit.

"Dani? Where are you going?" someone called behind her as she scurried through the crowd, the tears threatening to overflow

No, no. She wouldn't cry.

She wouldn't; she couldn't. Tanner wouldn't do this to her. He wouldn't leave her when he knew she needed him as much as she did. He said he wouldn't abandon her. And right before Valentine's Day?

*You aren't relationship material.*

The boiling sea of despair rolled to the surface, and though she tried to force it back into its haunting depths, it was no use.

As soon as she burst through the pub's glass doors, the sea overflowed above the walls she had built for herself. She slumped against a neighboring building and shook with grief, drowning in her tears.

Tanner should have been there holding her, caressing her, taking her pain away.

But he wasn't.

No one ever was.

# Twenty-Three

*February*

I T WAS JUST A BREAK. JUST TEMPORARY. AFTER A WHILE, DANI WOULD be back with Tanner as if nothing had happened. That was what she kept telling herself the next few days as she sat through her classes, staring into space.

But even if it was just a break, it still hurt.

She had ruined things with him. Dissatisfied him. And now he didn't want her.

Why had she been so afraid of sex? She had wanted it so badly, even led him on. But no—she had panicked right in the thick of things, denying him at the last minute when he had waited patiently for so long.

Why was she such a coward? She'd run back to Tanner and give it to him if that was all it took for them to be together; to seal the bleeding wound gouging her heart.

The thoughts continued to plague her as she woke to her 6:30 a.m. alarm Thursday morning and dressed for her arraignment. Tanner wouldn't be there to support her today when she professed her innocence and went to war with Dom the police officer. What was the point of anything if he wasn't there to celebrate in her successes and comfort her during the hard times?

Carolyn knocked on Dani's door and stuck her frazzled red head through the frame. "Hey, Dani, are you almost ready?"

Dani nodded as she shrugged on a green, long-sleeved button-up blouse above her slacks. "Yeah. Just have to do my make-up and then I'm good." She grabbed a brush from her bedside table and stared in her closet mirror at her saggy eyes and drooping cheeks. Makeup had never seemed so useful. "Thanks for offering to drop me off today. I could have called an Uber, you know."

Carolyn gave a sheepish grin and opened the door wider. She was already fully dressed in jeans and her usual baggy sweatshirt. "No problem. I didn't want you to pay for an expensive Uber ride all the way to La Cienega! Although you'll have to get a ride home afterward 'cause I have class."

After masking her defeated features with a bright display of blush and mascara, Dani followed Carolyn down the stairs and out of the apartment toward Carolyn's Toyota Camry. "It seems stupid to go through a trial for one hundred dollars," Dani muttered once they were inside.

"You're gonna be fine," Carolyn urged with an optimistic smile as she dug the key into the ignition. "Don't forget to ask for an attorney 'cause you're a poor college student. He can subpoena the other two cops who will corroborate your story about Dom's drinking and Haley and Mitch ditching you."

Dani stared out at the foggy, darkened sidewalks as Carolyn drove down Hoover and onto the already traffic-heavy freeway. Dom's scrawny partner surfaced in her mind.

*"Dom," he warned again with a frown as Dom tightened the cuffs on Dani. "This is a bit much."*

*"You're not gonna say anything about me drinking," Dom muttered.*

Dani slumped against the armrest. "The officers won't corroborate my story. Dom will pressure them not to. I'll just have to hope the jury believes me alone."

Today wasn't looking so promising anymore.

Carolyn shot her a skeptical look. "What are you talking about? Sure they will!"

Dani feigned a reassuring smile. It was no use arguing with her.

She took a deep breath as a weak stream of sunlight peeked through the clouds, warming her chilly bones. Maybe she could be more optimistic like Carolyn. Dani would ask for a lawyer, and he or she would help collect as many witnesses as possible. If Dom didn't want the word to get out that he'd abused his power, he was in for a fight.

Today was the first step on her road to exoneration.

The condensation clogging the windshield slowly diffused as they drove out of the city and into the suburbs on the southwest side. Packed concrete buildings gave way to patches of grass and cozy neighborhoods, and parents walked their children to school on the sidewalks.

Finally, Carolyn pulled in front of a large glass building and turned to Dani with a wide grin. "Good luck!"

Dani unbuckled her seatbelt and shouldered her purse, expelling a long sigh. "Thanks. I owe you one." She stepped out of the car and breathed in the fresh, salty air. It smelled as if it was going to rain. Sure enough, the sun seemed to disappear behind darkened clouds as she made her way up the concrete steps, lawyers and other nicely dressed people scurrying past her toward the giant glass doors ahead.

She paused, glancing over her shoulder to watch Carolyn's Toyota Camry disappear down the street, leaving Dani alone once again. With a deep breath, Dani turned back to face the intimidating circular structure where her fate lay waiting.

A light sprinkle began drizzling on her shoulders, and Dani shivered, folding her arms tightly against her chest. She hadn't thought to bring a jacket. California weather was ninety percent sunshine, so she had gotten used to dressing lightly wherever she went.

But now, of all days, it had decided to rain?

The trek up the steps to the glass doors seemed a mile longer as the rain dampened her blouse sleeves. She kept her head down, praying her makeup wouldn't get ruined. As she approached the glass doors, a man in a suit walking beside her smiled and darted forward to pull the door open for her.

"Thank you," she managed as she ducked through the doorway.

"Of course, miss." He nodded and entered the building after her, swinging his briefcase forward. When she glanced back at him, she started. He had a handsome, thirty-year-old face with long dark lashes. A neatly trimmed beard ran up the length of his jaw and connected with short, silky brown hair. He almost looked like…

"Jury duty?" he asked as they entered the line for security, flashing a playful smile in her direction.

Dani bit her lip. "Um…no. I have an arraignment." She grabbed a bin from the table, placed her purse and cell phone inside, and set it back on the conveyor belt.

The man arched an eyebrow. "Ah, pardon me. I just assumed…" He set his briefcase on the conveyor belt with a frown and fumbled with his wallet and keys.

"It's okay," she consoled, shifting her weight. His innocent assumption was warranted after all. She was a young college student who had no business being a defendant in court.

They pushed their bins further down the line. "I hope everything goes well," the man murmured from behind.

Dani turned to him and smiled. "Thanks. It will." She caught his grin before she turned and stepped through the metal detector. After being checked out by a female officer, Dani collected her belongings from the bin and followed signs down the busy hallway for courtroom 203.

Things would be better after today. If that lawyer thought she didn't look like a criminal, then what did she have to fear from a jury? When her innocence was proven, maybe her parents would finally realize Dani wasn't as bad of a daughter as they thought.

*But you were three years ago,* the sinister voice whispered. *Who's to say you're any different now?*

Dani shuddered as she headed up an escalator and continued down a long hallway. Unlike the other bustling hallways, this one was deserted. She stared down at the pristine marble floor, listening to her isolated steps echo off the narrow walls while she trekked deeper into the building's maw. Haley's accusatory face appeared in front of her, the captain's mascara dripping down her face, ruined by her tears. "You ruined me!" Haley yelled in a broken voice. "We should never have been friends. All you're good for is hurting everyone who gets close to you!"

Dani shut her eyes, willing Haley's face out of her mind. *No, Haley, you did this to yourself. It's not my fault. You should be the one who is sorry.* Dani couldn't let her self-doubt creep up on her again. It was past time justice was served.

"Miss Danica Torres," the judge began, staring down her pointed nose after reading the court process formalities. Her short dark hair framed disinterested eyes on a plump face. "You are here today for resisting arrest under Penal Code 148 PC, and theft by larceny under California Penal Code PC 484. How do you plead under the charge of resisting arrest?"

Dani eyed Dom, who stood at the end of the bench, waiting patiently with his hands folded. His badge gleamed brightly on his uniform, his burly body straight as a ramrod, his rounded face relaxed and respectful. It was a striking divergence from the inebriated, volatile officer she remembered from Black Friday.

She turned back toward the judge's desk and brushed the hair from her eyes. "Guilty, your honor." That was as much of a victory as Dom was going to get. She glanced back in his direction, but his neutral expression hadn't changed. Professional, calm—as an officer should be.

"And for the charge of larceny?" the judge continued in a firm voice, drawing Dani's attention back to the woman's piercing gaze, outlined by stringy curls and a wide chin.

Dani opened her mouth, her answer brimming on the tip of her tongue, but hesitated. *This is it. This is what you've been waiting for. Say you didn't do it. It was Haley and her cheating, scheming, piece-of-shit boyfriend.* A memory flashed of Haley's smiling, flirtatious face as she cozied up to the guys at the bar, and the guilty jab in Dani's gut returned.

*She's my friend. I can't ruin her life.*

*No, she isn't my friend,* Dani reminded herself sharply. Haley had stabbed her in the back. And it didn't matter anyway. Dani was innocent; Haley wasn't.

*But is Haley really to blame? She was only trying to please Mitch. Wouldn't I have done the same?*

*Wouldn't I?*

"Miss Torres?" the judge repeated, straightening in her leather chair behind the raised desk.

"Guilty," Dani whispered weakly. Mitch deserved to go to hell, but Haley… She didn't deserve punishment for just trying to be loved by him. Dani wouldn't be the one to ruin their relationship. Haley would have to realize on her own that she deserved better than Mitch.

The judge raised her thin eyebrows and peered at Dani with grim authority. "The defendant pleads guilty to both charges. Because this is for a measly one-hundred-dollar bill,"—she eyed Dom with distaste—"I'll settle with a fine of six hundred dollars." She pounded the gavel on its block, the ear-splitting echo around the vacant chamber sealing Dani's fate. "Though I must remind you, Miss Torres, your record was not completely clean before this incident, and I'm alarmed to see an aspirational, young college student such as yourself continue to make unwise decisions. Next time, you very well could end up in jail, throwing away your future for good." She pursed her thin lips in a manner not unlike Angelina Torres, and Dani's chest tightened.

Her mom would not be happy to hear she'd have to transfer more money to Dani's account.

When was her mom ever happy, for that matter? But now, Dani had given her more reason to be angry with her. *God, what did I just do to myself? My mom's reaction is understandable, but Carolyn and Emma will be bewildered.*

Dom didn't make eye contact as the bailiff led Dani out of the courtroom, her feet weighing her down like bricks. She clutched the edge of her blouse and forced her face to remain calm, refusing to show any emotion although a fiery burn had crept up her throat.

*Guilty. Guilty. Guilty.* The tiny voice followed her all the way through the marble hallways and through the double glass doors. She stopped in her tracks as the pounding rain jerked her from her thoughts. She huddled underneath the overhang, digging her shaking fingers into her pocket to order an Uber on her phone. The action sent a ripple of despair through her limbs. This time, Tanner wouldn't be there to pick her up and save her from her troubles.

*There was a reason Tanner left you.*
*Guilty. Guilty. Guilty,* the voice echoed.

*February*

ON VALENTINE'S DAY, DANI SPORTED HER RED AND GOLD lacrosse shirt, black tights, and white Vans. She had been saving a knee-length satin red dress to wear today for months, but what was the point when there was no one to wear it for?

She swallowed a lump wedged in her throat and swerved her bike around the trickle of students on the campus path, trying to ignore the smiling girls and guys holding heart-shaped balloons.

*Valentine's Day, a.k.a. Singles Awareness Day*, Dani thought as she sped around the smiling couples holding hands. Tanner should have been buying her flowers and walking hand-in-hand with her like them. As hard as she'd tried not to think about Tanner, the part of her that still loved him overtook the rational part of her brain. What was he up to right now? Probably on his way to football practice since it was almost noon. Was he thinking about her at all? Surely it wouldn't hurt to shoot him a quick text to let him know she still cared about him.

Parking her bike in front of the large arched Dornsife building, she did just that and waited anxiously for a response. The four agonizing minutes she waited were long enough, and she slipped her phone into her pocket as the sinking feeling in her chest worsened.

Maybe he was just busy talking to one of his buddies as he walked to practice. He'd respond eventually, right?

*What am I doing? He wants time* away *from me.*

Looking up, she spotted Chase walking down the path in a red button-down collared shirt and jeans. His usual dark, floppy hair was combed back nicely, his slim face beaming like the sun as he clutched a bright pink bag in front of him.

He caught her watching him and cocked a brow, then recognition spilled across his lips. He smiled and meandered off the path in her direction.

"Hey, sorry I forgot your name. Danice, right?" he asked as he approached the bike rack, his brown eyes boring into hers unabashedly. The inch she had in height difference on him was amusing enough to pull her from her melancholy thoughts.

A small smirk crept across her lips. "Close enough."

He flashed a wide smile. "Awesome. Can I ask you a question? Do you know what time Emma's econ class gets out today? I want to surprise her."

His words tugged at the sinking feeling in her chest, but she managed to mask her emotions and give a shrug. "I can text her."

He lit up like a little kid being offered a cookie. "That'd be great, thanks!"

Dani pulled out her phone and, seeing no response from Tanner, breathed out a small tremor. Her fingers quickly typed out a text to Emma. She was probably at the apartment still; Dani always left before her on Fridays.

A few seconds later, her phone buzzed, and she scanned her room-mate's reply. "She said 2:30."

Chase's eyes twinkled, and his wide smile illuminated his face again. "Perfect. I hope she likes Reese's."

*Why had Tanner never seemed that enthusiastic around me?* Dani forced a small smile. "You can never go wrong with chocolate. I'm sure she'll love it."

He beamed back at her.

For hanging out with a bunch of spoiled rich kids, Chase seemed like a decent guy. She remembered how he had scanned Dani and Carolyn up and down at the frat party in a shallow act of disapproval, but maybe she had judged him prematurely. Dani was just glad he and Emma seemed to be getting along so well.

"Oh, by the way," Chase started, interrupting her thoughts, "my buddy Kyle has a thing for you but doesn't have the guts to ask you out. He's a cool guy, plays on the baseball team."

Dani's stomach plummeted. "Kyle…Walker?" Her mind flicked back to the tall, handsome guy Carolyn had been rattling off to at the frat party.

"Yeah, that's the guy. He'd kill me if I told you, but he'll never make a move. Just thought I'd let you know in case you're interested."

*Shit. Carolyn is going to hate me.*

Chase waited with a smug grin as Dani wracked her brain for a valid response. All that came out was, "Damn."

Chase cracked his knuckles, his expression optimistic. "You should see him, gushing over your lacrosse skills like a little kid." He shook his head with a small laugh.

Heat rushed to Dani's face, and she scratched her cheek. *Kyle talks about me? Tanner never gushed about me like that to any of his friends. Except when he bragged about my hotness to his roommate who looked at me like I was his favorite toy.*

"Like I said," Chase continued, "he's super chill. I can set something up if you want. Just let me know."

"For sure," Dani lied, forcing a smile.

"Cool. Catch you later, Danice." He nodded and continued bouncing down the path along with all the other happy couples, swinging the pink bag by his side.

Dani threw her head back in defeat, wringing her fingers through her hair. Maybe she should just avoid telling Carolyn altogether and spare herself from the redhead's wallowing.

As she walked up the brick steps and into class, she couldn't help thinking how badly she wanted someone like Chase in a relationship. Someone to be there when she came home late from lacrosse practice, showering her with treats, cheering her on during her matches, and running up to hug her after she shot the winning goal. She'd imagined Tanner doing it many times, but he hadn't come to her game.

*Yeah, that was* after *I cock-blocked him, remember?*

Still, he hadn't ever seemed as head-over-heels as Chase.

Was that what being in love looked like? She thought she was falling in love with Tanner, or coming close to it. She definitely had a strong attraction to him and cared for him as a partner should.

So why did Dani not light up the way Chase did when thinking about Emma? Maybe every relationship progressed differently.

Regardless, Dani wanted a relationship like Emma's more than anything.

Hell, she wouldn't mind dating this Kyle Walker guy during her and Tanner's "break" if Carolyn wasn't so infatuated with him. Another image of him popped up in her mind: his curly hair fell over dark lashes as he gripped his drink with his broad, lean build, basically the "dream guy" image every girl imagined.

Dani shook her head as she took her seat in the back of the classroom, the rest of the chairs filled. Kyle was off-limits; Dani would have to look elsewhere. Tanner wouldn't have minded—they were on a break, so they could date non-exclusively.

She gazed out the nearby window, tapping her pencil as she watched a girl kiss her guy on the cheek.

Who was she kidding though? Since school had started again, she didn't have a free minute in the week to spend hanging out with friends, let alone *dating* full-time. School and lacrosse and prepping for the MCAT—it all was killing her from the inside out, and she'd be lucky if she made it through the rest of the month, not to mention the rest of the semester.

"Good morning, everyone," Professor Johnson greeted the class with her British accent, hands folded in front of her long green dress and matching spectacles. "I'm sure we're all very tuned in to the coronavirus news on our smartphones, but for those of you who don't already know, the World Health Organization declared a global health emergency a few weeks ago."

The class sat in silence. By this point, everyone had probably heard the news.

"Additionally, yesterday, a cruise ship that had over six hundred infected patients was finally allowed to dock. There has been a lot of speculation over whether preventing docking was effective in containing the virus as it also trapped hundreds of people in close quarters with those infected."

Johnson walked over to the smartboard and pulled up a slide showing several microscopic images. "I thought, with scientific questions evolving daily about the predictability of this virus, it'd be prevalent to jump ahead to chapter four and learn about how viruses multiply and spread at the molecular level.

"Now, as you all know," she went on, pulling out a laser pointer, "pathogens are aerosolized in tiny particles that survive on air currents over great lengths of time. Pathogens can transmit in the air when an infected person coughs or talks, or can be aerosolized by equipment or dust such as nontuberculous mycobacteria or aspergillus…"

Johnson changed the slide to images of several molecules paired with medical equipment and diagrams of people coughing. "This coronavirus, specifically SARS-Co-V-2, leads to the new disease, COVID-19…" She paused to write the name on the board. "What's alarming about this coronavirus is that there are still a lot of unknowns. However, because this virus has demonstrated an ability to spread more quickly in comparison to other diseases, we can assume it has a particularly high level of contagion."

The next slide showed a table comparing two viruses.

Johnson pointed her laser to the virus on the left. "Let's look at 'Type A' of the flu, for example, which many of you may have battled before. According to the CDC, its incubation period is one to four days, and contagion can start one day before symptoms appear and up to five days after the symptoms disappear." Her laser circled the virus on the right. "SARS-Co-V-2, on the other hand, can be assumed to have a higher incubation period, which would account for a higher rate of infected people, as people have more time to spread the infection before they start showing symptoms."

She set down the laser and flipped off the slideshow. "Now, turn to page 58, and we'll take a look at the molecular construction of viruses…"

As Dani flipped open her textbook, she made a mental note to chat with Dustin about the coronavirus the next time she saw him for med school counseling. This contagion lesson was a little more informative than the rumors going around, but it still seemed overhyped to her. Why should people be freaking out about a few respiratory symptoms similar to an average-day cold?

Her head drifted up from her textbook. When *would* she meet Dustin again?

She'd text him after practice that night.

*Twenty-Five*

*February*

"YOU SHOULD READ UP MORE ON PHYSIOLOGY TO BE READY for the MCAT by summer," Dustin addressed Dani the next afternoon as he sifted through his bowl of noodle soup. He stretched his leg into the sun from where they sat at a small table at the center of the Village, their usual meeting spot.

He wore his scrubs. Luckily, he had found time to meet her before the start of his clerkship again. "Other than that," he continued, "you just need to continue having study sessions every weekend to prepare."

Dani's voice dripped with sarcasm. "Right. During the few hours of the weekend I have free when my ass isn't getting kicked by lacrosse." She swirled her caramel Frappuccino and took a drink. "Ugh, I'm gonna be dead. I have games every weekend from here on out through April."

Between classes, lacrosse practices and games, and studying for her MCAT, she barely had time to sleep. She had forgotten how much more pressure the games added to her already busy schedule, and she was easily exhausted all over again. The one good thing about her exhaustion was it kept her distracted from the roller coaster of emotions triggered by Tanner's absence and her parents' neglect.

Dustin raised his palms in an innocent gesture. "You're the one who got yourself into this mess with the med and sports thing," he noted.

"Shut up." Dani rolled her eyes, her lips teasing upward as she flipped her hair over a shoulder. "You keep saying that, but you did the same thing with basketball, remember?"

"Uh-huh. See how fun it is?" He sat back and wiped some soup off his smiling mouth. "Speaking of sports, though, you were awesome last weekend. I stopped by."

Her heart fluttered as she remembered Dustin and his sister cheering from the sidelines. She perked in her chair. "I saw you! I was surprised you came all the way from Culver City."

He tilted his head. "Mel had a softball game at the field nearby. After it ended, I thought I'd catch the end of your match. Sorry I didn't say hi—we had to head home right after." His eyebrow raised and a playful smirk stretched across his face. "I didn't know you were such a beast at lacrosse."

Dani twisted her straw and shifted in her chair. "Well, I *was* MVP of Montana's High School Lacrosse League. And as a junior." She fluttered her eyelashes ostentatiously.

His lips quirked, and he leaned on his elbows. "Wow, impressive. I was wondering where that feisty, confrontational attitude came from when the ref called a penalty on you."

"Oh, you saw that?" Dani's face flushed a furious red, and she rubbed her sweater sleeves. "I can get pretty heated in the moment."

He laughed, and Dani shrugged, taking another sip of coffee as she avoided his eyes. Her gaze flicked to his after a moment.

"Oh, I meant to ask you—have you been following the latest on the coronavirus?"

It had been almost a month since the United States confirmed its first coronavirus case, but the virus hadn't shown any signs of slowing around the world. Europe had suffered an alarming infection spike, while countries in Asia with high infections were implementing business and school restrictions that inhibited close contact with others.

Dustin sipped up a noodle, splashing soup broth onto his cheek in the process. She smirked as he wiped his face with a napkin before responding.

"Yeah, of course. All the hospitals' health experts, including Keck, have been following guidelines issued by the CDC, watching for any symptoms and respiratory illnesses that may be associated with COVID-19. It's serious stuff."

Dani wrinkled her mouth, twisting her straw again. "It can't be as bad as the news is making it out to be though…"

Dustin scratched the stubble on his jaw. "My mom said all the major health-care providers' leaders have been on clinician calls with the California Medical Association. They've had to read up on the DHHS's Pandemic Influenza Plan so they're prepared when the outbreak hits."

"When," not "if." Dani's professors had already confided the outbreak would spread across the globe considering there wasn't adequate testing, contact tracing, or knowledge about the virus, but hearing it from Dustin seemed to give it more validation. He had this aura of confidence and promise that set her on edge and triggered a sliver of fear up her spine. *And* his mom was an ER nurse at Olympia; she would be the first to know about an impending crisis.

Was it possible the virus was more serious than she'd believed?

Her brows drew, and she folded her arms on the table. "My teacher said it's more contagious than the flu, but I don't get why it's such a big deal if it spreads quickly? It doesn't sound all that bad if you get it, nevermind the one percent death rate. The media *is* overhyping a lot of it." The news had shown daily horrific videos of people in other countries hooked to ventilators, families weeping, and streets as vacant as ghost towns.

She shook her head. There was no way the virus could get as bad here as it was in those other countries. This was the United States of America, for crying out loud!

Dustin sighed and scratched his chin. "Yeah, but it's not so great if you have someone in your family who is over the age of sixty or has pre-existing conditions. Even if the fraction of high-risk patients is just twenty percent, if only half the US population gets infected, that's thirty million extra people in our hospitals."

Dani frowned as the image of her lacrosse team lifting the PAC-12 championship trophy was swept away by images of masked citizens panicking to and fro in an apocalyptic mess. "Well, I guess people should just eat more vitamins," she joked, but Dustin didn't laugh.

"This virus is doing more than just affecting physical health," he went on. "Jessie—Dr. Turner's son, if you remember—told me one of his buddies is doing an article about racism that sprung up recently against Asian Americans. A lot of it has been incited from politicians labeling COVID as the 'Chinese Virus' or 'Kung Flu.'"

Dani twisted in her seat and averted her gaze as she recalled what had happened to Noemi. "Racism is terrible, period. It's a shame that people are taking a few political jabs to extremes. I mean, China *is* to blame after all. They need to be held accountable."

Dustin raised his head from the bowl of soup. "Regardless of who's to blame, how many problems has name-calling solved, in the end? I don't care what your political affiliation is. It's unnecessary, immature, and does nothing to fix the issue, only exacerbates it. If you're in a position of power in the middle of a crisis, you better solve the damn crisis instead of pointing fingers."

Dani pursed her lips and dropped her gaze to the table, resisting the urge to comment. She didn't want to get into a heated argument with her mentor over racism and politics; maybe it was best to keep her mouth shut.

A minute of sticky silence strung between them. Dustin twirled his noodles, brow furrowed, while Dani downed the last of her coffee, avoiding eye contact. When her phone buzzed against the metal table, she jerked in her chair.

It was Haley. **What the hell, Dani? Mitch was arrested today cuz he's on probation, but I got off with a free pass. Even after I apologized a million times, you go and tattle?**

Dani arched an eyebrow and opened the text to send a reply, but her fingers hovered over the keypad. A small flurry of satisfaction dropped in her gut at the thought of Mitch behind bars.

And that douchebag had been on probation? He was an even bigger crook than she thought. Dani had only spared him because of Haley, but she'd hoped the lacrosse captain would come to her senses and ditch the guy soon, which apparently hadn't happened.

Why had Haley continued to stick up for this piece of shit? Even after everything Dani had done for her, somehow, it had been for nothing.

"What's up?" Dustin asked, seeming to note her hesitation.

She set her phone on the table and rapped her fingers along her arm. "Nothing."

He narrowed his eyes, studying her intently for a long moment. Then with a shrug, he shook his head and returned to his soup.

His subtle disappointment struck a chord with her. Should she tell him? She kind of wanted to see how he would react.

Dani lifted her cup and inspected the "Dulce" font on the side. "Back in November, I got arrested."

The smooth tones of Dustin's face hardened as he drank in her words, then he laughed.

Dani frowned. "I'm serious. I was charged with petty theft and resisting arrest. I have a misdemeanor on my record." *But that's not the only thing…*

His smile teetered, and he leaned back, eyebrows drawn with incredulity. "Really? What the hell did you do, Dani?"

She gave a small shrug and folded her arms. "Why does it matter? Go ahead and yell at me for being a horrible person and making bad life choices, yadda yadda."

His teeth grazed his bottom lip for a silent moment. "I don't believe you were arrested. It's not like you."

She dug her nails into her arm as a jolt of guilt rattled her spine. "How would you know?" She was surprised at the venom dripping in her tone.

His disbelieving expression contorted into a scowl. "Because you wouldn't do something so stupid. Especially something that risks your chances of getting into med school." He looked her up and down as if weighing her soul. "And you're a decent person. Not a damn criminal."

For a moment, Dani was shocked at his conviction, but then a wave of dark emotions threatened to sweep from her core.

He didn't know what else she'd done. If he knew, he wouldn't think she was so decent after all.

She blinked back the pressure building behind her eyelids, her lips tightening as she met his calm gaze. "You don't even know me, Dustin. Maybe I *am* a cold-hearted criminal who stupidly risked my chances of getting into med school."

And with that, she grabbed her cup, slung her backpack over her shoulder, and stormed off, her eyes burning from her refusal to let the tears fall.

# Twenty-Six

*February*

**"C**AN YOU PICK UP MEL AFTER YOUR CLASSES TODAY? JANINE has to leave practice early for some reason," Rachel reasoned through Dustin's phone.

He pressed the phone to his shoulder as he dug in his laptop for his keys, not really listening to his mom as his mind tried to grapple with Dani's sudden outburst. He'd been on his way through the Village after their conversation when his mom had called, interrupting his thoughts.

"Dustin?" his mom urged.

He wracked his brain to find her initial question as he approached his car parked alongside the curb.

Mel, she had asked him to pick up Mel.

*Shit.* "I don't get off till about seven." He rarely picked up Mel from practice. Although the softball field was just a ten-minute drive from Keck, his classes usually ran later. Thank goodness Janine, one of the other moms, also lived in Culver City and was able to drive Mel to and from practice most days.

"That's fine. I'll ask Eleanor if Mel can stay at her place until then. And could you pick up some bread and PB and J for Mel when you get the chance?" People talked amicably in the background through the line, and there was the crunching sound of someone eating potato chips. She was probably in her hospital's break room.

"Sounds good." He hung up and glanced at his watch as he stopped in front of Bank of America, the last building before Hoover St. He still had time to kill before his clerkship started. Might as well grab the PB and J at Target while he was here.

As he turned on his heel toward Target across the path, his thoughts returned to Dani. He couldn't believe she had been arrested. She'd even said it nonchalantly, as if she wasn't ashamed of it. It baffled him. It was way out of character for her. When they were volunteering at the hospital, he had seen someone who was driven, humorous, and passionate about the medical field. It wasn't the kind of description that fit a criminal.

But did he even know her? They'd only met a handful of times over the past few months. But why would she do something so irresponsible, so stupid? She was one of the smartest people he knew, but did she really fail to make common-sense decisions when it came down to it?

Maybe she had been right in telling him she wasn't who he thought she was.

Just like his mom had been right about his dad.

Dustin grabbed a basket from the store entrance and browsed the grocery aisles for sandwich items. The relatively empty store probably meant most of the students were back in class after their lunch breaks. Turning down the condiments aisle, he saw two tall, fit guys talking quietly at the end of the shelves. One of the guys held a six-pack of beer, and Dustin recognized him from USC's basketball team this year.

Dustin walked down the aisle to where the peanut butter was located.

"The lacrosse team is playing on Friday. You gonna go?" the basketball kid asked. Dustin tried to keep his focus on comparing peanut butter prices.

"Why would I want to?" the other guy replied with a snort.

"Dude, you've been *obsessed* with the girls on that team. I thought you were still interested in that one chick even though she kicked your ass at PSK's party."

Dustin's ears perked up. *What the hell?* Dani had confirmed she'd been the one to kick a guy's balls at the PSK party after one of Dustin's friends had shared the news with him. Could she have kicked one of these guys?

He glanced over at the two undergrads. Their backs were turned slightly, so he was hidden from their view.

"She won't be playing. I got her suspended." The statement was quiet, barely audible.

Dustin froze as he crouched to scan a peanut butter label. No way. Dani hadn't told him she had been suspended.

But then again, she hadn't told him she'd been arrested four months ago either.

The basketball guy laughed. "No shit? So much for the suspension—she's been playing in all the games. And she's a *beast*. Assisted, like, four goals last game."

Dustin took a step forward so he could get a better look at the guys. The one he didn't recognize, a tan surfer-looking guy with messy blond hair, scowled.

"It's the damn athletics director. My dad bribed him to get her thrown off the team completely, but I guess the guy was too afraid to follow through."

This dick had bribed the athletics director? Who the hell did he think he was?

Dustin picked up a cheap jar of peanut butter and placed it in his basket, then sauntered up to them. "Hey, yeah, I heard that girl got suspended."

Both of them narrowed their eyes and scanned him up and down.

The basket slid down his arm as Dustin put up his hands innocently. The lie came easy to his lips. "I'm in Phi Sigma Kappa." He turned to the surfer guy. "I saw what she did to you at the party in September. What's her name again?" Dustin had to be sure.

The scrutiny in the surfer guy's eyes relaxed before he ruffled his shoulders and ran a hand through his blond hair. "I shouldn't be talking about this," he muttered under his breath, but when Dustin didn't budge, he sighed. "Danica Torres. She's a crazy bitch. The girl came up to me after her practice in September and threw her phone at me."

Dustin stiffened, his teeth grazing his bottom lip. *Damn. She didn't say that either. Who is this girl?* "Sounds like you picked the wrong chick to fight with," he replied with a snort.

Basketball Guy chuckled. "Yeah, Peter, she really kicked your ass."

The sandy-haired guy, Peter, scrunched his face into a pathetic scowl. "She's the one who came on to me at the frat party, man. All flirtatious and shit. It was pretty convincing though." His lips twisted into a cunning smile.

Dustin's eye twitched at the thought of this ass-hat putting his hands on Dani. He quickly relaxed his face to hide his contempt. "Damn. Too bad you two didn't work out."

Peter scoffed. "I don't even care anymore, bro. I heard she's been sleeping with Tanner Stevens—you know, that wide receiver from PSK? According to him, she's a disappointment under the bed sheets. I don't go after girls with a weak pussy."

Peter didn't have time to react as Dustin's fist slammed into his smirking face, hurling him backward into the empty aisle.

"What the hell, bro!" Peter's friend protested, eyes wide in shock. He stepped forward, his knuckles turning white on the beer pack as he braced in a fighter's stance.

Dustin shoved him, and he fell back easily into the shelves of condiments, knocking some mustard bottles to the floor. The guy stumbled to his feet yet still somehow managed to retain his hold on the six-pack, of course. He raised an arm in defense.

"Chill, man!"

"Get the hell out," Dustin growled in a murderous tone. The shopping basket handle cracked in his furious grip, his other hand throbbing painfully from the punch. The two guys probably could have taken him together, but they were shaken.

The basketball guy shrank into himself, his eyes pleading for mercy. To his side, Peter slumped in a daze, his nose a broken, bloody mess.

Peter's buddy dragged him to his feet, and they both shuffled away, beer still in tow.

"So how were the Casters?" Dustin asked Mel as he shifted his car into gear and headed out of the eastside neighborhood. This part of town was sketchy at night; the scattered lampposts casting dim light on graffiti-covered walls and windows secured with metal bars. A few late-night wanderers stalked the street corners, their faces hidden by darkness. His mom had always taken care to steer Dustin and Mel clear of the eastside past dark. Well, most parts of L.A. for that matter.

"Lexi's cool, but her mom is *blech*," Mel responded from the passenger seat with a disgusted scrunch of her lips. "She's too peppy and overly nice. I can't stand her." Her long brown hair was coming out of its braid, and her dirty softball shirt and cleats were bound to leave a mess on the seat for him to clean up later. She really should've been in the back seat anyway, but when she climbed into the front, he had been too tired to argue with her. His long shift had drained him of energy once again.

He let out a slow exhale as he pulled onto the traffic-heavy 10 freeway. He still had a ton of studying to do before his pediatrics shelf exam later that week. Unfortunately for him, the past few shifts hadn't been smooth; his sluggishness to recall the proper prescriptions today for his last few patients highlighted just how underprepared for his exam he actually was.

*Just a few more months, and I'll be done.*

Dustin licked his lips, clearing his head, and forced a smirk at his sister. "Wow, a whole day with an overly nice person? Sounds like torture." He tsked. "You know, if you played in the Culver softball league, you wouldn't have to deal with Mrs. Caster's cuteness."

Mel tilted her head and wrinkled her nose. "But the Culver league sucks! I'd rather play on this team, regardless if I have to put up with Mrs. Caster. I just hope I don't have to stay at her house again anytime soon—she tried to paint my nails!" She curled her feet up on the seat as she peered out at the passing headlights. "I always thought she was crazy. But not *that* crazy."

Dustin pursed his lips, his thoughts drifting to Dani. She'd always come across to him as bold and assertive, but after today, he was beginning to think he'd underestimated her daring side in more ways than one...

"What happened to your hand?" Mel asked, eyeing his gauzed knuckles.

His hand throbbed on cue, and he flexed his fingers on the steering wheel, biting his lip. As soon as he left Target earlier that day, his knuckles had bruised an ugly purple color, so he'd bandaged them in gauze at the hospital and told coworkers he'd cut himself picking up a broken lightbulb.

Dustin pondered his response, then pursed his lips. He was tired of the damn bulb story. "I beat up some guy at the grocery store—oh, which reminds me…" He shuffled his wrapped hand behind the back seat, wincing as his skin stretched, and tossed the grocery bag onto Mel's lap. "Got your sandwich stuff for school. It took a bloody fist, so don't forget it."

"Yes, finally!" Mel exclaimed. She inspected the peanut butter and jelly, then shoved them back into the bag as if she approved.

The next few minutes commenced in silence as they inched along the freeway, staring at the bumper of an SUV. Dustin's fist continued to throb, and he found himself replaying that afternoon's events over in his head like he had been all day.

"Hey, Mel," he said after a moment.

"Hmm?"

"What do you think of Dani? You know—the blond girl who carpooled with us during winter break."

Mel shrugged as she gazed out at the darkened streets. "She seems cool. Why? You like her?" She gave a cock-eyed grin.

He snorted and scratched his jaw. "No. I'm just curious of your opinion. What if I told you she is kind of hot-headed, deceitful, and gets in fights?"

"Uh, isn't that a pretty good description of you?" Mel shot him an accusatory glance, nodding at his bandaged hand. "Don't be a hippo-creet."

His mouth slanted. He couldn't deny he was innocent of any of the three descriptions. "Touché." But Dani…she had also committed theft.

Mel rolled her shoulders and kicked her feet onto the dashboard. "I think it's kinda cool that she's a rebel. It shows she's tough."

Dustin shook his head, a smirk drawing from his lips.

His little sister was always the wrong person to ask.

*March*

"YOU FOLKS ARE GETTING A LOT OF INFORMATION OUT THERE, so it is important you check your sources," Dr. Turner said one March afternoon, his serious eyes circling the class to draw each person's attention. Dani supposed it was an appropriate statement coming from him, considering his son was a journalist for the *LA Times*.

Thanks to Carolyn, Dani was well informed of the continuing spread of the coronavirus. Seattle had recently confirmed what was apparently the first coronavirus-related death in the United States. When global cases approached 100,000, the president issued a "do-not-travel" warning to highly infected countries. By March 3rd, the World Health Organization had reported 3,000 deaths, prompting California's governor, Gavin Newsom, to declare a state of emergency the next day.

Turner pushed the glasses back on his large nose and folded his arms. "In light of the seriousness of the outbreak, I should warn you all, it is quite possible the university may suspend in-person classes for an indefinite period of time."

Dani's gut clenched as a murmur of protest flooded around the room. She glanced around to see students' shocked and disbelieving faces reflecting her own. Dani was still not willing to accept the virus was as bad as the news made it out to be; there was no way they were contemplating shutting down the school!

Turner meandered in front of the whiteboard and leaned his large frame against the lectern. He peered at them with dark, somber eyes.

"This, of course, has not been confirmed, but as I'm sure you are all aware, schools would be one of the most dangerous incubators of the virus should one of you become infected."

He paused and scratched his bald head. "What is even more frightening is that the numbers you are seeing on TV of cases and deaths are weeks behind what the virus has actually affected. I am highly urging the school to jump ahead of this thing and make the necessary precautions to sustain human life. I cannot stress how important it is that each one of you also takes the guidance of the CDC seriously, because this is a truly unprecedented situation, and I want you all to stay safe." Turner's chest heaved in a deep breath. "All that I'm saying is, be prepared. We're not sure how long this pandemic will last, and Lord knows to what degree."

Trepidation rattled Dani's limbs as she processed Turner's words. She had struggled for most of her life to learn anything online; she had a hard enough time focusing in person as it was.

And what about lacrosse?

Her team had been on a roll so far throughout March. They had slaughtered Boston College in a whopping 18–9 victory and burrowed through their next three opponents in a similar fashion. The girls were on the road to a solid spot in the PAC-12 tournament, inching closer to the first-round playoffs in mid-April.

So far, the team was undefeated this year. How would a break in games affect their standings in the PAC-12 tournament? Would the matches be readjusted if some dates were cancelled?

Dani's thoughts plagued her for several days as she went to and fro between classes, completed assignments with Carolyn, ate late night dinners, and suffered through lacrosse practices. As news came in about states' escalating restrictive measures in response to the virus, Dani's trepidation only grew.

Dani trekked through the locker room pulling her sweaty shirt over her head after lacrosse practice later that week. She felt her phone buzz against her thigh and fished it out of her pocket, scanning the screen in her sports bra and shorts. Her body crumpled onto the bench, her heart dropping ten flights. She reread the email two more times, but the message read the same every time:

*USC will continue online classes after Spring Recess, from 3/22 to 3/29. All on- and off-campus events will be canceled or postponed to a later date.*

Dani felt as if the air had been sucked from her lungs. She had been warned time and time again by Dustin and all of her pre-med teachers that school closures were only a matter of time, but she still believed it wouldn't happen. Dani had held onto the hope travel restrictions and airport screening would be enough to contain the virus.

But she was wrong.

"Holy shit," Taylor murmured from across the aisle, and Dani looked up to see her staring at her own phone. "I can't believe this." The other girls paused in the midst of pulling shirts and pants on and looked up, alarm in their eyes.

"What?" Haley asked as she hovered above Dani, shooting a glance at Taylor. She grabbed her phone from a side pouch inside her locker, and her jaw dropped as she scrolled through the message. "What the hell! Are they postponing our games? How do they expect us to cram three more into April?"

Dani dropped her head in her hands and tried to swallow the burning sensation in her throat.

This *had* to all blow over soon.

She wouldn't accept her lacrosse season was lost.

*March*

DANI SHIFTED UNCOMFORTABLY ON THE COUCH BESIDE ALISHA as *The Princess Diaries* played on the TV screen. She had thought the comedy would provide some lighthearted entertainment while Emma and Carolyn went out shopping, but a knot tightened in Dani's chest as Princess Mia read the letter from her father:

"Amelia, courage is not the absence of fear, but rather the judgment that something else is more important than fear. The brave may not live forever, but the cautious do not live at all…"

Dani coiled into the cushions, the small apartment living room drifting away as her head swam with a memory of her own father's life lessons.

*Franc Torres waved a thick finger in front of his bloated face as he growled, "Get back on that damn field, Danica! You'll never get anywhere in life if your ass is planted on a couch half the day." He folded his arms where he stood by the back door, waiting for her to move from the couch.*

*"I just wanted to chat with my friend! Give me a second to relax," she retorted, snapping her head back to the cute guy sitting beside her. After weeks of friendly banter between classes, she had finally been able to coax him over to her house—in accordance with her dad's strict stay-at-home rules as usual.*

*Franc scanned Vincent in a long, judgmental sweep. "El es un pedazo de basura, mija," he scoffed. He's trash, daughter.*

*A mixture of shame and anger boiled deep within Dani's gut, but she said nothing.*

*Vincent's eyes shifted nervously from her to her dad as Franc hovered above them, mustache twitching beneath his hard stare. "Uh, actually, it's cool. We can hang at school," he mumbled.*

*He stood and turned to leave.*

*Dani grabbed his arm, halting him in his tracks. "Vince, wait—"*

*He shook her off. "You look like you have important 'life stuff' to do," he whispered with a nod at her dad.*

*Dani shrunk back as Vincent shuffled across the living room and out the door. She had been trying to hang out with him for the longest time, but her dad made sure she was always under his nose when she wasn't at school.*

*Franc folded his arms in front of her and shook his head. "Smart move on his part. You aren't relationship material anyway. You don't commit to anything…"*

Dani shook her head and was back in her apartment. *You aren't relationship material.* The words echoed in her mind as her thoughts shifted to Tanner. What was he doing right now? Did he miss her during spring break? What about since Governor Newsom's stay-at-home order for the past few days? Or was Tanner having a blast being free of her?

The thought left a deep gouge in her heart. Maybe she should have come clean and just told him why she was holding back. It was her own damn fault. She should apologize and ask for forgiveness, meet up with him to talk things through. She'd be a good partner, an honest partner, and he would welcome her back with open arms, proud of her for recognizing her mistakes.

Because she couldn't survive this loneliness; this perpetual self-doubt nagging her mind every day. He was someone she could talk away her problems with. He was someone she could vent to about her lacrosse season being torn up, or how her parents wouldn't understand her and made her feel undervalued.

He still cared, didn't he?

She pulled her phone out of her jeans pocket and tried texting him again, though it was probably moot. She needed him to console her, to cuddle with her and tell her everything would be okay, that lacrosse would return soon, and life would go back to normal.

But his continued absence only made her throat constrict tighter.

Was she so undeserving of a boyfriend? *Yes, Dani, you did this to yourself. You act like you're so tough and have everything together, when in reality, you're a weak, pathetic piece of trash. Just like your parents and Tanner and friends think you are.*

*That's why Tanner left you. You don't deserve him. You don't deserve anyone.*

"Why are we sitting through this lame-ass movie if you aren't even gonna watch it?" Alisha murmured from the end of the long couch, pulling Dani from her thoughts. Alisha planted her feet on the coffee table, peering at Dani through a tangled mess of short curly hair.

Dani's own dirty-blonde hair had grown excessively long since she last had it cut in the summer. It was a dumb thing to be worried about, but it was just a small enough worry to push her frail state over the edge.

Dani swallowed with difficulty. "Sorry. I was just thinking about… the pandemic."

Another memory flashed of her father glaring at her from across the dinner table several years ago. *"If your damn head wasn't always in the clouds, you wouldn't need a lacrosse scholarship to get into college. Get your shit together, Danica!"*

She doused her fuse of emotions with a sharp bite of her tongue.

Alisha's bored gaze returned to the movie. "I'm sure everything will be back to normal in a few weeks. This whole shutdown thing is bullshit. It's not worse than the flu, so who cares if we get sick?"

Dani sat up straight, a spark of hope igniting at the realization she wasn't alone in thinking the virus was overhyped. "That's what I keep saying!"

"I never go to the hospital when I'm sick anyways." Alisha pulled on a strand of curly hair. "My parents are super worried though. It's so stupid."

Dani's parents, however, were on Dani's side for the first time, surprisingly. They had wanted her to come home during the school closure, but Dani had told them she wasn't eager to stand in five-hour airport lines to be screened for the virus. Travelling anywhere had become a nightmare since the president declared a national emergency on March 13th.

Funny how all the airport crowds were happening when the CDC was advising people to stay out of large crowds.

The front door opened, interrupting their conversation. Emma popped through with two huge bags of groceries and called, "Hey guys!" across the kitchen.

Dani whipped her head around, forgetting the heated argument she had been building into. "Hey, you need some help?"

"I think we got it," Emma replied, setting the bags on the kitchen counter.

Carolyn followed through the front door a moment later, also carrying two large bags. "I can't believe they're out of toilet paper!" She scrunched her freckled face in disgust. "I'll need to go out again tomorrow. Early."

"Damn," Dani huffed. "Did they have much food?"

"Not much. All of the meat and dairy products were gone when we got there," Emma answered as she unloaded fruit, snacks, and canned food into the refrigerator and cupboards. Her dark head bobbed up and down through the bar window.

"What the hell is wrong with people?" Alisha muttered. "They're acting as if the world is ending."

"Yeah, it's totally insane." Emma shut the refrigerator door and put her hands on her hips. "Luckily, we'll survive with what we got. I asked one of the store attendants how early the dairy sells out, and she said it's gone within twenty minutes of the store opening."

"Shiiit. Guess no more cereal for a while." Dani sighed and slouched back into the cushions.

"I mean, I guess it could be worse," Carolyn piped in. "You know, like, none of us are dying from the virus."

Dani shot her an appalled look. "Hon, you need to get your priorities straight. Cereal is way more important."

Carolyn, Dani, and Emma laughed while Alisha's lips curved upward.

After Emma and Carolyn had unloaded the rest of the groceries, Emma asked, "Hey, anyone up for going to the beach? We should go before they close it down too! I haven't been able to go since my crazy school schedule, but now we have all this time to kill…"

*The beach?* A wave of nausea bubbled in the pit of Dani's stomach at the mention of the words. She'd made a conscious effort to avoid the beach ever since first visiting Santa Monica during her freshman year.

Carolyn shot Dani a worried look, then turned and pointed to her own heavy torso. "You think this body is beach-appropriate?"

Emma blanched. "We don't have to sunbathe. Just walk around, you know? Dani?"

If it were any other place, Dani would jump at the opportunity to get outside, especially after having been cooped up indoors for so long. But the beach… She bit her lip and forced the rising nausea away.

"I think I'm okay." When Emma raised an eyebrow in surprise, Dani muttered, "I…hate sand."

Great excuse.

*March*

Dustin's sigh deflected against his mask as Dr. Kerrigan allowed him to peer over his shoulder at the computer's patient reports.

Diagnoses were always the worst part of his clerkship shadowing.

"All right, Mrs. Riley," Kerrigan began in his muffled baritone voice. He swiveled in his chair to face the slim, freckled woman and the five-year-old red-haired boy on her lap. "After looking at the test results, it appears your son has higher than normal nitric oxide levels, which is a sign of asthma. About how many times a week would you say he shows symptoms of breathing difficulties?"

The woman shifted uncomfortably on the operation seat as her son continued playing with his iPad, oblivious to the concerning circumstances surrounding him. Like Dustin had been, not so long ago.

"Hmm, not often," the mom answered softly. "It usually shows up when he visits his father once every month."

Kerrigan scratched the scruff of beard poking out from under his mask as he leaned back in his chair. "Got it. Does his father have any pets in the house?"

"He recently got a dog. Maybe that's why?"

"Bingo. I think we have our answer." Kerrigan pushed back his glasses and swiveled back to the computer, his fingers flying across the keyboard. "I'm going to diagnose your son with a mild persistent case of asthma and prescribe him some medication. The good thing is, we can prevent the attacks by keeping him away from the dog. Hopefully, your son can visit his father elsewhere, or the dog can be relocated if possible."

The woman nodded after a moment as if she was unsure. Dustin was oddly reminded of his father's reaction when his mom had tried to keep him away from visiting Dustin and Mel. Derek had made many sacrifices for them, including turning down business promotions to other states so he could be with his family. Staring at the nervous red-haired woman before him, he wondered if her partner would make any similar sacrifices for the sake of his son.

Dustin looked over his clipboard at the cute boy sitting on his mother's lap. He had his mother's bright red hair, pudgy cheeks, and small green eyes. He was seemingly unaware of his predicament as his gaze remained fixed on the iPad.

*I wish you the best, kid.*

Kerrigan turned to face the woman once again, and his smiling eyes turned serious. "Also, Mrs. Riley, you should know that your son is at high risk of a severe reaction to COVID-19. In future checkups, we will coordinate so you don't have to come inside the hospital and risk exposure from other patients. It is critical that you two continue to stay home and do not come into contact with people outside of your current living situation."

The woman's eyes widened above her mask, and she gripped her son tightly.

Dustin shifted his feet as the weight of the boy's situation sank in his chest, shifting his thoughts to his own family. He wished he could somehow promise the woman and her son that everything would be all right, that they would all get through this together. Virus and family hardships both.

But did he really believe that?

After Kerrigan and Dustin bid the woman and her son farewell, Dustin followed the pulmonologist out of the patient room and down a hallway, his mind wandering.

It had been three days since classes started again. Although most of USC's classes had switched to online lectures following spring break, Dustin's clerkship was one of the few exceptions since it required students to report to the hospital and treat patients. However, Keck's department chair had emailed during the break, stating that the clerkships were subject to change as they monitored the coronavirus situation.

It left him with a nagging worry in the pit of his stomach. It was almost too much to hope things would go on as they were.

"So how are you feeling with pulmonology so far? Any questions?" Kerrigan asked as he led Dustin to a physician's desk in a small office.

Dustin believed he had done well on the shelf exam the week before spring break. He was in the home stretch of his studies and would be continuing on to his final clerkship, family medicine, before graduating in May.

He shook his head as he set his clipboard on the desk. "I'm just concerned about how the pandemic will affect my studies."

Kerrigan gave a long sigh and pushed his glasses up the ridge of his crooked nose. Even with the health cautions against touching your face, some habits just couldn't be broken, Dustin supposed.

*Damn, I just jinxed myself.* Dustin ground his teeth as Kerrigan gave him an apologetic look.

"That's just what I was just going to bring up. Unfortunately, the number of incoming COVID cases has been rising exponentially at a rate we can't maintain, and physicians are being pulled from other departments just to help monitor patients. The clinicians were also briefed this morning that after today, we can no longer have students come into contact with any patients with fevers or respiratory infections, regardless of the cause. There are still too many unknowns about this disease."

He paused, and Dustin's gaze dropped to the floor. "I'm sorry, Dustin, but starting tomorrow, we are transitioning all students to continue their clerkships from home. I presume your shadowing will be transferred to Zoom or some other means. This is an unprecedented situation, and my colleagues are having to sort through new changes in the hospital as we speak. I wish the situation was different."

Kerrigan's words faded to oblivion as Dustin's chest tightened. Since the beginning of med school four years ago, Dustin had looked forward to his final semester when he would finally accept his master's degree. Now, he couldn't help but recognize he was in the worst possible scenario leading up to graduation.

How was he supposed to practice treating patients from a webcam? Or work with anesthesiology tools in an operating room when he was trapped in his bedroom?

"There is more news," Kerrigan continued. "The department chair may expedite the graduation for fourth-year students as it's looking like hospitals in Los Angeles may soon be overwhelmed, and they could use extra help."

Dustin nodded mechanically, but his mind raced.

An expedited graduation? A recruitment that landed him a job in the medical field and negated the need for his residency? Such news should have made Dustin leap for joy, but it triggered an alarming train of thought.

As if it wasn't bad enough that his mom was already working over-time to the point of depression, now he would be too? Mel was already having a tough time being separated from her mom; Dustin was all Mel had left. But long hours and COVID exposure meant staying away from her, as well as Bettie…

In another universe, Dustin would be ecstatic at a speedy recruitment. But not like this… Not like this.

His throat was dry as he swallowed and met Kerrigan's optimistic stare. "Thanks for the update, Doctor. I'd be happy to help the health-care workers in any way I can."

Kerrigan's eyes shimmered. "You're a good kid, Dustin, always seeing the bright side of things." The pulmonologist ruffled some papers on his desk before sharing a reassuring smile. "Regardless, we'll all get through this together."

Where had Dustin heard that before?

Later that week, Dustin sat perched at his desk, poring over a textbook of family medicine practices. He read and reread the protocol for an asthmatic person having bad reactions to amoxicillin, but none of the words on the page seemed to stick.

The news of a possible expedited graduation had only piled extra pressure onto his studies. How much time would he have left to study for his final NBME? Would he even pass his exam with all this added stress?

He found himself pondering the irony of his sister's words several months ago.

*"But what if you don't graduate?" Mel asked as she biked alongside him.*

*He tossed his head back in laughter, tugging Max away from a tree. "That rarely happens for students who get accepted into a residency…"*

As if Kobe Bryant's death this year wasn't bad enough, now this virus madness.

It was all too much, too fast. He should be spending his final weeks of med school in a hospital, not crunching studies in his bedroom, crouched over his textbook like some high-school student. No freshly graduated med student should be thrust on the front lines of a pandemic, battling a deadly, unknown virus—

"Dustin, let's play a game or something," Mel blurted from his doorway, jarring him from his thoughts. Her head poked into his room, her long brown hair falling over her shoulder as she blinked her large brown eyes at him.

He glanced at the clock: it was past 10:00 p.m. "Not now, Mel. It's late. Are you done with your homework?"

Mel rolled her eyes. "I told you, my teacher only gave us two assignments this week, and I finished them yesterday." She invited herself into his bedroom and plopped onto his bed, kicking her feet up. "Come on, let's do something! I'm tired of watching TV."

"I'm busy. Go play with Max or something," he muttered. On cue, Max trotted into the room and propped his front legs on Dustin's lap, barking and drooling on his sweatpants. "Dammit, Max!" Dustin shouted.

"See? Max is bored too," Mel chirped, leaning her chin on a hand.

A car door slammed outside, and Max whirled out of the room, barking excitedly.

"Sounds like Mom!" Mel shot upward and popped to her feet. She dashed out of Dustin's room and down the hallway.

"Shit, Mel, come here!" Dustin bolted out of his chair and scrambled after her.

"What? It's just Mom," she responded with a twist of her lips as he came up behind her.

When the door cracked open, Mel stepped forward. Dustin grabbed her shoulder, halting her momentum, and tugged her back by the wall. She flicked his hand off her and wriggled away as Max circled in front of the door, wagging his tail a mile a minute.

Rachel's voice crept through the doorway. "Everyone away from me!" After poking her head through and confirming Mel and Dustin were clear, she stepped into the house and pulled the door shut behind her with a gloved hand. Her brown hair was up in its usual tight bun, and she wore an N-95 mask to match her scrubs, her purse slung over her shoulder.

She tilted her head at Dustin with the mannerism of a drill-sergeant. "As soon as I get into my bedroom, take the Lysol and start cleaning the doorknobs."

Dustin nodded, used to the daily routine after Rachel came home from work. Mel, on the other hand, was usually asleep when Rachel came home and hadn't fully adjusted to the strict measures Rachel had put in place since last week. The difficulty of restraint was evident in Mel's somber face, and Dustin could tell she wanted to run into her arms like she usually did.

Despite Rachel's protective measures, he wasn't sure how effective they were. Even with all of the handwashing and disinfectant wiping, unless Rachel stayed in the garage and refused to enter the house, they would still be risking some type of exposure to her.

She offered a weak smile and strolled through the hall into the back bedroom, locking the door behind her.

Mel's eyes drooped as soon as Rachel had disappeared. "Sorry, I forgot."

Dustin headed to the cupboard beneath the kitchen sink and pulled out the Lysol. "It's okay. Just try to remember the next time you're up late. Not that you should be," he added in a patronizing tone. He pulled on a pair of latex gloves and closed the cupboard. Max sniffed at him curiously as he walked to the front door and wiped the handle. "Sit, boy," Dustin ordered with a point of his finger. The dog whimpered and squatted on the carpet by the entryway.

After he had wiped all of the doorknobs, Dustin joined Mel on the couch and turned on an episode of SpongeBob, forgetting about his studies.

A half hour later, Rachel came out of her bedroom in a mask, T-shirt, and pajama pants, holding a trash bag with her scrubs inside, presumably. She disappeared behind the kitchen counter and into the garage. The laundry machine revved to life before she came back into the living room and slumped on a barstool, her hair damp and eyelids heavy.

Mel scooted to the edge of the couch and stared at their mom with large, somber eyes.

Dustin leaned on his knees, folding his hands. "You okay, Mom?" he asked, furrowing his brow.

She smiled back at them, but the reassurance in her expression drained until she dropped her head into her hands.

Dustin switched off the TV and crossed the room to sit on the barstool beside her, lost for words. Mel followed suit, approaching Rachel and placing a tentative hand on her arm.

"Don't come close to me without a mask, baby," Rachel managed, her muffled voice breaking. "I know it's hard. I'm sorry,"

Mel's eyes dropped, and she pulled her hand away slowly but made no move to retrieve a mask. Dustin's throat closed up at the sight of the two of them so broken up. He squeezed Mel's shoulder as she asked softly, "Mom, what's wrong?"

Rachel raised her head and uttered, "Today…was the worst day of my career." Tears slipped noiselessly onto her mask as she sniffed back a sob.

Dustin and Mel exchanged worried glances before resting their gazes back on their distraught mom.

She met their faces with puffy eyes and wet cheeks. "In my twenty years of nursing, I've…" Her chest heaved as she struggled for words. "I've never had to watch a person…say goodbye to their loved ones over FaceTime." Her head fell back into her hands as she choked on her last words, and she broke down weeping.

Dustin's chest constricted as he grappled with wanting to close the gap between them and heeding Rachel's precautions to minimize exposure to the virus.

But they were already close—too close for the virus to be concerned.

*Screw it.*

He wrapped his arms protectively around her, pulling her into a tight hug. The act seemed to make Rachel forget about her own rule, and she clung to him as she trembled, her hands fisting into his hair.

Mel sniffled and joined the hug, squeezing the both of them.

"If anything were…to happen…to me…" Tremors rocked Rachel's body as she forced the words out. "I don't know what I'd do if…I couldn't see you two."

A searing burn rose behind Dustin's eyelids as his mom's sobs vibrated against his chest and his sister's fingers clutched at his side. He could only whisper consoling words as he tried to be the rock for both of them to lean on; the rock his father hadn't been.

*We'll all get through this together.* The recurring thought taunted him now as he grappled for consolation.

*We have to.*

*March*

THE WARM, PUTRID SMELL OF BLOOD BURNED HER NOSTRILS, THE WET *grass dampened her knees in the cold night fog. The choked cries of someone gasping for air, the ear-splitting shriek of a woman bellowing in the distance…*

*Dani's body shook as tears raced down her cheeks, and her chest vibrated with sobs. Her hand reached down to cling to an arm—*

Dani blinked away the memory and turned to Carolyn on the couch. "Want to go for a run?" she asked, setting aside her empty cereal bowl on the coffee table. "My legs have been itching to get some exercise after two and a half weeks of quarantine." *As if the nausea stirring in my stomach isn't the real reason… Since the stay-at-home order, my thoughts have wandered too much. I'm afraid of another flashback.*

But her legs *were* bouncing with pent-up energy. Going from

Winston death workouts to quarantining was starting to have some serious physical side effects.

Carolyn raised her head from the novel in her hands to shoot
Dani a look that said, "Yeah, right!" She rotated on the cushions before
resubmerging herself in the book.

Dani tossed her hair over a shoulder with a scoff. "Come on,
you've been reading all week!"

Carolyn's green, disinterested eyes met Dani's over the pages. "It's
for my humanities course! And we've already had the discussion about
my amazing, fit body." She poked her stomach like she did so many
times and crinkled her nose.

Dani rolled her eyes. "You can ride my bike beside me."

A low grunt was Carolyn's only response.

Dani flicked her gaze up the stairs, wondering if Alisha might
want to get outside. The girl had been locked away in her room for the
past few days...

"I'll go!" Emma popped out from the kitchen, wiping a hand on a
towel. "Though I haven't been in shape since I played volleyball in high
school. Guess there's no better time to get some exercise, huh?"

Dani brightened and stood from the couch, lifting her cereal bowl
from the side table. "Awesome. Leave in five? I still gotta change."

Emma grinned as she started up the stairs. "Yeah, sure!"

After rinsing her bowl, Dani skipped upstairs to her room, glad for
the change in quarantine scenery. When she wasn't Zooming her professors or completing assignments, her days were consumed by sitting
on the couch all day watching Netflix—but her mind so often drifted
elsewhere.

She met Emma back downstairs in a tank top, spandex shorts, and
running shoes, her hair tied back in a ponytail. Emma wore stretchy
pants and a bright orange T-shirt with the words "San Miguel," her El
Salvador hometown, stitched across the front in huge block letters.

"Let's go, girl!" Emma flashed a bright smile and led Dani through
the front door.

The sun shone dimly through a blanket of clouds as the two of
them jogged through the neighborhood and along the perimeter of the
eerily closed campus. The sidewalks, which normally bustled with students whizzing by on skateboards and bicycles, was now oddly vacant.
The ghost-town scene reminded Dani of her parents' house, where

pedestrians on the long roads were far less common, the neighborhood houses spread far apart.

Emma made it as far as the first corner on Jefferson and Vermont before she slowed to a walk, not able to keep up with Dani's lacrosse-conditioned legs. She threw her hands on her hips, her face tomato red.

"Phew…that was killer."

Dani cracked a taunting smile as she rounded the giant university corner sign with her panting roommate. "Now you have a taste of what I felt like coming home from practice."

The thrum of energy pumping through Dani's veins was exhilarating. She hadn't realized how much she'd missed the daily burn of lacrosse practice. That life seemed distant now; a faraway dream in a utopian society.

She tucked a hair behind an ear. "Winston had us run at least one campus perimeter and a mile every day, plus suicides at the end of practice in the off-season."

"I don't know…how the hell you did it… I would have quit the first day!" Emma's eyes perked before she heaved a huge breath. "Damn. That felt good though after being cooped up inside for weeks. It's like I forgot there is actually a world outside."

"Yeah." Dani glanced out at the empty streets and bit her lip. A few cars rolled past, but otherwise, there wasn't any traffic. Across the way, the metro pulled up into an empty station. *I've watched too much of* The Walking Dead, *Lord help me.*

Emma stopped when they reached the intersection of Vermont St. and the southwest campus corner. "I take back my thinking it was a good idea to do a campus perimeter. Why don't we jog back up Vermont instead? I'll try to keep up this time."

Dani shrugged, and they turned to head back in the direction they came. She barely broke into a sweat as she led Emma in a slow jog. "I can't wait for them to open all of this back up," she noted after a while.

"Me neither, though honestly…I think we'll be quarantined for the rest of the school year," Emma huffed.

Dani's brows tightened. "That's ridiculous. People are sick of staying inside. And the seniors have to graduate at some point!"

They turned right on Jefferson St., heading by the Village in front of USC's north gate.

"Dani…the cases keep rising, and we're en route to follow Italy." Emma's labored breaths only worsened with every stride. "Have you seen what's been happening to them? They're having to *triage* people. They're deciding who to save and who to let die."

Dani's eye twitched, her lips pursing. "The US isn't as bad, and we can open our economy safely to combat the virus if people are so worried about it. I have to finish my lacrosse season! We were undefeated up until this point. We can't just let it all go to waste!"

Emma slowed back down to a crawl and eventually stopped, taking a moment to even her breathing as she bent over. Dani turned and stopped as well, shooting her an exasperated look.

Emma straightened and stared at the sidewalk. "I don't think your lacrosse season is coming back, Dani. I know it's hard to grasp, but—"

"It damn well is coming back!" Dani shouted, her fists balling. Her left eye twitched again. "Lacrosse is everything to me! I need it!"

Emma furrowed her brow and tucked a sweaty strand of brown hair behind her ear. "I'm sorry about that. Really, I am. I'm taking a hit too." She rubbed her arm and shifted her weight. "I'll be missing out on some interviews I had scheduled with business executives who were supposed to fly out for the career fair. Since the virus came, everyone's lives are being put on hold."

Dani fought the burn creeping up her throat. "There's more to it than just that. Lacrosse isn't just a 'sport I worked hard for.' Even though my parents treated it like a religion, to me, lacrosse is the one thing I'm good at. It's kept me grounded and happy. It's…" She choked on her words as tears neared to spilling over.

She couldn't break down in front of Emma.

Dani spun, her eyes trained on the sidewalk as she continued down Jefferson St., Emma trailing quietly behind her.

Loud chanting and cars honking up ahead drew Dani's head up. Some students were chanting in front of the USC gate across the street from the Village, signs thrust high in their hands. The wording on their signs became clear as Dani and Emma came to a stop at the intersection:

"Let us out for Commencement 2020!"

"Liberate USC!"

"Don't let the cure be worse than the problem itself!"

Dani recalled the president saying something on the news similar to that last sign. For some reason, that particular phrase embedded itself in a nook of her mind: *The cure cannot be worse than the problem itself.*

*The problem is worse…*

*Not the cure…*

Dani's hand darted up to scratch her cheek. "At least these people get it," she muttered.

Emma wiped the sweat from her forehead and planted her palms on her hips. "They're not wearing masks or even bothering to social distance."

The protesters consisted of mostly upperclassmen but included some freshman and sophomores as far as Dani could tell. A tall boy caught her eye: Kyle Walker, the baseball guy who apparently liked her, shouted among the crowd, brandishing a fist in the air.

And beside him, sporting a wide grin beneath his dark, floppy hair, was Chase.

"No," Emma muttered. "*Tienes que estar bromeando.*" *You gotta be joking.* Her plush lips tightened into a thin line, her eyes hardening. "I told him it wasn't safe to be out in crowds. And he promised he'd wear a mask."

Dani grimaced. The only times she'd heard Emma speak in Spanish was when she was angry. And Emma didn't get angry often.

Dani followed Emma's glare back toward Chase, who waved at a few honking cars, whooping along with Kyle and the other students. He didn't appear to notice his girlfriend stiffening a ways down the path.

Scanning the crowd further, Dani's lungs tightened when she caught sight of Haley's glowing face skirting around the whooping students. The lacrosse captain stepped to the front of the crowd, holding a sign with red block letters: "Let my undefeated lacrosse team compete!"

A sudden surge of pride for Dani's teammate flooded through her limbs, masking any flutter of animosity toward the lacrosse captain.

Maybe Dani had shunned Haley long enough. After all, a small part of Dani had risen up to protect her teammate in court, so perhaps it was time to patch up their friendship.

As Haley raised her sign and shouted at passing cars, Dani recalled Haley's frustrated comments months ago when they had waited in line at Uniqlo. "*Some people think they're so entitled, putting themselves first at the expense of everyone else.*"

She was right, even now; one person's lone happiness at the expense of everyone else wasn't fair. Just like their lacrosse season coming to a halt wasn't fair. Just like seniors being denied graduation ceremonies, job interviews, and career developments wasn't fair.

It all shouldn't be sacrificed for a few sick people.

Cars weren't banned because of a couple fatal car accidents, and liquor wasn't made illegal because a few dumb people drank irresponsibly. That was the price society paid to continue with convenience.

Dani's eyes followed Haley as the captain approached a huge yellow flag bearing a snake emblem and the words, "Don't tread on me." Dani raised her head to see who held the flag and caught a glimpse of sandy hair—*Peter*. Her stomach roiled at the sight of him.

Peter glanced across the path and met Dani's seething stare. He flashed the most cunning, pathetically stupid smile she'd ever laid eyes upon.

Haley followed his gaze and upon seeing Dani, faced Peter with a sharp twist of her red lips. She traced a finger along his chin and whispered something in his ear, making him laugh.

Was she flirting with him? Not that it surprised Dani—Haley flirted with everyone—but why this douchebag? She knew what he had done to their team; to Dani!

And then she understood. Haley was still pissed at her for Mitch's arrest and didn't believe Dani hadn't turned him in. Haley was flirting with Peter, purposely, to hurt her.

As if Dani hadn't been hurt enough.

Resentment for the captain returned tenfold in a sudden rush. This was the friend who had cheated her, betrayed her. Of course Haley would accompany herself with someone as sick as Peter. Of course she would sink that knife deeper into Dani's back.

And Dani had considered forgiving her a moment ago!

Dani's cheeks fumed, and her praise for the entire group melted away. She grabbed Emma's hand. "Come on—let's go before these shitheads make me puke."

Emma scoffed toward the group in agreement as they continued across the street to the Village, though Dani knew they were upset for different reasons.

When they returned to the apartment, Carolyn was in the same spot they had left her in: on the couch, although her book had moved to the coffee table, and her eyes were trained on the TV.

"Alisha in her room still?" Dani asked, pouring herself and Emma a glass of water from the refrigerator.

"No, she left shortly after you two," Carolyn answered, her gaze still fixed on *Grey's Anatomy*. "She didn't say where she was going. I hope she stays safe and acts responsibly."

Although Dani disagreed with the whole quarantine situation, she had still complied with mask orders and obeyed distancing rules out of courtesy.

Alisha, however, was not one to typically mind about courtesy.

Later that evening, Dani sat alone at the kitchen table with leftovers from Carolyn's failed attempt at chicken enchiladas the previous night. Halfway into her meal, the front doorknob jostled, and Alisha stepped through the doorway.

Dani straightened, her fork pausing halfway to her mouth. "Hey, girl, where've you been? Out with Noemi?" Her eyebrow raised when she caught sight of the mask tucked snugly over Alisha's face.

"Yeah, we went out on a walk," she muttered as she removed her mask.

Alisha, on a walk? With a *mask?*

Dani set down her fork. "You've been gone a long time. Everything okay?"

"Just had to get out, get my mind off things." Alisha headed to the kitchen and helped herself to Carolyn's leftovers from the refrigerator. She scooped some enchiladas onto a plate and heated them up in the microwave.

Dani bit her lip as Alisha slouched on the countertop with folded arms, allowing a silent minute to tick by. Her brown eyes hung haggard beneath her thick curls, her lips pressed in a tight line. Finally, the microwave beeped, and Alisha brought her plate to the table, plopping onto the chair across from Dani before digging into her meal.

Dani picked up her fork and followed suit, not knowing what to say. Well, she never really knew what to say with Alisha for that matter. The girl was a detached enigma.

"I didn't think you were the 'walking' type," Dani teased, taking a bite.

"I'm not," Alisha started. Her mouth opened and closed as she tightened her grip on her fork. "My mom has it. The virus."

Dani's jaw dropped, and her food nearly spilled out of her mouth.

So that was why Alisha had come out of her room sparingly for the past two days. Dani had thought she was just tired of hanging out with her roommates.

She twisted a strand of hair. "Shit. Is she okay?"

Alisha shrugged and rested her chin on a fist, her eyes focused on the strip of chicken she twirled around with her fork. "Yeah. My dad took her to the hospital to get tested after she got a fever. She had a hard time breathing, so they kept her there the past few nights. My dad was really worried and said it was possible they'd have to intubate her, but yesterday, she improved, so they might release her soon." Her face was blank as she took another bite.

Dani let her chew and swallow as she absorbed the weight of Alisha's words.

Alisha dragged her enchilada across her plate. "When I spoke with her earlier today, she looked as white as a ghost. She said battling COVID felt like she was drowning…" Alisha's lips pressed into a frown as she met Dani's timid gaze. "This virus, Dani, it's a gift straight from hell."

She paused again, and Dani's stomach coiled as she remembered their exchanged comments weeks ago about the virus being "over-hyped." The nausea was followed by a wave of regret for not checking in on Alisha during the past few days. Her roommate had suffered while Dani had watched Netflix thirty feet away, absorbed in her own dismal life concerns.

*Failure after failure after failure…*

Dani inhaled a shaky breath and scratched her cheek before resting her eyes back on Alisha's shadowed face.

Alisha turned her head into her hand, her fork clinking against the plate. "I seriously thought for a day she wasn't going to make it. When I last talked to her before she was symptomatic, I screamed at her about some stupid thing. It all happened so fast; she was taken to the hospital before I knew what was happening. And I didn't answer my dad's calls until after she had been hospitalized for a day, all because of a dumb fight." The levelness in her voice wavered. "I hate myself for it…"

Alisha's words stirred the slumbering beast deep in Dani's gut. The monster poked around the dark depths of its confinement, testing its chains.

A lump inched its way up Dani's throat. *I need to console her, tell her—tell her what? That I understand what it's like to have a difficult relationship with your parents? Admit everything about my past?*

Dark images from that horrible night boiled in her core, threatening to resurface. *No, not again.*

She bit her tongue, forcing the monster back into its peaceful oblivion. *Why would Alisha want to even talk with someone like me? What have I done to earn her trust? Anyone's trust?*

*I've done nothing.*

Dani's throat burned as she swallowed. "I'm glad she's doing okay. I'm here for you if you need anything." The statement tasted sour coming out of her mouth.

Alisha glanced up at her and gave her the smallest hint of a smile. The tension in Dani's stomach relaxed a bit as a part of her warmed from seeing a soft side to Alisha.

She locked her legs and forced a smile in return.

Dani lay on her bed after dinner, images of the protesters floating through her head along with Alisha's shocking revelation at the dinner table.

Maybe this virus was a little more dangerous than she thought. If Alisha, a hard-minded person who had been fed up with the stay-at-home order and health precautions, had completely flipped and believed this thing was a serious threat, what did that mean?

Still, Alisha's mom was the only person Dani had known, and indirectly, who had gotten the virus. According to the news, an overwhelming majority of diagnoses involved mild symptoms. Dani imagined consoling Alisha with that brilliant, reassuring statement: *Don't worry, the virus only kills one percent of the population; don't bring up your guard just because your mom got sick!*

Instead, Dani had told her she was there for her if she needed anything.

But that was a lie.

She hadn't been there completely for anyone in a long time. She hadn't dared to expose her past and allow herself to be vulnerable to others, so why should she expect vulnerability from anyone else?

She shouldn't expect vulnerability from anyone else, because the walls to her own heart would remain strong, impenetrable.

Because when the cure was worse than the problem itself, you didn't have a choice.

*March*

DUSTIN CLOSED HIS LAPTOP AFTER STUDYING ANOTHER VIRTUAL shadowing from a Keck physician, feeling more and more useless with each day that dragged on. It was Saturday morning, the final weekend of March, and he had now been studying from home for two full days now since his clerkship transitioned to online.

He stretched back in his chair and peered out the bedroom window. The bright morning sun offered a hint of optimism in what was now becoming a swirling vortex of fear and chaos.

Every night, his mom came home late in the same exhausted, defeated state, relaying more heartbreaking stories of patients suffering alone in the ICU unit. She deserved a break. She deserved to be home with her son and daughter during this crazy, fearful time.

But of course, Rachel's perseverance was unfazed.

She kept going back to the hospital with an unhindered determination, day after day. Her justification echoed in his mind: *"Anything I can do to save just one more life will have made a difference."*

As concerned as he was about being thrust onto the frontlines, the health-care workers needed all the help they could get. He would do it for the families who waited in trepidation as their loved ones suffered in hospital beds.

He would try to be that difference, like his mom.

Dustin stood and ran a hand through his hair before opening his door. He glanced across the hallway to Mel's bedroom. It was 11:00 a.m. She must be up by now. Then again, she had been staying up late to welcome Rachel when she came home.

Although he was eager to graduate and start aiding the hospitals, his chest tightened at the thought of leaving Mel for so long. He wasn't eager to separate her from himself when her mom and dad were both now scarce in her life.

He meandered down the hallway to the living room and sank into the sofa, his eyes creeping to where Max slept peacefully on his bed in the corner. The golden retriever probably wouldn't be ready for a run for another hour.

Dustin reached for the remote and flicked on the TV, anxious to see a quick news update. These days, the rising cases and death toll had only worsened his worry about his mom and the daily risks she took.

He held his breath as he read the CBS headline: 6.6 MILLION AMERICANS FILED FOR UNEMPLOYMENT LAST WEEK. The young news anchorman gave unemployment comparisons to the Great Depression while images of "closed" signs on small businesses flashed across the screen. Next, a "rising cases" graph ranked the United States in a relatively poor state in comparison to other countries. "Worldwide cases have topped one million with over 53,000 deaths, and the United States have accumulated over 245,000 cases and almost 6,000 deaths, according to John Hopkins University…"

Dustin switched the channel to KCAL9 and saw a different headline: INMATES RELEASED FROM LOS ANGELES COUNTY IN RESPONSE TO CORONAVIRUS OUTBREAK. His lips pressed, and he turned up the volume.

"The City of Los Angeles has released approximately 1,700

inmates who had less than thirty days left in their sentences and were jailed for non-violent crimes. County officials have warned that an outbreak in the jail systems could be devastating as the living quarters are tight and pose a high risk of spreading the virus. Although no inmates have tested positive, inmates have been worried about a lack of health precautions…"

He shut off the TV and rubbed his neck.

His dad was in for non-violent crime and might get released early. But if his jail contracted an outbreak, his dad would be high-risk as a smoker in his fifties.

Dustin clenched his fist but found his mind drifting to the conversation he had with Dani about his dad. He'd told her that given enough time, people could change.

Did he still believe it though?

Thinking about Dani made him frown. During their last mentor meeting in February, she had denied the virus's serious health effects, and that was exactly the type of attitude that helped spread the virus and put health-care workers, including his mom, at risk. That was the type of attitude that dismissed the people who were dying alone in hospital beds while their loved ones cried goodbye from an iPad.

He sighed. If she was planning on going into the medical field, she would have to start listening to science.

Running his hand through his hair, he walked back to his room and slumped at his desk. His eyes scoured his clerkship notebooks before pausing on the large manila envelope he'd shoved between some books on the top shelf. He pulled out the envelope and flipped through the pages he'd partially filled out.

After pondering what he'd heard from Peter Harrison at Target, he'd begun filing an inquiry to USC's human resources department about a possible bribery scandal involving the athletic director. Since the transition to online learning, however, he hadn't found the time to pick up the documents.

He scratched his chin before setting the envelope aside. His studies were more important right now.

Well, maybe his brain just needed a break from everything for a while.

Dustin slipped his phone off his desk and called Jessie.

His friend answered in two rings. "Hey, bro, what's up?"

"Hey, man. Just wanted to call and see how you are doing."

Jessie's light snort was a familiar, comforting sound. "Same ol', same ol'. I started working from home mid-March, right when all this virus shit obliterated everything. Now we're just trying to find new ways to milk the same cow. This damn virus killed all the good stories. No sports, no concerts, no lady on meth that tracked down and shot her ex-husband…"

A smile cracked across Dustin's lips—the first in a few days. He didn't blame Jessie for wanting a change of scenery since the coronavirus's all-consuming, depressing stories had consumed their lives.

"But right now, I'm doing a piece about how hard the Black community is being hit," Jessie went on. "It's crazy, man, get this: Thirty-three percent of hospitalized patients are Black, though we make up only eighteen percent of the population."

"Shit." Dustin scratched the stubble along his jaw. "Why is there such a huge discrepancy?"

Jessie sighed through the phone. "We make up a large percentage of the 'essential workforce.' You know, drivers, grocery workers…the same people who have to put up with the anti-maskers who think the virus is a hoax. And companies are moving slow to implement proper safety measures."

Dustin leaned back in his chair, licking his lips. "That's…insane. They deserve proper safety measures if they're being forced to risk their health every day."

"Yeah, man. There's a lot of shit going down." He paused, the sound of ruffling papers drifting through the line. "Anyway, how's the fam?"

"Mel's good. My mom is having a tough time though."

Jessie knew about Dustin's dad but respectfully never brought it up. Dustin appreciated him for it.

"Damn, health-care workers deserve more respect in this country," Jessie said softly. "There's actually a protest organized by health-care workers scheduled for this afternoon at one of the hospitals downtown. I'm supposed to head there today to take pictures for a colleague…"

Dustin recalled the other protests that were happening around the country in demand of reopening the economy. Apparently, two months locked inside with an abundance of free time was worse than people getting sick and potentially dying—at least for those who had the luxury of not having to decide between putting food on the table or paying rent.

"Which hospital?" Dustin asked.

Angelina Torres tugged her dirty-blonde hair through Dani's laptop screen, frowning. "I can't stand my hair being past my shoulders," she moaned. "I don't understand why they can't even open the salon."

Franc sat silently next to Angelina on their living room couch, his dark hair also growing long over his hardened eyes. He stared at the floor, folding his hands, as his wife continued beside him.

"All this staying indoors has been ridiculous. We finally went out to a community bonfire the other night."

"Did you socially distance?" Dani asked, picking a fingernail as she kicked her legs behind her on her bed.

Although the whole quarantine situation still frustrated Dani, it couldn't be all that bad to practice *some* safety measures while you had fun with friends, right? In the week after Alisha told her what had happened to her mom, Dani couldn't help but be afraid, if only a tad, of her parents getting the virus.

Her mom leaned forward, a reassuring smile tugging her lips. "It was fine, Dani. None of us had symptoms, and we were just with close friends."

Dani bit her lip. "Well, I think it doesn't hurt to be cautious."

Her dad hadn't said a word the whole time, just scratched his beard and frowned while Dani and her mom talked. Each time Dani talked to them, she felt like she was communicating through a glass barrier. There was still a disconnect, but she had to admit it was a good sign if one of their conversations hadn't erupted into arguing and overblown emotions from the start.

"How has school been going?" Angelina brushed back her long bangs.

"It's all right. Just daily Zoom sessions and a bunch of research papers. Nothing crazy."

Her mom shifted on the couch. "I am so sorry your lacrosse matches have been postponed. We were looking forward to flying out to see you play!"

The corner of Dani's mouth tugged upward as she glanced down. "I wish you could see me play too. I think our next match is…" Dani scrolled through her phone to find her lacrosse schedule. "Syracuse," she finished with a swallow.

Her dad's fists clenched, and he silently stood from the couch. Angelina's eyes softened as she watched him leave.

Dani sucked in a breath as a wave of emotions boiled to the surface. He always did things like this, dismissing himself from a conversation without so much as a word.

*"Don't let people control you."*

The echoing words stirred a boiling anger deep in her core—a familiar anger that had festered uncontrollably over the years. She had persevered through her own self-doubt with those words, past her dad's concerns and ambitions for her.

But it was the conversation with Dustin on the way home from the volunteer program in January that tamed her anger. *"Sometimes, given enough time, people do change."*

How much time does a person need? She had waited so long, *so long*, for her dad to have a change of heart. It didn't seem he was any different now than he was three years ago.

Maybe he would never be proud of her.

Her wavering emotions spiraled into a wave of guilt, and she squeezed her eyes, fighting back the constricting pain in her chest.

"Honey," Angelina started.

"Never mind, Mom," Dani murmured, rubbing her brow. She couldn't bear to look into her mom's somber eyes. "I'll call you another time. Talk to you later."

Dani shut her laptop and rolled over, the sunlight through her window warming her legs. Maybe it'd be good to go for a run today to get her mind off things.

She swallowed against the soreness in her throat and pulled her textbook from the floor, flipping through to a tab she had marked for her research paper.

Why was it so hard to talk to her parents? Even when she was on her meds, her parents somehow managed to make her feel torn and helpless.

Alisha's relationship with her own parents seemed to fare better than Dani's relationship this past week. Alisha had come out of her room more often since their talk at the dinner table and had informed them a few nights ago that her mom had fully recovered from COVID and left the hospital. The girls had all celebrated by ordering pizza and some champagne, and Alisha had been more engaged than Dani had ever seen her, for Alisha's standards.

Dani's stomach churned as Alisha's faint smile surfaced in her mind. She felt guilty for not telling her roommates everything—about her parents, about that dark night three years ago. But each time she tried to gather the strength to retell her past, the monster jolted inside her, and the overwhelming rush of despair and self-hatred threatened to swallow her, so she forced the memories back down.

*The cure cannot be worse than the problem itself.*

A pang in her chest snapped her attention back to her textbook. Why was it getting increasingly harder to focus all the time?

Her phone buzzed next to her on the bed, fluttering a dimmed hope to life in her chest. Maybe it was Tanner texting that quarantine had him thinking about her and he wanted to finally make up after all this time.

Her eyes raked the phone screen.

It was Dustin. **Want to meet downtown for a health-care protest?**

Dani bristled on the bedcovers. She hadn't talked with Dustin since their last mentor meeting in February. Her lips tightened as the brittle memory resurfaced. He wanted to hang out with her? Even after she walked out on him?

She twirled her hair, contemplating. She wasn't too sure about taking the side of the people who were arguing *for* strict quarantining measures, but maybe it would be a good distraction from herself. And it would be good to see a new face after being locked away in her apartment with the same three people for so long.

Her fingers danced across the phone screen. **What time?**

# Thirty-Two

*March*

At a quarter to two, Dani hopped into an Uber and headed to PIH Health Good Samaritan Hospital downtown. She had dressed in light clothes to combat the warm California sunshine, skinny jeans rolled up to her ankles and a black-and-white striped T-shirt to match her black sneakers. A green handkerchief tied around her nose and mouth constituted a makeshift mask.

When Dani stepped out of the Uber near the hospital ambulance zone, she was greeted by a crowd of health-care workers in scrubs and lab coats, spread a safe distance apart. They all wore masks and held signs that read, "I stay at work for you. You stay at home for us," and, "More PPE for frontline workers!" Each of them stood in rigid silence, a stark contrast to the protest scene in front of USC.

In front of them, photographers and journalists snapped pictures, all wearing masks as well. A small crowd formed on the sidewalk where onlookers had gathered to watch the silent protest.

She spotted Dustin among the protesters in the back—one of the taller ones in his blue scrubs and a mask. He was chatting with a tall, handsome Black man in dark jeans and a blazer. A high-tech camera hung around the man's neck, and a leather satchel hung over his shoulder.

She made her way across the grass toward them, skirting around the onlookers and photographers. After a moment, he looked up and caught her eye.

"Dani!" he exclaimed in a muffled voice.

She nodded awkwardly as she approached, resisting the urge to hug him in greeting.

In the month since she'd seen him, his hair had grown longer, and the short bangs he normally gelled back curled over his forehead. The blue fabric covering his mouth brought out his blue eyes. Ocean blue, she noted.

He squinted, and she realized he was smiling. "I'm surprised you came. I didn't think this was…something you'd be interested in."

Dani's mind flashed an image of his stunned expression when she'd debated him over the seriousness of the virus. She bit her lip. "No, I'm glad you invited me. I was losing my mind at my apartment." She glanced at the grass and shifted her weight. "But…I'm more happy to be able to show support for our health-care workers."

How odd that phrase must've sounded to his ears, not to mention her own, considering she had opposed social distancing and mask-wearing just a week ago.

She sighed through her mask, and her hot breath splashed back into her face, adding to the discomfort already provided by the hot sun. *Damn, these things are annoying to wear.* "I am…kind of starting to get the precautions over the whole COVID thing. I was being stupid."

His eyebrows arched briefly. "Thanks for showing your support." He gestured to the photographer standing next to him. "Dani, this is Jessie. You already know his dad."

"Nice to meet you." Jessie's brown eyes shone from above his mask.

Dani clasped her palms. "Likewise. I've heard so much about you and your writing for the *LA Times!*"

His hand waved dismissively. "I try." He turned to Dustin. "So she's the young med mentee?" Dustin lifted a shoulder, and Jessie's head swiveled back to Dani. "I heard you have some dope lacrosse skills!"

Dani's cheeks heated, and her lips perked. She folded her arms and raised an eyebrow at Dustin, and he gave a guilty shrug.

Jessie whistled. "Damn, this is good shit!" His cheeks lifted as he pulled up his camera and snapped a picture of the two of them. "If you want that picture for a Christmas card, it'll be thirty bucks," Jessie teased.

"Thirty bucks my *ass*," Dustin said, rolling his eyes. "How much would a picture of *this* cost?" He held up his middle finger.

Jessie shot him a sly wink. "A'ight, I guess my services aren't needed here. I'll go bother some peeps who actually *want* their pictures taken." He spun on his heel and made his way to the front of the crowd, snapping pictures of a few nurses.

Dani stifled a laugh, shooting an amused look at Dustin. "You two are such *pleasant* friends."

He smirked and shook his head. "You should've seen us playing basketball when we were undergrads. Our coach sat us out for cursing at each other during games."

A giggle burst from her chest. "Seriously?"

He nodded and held up a finger, digging into his pocket with his other hand. His eyes widened as he scanned his phone screen. "Well, damn."

Dani bristled, rubbing her elbows. "What is it?"

His hand reached up to tug on his mask. "It's actually happening. The dean just sent an email that all fourth-year med students will have an expedited graduation and given a special license to aid in working at LA hospitals."

Dani's jaw dropped. "Oh, wow!"

Dustin, working as a licensed physician so soon? The thought of him getting to finally practice the profession he'd worked so hard for sent a flurry of happiness through her.

He rubbed his neck, not seeming to share in her enthusiasm. "Yeah, it's exciting…but being thrust into the workforce in the middle of a pandemic is not exactly what I prepared for. And I'm not too eager to leave Mel when my mom is already gone for most of the day…"

Just like that, her happiness for him dissipated. She gripped her elbows, the image of Dustin surrounded by coughing, suffering patients washing away her smile as quickly as it had come.

A memory of Alisha's broken demeanor surfaced, tightening Dani's chest. Alisha's mom hadn't even had any pre-existing conditions, yet she had been close to intubation. Would Dustin be protected enough from the virus? He was young and fit, but would it be enough?

She tucked a loose strand of hair behind her ear. Maybe she could still give him reason to be happy; optimistic. "Well, regardless, you're two weeks closer to your graduate degree. And you get a special ticket into the workforce! That's pretty cool. I wish I had a job just handed to me."

He opened his mouth, but chanting down the street stifled his response. Dani stepped around a nurse to see a small crowd of loud protesters turning a corner one block down. They were heading toward the hospital, unmasked, brandishing American flags and signs not unlike the ones she saw the students holding at USC: "Liberate America!" "Let us work!" "The cure cannot be worse than the problem itself!"

The appearance of that sign made the nausea in her gut return in a sickening swirl. She retreated behind the nurse to Dustin's side and dropped her gaze to the grass, trying to block out the subtle throb building behind her ears.

"Are you okay?" Dustin asked. His soft fingers lightly traced her arm.

She nodded but kept her head down, her pulse quickening.

*Breathe. Just breathe.*

The chants grew louder, and she glanced up to see the photographers snapping away at the oncoming protesters. A murmur rose among the nurses and onlookers gathered in front of them.

Jessie came into view, fumbling with the folds of his satchel as he approached Dani and Dustin. He nodded at the marchers. "Looks like you guys got company."

The protestors kept advancing, an endless stream of American flags and flaunted signs rounding the corner. The photographers and onlookers stepped aside to allow some protesters through, recreating the Red Sea parting for Moses. Many of the health-care workers didn't flinch, calmly raising their signs, even as some protestors came face-to-face with them.

Not every worker, however, showed restraint.

"Put a mask on!" one of them yelled at an approaching protester.

A few other doctors stepped forward, scowling.

"This isn't a game!"

"People are dying!"

"Go to hell!"

One of the opposing protesters flashed his teeth and flaunted his "Make America Great Again" sign in front of a nurse. "We choose life over fear of death! Freedom over oppression!"

Jessie and other photographers clicked their cameras furiously as the protestors clashed, capturing the heat of the moment.

The throbbing behind Dani's ears escalated to a sharp pounding, and her hands started to tremble. The sign reading, "The cure cannot be worse than the problem itself!" kept inching closer, weaving its way around the photographers to the back row of nurses where Dani and Dustin stood.

A siren blared, and she glanced up to see a police car pull up the drive adjacent to the protestors. An officer stepped out in a mask, raising an intercom.

"Let's make sure we keep a clear path to the hospital, folks," his voice blared. "This is also a reminder that the state of California has issued a stay-at-home order in an effort to contain the virus. We won't force you from your protests, but let's respect everyone's safety and keep things under control."

The unmasked protestors slowly retreated from the close proximity of the nurses, and the tension in the air relaxed a little. The lanky protestor who held that particular sign turned away and marched back into the street, following his other comrades.

Dani released a breath she didn't realize she was holding. The pain in the pit of her stomach and the pounding behind her ears eased a bit.

Maybe coming here was a bad idea.

Another siren echoed off the surrounding buildings. Dani expected a second police car to join the first, but this time, it was an ambulance that sped around a corner.

"Out of the street, folks!" the cop shouted through the intercom over the wail of the siren. The ambulance swerved behind the protestors and headed up the drive to the front of the hospital.

Several nurses rushed out of a set of double doors from the main building to meet the ambulance as it sped up the pavement. They wore long protective gowns, gloves, and face shields—biohazard gear that reminded Dani of the doctors in *Outbreak*.

Two EMTs threw open the ambulance doors from the inside and hopped down, wheeling out a young, motionless blond man on a gurney. A breathing mask was clasped over his mouth, and a portable ventilator trailed from the ambulance behind him.

The guilt and anxiety she had fought to lock away for three years rattled her core. Her knees buckled, and she clenched her gut, her head whirling.

Everything faded into darkness.

# Thirty-Three

*March*

The flashback washed over her in a rush of horror, the images dancing across her eyelids in vivid detail: a girl in a plaid shirt, her dad's dark eyes staring at her in terror, her body shaking with shock… The monster chained in the pits of her stomach rose from its slumber, pulling her, dragging her into a dark, endless abyss.

Someone patted her cheek, and her eyelids fluttered open. The blurry figures in front of her slowly came into focus.

Dustin hovered over her, his eyes awash with concern, as a small crowd of nurses and photographers peered around him. A few quiet murmurs and gasps met her ears.

"Is she okay?"

"What happened?"

"Does she need some water?"

"I already told you, give her some space, please," Dustin ordered, his tenor voice brimming with anger.

Something soft behind her back and neck was propping her on her side. She slowly sat up and held her head, her mind spinning furiously. She took in the feel of the grass beneath her sweaty legs, the bright sun reflecting off the hospital's glass windows, and the faint scuffle of the dispersing protestors.

It all came back to her in a rush: the conversation with Dustin about his expedited graduation, the policeman warning the protesters to keep the peace as a taunting sign inched ever closer to her…the boy on the gurney—

She climbed to her feet and dug in her pocket for her phone.

"Dani? What are you doing?" Dustin stood beside her, alarm flooding his eyes. He was wearing a different shirt than before, a thin white shirt, but the same blue scrub pants. Dani shoved the small detail aside and swiveled on the grass.

Dustin's hand darted to her back. "Slow down before you pass out again. It looks like you had a small seizure or panic attack. You should get checked out."

Dani ignored him, the familiar wave of nauseating grief rushing toward her. She had to get away, block it out, do anything to get the overbearing darkness out of her head—

Her sweaty fingers finally pulled the phone out of her pocket, slipping frantically across the screen. What was she searching for? Uber. She tapped on the widget and ordered one. The driver would be there in two minutes.

"Dani, what's wrong?" Dustin asked, confusion and worry etched onto his face. "Talk to me."

"I'm sorry, I—I have to go." Her voice shook as she tried to push back the haunting memories. "I have to get home."

"Okay, I'll drive you." He placed a warm hand on her arm. "You should slow down, take a breath."

She shook him off. "I have to go." He reached for her again. "Just— stop!" she yelled, swiveling sharply away from him. A sultry breeze flushed her cheeks as she scurried toward the edge of the street, weaving through the startled group of nurses, onlookers, and photographers. She didn't know how long she was passed out for, but it looked like the crowd of protestors had dwindled.

"Dani, wait!" Dustin shouted after her as her Uber pulled up.

She hopped inside and slammed the door swiftly behind her. "Drive, please!"

The last thing she saw was Dustin's frantic, ocean blue eyes staring after her as the Uber whisked her away.

She tore her gaze from the window, dropping her head into her hands as her heart raced.

A low, distorted voice came from the front seat.

"What?" she choked, forcing her head up.

"You have an address, Miss?" the driver asked again.

"West 23rd and Hoover." It came out as a barely audible whisper.

The Uber driver said nothing else as he drove through the empty streets. Dani squeezed her eyes shut, trying to block out the images from the hospital that had triggered her flashback. A throbbing behind her ears pounded in a soft rhythm, keeping pace with the click of the car's turn signal.

She curled into herself as the nausea clawed its way through her gut, snipping away at her insides.

*Breathe, Dani. Breathe.*

Her breaths were labored, her heart hammering through her chest as her body convulsed for the entirety of the ride.

As soon as the driver dropped her off at her apartment, she darted to the front door and threw it open, tearing off her mask. Emma's greeting from the living room was left unanswered as Dani dashed upstairs to her room and locked herself in. Diving onto her bed, she stuffed her face into her pillow and finally succumbed to the enormous wave of grief she'd been holding out against.

She wept.

And wept.

Dani stayed locked in her room for two days, ignoring her roommates' pleas to come out. Their only confirmation of her existence was her choked sobs through the bedroom door.

Her phone buzzed with texts from Dustin until she turned it off and threw it into the closet. She didn't come out to eat, her only food the box of stale Cheez-Its she found lying in the corner of her room from a month ago.

Dani was a wreck. The boy on the gurney had ignited a swarm of memories that threatened to drag her into oblivion. She couldn't think, couldn't function, without seeing his motionless form, a breathing tube slapped onto his pale face. Little reminders popped up wherever she looked: her lacrosse stick leaning against her door frame, the USC sweatshirt draped over her chair, the med school brochures she had piled on her desk…

During the second afternoon of her caved isolation, waves of self-loathing battled with the sailors of self-pity. She desperately longed for the consoling moments she'd had with Tanner after she was arrested. Dani needed him again to hold her close and trace those comforting circles on her hips as she spilled her tears.

But even he wasn't here for her now. He didn't want her.

And he didn't deserve someone like her.

She eyed the drawer in her bedside table where her meds were stored for the millionth time in the past thirty-six hours. Maybe it was time to admit she wasn't strong enough without them.

*No. It's almost been a year. You don't want to start that robotic cycle all over again!*

Dani rolled over and stared at her bulletin board of lacrosse pennants and high-school memorabilia through glassy eyes.

Why couldn't things go back to the time before that terrible, life-changing incident three years ago? Her chest spasmed as the horrific images from that night threatened to resurface once again…

A knock sounded on the door, jolting her back to the present. "Dani, please let me come in, or I'm going to call your mom." Carolyn's voice was etched with worry. "You've been in there way too long. You're scaring me."

Dani closed her eyes and uttered a small noise in response.

"Dani, I'm serious. Please open the door. Let's talk about it."

Carolyn had seen her depressed during their freshman year, so it made sense that she was on high alert, moreso than the other roommates. Still, talking about it was the last thing Dani wanted to do right now. It would only reignite those memories, plunging her further into the darkness and perpetuating this pathetic cycle of despair.

"I'm not leaving," Carolyn warned.

After a long moment, Dani sighed and eased out of bed, steadying herself as nausea crept to her head. She dragged her feet to the door and unlocked it before trudging back to slump on the bed.

Carolyn entered wearing an oversize T-shirt and sweatpants, her bright red hair tied up in a loose bun. She shut the door behind her with one hand, holding a bowl of mac 'n' cheese in the other. Her nose wrinkled at the Cheez-Its and dirty clothes spilled across the floor.

Sinking on the bed beside Dani, she held the bowl in front of her. "I brought you some sustenance," Carolyn offered with a smile.

Dani's stomach rejoiced as the cheesy goodness filled her nostrils. Was she so malnourished that even Carolyn's cooking looked exquisite? She took the bowl tentatively and tried to hide the guilt that washed over her face as she raised the spoon to her lips.

Carolyn brushed Dani's long, messy hair behind her ear. "You know, as impressive as it may be that you've been off your meds for almost a year, I still think you should take them. You don't have to prove to me or yourself or anyone that you can survive without them." Her voice softened, and she rubbed a freckled arm. "No one is all-invincible; even Simon Belmont takes a hit every once in a while."

Dani lifted the fork to her mouth and paused, raising an eyebrow at the *Castlevania* reference.

Her roommate scratched her nose. "Yeah, I looked it up to try to impress you. Not the best line, sorry."

A small laugh escaped Dani's mouth. It was the most life that had come from her in two days.

Her gaze locked on the drawer that harbored the small orange bottle of pills she had tucked away for eight months. "You know, the meds *have* been tempting after the past two days. I considered taking them again…but I can't. My misery is…part of the natural grieving process, right?"

She wanted to say she needed to suck up her self-pity and get over herself, but the words probably wouldn't have sat too well with Carolyn.

Carolyn folded a leg over her knee. "Maybe it is, but what you've gone through isn't typical for every college girl. I'm sure a doctor would have a better response to all this. Regardless, it's not healthy to be locked up by yourself for so long, you know." She shifted on the bed. "When I got upset as a kid and wouldn't come out of my room, my mom would say I'd miss the family trip to Disneyland. Do I have to threaten you with a missed trip to Disneyland when it reopens?" Her green eyes quirked upward.

That wrought a smile from the corner of Dani's mouth.

When they first became roommates, the two of them had promised to make a trip to Disneyland before they graduated. They hadn't yet found the time to go, as Dani always had summer training for lacrosse, and Carolyn always had some school event to go to when she came back from break. Disney was closed now, however, but Dani didn't want to point out the dire chance of it reopening so soon.

"I'm sorry," Dani said softly, setting the bowl beside her thigh on the bed. "I've felt like shit the past few days, and I didn't want anyone to see me like this. I don't want you to feel sorry for me."

Carolyn scanned her disheveled features. "I don't blame you. You look and smell awful."

Dani laughed weakly.

"So tell me, what happened on Saturday?" Carolyn paused and bit her lip. "Did Dustin…hurt you?"

If she were in a happier mood, Dani would have found Carolyn's question comical. Instead, she winced as she remembered Dustin's defeated blue eyes as she pushed him away and fled from the hospital. She glanced at her closet where her phone was buried among her clothes, his messages left untouched.

Dani swallowed a burning lump in her throat. "No, not at all. I blacked out after—after I saw a boy on a ventilator…being gurneyed into the hospital." Dani clenched her hands into fists as wheezing gasps echoed in her mind, twisting a knot in her chest tighter and tighter. Her head dropped, and tears spilled down her cheeks. The bed shifted, and Carolyn's arms embraced her, easing Dani's constricted breaths.

After a minute, Carolyn said softly, "I can't imagine the pain you've gone through, and nothing hurts me more than to see you this way." She rubbed her hand along Dani's back. "Would it cheer you up if you came down and watched a movie with us? Heck, let's watch *Castlevania!*"

Dani rubbed her eyes with her wrist, sniffing back a sob. "Maybe later. I think I still need some time alone."

Carolyn squeezed her shoulder. "Sure, you take as long as you need. But no more locking the door, and holler if you want more food." She smoothed her shorts along her legs as she stood and headed toward the door. Her hand paused on the doorknob, and she turned to offer Dani a hopeful smile. Then she pulled the door closed behind her, honoring Dani's request and leaving her alone once again.

# Thirty-Four

*March*

T HE NEXT MORNING, DANI ROLLED OUT OF BED TO RETRIEVE her phone from the closet and turned it on. There were four texts and two missed calls from Dustin.

She sat on her bed as she scrolled through a few of his messages from the past two days, which were spaced out from the minute she had left him at the hospital to last night.

**Hey, just wanted to check in with you.**

**Are you there? Let me know how you're doing.**

**Just want to know if you're okay. Call me when you get the chance.**

**Please call me Dani.**

A wave of guilt washed over her as she pictured him perched over his phone for forty-eight hours, worrying about her.

He only wanted to know if she was okay. She should tell him the truth—she at least owed him that after blacking out and fleeing from him in a hurry without an explanation. Though he wanted her to call, she wasn't sure she'd be able to stop herself from breaking down during their conversation.

Dani began typing a reply. **I'm sorry. I've been suffering from PTSD for three years...** She stopped typing as dark images flashed through her memory. The monster shackled deep within her core shifted in its cell, jolting an ice-cold tremor through her spine. She swallowed bile to force the pain away.

Her shaking fingers clumsily deleted her response and typed out a different message. **Hey, sorry for the late reply. Thanks for checking in on me. I'm doing okay.**

Her phone vibrated after seconds. **You sure you're okay?**

Dani blinked back the tears that burned her eyelids. **Yes, I'm sure. Just got a little light-headed from the heat.** She wasn't sure how convincing that sounded, especially if he connected this hospital episode with the last time she had left abruptly at their mentor session.

She added quickly, **My roommate has been taking care of me. Good. I'm glad :)**

His smiley face loosed a tear from her eyelid. How long could she go on hiding from people? From Dustin, from Emma and Alisha, when they only wanted to help?

*The cure cannot be worse than the problem itself.*

She swallowed a boulder and stood from the bed, just as her phone buzzed in her palm again. **Let me know if you need anything. I'll always be here if you need someone to talk to.**

This time, the tears flowed freely down her cheeks.

*If only it were that simple, Dustin.*

Later that day, Dani crept down the stairs in her pajamas, appeasing her angry stomach's demand for food. She peeked around the corner at the bottom of the stairs to see Alisha lounging on the couch, her feet sprawled on the armrest, as she stared at the TV.

When Dani took a step into the kitchen, Alisha propped her legs down from the armrest and turned toward her. "Hey, it's good to see you."

Dani looked down at her slippers and rubbed her arm. "Thanks. You too."

Alisha turned her head focus to the TV, not commenting further, and Dani silently thanked her for it. She shuffled to the kitchen and grabbed a bowl and a box of fruity pebbles from the cabinet, her stomach growling ravenously.

The squeak of the front door opening jerked her head to the entryway. Emma bustled inside with a grocery bag on each arm, her purse slung over a shoulder. She stopped in her tracks when she saw Dani, her eyes widening. "Dani! You're alive!" Her thin lips stretched into a smile, and she kicked the door shut behind her.

Dani slanted her mouth briefly as she grabbed a milk carton from the refrigerator and poured the last of the milk into her cereal.

Emma dropped the bags onto the counter. "Oh, good. I got more milk just in time. I figured I'd grab some while I was out shopping for spaghetti. Luckily, Trader Joe's has a limit of one gallon per person, so we don't need to get up super early for milk anymore." She began unloading the groceries into the cabinets, her long brown hair whipping back and forth as she skirted around the kitchen.

Dani fished a spoon from the drawer before collecting her bowl and heading to the table by the front door.

"Is everything okay?" Emma's concerned voice halted Dani before she sat down.

"Um, yeah," Dani muttered over her shoulder.

"That's good. I was beginning to worry. You know, if it's boy problems, I'm always down to chat."

Dani bit her lip and turned to face her concerned roommate, trying to hide the disdain from her face.

Emma offered a hesitant smile, grasping her elbow. "Not that I'm an expert on boys… I just… Sometimes it's nice to vent about them, you know? Anyway…" She grabbed some cans from the grocery bag and ducked below the counter, frowning as she opened a lower cabinet. "Ugh, I hate this tiny kitchen. There's barely any room for groceries for two people, let alone *four*…"

Dani turned her head and scoured the couch where Alisha was curled up. Scratching her cheek, Dani sauntered in Alisha's direction and paused in front of the coffee table, sighing. "Mind if I join you? It's a bit…quieter over here."

"Sure." Alisha hiked her feet off the cushions and cleared the pillows so Dani could sit.

Dani smiled and sank into the couch. "Thank you."

Alisha said nothing as Dani munched on her breakfast and fixed her gaze on *National Treasure*. Alisha's silent presence was soothing, providing a nice break from the energy wafting through the kitchen.

After a few minutes, Emma emerged from behind the bar, wiping her brow on an arm. "Hey, Dani, do you want to join my study session with Carolyn later?"

Alisha rolled her eyes, sliding her bare foot along the coffee table. "Let her be, Emma. She'll engage when she's ready."

Both Emma and Dani bristled at Alisha's interjection, and Dani couldn't ignore the subtle warmth easing her limbs from Alisha's defense.

Emma's bracelets clanged as she brushed her long bangs out of her face, her lips tightening. "Okay, no worries. Let me know if you need anything, Dani," she said softly before disappearing up the stairs, Alisha's skeptical eyes trailing her.

Dani twisted a lock of hair and dropped her gaze. When Alisha had been locked away in her room, none of them had bothered to check in on her. She set her bowl and spoon on the coffee table, guilt jostling her gut. "It's not fair how when you were alone in your room…you didn't get as much attention. I'm sorry for that," she said quietly.

Alisha jerked her shoulder. "It doesn't bother me. I prefer people to not pamper me."

Dani scratched her arm. Alisha had always gone with her daily routine not expecting anything from anyone, but here Dani was, getting all this attention and still feeling cut off; alone.

How could Alisha be so strong and independent? How did she not envy Emma and Carolyn's overbearing care toward Dani?

Didn't she want to feel included; cared about?

*Of course she does, just like any human being. You wanted to be alone just as much as she did, remember? Maybe we aren't as different as I thought. Maybe it's time I opened up to her.*

As Dani warmed to the idea of confessing her past, the sign from the protest crept to her mind like a sickening poison: *The cure cannot be worse than the problem itself.*

She sucked in a deep breath and picked up her spoon, poking at her soaked fruity pebbles.

Alisha broke the silence and gave Dani a sideways look. "Do you want to volunteer with Noemi and me at a food bank? Maybe you could use some fresh air, get away from the apartment."

Dani straightened, drawing her brows. Since when had Alisha started volunteering at food banks?

Alisha twirled the drawstrings of her sweater as Dani returned her focus to her roommate's offer. Maybe Dani did need some fresh air… but the last time she went outside, she nearly had a seizure.

It was too soon.

"I think I'll pass," she replied with a dip of her eyes.

Alisha shrugged, turning back to the television, and a twenty-pound brick sank in Dani's stomach.

Thirty-Five

*April*

DUSTIN LOCKED HIS HANDS ABOVE HIS HEAD, SHIRTLESS AND panting as he waited for the cross signal by Veterans Memorial Park. Max wagged his tail beside him, enjoying the cool April evening's run after being cooped up inside for a day.

Yesterday, the golden retriever and Mel had stayed with Bettie while Dustin took his long-awaited five-hour clerkship exam in his room, free of any distractions. The past two weeks had been a nightmare; since Dustin received the email about the expedited graduation at the protest, he'd had to crunch his last four weeks of studying into two. His eyes still burned from the late-night hours reviewing videos and family medicine notes.

He only hoped it was enough to earn him a passing grade on his final NBME.

He heaved a deep breath, pacing as he stared at the red signal. There was nothing more he could do. He'd taken his final exam. Now he could only wait anxiously for the next three weeks until his results came back, when the fate of his medical career and family situation would be decided.

The signal turned green, and Dustin yanked Max's leash, jerking the dog away from a squirrel scurrying up a tree. Max barked and galloped alongside Dustin down the final blocks to their house, a mesh of pink and purple coloring the sky as the sun dipped below the horizon.

Dustin breathed in the cool Venice Beach breeze, trying to concentrate on the syncopation of his exhales and the patter of Max's paws on the sidewalk. Running always helped with clearing his mind and releasing the tension from his muscles, but today, all it seemed to do was make him stress more about his damn exam.

When Coldplay's "Paradise" wafted through his AirPods, the lyrics about a girl running away from a heavy life through her sleep shifted his thoughts to Dani.

Although it had been a few weeks since she fainted at the hospital protest, he remembered the scene as if it had happened yesterday. She'd fidgeted and turned white when those "open up" protestors approached, and he'd barely lurched to catch her in time when she'd collapsed. After checking her vitals, he'd concluded she'd had a panic attack or some form of epileptic seizure. All he'd been good for was taking off his scrub shirt and easing it behind her neck and back to prop her up on her side.

It had scared the shit out of him.

He'd texted and called her for two days after the incident, until she finally responded saying she was all right, just light-headed from the heat.

Like hell she was all right. She had looked anything but that.

But if she kept shutting him out, the only thing he could do was trust her roommates were caring for her like she said.

As he crossed the last few blocks to his house, his thoughts drifted to the investigation report he'd begun filing against Peter Harrison's dad in her defense. He made a mental note to continue the report now his NMBE was finished.

He jogged up the cracked driveway past his Honda Accord, dropped off Max inside, and headed next door. His fist knocked twice on Bettie's hard pale wood before her muffled voice beckoned, "Come in, Dustin!"

He pushed open the door, feeling a bit awkward as he stood there, sweating and shirtless. Scanning the small, floral interior, he spotted Mel sprawled with her feet up on the couch, her large brown eyes locked on the TV. Movement from the kitchen shifted his gaze to Bettie's welcoming smile as she came around the kitchen counter, wiping her hands on a towel.

He displayed his best warm grin. "Thanks for watching her, Bettie."

His neighbor's bright pink lips bolted upward. "Of course. She's a doozy," she assured with a wink.

Dustin nodded to his little sister. "Mel, let's go. I'll make dinner."

"Don't worry about that. I'm making tacos now," Bettie interjected, swatting a hand. "You go and clean yourself up and then join us."

He licked his lips, the smell of ground beef making his mouth water. He forced a sigh. "It's all right. You cook for us all the time. And I shouldn't be exposing you to—"

Bettie stepped forward and stood on her toes to plant a kiss on his cheek. "There. Now I've exposed myself whether you like it or not. I've only got so much time left on this planet anyways!" She planted her hands on her hips. "Now, quit your arguing and meet us back over here in fifteen minutes. I made plenty for the three of us." She waltzed back into the kitchen before he could object.

He glanced at Mel, who only smirked and shook her head. They both knew there was no arguing with the old woman. Since her husband passed away a few years ago, she had made it her goal to spoil Dustin and Mel as her own, especially since Rachel had been working longer hours during the COVID crisis—not that it was much different than her rigorous schedule before.

Dustin's lip curved. At least he wouldn't have to scramble for dinner for Mel.

He returned home, showered, and shrugged into some sweatpants and a T-shirt. After filling Max's bowl with some kibble, he stepped through the front door just in time to see his mom crawl out of her silver Acura parked in the driveway, masked as usual.

"You're home early!" he exclaimed.

She gave a weak shrug, dark bags dipping beneath her sunken eyes. "I got lucky today. You going out?" He noticed a shallow indent on her forehead, probably from wearing a face shield all day.

Dustin shoved his hands into his sweats' pockets. "Bettie is cooking dinner for us. You should come grab some food."

Rachel swung her purse over a shoulder and shut the car door behind her. She trudged up the driveway and stopped a good several feet in front of him, her lips pursing as she folded her arms. "That sounds nice, but we should all be keeping away from Bettie as much as possible. You know she's in the high-risk category, Dustin."

He raked a hand through his damp hair, his mom's accusatory stare weighing him down. "I know, but she insisted. And she took care of Mel for the past two days anyways, so it's not like Bettie has been completely isolated from us… She just wants some company."

Rachel's posture stiffened, her fingers squeezing her elbows. "Damn, that woman. I know how stubborn she is." She rocked on her heels before her brown eyes softened. "You two go ahead. I've been in the hospital every day—I'm too much of a risk for her."

Dustin bit his lip, analyzing the dark bags seeping beneath her sunken eyes, the sag of her shoulders. "You're sure? You should join. It'd be nice for us all to eat together."

She tsked and smiled, making a shooing motion with her hands. "Go on, Dustin. Don't worry about me! You all have fun."

He sighed and stepped aside, allowing her to pull open the front door and disappear inside. His gaze fixated on the pavement where Rachel had been standing seconds ago. She deserved some quality time with her family over a nice dinner after working tirelessly day and night. It wasn't fair.

But his mom was right. He shouldn't even be going over to have dinner with Bettie; the risk was high enough with Mel seeing her. The woman was well over eighty years old. She *was* strong and healthy for her age though. And she'd made it clear she'd like to spend her remaining years in good company. Shouldn't they respect her wishes?

He clenched his fists at his sides. Damn, listen to him. He sounded like he didn't care about Bettie's health.

Dustin cursed at himself as he walked across the lawn to Bettie's porch, shaking his thoughts away.

The mouthwatering aroma wafting through the doorway temporarily stripped away his concerns. Bettie stood by the stove, loading plates with savory tacos, salad, rice, and beans.

"Just in time!" She beamed as he entered the kitchen.

After he and Mel had filled their glasses and sat at the table, Bettie folded her hands, gesturing for them to do the same. "Lord, please help us through these difficult times. May you watch over Rachel and all of the health-care workers while they endure long hours. Give them the strength to keep going. And thank you for the small blessings you give us all, like joining the three of us for dinner amid a raging pandemic."

*Except there are two Mottleys missing at this dinner.*

The sour thought penetrated his consciousness as Bettie unfolded her hands and they dug into their food. Dustin savored the crunch of his mouthwatering tacos while Bettie indulged Mel with small talk about her school. The scene before him of his sister and neighbor exchanging grins and enjoying their meal seemed so normal, it felt wrong. His mouth twitched, prompting grease to spill down his chin.

Why couldn't he just enjoy the small things life had to offer?

*Because my dad is a sex offender, and my mom is paying the price of a national health crisis that people aren't taking seriously.*

He wished things could go back to the way it had been before his dad committed assault—when his mom didn't need to work long hours, and the four of them could gather around the dinner table on Saturdays after Mel's softball games. Even if his dad's visits had been limited, at least it was a time when they could pretend things were all right.

"Thank you for cooking dinner, Bettie!" Mel spurted from across the table, her mouth full of food. "You're the best."

Dustin swallowed and wiped his mouth, bringing his attention back to the present. He forced a smile. "Yes, thank you, Bettie. The food is great."

Bettie had outdone herself as usual—the taco meat and shells had been cooked nice and crispy, just how Dustin liked them. He knew she had spent hours preparing to make everything from scratch. He could at least be grateful for her hospitality instead of moping around like a conceited asshole.

The old woman waved a hand, her thin lips perking. "Don't mention it. I just wish Rachel were able to enjoy it with us."

Dustin's teeth grazed his bottom lip. "She actually came home early today. I ran into her as I was leaving the house." He twirled his fork in the beans on his plate. "But she doesn't want risk exposure by coming over here."

Bettie's face scrunched into a sharp scowl. "How many times do I have to tell you folks not to worry about me? I've lived a wonderful life, and I'm not about to waste the precious time I have left locked away in my home. Besides, Rachel deserves to have someone cook for her once in a while. She works too hard. At least take some leftovers to her when we're finished."

A grin stole across Dustin's lips as he bit into a taco. "I will. She loves tacos." He sipped his tea before turning back to Bettie. "But enough about us. How are your kids doing with COVID?"

Bettie covered her mouth as she chewed. "They are doing well. Noah and Keith are working from home, but June was laid off. Fortunately, her husband is still working, so they're managing."

"That's good," Dustin reasoned as he grabbed another taco shell from a plate and began loading the fixings.

Bettie nodded as she refilled her glass with some tea. "Noah's wife, Harriet, is a teacher. She says a few of her sixth-graders do not have access to technology, so it's been complicating online learning. She's eager to get them back in the classroom in the fall but is worried it'll be impossible to keep them socially-distanced in those small rooms." She wrinkled a brow and reached for the salad tongs. "There are still too many unknowns. I just hope it doesn't significantly affect kids' progress in school."

Dustin raised an eyebrow to his sister. "Mel's class has been having the same issues, right?"

Mel took a sip of her tea. "Yeah, I don't like online learning. My teacher said it might continue through the fall though."

Bettie smiled as she poured Thousand Island dressing on her salad. "At least Mel has been fortunate enough to access the internet and food at home. Many other kids cannot say the same, unfortunately. It is especially hard for those who depend on school for their meals." Her pink lips fell into a frown. "It is such a shame to see so many kids be denied the basic learning tools as others just because of their difference in socioeconomic status. Everyone deserves the same opportunities, especially in something so critical as education."

Dustin dragged his fork through the beans on his plate. "It is a shame. Mel and I are really lucky."

They ate the next few minutes in silence, Dustin's personal woes taking a side seat to the images of families struggling to educate their children and put food on the table. This pandemic was hitting everyone differently, some harder than others. He stole a glance at Bettie's pale, wrinkled face and his sister's bright pudgy cheeks, smiling to himself. The food tasted slightly better as it slithered down his throat, caressing the empty pit in his stomach.

When they finished, Bettie stood and collected their dirty plates. "Will you two do me a favor and clear the table?" she asked, retreating to the kitchen sink with the plates in hand. "There is Tupperware in the cabinets for the leftovers."

Dustin reached for the salad bowl and paused as his phone vibrated. He pulled out his phone while Mel brought the trays of remaining beans and tacos to the counter. "Are you gonna help me?" she asked.

"Hold on, I'm just checking something…" His heart raced as an email from the dean flashed across his phone screen, titled, "Hospital Inquiry." He opened it and read the first few sentences, his breath stilling in his lungs.

"What is it?" Bettie asked above the stream of running sink water.

He reread the email just to be sure he wasn't imagining things and looked up. "I'm…being asked to fill out a form about a hospital assignment."

Bettie stopped scrubbing and raised her head, her brows drawn. "I thought you wouldn't get your exam results for another three weeks?"

Dustin curled his lip, disbelief shooting through his veins. "I thought so too, but it looks like the dean is pushing things a bit faster. Apparently, fourth-years will be temporarily licensed for elementary medical practices while we await the results of our last NBME. Hospitals in Los Angeles want to recruit us as soon as possible." He heaved a deep sigh. "I guess I don't have to worry about my fellowship this summer anymore. Going straight to the workforce, anyway."

Mel looked up with wide eyes after setting down the empty salad bowl by the sink. "So you're a nurse!"

He gave a small laugh, the declaration sounding odd to his ears. "Sorta. I'm guessing I'll be working low on the totem pole under strict supervision, probably aiding with screening or something."

Bettie walked over to him and put a hand on his cheek. "Dustin, that's fantastic! All of your hard work paid off. You did it!" She squeezed his shoulder, grinning widely, before the joy in her face fell a moment later. "Though, I wish with all of my heart that the circumstances were different—that you'd be able to celebrate properly."

Dustin's expression stayed stagnant. Eight long years of intense studying, social sacrifices, and countless sleepless nights were over. Gone like that. He had finished school.

He'd pictured this moment a thousand times in his head, but he'd never imagined it'd be like this: an expedited graduation in the middle of a pandemic.

He wouldn't be able to walk across a stage with his peers, he wouldn't be able to go out to bars with his friends and get wasted in good company. His aunt and uncle wouldn't be able to fly down to see him and congratulate him on his hard-earned degree. He wouldn't be able to take the cruise Jessie had promised in celebration.

Yet despite all that, his lips slowly stretched into a smile.

He would be a licensed clinician. Even if only temporary.

He would be back in a hospital, doing some good for the world. He would help save lives, and support his family in the process.

Maybe his mom could finally take some time off.

He had done it.

## Thirty-Six

*April*

Following Easter Sunday, Dustin drove to his first shift as a probationary licensed practitioner at Olympia Medical Center, leaving Bettie to watch over Mel and Max. His mom had pulled a few strings to get him recruited by her hospital so he could start working the next week.

When he arrived at Olympia, clean-shaven and showered, a nurse provided him with long personal protective equipment, a face shield, an N-95 mask, and gloves. A supervisor stationed Dustin in a make-shift tent near the main lobby entrance and tasked him with testing patients who showed symptoms of COVID-19.

It was a low-level role just as he had predicted, but he was thankful regardless for being handed one of the lower-stress jobs in the middle of a pandemic.

After a few walk-through screenings, Dr. Leopold, Dustin's supervisor, led him to the computer at the end of the tent. "Just remember to confirm several of the symptoms before you go ahead with the COVID test," he lectured as he logged into the system. "And as you already know, we are low on PPE, so limit contact. I will be walking up and down the aisle monitoring several different screenings, so just wave if you need me."

Dustin nodded, itching to adjust his tight facemask but refraining from touching his PPE as Leopold had advised.

"Great to have you on board, Dustin." Leopold's cheeks lifted before he left Dustin to his assignment and strolled along the pavement to address another nurse.

Dustin sighed as he turned to the computer, his warm breath fogging his face shield. He scrolled through the list of patients and check-marked the next person before stepping through the tent flap.

A minute later, a slightly overweight, older man with a handkerchief mask shuffled to the curb from the foggy parking lot.

"Eli Normand?" Dustin asked as the man approached.

The man nodded, his breaths labored. "Yes, sir."

"Hello, Mr. Normand. My name is Dustin, and I'll be screening you today." Dustin gestured inside the tent to a bench against the wall. "Have a seat right there while I take your temperature."

The man followed Dustin inside and sat as Dustin fished for the Resistance Temperature Detector on a nearby desk. He raised the RTD to Eli's forehead, and after a moment, the scanner displayed a temperature reading of 100.5.

Dustin stepped to his computer to type in the reading. "How have you been feeling, Mr. Normand?"

"I've been feeling a bit feverish for the past few days." His voice was deep and cackly through his handkerchief.

"All right. Any other symptoms? Nausea, body aches, runny nose…?"

The man wrinkled a thick brow. "Let's see… I haven't felt nauseated, but I have had body aches and a runny nose." He pulled his handkerchief higher along his nose. "And…uh, my breathing hasn't been so good lately."

Dustin's fingers flew across the keyboard. "Okay, sir, I'll go ahead with the COVID-19 nasal test as you seem to be showing the relative symptoms. And your fever is higher than normal."

Eli straightened and inhaled a deep breath. "Sounds good to me."

Dustin unwrapped a test kit and pulled out a long swab. The man grimaced when Dustin ran the length of the swab down his nose and pulled it out a few seconds later.

"What is your age, sir?" Dustin asked as he inserted the swab into a small tube.

"Seventy-four and countin' if I live long enough!" He chuckled, and Dustin flashed a small grin.

"Fantastic, sir..." Dustin scanned Eli's profile, and he swallowed. The man was a regular smoker. "Have you been in contact with any family recently?"

The man's brow tightened. "Yes. My son lives with me and has been taking care of me since I hurt my back a few years ago."

Dustin scrolled through the man's family history. "Your son's name is Matthew? And you also have a wife, Joanna?"

The man's eyes dropped, and his tone lowered. "Joanna passed a month ago, sick with COVID after being intubated for weeks..."

Dustin turned to meet the man with sad eyes. "I'm so sorry, sir. My deepest condolences," Dustin said softly. If worst came to worst, Eli may soon be battling the toughest fight of his life, alone in an ICU bed while his son lost sleep at home worrying about him.

The despairing image shifted Dustin's thoughts to Mel, and his throat burned at the visual of her crying alone if he or his mom contracted the virus.

Eli expelled a long sigh. "Being separated from her was the worst feeling I've ever experienced, and I don't wish it on my worst enemy. I couldn't be by her side in her final moments..." His voice cracked, and he closed his eyes. "I just hope my son doesn't have to go through it again with me."

Dustin's heart broke at the memory of the tears streaking down his mom's face as he and Mel held her close. *Today was the worst day of my career... I've never had to watch someone...say goodbye to their loved ones over FaceTime.*

He didn't know what to say. His lips tightened, and he glanced at the ground, searching for an appropriate response. "Don't worry, Mr. Normand. We'll do our best to make sure you get safely through whatever lies ahead, okay?"

Eli gave a small nod, but his eyes betrayed him.

Was this the kind of dismal hope his mom dealt with on a daily basis? Sick COVID patients who came in already having lost loved ones to the virus? Dustin was by no means a therapist or mentally prepared to deal with this kind of devastation on such a widespread level.

So what kind of hope did Dustin have to offer? The man was high age, overweight, and a smoker. He was already having trouble breathing.

The odds didn't look good for him.

And he knew it.

Dustin's chest constricted as he met Eli's somber gaze. If there was one thing he wished he had studied more in his clerkships, it was how to stay strong and maintain optimism in the face of so much suffering and turmoil.

No wonder his mom was so stressed and overwhelmed with emotion.

And this was his first day.

*April*

DANI LAY FORWARD ON HER BED, KICKING HER LEGS BEHIND HER as she typed her biology essay. The late morning sunlight shone brightly through her window, warming her toes while she hovered over her laptop.

It was the second to last week of April, and Dani felt loads better than she had at the beginning of the month. For the past few weeks, she'd stayed on top of her classes, celebrated a mild Netflix-filled Easter with her roommates, and helped Emma bake a cake for Carolyn's birthday.

She had found things in the quarantine life to be happy about.

She typed a few more paragraphs before shutting her laptop and plopping back onto the pillow, tired of writing. Snatching her phone from the bed, she scrolled through Spotify, searching for some good music.

*What was that song I liked from Dustin's car radio?* When she found "Angela" by The Lumineers, she attached her earbuds and tapped on the song. As the lush melody flooded her ears, she hummed along, rapping her fingers on her arm. The bittersweet acoustics and somber lyrics led her thoughts to things she had taken for granted. Things that distracted her from her past, such as laughing with her teammates in Wahlburgers and getting her butt kicked in a game of cornhole with Dustin.

The thought of Dustin expelled a deep sigh from her. It had been almost a month since she'd last seen him, and she was beginning to miss his sarcastic remarks and lame jokes. He'd mentioned a week ago via text that he'd started working as a COVID screener at Olympia Health Hospital. Although Dani was happy for him, the rising COVID cases worried her. She hoped he was staying safe.

When the song ended, she rolled off her bed and scuffled to the bathroom to relieve her bladder. On her way back down the hallway, Alisha stepped out of her room.

"Heading out?" Dani asked, pausing in front of her. Her roommate's curly hair was tied back in a short ponytail, revealing the pale, round planes of her face. A sleeveless shirt was draped across her torso, and ripped jean shorts shaped her short legs.

Alisha pursed her lips. "Yeah. Noemi and I are working at the food bank again. Wanna come?"

Dani shifted her weight, thinking. She still had an abundance of time to finish her biology essay—it wasn't due for another month anyway. Plus, wasn't she feeling well enough to get outside again?

"Sure," Dani answered with a shrug.

What could it hurt?

Around 1:30 p.m. Alisha and Dani took an Uber to Los Angeles Regional Foodbank, just southeast of downtown. The Uber passed a long line of cars waiting outside the food bank, and Dani gawked at how many people depended on these volunteers every day.

When the driver pulled up beside the curb in front of the warehouse, Dani and Alisha stepped into the warm spring sun. Noemi waved from underneath a large tent.

"Hey!" a high voice greeted.

The roommates turned to see Noemi waving at them from underneath a large tent full of volunteers. She placed a clipboard on a table and crossed the pavement toward them, a small spring in her step.

"Hey," Alisha replied as Dani smiled beneath her mask.

Noemi lifted a shoulder, her eyes sparkling. "Good to see you both!" Her dark hair was tied in a long ponytail, having grown lengthy since Dani last saw her at the food court in January. She wore jeans and a green neon T-shirt with the food bank's logo of two hands lifting a bowl.

Noemi turned and gestured behind her. "You guys can follow me this way." She led them toward one of the large tents further down the walkway. "I'm glad you decided to come along today, Dani."

Dani rubbed an arm. "No problem. I figured it's good to get outside. I didn't even know you and Alisha still went! Alisha has a sort of skill of slipping out of our apartment unseen. She could be an escape artist."

Alisha snorted as they approached a table stacked with dozens of boxes of canned food, fruit, and bottled water. "You guys are the ones who always make a huge fuss when you leave the apartment." Her voice pitched up an octave in a mocking tone. "'Oh my god, Emma, did you happen to see my brush? My hair is disgusting!' 'What in the hell are you wearing, Carolyn? Is that supposed to be an outfit?'"

Noemi erupted into giggles, and Dani couldn't help but laugh too. "That sounds exactly like us," she snickered.

A smug smile tugged at Alisha's lips.

They came to a stop at one of the tents where a trickle of masked volunteers walked back and forth from out of the warehouse, heaving small crates of food. "So what do we do?" Dani asked, eyeing the table of crates and cardboard boxes.

Alisha pulled a pair of latex gloves from a box on the table and handed it to Dani. "Pretty much just deliver the sorted cardboard boxes to each family. The damn line of cars gets longer every week."

"Seems easy enough." Dani pulled two gloves from the box and set it back on the table. "How'd you both get into it?" she asked as she stretched her fingers into the latex.

Alisha shared a smug look with Noemi. "Noemi actually got me into it. She's one of the organizers for Thursdays."

Dani's eyes widened at Noemi. "You're an organizer? That's awesome!" Apparently, Alisha wasn't the only one full of surprises.

Noemi shrugged. "It's always nice to give back, you know?" She pointed to a table further down the tent. "You guys can probably join the group over at Table 2. They could use more help on that side." She plucked a pen and clipboard from the table and smiled. "I'll leave you guys to it!"

As Noemi busied herself with greeting some new volunteers, Dani and Alisha walked to Table 2, where a small group of volunteers had assembled.

A slim, dark-skinned boy in his late twenties brightened as they approached. "Hey, Alisha! Brought a friend?"

Alisha nodded. "Yep. This is my roommate, Dani."

The boy grinned and put his hands on his hips. "Nice to meet you! I'm Warren. Glad to have you here!"

Dani smiled, and Warren stepped aside to allow the introductions of several middle-aged men and women alongside a few other college students, who greeted Dani with friendly smiles and the new standard "elbow-bump". It turned out the volunteers were all regulars—one teacher, three recently laid-off men and women, and one hair-stylist business owner who wasn't sure if she'd stay afloat—who had signed up for the food bank as soon as the lockdown commenced.

"Everyone here is pretty chill. Warren's the only one who's annoyingly in your face all the time, but he's cool." Alisha muttered as the volunteers got to work shoving boxes along the table or making trips to the warehouse. "Still, his social butterfly crap pisses me off."

Dani chuckled, following Alisha's line of sight to Warren who was chatting with another college guy. He seemed friendly enough. Dani continued scanning the rest of the optimistic group of volunteers and was jostled by the sudden longing in her heart.

She hadn't realized how much she'd missed the sense of family from being on a team. It had been practically two months since she'd competed in a lacrosse match, but this team environment was different. It lacked the angst and pressure of competition, the roar of a crowd, the adrenaline from an opponent chasing you up the field.

Here, it was serene, supportive, and humbling.

It was a good kind of different.

After a few minutes, Noemi signaled for the cars to begin driving up, and the volunteers got to work.

Dani took a box of canned food and fruit over to the next Toyota van waiting in line, and a middle-aged Hispanic woman smiled through the open window. "*Hola, señorita.* Please place in back door."

It took a second for Dani to understand the lady's words through her thick Spanish accent. She nodded, opened the side door, and placed the box on the seat. A baby cooed in the car seat on the opposite side, and three small kids poked their heads out of the back seat, curious eyes peering at her.

"*Siéntate, bebes,*" the woman told them, and they quickly plopped down into their seats. "*No molestes a la chica. Ella ha estada trabajando todo el día.*"

Dani smiled at the kids. "It's okay, ma'am. They aren't bothering me. And my day actually just started." The woman raised an eyebrow and nodded. It wasn't the first time someone had been surprised at Dani's small Spanish comprehension. She supposed her white skin had something to do with it.

When Dani slid the van door shut, the lady poked her head out the window. "*¡Gracias, señorita!*" She flashed a wide smile before driving away.

Dani bit her lip as she watched the van disappear down the street. How often did that mother come to the food bank? What about a husband to help out with the family? How could she feed these four children every day if she was just relying on food banks?

She grappled to understand the different family scenarios as she carried a box to the next several cars. Each driver thanked her with a wide smile and gracious words, as if the box of food was an early Christmas present.

How many times did these people come through these lines? Were they not getting stimulus checks? Was that not even enough to pay for food and rent as they searched for new jobs?

Well, Los Angeles *was* expensive…

As Dani continued trekking from tent to car, a colorful variety of races greeted her—White, Hispanic, Asian, Black, Pacific Islanders, and Latino. She had always known Los Angeles was a richly diverse city, but seeing such a variety of representation up close hit hard how far she was from Helena.

Back home, the demographics were drastically different. Whites made up ninety percent of the city, and now that she thought about it, there had only been a few dark-skinned people in her high school class. Her friends and neighbors had all been white; so were her teachers. She supposed she'd noticed a shift in demographics when she first came to

USC, but somehow volunteering now illustrated that realization even more—like she was crossing some invisible barrier.

It felt odd; like she was suddenly in a different, unfamiliar world.

After an hour or so Noemi crossed her path as Dani returned to her table from the line of cars. "Hey Dani, you and Alisha can take your break now," she said with a friendly smile.

"Oh, cool." Dani reached under the table to grab her hydroflask as Alisha came up behind them. Dani turned to her roommate and popped the question she had been pondering all day. "So, how did Noemi convince you to help out at a food bank? I never took you for the volunteering type—no offense." She lowered her mask and took a long sip of water.

"I never took you for the volunteering type, either," Alisha jested with a snort, and Noemi gave the two of them a curious look.

Dani's lips tugged into a challenging smirk. "Touché."

Alisha leaned back on the table and stared out at the line of cars as the volunteers ran to and fro beside them. A few silent seconds ticked by before a small sigh escaped her. "I wasn't the volunteering type. I just felt like shit after that day my mom got sick, and, to be honest, I wanted to assure myself I was doing something for her. I wanted to help fight against this damn virus, but I didn't know what to do. That was when Noemi suggested I should volunteer with her." She exchanged a look with Noemi, who shrugged.

Dani folded her arms at Alisha. "A few weeks ago, you were against social distancing, but now, look at you—wearing a mask and gloves." She smiled tauntingly.

Alisha narrowed her eyes. Her mask made it hard to tell whether she was glaring or smirking. "Well, I guess I didn't take the virus seriously till I saw it hurt my mom."

Dani bit her lip, reflecting on her recent worries about Dustin and her parents' exposure to the virus. She clawed at her cheek. "I get it. To be honest, since you said your mom got sick, I think I've been more cautious too."

Alisha nodded, her blank eyes trailing two volunteers who rushed by carrying a crate of bottled water. "Yeah. It's a shame how we ignore shit until it affects us. Since I became friends with Noemi, I started noticing more messed up stuff in the world I hadn't noticed before." She exchanged a glance with Noemi, and the Filipino shuffled her feet.

Dani tilted her head. "What do you mean?"

Alisha dipped below the table to pick up her own bottled water. "She showed me how the pandemic has been hitting people of color harder than whites. I didn't really believe in 'white privilege' until Noemi pointed out the white people protesting against the shutdown with signs that said, 'I need a haircut.' A lot of whites argue that their 'right' to freedom is infringed when they have to wear a damn mask, while so many POCs are essential workers with lower socioeconomic statuses, and have little to nothing to fall back on when they lose their jobs."

Dani pursed her lips. "I saw a lot of white people in the food bank lines too, though. The pandemic is hitting everyone, not just POCs. Also, I think 'white privilege' belittles people's accomplishments. Some people would go further to argue that it's an excuse for some POCs to use when they haven't worked as hard, yet had the same opportunities as everyone else."

Alisha lowered her water bottle and shook her head, her dark curls bouncing across her face. "No. That's what I used to think too, but you're missing the point." She shared a look with Noemi.

Noemi tossed her latex gloves in a trash can and dug into her backpack at the foot of the table. She pulled out an orange, peeling it as she stood to address Dani. "I know 'white privilege' sounds... mean, but think of it like this: There is privilege in lots of things—wealth, height, gender... But most people who have privilege don't realize they have it unless it's taken away from them. All 'white privilege' means is that white people are generally shielded from obstacles that are more likely to hinder people of color. It doesn't mean your accomplishments are a direct result of your whiteness alone."

Warren stopped behind Noemi as he passed them, raising a playful eyebrow. "You guys having the 'race talk?'" He strolled into their small circle, wiping his dark, sweaty forehead with an arm. "This outta be good."

Alisha made no attempt to hide her eye roll, but Warren only laughed.

Noemi's eyes squinted in a friendly smile toward Warren. "We were just talking about how POCs face more obstacles to success than whites. You should tell Dani about what you said the other day."

Dani shifted uncomfortably on her feet, hugging her hydroflask to her chest as Warren turned to face her. He grinned beneath his bright blue mask, but then his smile slipped away and his brown eyes turned serious. "So, as a small preface, I'm always up for talking about race stuff, but not all Blacks would say the same. Americans have an obligation to themselves to do the research about their country's history, but it's often Blacks who end up educating them on the racial scars of the past, and over the centuries it's really taken a toll on us." His serious gaze morphed into a smirk. "But I'm being presumptuous—my apologies."

Dani sucked in a deep breath, brushing off his comment. "I just think today is different than it was decades ago. I'm not saying there aren't still racists out there, but the opportunities today as a whole are way better for the majority of Blacks."

Warren nodded. "Well, opportunities may be better for some Blacks who are in the right places with the right motivations, but the same opportunities given to whites don't extend to the majority of Black people, unfortunately. Today, yeah, opportunities are better on paper, but the effects of slavery and Jim Crow still largely persist today—if not as blatantly—and create an obstacle for POC access to wealth and power. Like voter suppression, for instance."

"But how can you prove those opportunities are denied to them because of widespread racial discrimination?" Dani countered. "What if there are other factors involved?"

Warren's eyes danced as he adjusted the mask on his face. "All right, I'll give an example that proves that a large, disproportionate number of Blacks have harsher prison sentences than whites for the same crime: Look at Nixon's 'War on Drugs.' Whites had been snorting powder cocaine for years. It was the 'cool' thing in Hollywood. But when crack cocaine became widely used by Blacks because it was more affordable than powder cocaine, suddenly there was this explosive political rhetoric about getting 'criminals' and 'thugs' off the streets. There were harsher prison sentences for crack convicts—i.e. Black people—though crack was scientifically not more dangerous than powder. This 'thug' rhetoric sent millions of Black men to jail, and basically labeled Blacks as criminals."

Dani wrinkled her mouth in thought. "Okay. But isn't there higher crime, gang violence, and drug usage among the Black community?"

Warren flashed another grin. "That's actually not accurate. Around the same level of crime is committed within poor white, Black, and Asian communities, but more Blacks go to jail because there is a higher police presence in Black neighborhoods. Why is that? Doesn't make sense." He shook his head. "And let's look at the factors that led a larger portion of Blacks to grow up in unstable, 'high-crime' communities in the first place: After the Civil War, Blacks were barely recognized as citizens, so most didn't have any sort of family inheritance, or much property for that matter. And then redlining during the Great Depression deemed certain areas unfit for loans, which were mostly poor Black neighborhoods. Many Blacks who demonstrated high potential and scholarship couldn't get loans for a good education or houses due to the community they grew up in. Disproportionate racial poverty as well as the propaganda that most Blacks are uneducated, crime-driven thugs passed down for generations." He wiped his brow again and shifted his gaze to the growing line of cars behind them. "These are hidden discriminatory things that you wouldn't really think about if you didn't face them yourself, but that's why history is so crucial."

Noemi nodded as she bit into another orange slice, her soft expression trained on Dani. "'White privilege' doesn't mean your life isn't difficult; it means that in comparison to a POC in the same circumstance, your skin color may work to your advantage without you even knowing it."

Alisha set her plastic water bottle beneath the table, her dull brown eyes seizing authority as she straightened in front of Dani. "In some form or another, both of us have benefited from our whiteness whether we've noticed or not."

Dani pursed her lips, her thumb playing with the clip on her hydroflask. "But I'm not even fully white. I'm a quarter Hispanic. It's a shame people can't see past skin color."

Alisha scoffed as she plucked an orange slice from Noemi's hand. "Getting it now? How people treat you is all about skin color. Screw any other background you have."

Noemi glared at Alisha before turning back to Dani. "It goes for every community, really. I have other Asian American friends who haven't heard off-handed racist Asian comments like I have, and it's probably because they look more 'white' than Asian. On the other hand, sometimes it messes with their identity and makes them feel more isolated within the Asian community."

Warren gave a curt nod and hitched a thumb over his shoulder. "I'm not on break yet…I should probably get back to work. Anyway," he turned back to Dani, "I can't speak for every race or person, but you should read W.E.B. du Bois's book, *The Souls of Black Folk*. Maybe it'll give some perspective." And with that he headed back to the table and grabbed another box of canned foods, offering a joke to a passing volunteer.

Noemi's eyes fell to the pavement as she peeled off another slice of orange. "Sometimes it's as if the 'Black experience' overshadows all the other POCs," she muttered. "But at the same time, most of us POCs have gone through discrimination in some form or another, and we shouldn't fight for the spotlight when we are all just wanting equality."

Dani's teeth grazed her bottom lip. "Mmm, but what about all the *advantages* for people of color? Like the scholarships and stuff that help POCs get into colleges. What is the term…? Affirmative action. It recruits based on race, not skill. Don't you think that's wrong?"

As Noemi opened her mouth to respond, Alisha snorted and tossed up her hands, cutting her off. "You don't get it. Those systems are in place to *level* the playing field for POCs, not give them an advantage."

Noemi scratched her nose. "I totally agree that institutions should recruit solely based on skill, so at first I was on the fence about affirmative action, but it doesn't recruit *just* on race. There are other skill-based factors that it takes into account. Affirmative action is just aiming to diversify schools and expand minority representation in the workforce, making that ladder to wealth and power more accessible like whites have had it in the past."

"Us *whites* don't even realize how good we've had it," Alisha tacked on with a fold of her arms. "It goes beyond school and jobs. We've been able to just waltz through education and loans and housing, while POCs have had to work twice as hard."

Dani clawed her cheek as she absorbed Alisha's lancing words. "I don't think that's completely true. Although I may not have…recognized my good fortunes, I haven't 'waltzed' through anything in life. Everyone has their own share of struggles…"

Her throat burned as the laborious lacrosse practices and her haunting past bubbled to the surface of her consciousness, the countless hours consumed by tears and an endless, sinking pit of guilt …

The tears. There were *so many* tears.

Alisha bulldozed on in an accusatory tone, her eyes blazing. "Whatever you've struggled with, if you were a person of color, it'd be harder. Noemi has had to go through a lot of shit as an Asian American. It's insane."

Noemi took a deep breath and muttered, "Alisha, *stop*. It's okay. You shouldn't put her down. It's not fair to compare—"

"Oh, stop sugar-coating it. You're too nice all the time," Alisha cut off in a raised tone, and several passing volunteers turned in their direction. Alisha pivoted back to Dani, eyes blazing. "We have to educate ourselves. This country's system has been racist for centuries, and still is. I used to argue against it just like you, but the two of us wouldn't see it or complain when the system benefits us, huh? It'd be easier for you and me to just turn a deaf ear when we don't see the fear and discrimination for ourselves. People don't wanna believe in systemic racism because the concept undermines everything we've been taught about this 'equal and just country,' so of course it's easier for people to dismiss racism altogether."

Dani's stomach ached as she stared into Alisha's piercing brown eyes, astounded at her roommate's fiery words.

Noemi inhaled sharply next to Alisha, drawing Dani's gaze. Her jaw tensed as she glanced between the two roommates. "I think we should just…relax." Her fingers fiddled with the remaining two orange slices. "When I was back home in the Philippines, I heard the topic of racism in America was tense, but I didn't know it was *this* tense. It's okay to have a civilized discussion without yelling all the time." She shot Alisha another stern look, then tucked a dark bang behind her ear. "Honestly, everyone just wants to be treated fairly and given the same opportunities. Equality shouldn't be so hard for people to agree on."

Dani pursed her lips, avoiding Noemi's benign stare. Maybe she had a point. If Warren and Noemi had brought light to anything, it was that everyone had their own definition of equality.

After a heavy silence, a volunteer walked up and pulled Noemi to the side. Alisha spun back to Dani, her face a mask of steel. "People need to open their damn eyes and stop living in a fantasy world just 'cause it's more convenient for them. Ignoring problems isn't going to make them go away—it only makes them worse."

It was that comment that sliced Dani's chest the deepest.

When Dani and Alisha returned home later that evening after a silent Uber ride, they were greeted with angry shouts barraging through the apartment door.

Emma and Chase sat at the kitchen table, their heated words echoing off the kitchen walls. Carolyn was shrunken on the couch in the adjacent room, clearly distraught.

Emma glanced up at Dani and Alisha as they entered the kitchen, pausing for an instant before jumping back into the fiery conversation with Chase. "Come *on*. That horrible, tiny sacrifice of inconveniencing yourself is saving lives, you asshole! Do you think we want to be cooped up here?" Her thin eyebrows drew into a menacing glare.

Alisha wasted no time skirting past the kitchen table and up the stairs without a word as Dani stared at the fighting couple in disbelief.

Chase scowled, raking a hand through his dark hair as he leaned back in his chair. "You're being totally unreasonable. More people die from the flu and car crashes each year than the coronavirus! And anyway, just because a few people die in car wrecks doesn't mean we ban all cars and inconvenience everyone."

Dani grimaced. She had made the same arguments as Chase a few weeks ago.

Emma dropped her head in her hands and expelled a frustrated sigh. "¡*Dios mío!* You did *not* just compare this to that! None of those things have overwhelmed our hospitals to capacity in the span of a few weeks. And to rebuttal against the car ban thing, society has always agreed collectively to abide by measures that inconvenience everyone when it comes to peoples' health and safety. Just because a stop sign on a relatively empty street is an inconvenience, it doesn't mean you get to barrel through an intersection and ignore traffic rules!"

Dani brought a hand to her neck as a dull throb pulsed behind her ears. Noemi was right about one thing: everyone *was* arguing these days. About trivial things that didn't call for it. This pandemic had only been good for butting people's heads together and creating chaos.

She trekked to the living room and sank into the cushions beside Carolyn's balled figure. Dani raised an eyebrow at her roommate. "What's new?" she asked playfully, trying to block out the throbbing behind her ears.

"Ugh. They've been arguing for a half hour," Carolyn responded quietly, rubbing her temples. "I didn't expect things to get so out of control... I just wanted to watch my show!"

"Oh, the arguing is bothering you?" Dani's voice dripped with sarcasm. "I didn't notice."

Carolyn opened her mouth, but Emma and Chase's arguing rose a level, stifling her response.

If they didn't stop, Dani was going to her lose her shit.

She climbed to her feet and gave a loud clap. Both Chase and Emma's heads swiveled from the kitchen, the ensuing silence dropping like a depth charge. Dani's mouth perked at the couple. "Hey, so, it's been fun, but Carolyn and I want to wind down for the night, and it's kinda loud, soooo..."

Emma bolted up from her chair. "Guys, I'm so sorry! I didn't mean for this to get so intense." She glared at her boyfriend. "Chase—OUT." She pointed to the door, and he slowly rose, his lips pursing.

"So are we not going to resolve this?" he growled.

"I don't care right now. Just get your ass out of my apartment," Emma barked.

His eyes narrowed before he grabbed his jacket from the chair and exited the apartment. The front door slammed behind him, echoing through the townhouse.

Emma's tense shoulders fell limp as soon as he had left. She dropped her gaze and rubbed her eyes. "Sorry about that, guys," she repeated. "We've been having a lot of little arguments lately. Well, I guess they're not so little anymore... He was annoyed I wouldn't go with him to one of his friends' parties, and I told him the point of *quarantining* is to stay away from other people, so then he had the nerve to show up at our door and blah blah blah."

"Were you also concerned that he went to the 'open up' protest by USC?" Dani asked, settling back into the couch.

Emma's forehead wrinkled. "Oh, you mean the one we saw when we went running? Yeah. That was actually the first big argument we had." She tucked a bang behind her ear. "I probably didn't help things by calling him and his friends 'idiots.'"

Dani snickered, then covered her mouth and bit her lip. Probably not a good time to laugh.

Emma rubbed her temple. "Anyways, I'm dead. See you guys in

the morning. Hopefully it's quieter from here on out." She pivoted around the table and skulked up the stairs.

Carolyn perched upward as Emma disappeared from view. "Ah, finally! Now I can finish my episode of *Grey's Anatomy.*"

Dani grunted as Carolyn picked up the remote, her head still throbbing from Emma and Chase's argument.

From the few words she'd grasped through their spouting, Chase seemed to dismiss the seriousness of the virus, just as Dani had recently. Although Dani didn't wish harm on anyone, maybe Chase's perspective would only change if the virus affected someone close to him, like Alisha's perspective changed when her mom became sick.

*"We have to educate ourselves."* Alisha's comment from earlier rang in her mind like a clanging bell. Where had that come from? Dani bristled, biting her lip as her roommate's unsolicited words jabbed her. *"People need to open their damn eyes and stop living in a fantasy world just 'cause it's more convenient for them."*

Dani sank into the couch, the throbbing in her ears accelerating. *Failure after failure after failure.* She squeezed her eyes shut and clenched her hands into fists, but the throbbing was too much.

Where did that unfazed, confident, smart girl go? Perhaps it was all a lie. Maybe she *had* been living in a fantasy world all along, pretending to be stronger than she was. Maybe there was more dirty shit in the world Dani had been ignoring this whole time, like Alisha had said.

If anything, that statement rang true for at least one dark truth.

# Thirty-Eight

*April*

OLYMPIA WAS NEARING CAPACITY.

As the days dragged on into the final week of April, Dustin received word from his supervisor that the physicians were preparing to move patients into hallways. He tried to remain optimistic, but it was getting increasingly difficult.

Five minutes didn't go by without a siren blaring and an ambulance dropping off someone hooked up to a mobile ventilator. He never saw or communicated with his mom, as their break times varied day by day and they were restricted from touching their phones, lest they waste PPE equipment.

Every time he passed the morgue truck behind the hospital, the bodies were stacked higher than the previous day. There were outbreaks in local nursing homes. He'd been told some seniors passed away in ambulances while others remained unstabilized for weeks in the ICU. Few seniors made it off the ventilator.

Dustin cleaned his station after another long shift, his head filling with images of coughing patients throughout the day, when a familiar voice startled him from behind.

"Dustin? Is that you?"

He turned and came face-to-face with a girl in her mid-twenties wrapped in similar PPE garb from head to toe. Her mask obscured her lower face, but he would recognize her rectangular glasses and the twinkle in those brown eyes anywhere.

It was Lila Perry, his ex.

Dustin flushed tomato red and nearly dropped the bottle of sanitizer he was holding. "Lila!"

She tilted her head, her eyes crinkling. "It took me a second to notice it was you under all that PPE. I didn't know you were here at Olympia too!"

He shifted his weight and rubbed his neck with a gloved hand. *Dammit. Now I'm suddenly forgetting health and safety protocol?* His hand darted back to his side as he searched for words. "Yeah, I've been working here since Easter. Did you just transfer here?"

She nodded. "Originally, I was placed in observational care, but my supervisor reassigned me to COVID screenings 'cause you guys were getting pretty overwhelmed."

Dustin's eyes widened. "Observational care? Damn." He had thought all expedited fourth-years were sent to COVID screenings and other rudimentary positions. *Well, what did I expect. Lila's always been top of her class.*

Lila shrugged and bent to pick up a bin of gloves. "It was pretty boring, mostly. At least down here, you're meeting new patients every day." She retreated down the aisle with the bin, skirting around a few coworkers toward the storage room. She reemerged around the tent flap a moment later and walked back to his station. "How have you been?"

He resumed wiping the tables with a towel, trying to stay focused. "Uh, good mostly. It just seems to get more chaotic day after day."

"I'm worried it's not gonna get better anytime soon," she muttered. "Dr. Fauci says this is gonna be peak week for a lot of states. Hopefully the stay-at-home orders for the past seven weeks prove to be effective next month."

Dustin gave a long exhale. Dr. Fauci, the director of the National Institute of Allergy Infectious Diseases, was now becoming a public shaming figure for a large number of quarantine-weary Americans. People were latching onto any inconsistency or miscalculation of the virus to argue that the lockdown and mask precautions weren't were merely just an inconvenience instead of saving lives. But such distrust and hostility towards science wasn't new—the same anti-maskers had existed during the 1918 pandemic. "This is all so insane," he murmured. "Leopold said hospitals should be prepared for a second wave come summer, especially since many states are starting to release restrictions and places like Florida are letting their spring-breakers run wild." He followed Lila to the PPE disposal tent.

"Oh my god, why would states even consider opening!" Lila's pretty brown eyes widened behind her glasses.

A memory flashed of him kissing those soft lids as she cuddled against him on the couch in her apartment. He brushed away the imagery. *No. I broke it off so we could focus on med school. And a pandemic isn't the time to ponder romantics anyways.*

He watched her strip off her PPE and place it in a large bin, revealing her slim but curvy figure. He fumbled with the strap of his face shield as Lila unwound her long brown hair from its tight bun and combed her fingers through it.

"Ugh, I hate wearing these space suits all the time." She swung her purse over a shoulder and strolled toward the tent flap, turning to offer a timid smile beneath her mask.

Well, he assumed it was a smile, as he could only read the softness in her eyes.

Her tone was equally as soft when she spoke. "I'm glad I was transferred to your station. It's nice to see a friendly face."

He dropped his gaze as he stripped off his PPE garb and disposed it in the basin. "Yeah…I'm glad too. I'm sure you'll help me…retain some sanity."

She beamed and tightened her grip on her purse. "Good night, Dustin. See you tomorrow."

His eyes trailed her as she walked to the curb and stepped into an Uber. It was only when the Uber disappeared into the night that he remembered to collect his satchel from the grass.

He checked out with Leopold before heading down the dimly lit sidewalk to the back of the lot where his Honda Accord was parked. A weight dropped in his gut as he scanned the lot. It was still packed full of cars. He and Lila had been working tirelessly since 8:00 a.m., and although they had screened scores of patients, there were still new patients coming in all the time, albeit in smaller numbers during the night shift.

He would get up in nine hours to do the same thing all over again tomorrow.

He unlocked his Honda Accord and slid inside, his feet and calves aching from standing all day. Pulling out his phone, he checked his text messages from fellow med students, friends, and relatives:

**Stay safe out there!**

**God bless you and your coworkers!**

**Such a hero!**

Dustin skimmed through the texts until a picture message caught his eye. It was from Jessie. Dustin tapped the picture, and an image enlarged of him and Dani standing awkwardly next to each other at the protest last month. Dani was giving him an accusatory look, and Dustin was averting his gaze in a guilty shrug.

Underneath the picture, Jessie had written: **Got approved for next week's paper. Headline: Couples Going Mad During Pandemic. Keep an eye out.**

A hearty laugh escaped Dustin's lips. *Sonofabitch.* Jessie would mock him with that photo for the rest of his existence.

Dustin shoved his phone into his pocket and pulled out of the lot, his spirits somewhat lifted as Dani's smug expression mocked him in his mind's eye.

*Dammit, I still haven't had time to finish filing the report against Harrison's dad. Maybe I'll be able to resume this weekend.*

As he drove through the empty streets and passed the morgue truck of bagged bodies, his thoughts took a dark turn. Would some of the patients he screened end up in that truck? Would they be diagnosed with COVID and hooked to a ventilator in the weeks to come? Had he offered all the support and optimism he could?

Similar worrisome thoughts haunted him the entire drive, his grip tightening on the steering wheel as tension flooded his bones. When he finally arrived home, he followed his mom's daily sanitation routine, heading directly to his room for a shower, then disposing of his clothes in a trash bag and wiping all the doorknobs.

Feeling refreshed from his long, hot shower, he trudged next door in a Keck Medicine shirt, PJ bottoms, and a mask and gloves. His stiff limbs wanted nothing more than a nice long slumber, and they protested in pain with every minute he denied their request.

"Dustin!" his sister shouted as she opened Bettie's door, beaming up at him. "Took you long enough!"

"Shut up, dork," he teased weakly. "And where's your mask and gloves? That was the deal if you're gonna be around me and mom."

She rolled her eyes and dashed down the hallway.

Dustin shook his head before scanning the living room for his neighbor, who was lounging in her rocking chair by the door. "Thank you again, Bettie. I had another long shift today."

She winked. "Anytime, Dustin. Mel is such a sweetheart."

Dustin smirked as Mel pranced back into view, latex gloves on her hands and a blue Dodger mask tucked across her nose and mouth.

As he pulled the door closed, Mel waltzed ahead of him. "Ugh, I wish I could play softball again," she moaned, putting a hand on her hip. "Is this virus thing going to last much longer?"

He gave a weak shrug as he led her across the houses' adjoining lawns. "I dunno. I'm over this virus too."

Dustin followed his sister into their house and sank into the couch cushion beside her, rubbing his strained eyes. No sooner had he propped his feet on the coffee table than Mel sprung upward.

"Let's play Uno!"

Dustin tossed his head back on the sofa and sighed, his mask deflecting his hot breath onto his cheeks. "Nah, I'm dead. I worked twelve hours today. I don't think I can even make it to my room."

"Stop being a party pooper and come play with me." She marched over to the bookshelf alongside the wall and dropped to her knees. Shoving aside some novels and knickknacks, she found Uno and set it on the coffee table, sitting cross-legged on the floor.

Dustin watched her pudgy face brighten as she pulled out the cards and began dealing them clumsily in front of her, her latex gloves a bit too large for her small hands.

He grazed his bottom lip with his teeth. As much as he wanted to brush her aside, tear off his damn mask, and succumb to glorious sleep, he couldn't blame her for her perkiness. He and his mom weren't the only ones whose lives were being uprooted by the pandemic; Mel had been dealing with separation from her family for eighty percent of the week. Although Dustin was sure Bettie made her best effort to spoil Mel and amuse her throughout the day, there was only so much an elderly woman could do to entertain a nine-year-old ball of energy.

Dustin and Rachel were stressed as hell, but Mel knew that. Didn't she deserve a break just as much as they did?

And he promised he'd be there for her.

He expelled another deep breath, only to have his mask deflect it right back into his face again. He leaned forward on his elbows. "All right."

When her brown eyes lit up like the sun, his lips tugged into a smile. He picked up the hand she'd dealt for him and placed his first card. They went back and forth, Dustin barely able to keep his tired eyes from blurring out of focus. She placed back-to-back draw-four cards, and he had nine cards in his hand when Mel shouted, "UNO!"

"Dammit," he muttered, dropping his hand on the table. "Shit—I mean, darn." He scowled as his exhausted brain failed to watch his tongue. "You didn't hear that."

Whether she had caught his slipup or not, she didn't show any sign. She busily scooped up their cards and dealt another hand before he could object.

Mel beat him at two more games by the time the door opened and their mom stepped inside.

"Mom!" Mel shouted from the floor, making no move to approach her. She was getting good at remembering to not rush into Rachel's arms when she came home from work, though it still pained them all to restrain themselves from hugging.

Even that, now, was a privilege, it seemed.

"Hi, baby," Rachel mumbled, pulling the door shut behind her. He was used to seeing the dark bags sagging beneath her weary eyes, and the indent on her forehead from the face shield she wore was now looking permanent. A mask covered her mouth as usual, and he couldn't remember the last time he'd seen her round chin and full lips. Even when she was off the clock and with her family, she continued to make sacrifices to keep her children safe.

Dustin swallowed against the tightening in his chest. However hard he'd had it at work, his mom had ploughed through late-night shifts and health-care stress for as long as he could remember.

"Will you play with us?" Mel asked with hopeful round eyes.

Rachel set her purse on the table before placing both hands on her hips. It was a moment before she responded, her cheeks lifting. "Of course, honey." She glanced at the cards on the table and arched a thin eyebrow. "Ooh, are you playing Uno? You'd better watch out. That's my favorite game! Just give me a second to clean up, and I'll join."

They played another few rounds while Rachel showered, disposed of her scrubs, and cleaned all the doorknobs. It was a half hour before she finally pulled up a barstool and sat a few paces away from the coffee table, masked and gloved like always.

Dustin dealt their cards, and they played an intense round. Despite this being Dustin and Mel's tenth game or so, Mel was still as fiercely competitive as ever. She laughed when her hand forced Dustin to draw card after card, and when he reversed direction, Rachel forced him to draw again.

"Dang, Mom!" he protested as he picked up more cards.

Rachel chortled as she mixed her hand. "It's okay to admit you're getting your butt kicked by us ladies." She shot Mel a wink.

"Not for long," he surmised, pulling out a card. "Expect vengeance now I have the entire deck in my hand." He flopped a draw-four card in front of Mel, and she moaned. He made sure she didn't have a chance to recover by giving her draw cards the next three cycles. He was just starting to think he might win when Rachel threw her hands into the air.

"Ha! I win!" she shouted.

"What? You didn't even say Uno!" Dustin slapped his cards on the table.

She leaned back and folded her arms smugly. "That's how good I am. You two didn't even see it."

"Not cool, Mom!" Mel whined.

Rachel's neck craned as she stretched her arms. "Give me a break. You are such a cheater, Mel. I saw you peeking at our cards when it wasn't your turn." Her eyes glittered above her mask.

Dustin gaped at his sister. "Since she's a declared cheat, I revoke all of Mel's wins."

"I second that motion," Rachel agreed.

Mel scrunched her lips into a frown. "I am noooot," she moaned, and Dustin and Rachel burst into laughter.

The next morning, Dustin woke at 6:00 a.m. and changed into a fresh pair of scrubs. After he'd brushed his teeth and gelled his bangs back, he grabbed his bag and headed to the living room.

"Dustin," a voice whispered from down the hallway. He turned and spotted his mom poking her head out of her bedroom door. "Come here."

As he trudged through the hallway, her tone sharpened. "Not too close."

A small tremor simmered up his spine as he scanned her features. Sweat gleamed on her brow in the dim light of the morning sun, and fear was etched in her brown eyes.

"What is it, Mom?" he asked.

"Wake Mel and get tested first thing." She paused, and a heavy, foreboding tension hung in the air between them. Emotion clogged her next words, her voice hoarse.

"I'm sick."

Thirty-Nine

*April*

DANI SWEATED IN THE BEATING SUN AS SHE CARRIED BOX AFTER box to the endless line of cars at the food bank.

May was only a few days away, and Dani had never imagined by the end of the school year she'd be handing out boxes of food to families in the middle of an international health crisis. In a pandemic-less world, she'd be leading her undefeated lacrosse team to a PAC-12 championship right now.

But her lacrosse season was looking less and less important as the days wore on. Dani was beginning to feel ashamed for putting so much weight into the PAC championship when there were families struggling to put food on the table.

The next car in line pulled up, and a young woman leaned out the window with pleading eyes. "Hi, miss, do you mind if I have two boxes? I won't be able to make the trip tomorrow."

Dani balanced the box on her knee while she wiped sweat from her brow. The damn mask wasn't helping in this heat. "I'm sorry, ma'am, our policy is one box per family. It's first come, first served. Maybe you can have someone else wait in line for you tomorrow?"

Dani had helped out at the food bank a few times now with Noemi and Alisha, and she was used to families making desperate pleas for more than their fair share.

The lady squeezed her eyes shut briefly. "Please, miss, can't you make an exception just this one time?"

Behind them, the next car in line honked. Dani frowned as she opened the lady's back door and pushed the box inside. "I'm so sorry, ma'am. It wouldn't be fair to everyone else."

A honk sounded again, and Dani shot a frustrated glance at the driver behind them. The man was leaning out of his window, waving at her. Noemi skirted into view and brought a box to the man. She was usually busy monitoring the flow of things, but Dani was glad for her assistance to the impatient driver.

"Please, please, miss!" Dani turned her head back to the lady behind the wheel. She looked near tears. "I don't have anyone else to make the trip. My husband and I both work tomorrow…"

Dani took a step back. "I'm sorry. I wish I could help, but I don't have a choice—"

"Dani!"

She swerved as Noemi hustled up to her, a box jostling in her arms. Noemi lowered her voice and tossed her long ponytail over a shoulder. "It's okay, Dani. That other driver heard the lady begging for another box, so he offered half of his own box's contents. He only needed enough food to feed himself."

She handed her the box, and Dani craned her neck to see the driver behind the lady's car pull up next to them. He exchanged a wave with Alisha before driving away.

Dani stared after him before remembering to put the box in the lady's car.

"Oh, thank you, miss. Thank you so much!" the lady cried.

Dani shut the car door with a nod, and the lady beamed before driving away.

"I expected that man to be a whiny bitch, not generous," Dani mumbled to Noemi as they walked back to the tented tables.

"You really get both ends of the spectrum with this pandemic," Noemi said with a shrug. "A lot of people are suffering and frustrated, sure, but I've seen more compassion and generosity since working here. You and everyone volunteering are proof."

The compliment made Dani stiffen. She never would have volunteered here had it not been for Noemi and Alisha. But then again, Noemi's optimism offered a welcome contrast to the dark, shameful scars Dani had wrought upon herself.

Dustin's words echoed in Dani's ears as she walked side by side with Noemi back to Table 2. *Sometimes, given enough time, people do change.*

Maybe her mentor had been helpful in more ways than one.

She hadn't heard from Dustin in a while. Hopefully, he was doing okay.

Dani's chest tightened as an image surfaced of him working tirelessly in long protective gear, being coughed on by ghastly, sick COVID patients.

The sound of approaching footsteps jolted her from her haunting thoughts. She glanced up to see Warren join her and Noemi from behind.

"Everything good?" Warren asked. "I heard that guy honking."

Dani rubbed an arm as the three of them stopped in front of their table. "Yeah, he just wanted to help out the lady in front with some of his food."

Warren's brow arched. "Oh, that's good. I thought another one of those crazy LA mofos showed up." He patted Dani's shoulder. "But it's a good thing we have Dani to protect us."

Dani shifted her hips. "Well, I'm always good for cursing out people if you need me. It probably wouldn't leave a good rep with the food bank, though."

Warren tossed back his head, a sharp laugh bursting from his lips. "Hell yeah! I wanna see that."

"If this pandemic ever ends, just show up at one of my lacrosse matches."

Warren cackled again. "No shit? Save me a seat. I'm totally coming." He shook his head with a grin and continued toward the warehouse.

Dani cracked a smile as she reached beneath the table for her hydroflask. Of all the other volunteers, Warren was the one she enjoyed the most. As she watched him reemerge from the warehouse, a crate of boxes tucked under his arms as he chatted with another volunteer, Dani thought back to the conversation she'd had with him about race. Neither of them had mentioned the topic since, but thankfully the avoidance of the subject hadn't led to any further awkwardness.

She downed a sip of water and picked up another box before heading out to the next waiting car.

As she went back and forth to the next dozen cars, every driver thanked her with an appreciative smile, and Dani found herself inadvertently noting each person's skin color. Soon Carolyn's words about capitalism echoed in Dani's ears: "*It's like this mentality that there's an 'us versus them,' and success and wealth are the focus instead of healthy livelihoods and people's well-being... Just because people aren't successful doesn't mean they don't work hard; sometimes life just deals people unlucky hands.*"

In Carolyn's "us versus them," Dani saw how Warren would argue that Blacks or POCs constituted a large portion of "them," considering the higher poverty rate among POCs. "*Them*"... she pondered. *I.e.* "unsuccessful"... "other"... "slackers"... "drain on the economy"...

It got Dani thinking about the hard work in her own life. She had done everything right, practiced late hours into the day, and earned a scholarship, yet lacrosse and a normal college life had still been snatched from her.

And what about the people in line for food? Everyone's lives had been uprooted by the pandemic to some degree, regardless of how hard he or she had worked. The only difference was circumstance: Whereas she had lost lacrosse, maybe they had lost their jobs. Where she had lost access to in-person education, they had lost access to basic necessities like food.

Maybe Carolyn had been right; sometimes, no matter how hard you worked in life, you were dealt a bad hand. And Warren's argument compounded that not everyone played with the same, fair deck.

And perhaps, because of her own circumstances, Dani had one of the better decks. Perhaps, despite her losses, she won more often than not.

As she walked back to Table 2, she dared to think maybe her life wasn't so bad; she'd gotten a full-ride to school and had enough money from her parents to pay for a decent-sized apartment. Food hadn't even been a concern for her.

*Why was I ever complaining before? I was frustrated about so many dumb things. I already have so much.*

Her own problems didn't seem so important now.

When she reached the table, she leaned on her elbows and lowered her head into her hands, swallowing back a sharp burn in her throat.

Someone brushed her elbow. "You okay?" Alisha's hand came down on Dani's shoulder before slipping away quickly.

Dani wiped her face and met Alisha's concerned brown eyes. "Yeah. I'm good, thanks."

Before she could explain further, her phone vibrated in her pocket. She whipped it out with sweaty palms, thankful for the distraction.

Her breath caught in her throat as her eyes raked the screen.

*Tanner!*

She opened his message with shaking hands as her heart somersaulted in her chest.

**I've missed you, D. So much. Wesley is out tomorrow night. Wanna come by? I'll order some pizza.**

Forty

*May*

**M**Y MOM IS SICK.

The agonizing thought kept racing through Dustin's head as he scanned patient after patient outside Olympia Hospital. In the days since he'd returned to work, he had worried constantly about her, hoping he had left her enough food by her bedroom door and praying she was doing okay.

By some amazing gift from God, he and Mel had both tested negative after waiting several days in trepidation for their results.

It was a damn miracle.

Dustin had nearly broken down in relief, but his celebration was brief. Rachel refused to be taken to the hospital to be tested, lest she give Dustin the virus during the car ride, but Dustin had seen enough COVID patients to assume his mom had contracted the virus.

A young woman entered the tent with her ten-year-old daughter, shifting Dustin's attention back to the task before him. When both the mother and daughter expelled sneezes and raspy coughs, it was all Dustin could do to refrain from breaking down right there in the screening tent.

Dustin's deep breath fogged his face shield as he walked the woman and her daughter through the screening process.

*Mom is strong. Her fever will pass in a few days; she's not high-risk.*

*But neither are these two patients. What is the world coming to?*

More patients streamed in throughout the day, some worse than others. As hard as he tried to suppress his emotions, the nagging concern for his mom crept up on him with each young and healthy person he screened.

Rachel could easily end up being one of these people. And God forbid she be taken to an intensive care unit after a few weeks, treated by her own coworkers like one of the other nurses had been.

His mind took an ugly turn as he imagined her being tossed in the morgue truck he passed on his drive every night. This damn pandemic was a horrific contemporary rendition of an apocalypse. People were being left alone to die as all hospitals were prohibiting visitors. Loved ones were being denied a proper funeral and burial, breaking families' hearts.

His little sister's words echoed in his mind from so many months ago: *"You know that every time you swear, God gets angry… One day, He's not going to be able to hold all of His anger any longer, and we're all going to pay the price."*

Her statement had seemed funny at the time, but now, it held an eerie feeling of foretelling.

He swallowed with difficulty as his sister's sagging brown eyes flashed in front of his own. She had stared helplessly after him from Bettie's doorway as he left for work several mornings ago. It had been so hard for him to look her in the face and promise her everything would be okay.

Dustin's chest ached as he screened a healthy-looking man in his late thirties. Dustin had promised himself to look after Mel and be there for her when she needed him most, and now he couldn't even do that.

He bit his lip. He needed a seed of hope to hold onto—something he could use to inspire himself and other patients.

After dismissing the man, Dustin walked over to the computer and opened the patient database. Maybe Eli Normand's recovery could give him some hope. It had been two weeks since Dustin had tested the jolly man. Hopefully, he was feeling better. Maybe it would be enough to lift Dustin up and distract him from his constant worrying about his mom.

Dustin scrolled through Normand's file, his heart hammering eagerly in his chest. Bold letters at the bottom of the screen indicated a health update, dated a week ago: "Tested positive for COVID-19." His breath hitched as he scrolled further down the log. The most recent health update made him grimace: "Patient released from care April 28th—Deceased from pneumonia-related complications."

His stomach plummeted, and his eyes strained to hold back tears.

It was too much.

He tore away from the computer, skirted past patients and busy coworkers, and dashed out of the tent. His feet carried him along the perimeter of the PPE tent and down a small alley behind the hospital, away from all the sick, helpless patients.

Finally alone, he ripped off his face shield and mask to release the tension wrangling his body. His bellowing curse rebounded off every surrounding building, closing back in on him like a suffocating blanket. He slumped against the building and sagged his head in his hands as the world seemed to slip from under his feet.

What was the point of going forward when the end was just a dark, endless abyss?

Was there even an end to this nightmare? How many more months would this marathon last? Whatever the answer, he couldn't fathom surviving it without his mom.

The scuffle of footsteps sounded moments later from around the corner. He didn't bother looking up.

"You okay?" a soft voice inquired as the steps approached. It was Lila.

"No, I'm not." His words came out hoarse, choked, as he stared at the dirt beneath his shoes. "My mom is sick and bedridden after she dealt with COVID patients seven days a week. Every night after my shift, I drive by a truck that is loaded with dead people. We're working in a profession that watches people die every five minutes. How the hell can any of us be okay?" His Adam's apple bobbed precariously as he raised his head and met her concerned eyes.

His gaze shifted past her shoulder as a nurse appeared down the alleyway. Lila followed his line of sight and straightened.

"Matt, finish up for me, would you? Tell Leopold we'll be back in a minute," she ushered.

Matt nodded and spun on his heel, vanishing from view.

Lila turned back to Dustin, allowing a few seconds to tick by. She approached him cautiously and leaned against the wall next to him, a few paces away. After a minute, she pulled off her glove and inched closer.

"I'm here for you, Dustin, if you need me," she whispered, her hand stretching across the space between them and cupping his cheek. "I just wanted you to know that."

He sucked in a breath at the clear violation of health and safety protocol. What was she doing?

His mind battled with his emotions as her light touch washed a wave of warmth through him, rousing forgotten memories. His pulse picked up pace as he recalled the feel of her body spooned against his, her high-pitched laugh drawing a smile from him as they stole kisses during their clerkship breaks… He'd forgotten how long it was since he'd been touched like that, or how much he missed it.

When he didn't pull away from her hand, Lila smiled through her face shield, and he couldn't stop his heart from fluttering.

He'd told himself he wouldn't get involved with anyone this past year while he focused on med school, but now she was here, caressing him…maybe it was what he needed. Maybe he needed someone to hold him; support him through this chaotic time.

*Stop this, Dustin. What the hell are you doing? Your mom is already sick. Do you want to increase the risk for Mel and Bettie contracting the virus? Lila is just as exposed as you every day.*

He shouldn't be letting Lila touch him. It was completely brash and irresponsible. If his supervisor or anyone else caught them carelessly violating health and safety protocol, they'd be fired. But as much as his mind screamed at him, he couldn't get himself to push her away.

He stiffened as she brushed her thumb along his cheek, her brown eyes shining hopefully through her glasses. He gazed back at her with a heavy heart, his fingers itching to unwind her hair from where it sat in a tight bun atop her head. Lila looked beautiful even in her nurse's white screening garb, which could've passed for a space suit without the helmet. He yearned to tug off her face shield and pull her into his arms—but then the logical part of his mind jerked him back to his senses.

His hand darted to hers and dragged it off his cheek in a fluid motion. The hope in her eyes fizzled as he sidled around her.

"This is against protocol," he rebuked with a sharp twist of his lips.

As if he gave a shit about protocol right now. Or anything.

But this wasn't about him. This was about his mom. Mel. Bettie.

This was about Eli Normand and the families ripped apart each day as hundreds died alone in their hospital beds.

He owed it to them to keep pushing forward like his mom had even under the most despairing conditions. His damn personal feelings didn't matter in the context of everything else.

"We need to get back to work." Snatching his faceguard off the ground, he marched toward the PPE tent, leaving her standing dumbfounded by the wall.

# Forty-One

*May*

DUSTIN CAME HOME LATE THAT EVENING AFTER HIS SHIFT AND checked on Mel at Bettie's house in his usual routine. He stood a laughable distance away from the porch as Bettie opened the door. After being exposed to COVID patients all day, he was not going to take any chances risking Bettie's health, regardless of her objections.

"Hello, Dustin. How has your mom been doing?" Bettie asked, looking up at him from beneath her white curls.

He smiled faintly behind his mask. "She's been in a lot of pain regardless of the pills I give her. The fever is really getting to her, and she still has chills and a cough."

Bettie's face fell. "I'm sorry to hear that. Your mom is a fighter, Dustin. I pray for her every day that she'll get through this soon." She tightened her lips before swiveling her head over her shoulder. "Mel, your brother's here."

A moment later, footsteps scuffled from behind Bettie, and his sister's head popped around the door, her long brown hair spilling around her round face. Max's bark sounded from inside the house, and Mel turned to face the excited golden retriever.

"Down, boy!" she ordered as she blocked Max from bounding toward Dustin.

Dustin's lips quirked before he addressed Bettie. "Has Mel been good?"

Bettie glanced at Mel and smiled. "She's been a delight, keeping this old lady occupied. I don't know what I'd do without her."

"Can I see Mom?" Mel asked with wide eyes as she stroked Max behind the ears.

Dustin sighed and shook his head at his sister. "Mom can't see anyone right now. It's too risky."

"But you get to see her," Mel pouted, injury gushing in her soft brown eyes.

Dustin rubbed his neck. "I told you, I just bring her food and make sure she's okay. I can't be around her any more than you can."

Mel nodded slowly, looking away. It had been almost a week since she last saw their mom, and Dustin wished more than anything for them to be together, but Rachel was increasingly symptomatic. Her pale, frail state wasn't a pleasant sight.

After ten more minutes of catching up on the day's activities, Dustin walked next door and heated up a bowl of soup for his mom. He walked down the hall with the bowl in his gloved hands, a new N-95 mask secured against his face.

He paused at her bedroom door and knocked twice. "Hey, Mom, I brought some soup."

No answer.

"Mom?" He knocked again, fear washing through him as a heavy silence hung in the air. He hesitated, contemplating the risks of entering a contaminated room, before pushing the door open.

Rachel lay motionless on her bed under the covers, small wheezing breaths escaping her. She gazed at him with pleading eyes. "Dustin..." she choked.

His grip on the bowl loosened as his mind whirled into panic. He darted to her bed and set aside the soup on the adjacent desk. Terror spilled through his veins as he raked over his mom's features: her brow dripping with sweat, her face as pale as a ghost, her breathing shallow and labored.

He whipped out his phone with shaking hands and dialed.

"9-1-1," the operator answered. "What's your emergency?"

"Why'd you get olives?" Dani groaned through her mask, slumping on Tanner's couch as he opened the pizza box.

"So I can do this." Tanner picked one off a slice and dropped it down her low-cut top like he had on their first date.

Dani shrieked as the warm olive plunged down her shirt. "What the hell!" She plucked the olive from her skin and punched his rock-hard chest, though a laugh escaped her. She really needed to start wearing shirts that didn't give him such an easy target.

His attractive smile made her heart flip, and she took a moment to admire the smooth planes of his cheeks, the dark hair accentuating his silky brown eyes.

"You don't have to wear that damn thing while you're here." Tanner slipped the mask from her face and tossed it on the coffee table. His hand crept back to her neck and drew her hair around a shoulder, stirring the flurry of emotions in her chest. "Mmm, much better," he murmured.

Dani supposed it was stupid to wear a mask. It wasn't as if she was planning on keeping six feet apart from him anyway.

Tanner leaned back and rested an arm across the back of the couch, his thick biceps visible through his long-sleeved shirt. "How has quarantine been going?"

The memory of the protest at Dignity Hospital forced its way into Dani's mind, followed by those dark days of turmoil and depression. Bile rose in the back of her throat.

"Not so great. I've been really lonely without you." She stroked his arm and turned to face him. "I wanted to apologize for anything I did that made you feel…doubtful about our relationship. I never meant to hurt you."

"It's okay." His eyes softened. "I've been thinking about you a lot since the whole quarantine thing." He lowered his head and shifted closer to her, placing a warm hand on her thigh. "It made me realize how much

I've missed you, that what we have is real. What's that saying…? 'If you let something go and it comes back to you, it was meant to be.'"

She tilted her head in a small taunt. "Oh, how romantic."

A deep chuckle rumbled through his chest as he gently squeezed her thigh. "Don't get all swoony on me now. I'll skip dinner and go straight to dessert." He brought his lips to her neck and planted a tickling kiss.

"God, your lines are terrible," Dani snickered as she tilted her neck up, relishing in the skin-prickling frenzy she had missed for so long.

In one strong motion, he lifted her on top of him so her legs were straddling his waist. Her heart raced as his fingers eased under her shirt and trailed up and down her abdomen. She shuddered and tangled her hands in his messy hair, a ripple of pleasure bursting from her core. His hands dipped to her jean shorts, unbuttoning them.

In a frightening flash, she was teleported to the time he restrained her on his bed in January. Her pulse pounded in her ears as she recalled the sharp sting along her cheek from his slap and the trepidatious shake of her body when she was able to roll away from him.

She bit her tongue and shoved aside the memory.

This was what she wanted. She had nothing to be afraid of if she didn't push him away. He didn't deserve to wait any longer.

She had longed for someone to hold her and caress her and make her laugh the way he did, and her yearning had built up alarmingly high in the past few months. With every caress of his fingers, her breath hitched, and it wasn't long before her happiness came crashing down in a tidal wave of emotion.

When she began to tremble, he lifted his head to stare at her. "I'm sorry. Too fast," he apologized, pulling his hand away. "Listen, ah, I'm sorry for hitting you back in January… I just lost my temper a bit. But you're worth the wait."

She inhaled deeply, whimpering as she absorbed his words. He had always been so patient and forgiving with her. It made her heart ache harder for him.

Dani cupped his face and kissed him deeply. He returned her kiss with such tenderness her eyes watered. After a moment, he pulled away and stiffened under her when he read her expression.

"What's wrong?" he asked softly, brushing away a tear.

Her voice cracked as the words spilled out of her. "I love you," she whispered.

He wound his hands in her hair and kissed her trembling lips, pulling her into a tight embrace. She clutched at his shirt, convincing herself he was real, in the flesh. She relished in the warmth of his strong arms locked around her, the rise and fall of his chest as he breathed, the folds of their bodies melded together.

"I've never felt this way about anyone before," she said, her voice breaking. "You make me feel safe. *Wanted.* Like I'm a good person."

"Of course you're a good person," he murmured into her ear. "Why would you think otherwise?"

She pulled back from him slowly and dropped her gaze.

*Tell him. There should be no secrets between you. You can do it. He's here for you.*

"There's something…I should tell you."

He straightened and tucked her hair behind an ear. "You can tell me anything."

Dani traced a finger along his jaw, absorbing his serene, perfect brown eyes as she prepared for her next words. She let out a long sigh. "I've only told this to one other person, but…"

Tanner caressed her hip bones with his thumbs in those small, comforting circles, urging her to go on.

"I…"

The haunting memories bubbled to the surface, threatening to wash over her, and she dug her fingernails into his shirt, terrified he would slip away.

"In high school, I made a lot of awful, *horrible* mistakes, and I still live with their consequences today."

*The crumpled person emitted a wheezing sound. It was a man, and now she was closer, she could see…*

She searched Tanner's eyes, and when she saw compassion and understanding, she continued.

"I…"

*Say it like it is.*

*Say it.*

"I killed my brother."

Dustin stood in front of the Mottley house watching the ambulance disappear down the dark street with his mom inside. At the edge of the flashing red and blue lights in his vision, he glimpsed tears streaming down Mel's face while Bettie soothed her, squeezing her shoulders.

He stared blankly into the darkness long after the ambulance had vanished, fearing his worst nightmare was coming true. He had a terrifying thought that tonight was the last time he'd see his mom. The image of her pale face and weak, hollow eyes were ingrained into his memory, and he prayed to God she wouldn't leave him and Mel this way.

She couldn't—wouldn't—say goodbye to her children through an iPad from a desolate, distant hospital bed.

Dustin wouldn't survive it.

Bettie said softly, "Dustin, you can stay with us tonight, honey. And for however long afterward."

It was another long minute before Dustin turned to her, gave a small nod, and followed his neighbor into her house.

The three of them stayed up watching one of Mel's favorite movies, Disney's *Meet the Robinsons*, but Luis's longing for a family hit Dustin hard. He turned his head away from the screen and fought against the pain in his throat.

Mel stood from the couch to take the remote from Bettie, who had fallen asleep in her chair by the front door, Max's head resting by her feet. Mel shut off the movie and came to sit back down beside Dustin, quieter than a mouse. Before he could turn to her, she broke their "no contact" rule and wrapped her arms around him, resting her small head on his shoulder.

Dustin lifted a hand to push her away, fear rising at the thought of infecting his sister, but he couldn't bring himself to do it.

Mel never hugged him.

Her closeness tugged at some foreign piece of his heart, and Dustin cursed at himself before hugging her back with all the warmth he could give. They only had each other now, and in this last desperate moment, he couldn't deny her this small piece of love despite how hard he tried to talk himself out of it.

He squeezed his eyes shut, fighting to hold back tears. He couldn't cry; he needed to be that last rock for her to cling to, that last beacon of hope when the storm surged around them.

*Crying doesn't solve anything,* he told himself as pieces of his heart chipped away with every second Mel clung to him. *Don't cry, it'll only make things worse.*

But in the end, he cried.

Tanner's thumbs stopped circling Dani's hip bones. "You killed your brother? What...? Why aren't you locked up?" His eyes narrowed, and what was once compassion morphed into alarm and disbelief, then revulsion.

Dani's hands shook, and though she still clung to his shirt, she felt him slipping away. "Yes...but...I didn't mean to do it... I m-made some really bad decisions—" Her breaths quickened, and she tore her gaze away from him. She sounded like she was making excuses for an indefensible, atrocious act.

And she was.

"Shit," Tanner muttered. He crawled out from underneath her and combed his bangs out of his face. "That's one hell of a secret to hide."

She cowered on his couch as turmoil gushed through her stomach, her deepest scars now exposed. When Tanner finally raised his head, his expression spoke of disdain and disgust at the monster sitting before him.

"God, Dani. I can't believe this. You *killed* someone?" He paused as he searched her face. "How? Why?"

Dani's voice shook as the dark memories crawled to her consciousness. The words from her lips came out weak and distorted. "I—I made so many mistakes... I was so angry... I—I had been drinking and wasn't thinking c-clearly—"

Dani cut off as the nauseating images flooded her vision: Jeremy's pale, lifeless face, her hands coated in blood, her dad's judgmental glare... She squeezed her eyes shut, willing the images away.

She couldn't go on.

After a painfully long minute, Tanner's deep sigh met her ears. "Regardless of how it happened, why would you tell me this now, right after we got back together?"

"I w-wanted to tell you sooner," she sputtered as her eyes watered and throat burned. "I just...was afraid. I've always b-been afraid."

Horror distorted Tanner's once mesmerizing, sultry brown eyes. "Damn. I don't even know what to say…"

She opened her eyes and met his disbelieving gaze.

"How can you…live with something like that?"

"I d-don't know. I'm trying, I—" She choked back tears, struggling for words.

But it was no use trying to defend herself. She saw it in his face: judgment. It was what she had been afraid of—what she had been hiding from for three years—but she could no longer hide from a verdict she so badly deserved.

When she reached a hand to him in one last attempt to have him understand her, he pulled away. Her stomach heaved, and the dizzying nausea threatened to spin her world out of control.

"Shit," Tanner mumbled, brushing his bangs out of his eyes and turning his head. "Um…I want to believe I'm dating a decent, beautiful girl, but after this…I'm not sure if I really know you—especially since it took you months to tell me something this huge. I can't do this. I can't date a…murderer, as harsh as that sounds. Sorry." He averted his eyes as Dani's heart shattered with every word. "We're done."

She had to be dreaming. She would wake up and Tanner would be by her side, consoling her and shielding her from her dark pit of despair.

But that was fantasy.

And a horrible nightmare was her waking reality.

As much as she had tried to convince herself over the years that she'd moved beyond her past, she couldn't deny the truth any longer. Her past was a part of her. She had done this to herself; it was her own fault. Her despair, her shame, Tanner and her parents' revulsion—she deserved it.

She deserved all the hatred and rejection of the world.

Her body trembled as a wave of panic encapsulated her.

Tanner was right: it was a hell of a secret to hide. And his reaction was exactly how anyone should have reacted to the reveal of something so monstrous.

There was no cure, no hope, for something as dark and destructive as her.

She couldn't suppress the memories she had shackled down in

the darkest depths of her core. All the raw emotions she had locked away for so long broke free, swallowing her whole. Guilt, self-hatred, helplessness, and agonizing grief flooded every inch of her body, blocking out Tanner's face, and his dorm, and Los Angeles, and the world.

This time, she welcomed the darkness as it consumed her once more.

# PART II

*Forty-Two*

*Three years ago*

THE BELL RANG, AND AN EIGHTEEN-YEAR-OLD DANI strolled down the front steps of Helena High School, her best friend's arm hooked through hers. Students bustled around them on the pavement underneath the warm September sun, chatting animatedly with friends and scrolling through their phones as they waited for their rides.

"So have you decided on a school yet?" Natalie asked with a wide smile, batting her dark lashes.

Dani's mouth curved, her hazel eyes sparkling. "I can't decide between Penn State and Duke. I think I look better in blue—you think?" She looked down at her own blue-and-white plaid shirt.

Natalie's lips quirked, and she tilted her head playfully. "What about Princeton? Weren't you on the phone with them the other day?"

Dani twisted a strand of hair, wrinkling her mouth. "So Princeton said they'd offer a decent financial award, but only if I brought up my grades."

Her friend tossed her head back in a sharp scoff. "Well, we both know that isn't gonna happen. You barely pay attention to me when we're talking, let alone your teachers."

Natalie chuckled as Dani punched her shoulder.

When they approached the car pick-up line, Dani caught sight of her dad's large red pickup waiting at the curbside.

"Oh, shit, there's my dad. I gotta go before he starts throwing a fit." Dani slipped her arm from Natalie's and walked toward the curb, eyeing the large jagged dent in the truck's front bumper. Her dad still hadn't fixed it from when he'd ploughed some fallen tree trunks out of the road a week ago; road service was slow and unreliable where they lived deep in the outskirts of Helena, but it was a decent tradeoff for peace and isolation according to her parents.

Still, Franc Torres should've gotten the bumper fixed by now. Someone could be hurt if he or she wasn't paying attention and walked into the end of the sharp, protruding metal.

"You're going to the theater, right? I told Ethan you would be there!" Natalie called, whipping her brown braid around as Dani opened the passenger door.

"Yeah, I'll be there!" Dani's face heated as she tossed her backpack on the floor and shut the door behind her. Natalie had so generously invited Ethan to join their Friday night plans after tiring of Dani's gushing about him for weeks.

A smile tugged at her lips before she turned to her dad. "You can drop me off downtown by the McDonald's. I'll grab dinner there." She buckled her seatbelt and gazed at Natalie's retreating figure through the window.

Franc Torres shifted the truck into gear as soon as she'd buckled up and pulled away from the school. He gave her a flat look as he turned left onto the main street, heading in the opposite direction of her requested destination.

"You're not going downtown."

Dani's smile vanished. "What are you talking about? You and mom already agreed I could go."

His dark eyes tightened. "I had no part in that conversation."

Dani bit her lip and played with the hem of her shirt. *Caught red-handed.* She had only gotten confirmation from her mom about her plans today in the hopes her dad would have his hands tied. Evidently, her mom hadn't relayed the message.

Franc's knuckles turned white on the steering wheel. "This is what I mean when I say you go around being irresponsible! Partying all the time, going out with boys... You'll end up blowing everything we've worked on."

She rolled her eyes and huffed, "Dad, I'm just going to the movies, not a club." He was *not* going to mess up her date.

His thick mustache twitched. "You don't have time to be going out. You'll just have to tell them you aren't coming. You need to work on your footwork."

Dani whipped her head against the headrest. "I practiced a ton yesterday! I'm sick of you chauffeuring me around like a guarded princess."

"You still need more practice," Franc scolded. "More scouts are coming to the Helena tournament in a few weeks." The truck picked up speed as it continued down the road away from the theater—away from Ethan, who would soon be wondering why she ditched.

She threw her hands up. "What the hell, Dad! I have plenty of offers. I don't need to keep trying to impress scouts!"

"Syracuse will be there this time."

Syracuse was the top lacrosse school in the nation—the school her dad obsessed over as a lacrosse player himself. Dani didn't understand why her dad cared so much about his kids going to the most competitive school. He never once bothered to ask them what *they* wanted; it was always what he wanted.

Dani shoved her gaze through the window and tried her best to block out her dad for the remainder of the ride, but a dangerous rage bubbled all the while. Her dad was eating her life away, and he didn't even *care*. The only thing he cared about was lacrosse and controlling her.

Never mind what she or anyone else thought about it.

The long, winding drive beside Helena's whitebark pine trees felt longer this time. As soon as her dad pulled the truck into their driveway, Dani slung her backpack over a shoulder, hopped out, and slammed the door behind her. The gravel crunched under her heavy footsteps as she marched up the path to their large, two-story house.

"I expect you to be in the back yard in five minutes, Danica!" Franc shouted after her.

"Shut the hell up already," she said to herself in a low tone, heading up the stairs to her room. She tossed her backpack on her bed and grabbed a warm jacket and flashlight before skulking back down the stairs.

"Hey, where are you going?" Jeremy stepped in front of her by the living room sofa. His light hazel eyes peered down at her from under a red and gold USC hat.

"Anywhere away from Dad," she blurted as Franc came through the front door with a sharp glare. Dani pushed past Jeremy and out the back door as Franc yelled something behind her.

She hiked out across the expansive back yard and approached the beckoning forest, which provided a nice backdrop against the wide pasture on her left. A wall of tall Douglas fir trees blocked out the fading autumn sun as she trudged through a dense undergrowth of shrubbery and sharp twigs, not caring about the scrapes she'd feel in the morning.

She often hid out by the creek in the woods when she needed to escape her dad's overbearing presence, even when she knew she'd suffer the consequences afterward. He didn't know where her secret spot was, and he'd never find out. Only Jeremy knew where it was: far back in the woods behind the tall lodgepole pine tree with two odd crosses in the branches.

Sitting behind the protection of the lodgepole, she heard the scrunch of leaves behind her. Jeremy's head appeared from behind the large tree's base, a flashlight in his hand too.

Apparently, he also wasn't planning on going back anytime soon either.

He settled next to her, not speaking, and she lay her head against his shoulder, listening to his soft breathing and the low whistle of the wind through the trees.

After a few minutes, he broke the silence. "You know, I never really wanted to go to Syracuse."

She lifted her head and gazed into his soft hazel eyes. "You didn't?"

Jeremy had followed their dad's dream and attended Syracuse on a lacrosse scholarship, and Franc loved him for it. Her brother had been the perfect, obedient child Franc always wanted.

Now, Jeremy was admitting he never wanted that life?

He shook his head. "No. I wanted to go to USC."

Dani laughed. "I thought the only reason you wear that hat is because Audrey goes there." She hadn't yet met Jeremy's girlfriend; Jeremy had met her in Syracuse, and now Audrey was pursuing a master's degree at USC in biomedical engineering.

Jeremy's lips stretched into a smile at the mention of his girlfriend, and he averted his eyes. "I was the one who convinced her to go to USC, actually. USC has always been a sort of dream school of mine, but I didn't tell anyone because I didn't want to ruin Dad's plans for me. I've always wanted to go to California and see the beaches, study criminal justice, do something that would get me out of this shitbag town. Now, look at me—back in Helena, working as a server. But hey! At least I have a damn psychology degree!" He scoffed and dragged his shoe in the dirt. "I thought Syracuse would grow on me, but I never really liked the fast pace of the East Coast, the cold weather, and the exhaustion of lacrosse. The problem was, I didn't know how bad I screwed everything up until after I realized I'd wasted all my time."

His story of defeat was so contrary to the optimistic, prodigal, driven brother she knew. She half-expected him to shrug it off as a joke, but when she lifted her head to study the smooth planes of his twenty-five-year-old face, she realized he was sincere.

She sighed and traced a pattern in the cool soil beneath her legs. "I can't believe you gave up lacrosse after college. You could have gone pro."

Jeremy snorted. "Lacrosse is overrated. Who watches Major League Lacrosse who isn't Dad, Grandma or Grandpa?" He rubbed his lightly freckled nose and locked his hands over his knees. "Lacrosse was fun, but I only played it 'cause Dad's world revolved around it. He convinced me it was my best chance of getting into college."

Dani bit her lip, holding her tongue. She didn't think he'd opposed lacrosse *that* much. He was the one she'd enjoyed playing with after all this time!

After a minute, Jeremy looked up and held her gaze, his hazel eyes turning soft. "Don't let people control you, Dani. And don't let them tell you what you should or shouldn't want. Even if one of those people is Dad." He brushed a stray hair from her cheek. "Listen, you're smart, Dani. *Really* smart. Don't let your gift go to waste. I know you love lacrosse, but it's not going to land you in a professional career. Especially since you're a girl."

Dani shot him a glare. "What the hell is that supposed to mean, asshole? I'm better than most lacrosse guys!"

He took off his hat and smoothed his hair back, smirking. "You know what I mean. It has nothing to do with women being less skilled than guys—it's 'cause there isn't any money in women sports, as sad as it is…" His lip curved as he turned his head to stare at Dani's design in the dirt. "Anyways, my point is, do what *you* want to do, study where *you* want to study. Lacrosse will help get you there—you've got more than enough colleges lined up."

A timid smile tugged across Dani's lips. "Thanks for the advice. I didn't know you saw things that way." She thought she was the only one who thought her life was spiraling out of her control. It was nice to know she wasn't alone and someone supported her decisions. "I always wanted to pursue a lacrosse championship in college—on my own terms at *my* school of choice, not Dad's. But I didn't really think about what I'd do after college."

Jeremy tucked his hat over his ears and leaned back on his hands. "So where do you want to go?"

"Mmm, I was thinking Duke. It's a pretty good school, has a competitive lacrosse team, and is close to Grandma and Grandpa."

Jeremy tsked. "Damn. Duke, huh? For being such a rebel against Dad, I thought you would've at least picked one of Syracuse's rivals." He softly punched her shoulder, and she pounded him back, laughing. Then Jeremy's face relaxed. "But seriously, have you thought about looking into schools' pre-med programs? I thought you liked science."

She pursed her lips. "I guess I never really believed anything would come of it. And I'm terrible at studying anyways."

His eye roll was barely visible in the fading daylight. "You wouldn't have to study if you just paid attention the first time! You have an eidetic memory, for Christ's sake!"

"Yep, and you'd better watch it if you don't want me reciting the lines of all your least favorite chick-flicks." She squeezed his cheek.

The shadows enveloped them in darkness as hours trickled by, the two of them swapping stories. Jeremy spilled how much he'd missed Audrey, and was planning a surprise trip to see her in California once he saved up some more cash from table serving. Dani in turn told him about Natalie's shiny new Chrysler and how Natalie mocked Dani for her failed dating attempts, but somehow all of her stories ended up with her dad cutting her fun short and ordering her back onto the lacrosse field.

Stomachs grumbling, they finally stood and picked their way through the woods back to their house, the beams of their flashlights leading them through the dark.

Their mom's potato casserole simmered on the stove when they entered through the back porch. Angelina leaned against the kitchen counter, her expression stoic, as Dani and Jeremy loaded their plates with potatoes. Glancing across the room, Dani spotted Franc's head above the couch, turned away from them toward the TV.

The tension in the air was ever so thick as Dani and Jeremy ate in silence at the kitchen table, the clinking of their silverware and buzz of the television the only sounds of life.

Not long into their meal, Franc's deep voice rumbled, "You're grounded until after the Helena tournament."

The boiling anger that had dissipated earlier returned with a gut-wrenching explosion. Dani's fork clattered to her plate, and she glared at the back of her father's head.

"I'm done with this bullshit. I'm not going to Syracuse!"

He whipped his head toward her, daring her to speak again. "¿Qué acabas de decirme?"

She held her ground as her fist clenched under the table. "I said I'm *done!* It's not your decision! I'm going to Duke!"

Franc turned his head back to the TV. "We're not having this discussion again."

Dani's face scrunched into a distorted ball of fury. "I don't have a life thanks to you! Lacrosse isn't the only thing I enjoy, newsflash. You've kept me cooped up here for years, keeping me from doing anything else! I haven't been able to try new things and live a shitty, normal teenage life!"

Her dad's head swiveled to her again as he responded gruffly, "¡Cómo te atreves a harblarme con esa impertinencia! Everything I did was to keep you out of trouble, to keep you focused on getting into coll—"

"Have you even bothered to ask what I wanted? Your damn rules have done nothing but shackle me! You just can't get over your mom's death, so you have to take it all out on me!"

Angelina gasped behind her, and Jeremy stiffened out of the corner of Dani's eye.

Dani kept her glare focused on her dad as he stared back, emotionless. He scratched his mustache before standing to a menacing height and raising a thick finger at her.

"My rules are *there* because you've proven to be reckless without them. And you still fail to comply half the time." His tone raised in volume as his dark mustache twitched. "You've failed time and time again to do the right thing. Failed to practice when I say, failed to focus on college, failed to be home at curfew. Failure after failure after failure… You never learn!"

Jeremy sucked in a deep breath next to her, but she barely noticed.

Dani glared back at her dad, lips trembling. She stood from the table and stormed past him, trekking upstairs, feeling his eyes drill into her back the entire way. Finally inside her room, she slammed the door and locked it behind her, sealing the barrier between herself and a world she would sooner set on fire than face.

Seething, she whipped her phone out of her pocket and texted Natalie.

**Meet me at Sandero's at midnight. I need a drink.**

# Forty-Three

*Three years ago*

DANI STAYED LOCKED UP IN HER ROOM UNTIL 11:30 P.M. HER parents always went to bed around 11:00 p.m., weekend or not, so she knew she'd be able to sneak out unscathed.

She crept out of her room and down the stairs to the front door, quiet as a fox. Grabbing her dad's truck keys from the key rack, she slipped outside.

A blanket of fog had crept into the chilly night air, and she clutched her leather jacket over her plaid shirt as she hopped into her dad's truck. The engine sputtered to life, and she prayed her parents slept through it. Cars this far out of town were sparse, and any human noise at this time of night by their house was sure to rouse suspicion.

Their bedroom window remained dark, thankfully, as she pulled her dad's truck out of the driveway and meandered down the road in the foggy darkness, away from Franc's controlling, overbearing presence.

Her dad couldn't stop her this time. He had it coming to him; he had done this to himself. If he wanted her to stay away from distractions like partying and drinking, she was going to do them. She was done being controlled by him. His stupid grounding rules meant nothing to her. From now on, she would play lacrosse when she felt like it. Hell, maybe she'd even take Jeremy's advice and start looking at med schools.

Dani pulled off the highway and continued down the busy downtown street. It was Friday night—all of the clubs and bars were sure to be packed.

She deserved to have some fun once in a while, to break some rules and have a drink. Dani had only drank once before, and that was when her dad had offered it to her. She hoped she looked old enough that the bartender wouldn't ask for her ID. Although she was eighteen, she might be able to pass for twenty-one with her dark eye shadow.

Dani pulled up to Sandero's and parked next to Natalie's silver Chrysler.

Pounding music met her ears as she approached the entrance and peered inside.

Sure enough, the pub was a raucous party. A DJ blasted music on a small stage in front of a crowd of rowdy dancers, flashing lights driving the energy in the room. Beyond the dance floor, a sea of giddy twenty and thirty-year-olds laughed and clumsily tossed back their drinks as they chatted animatedly with friends and colleagues.

Swerving around the dance floor, she spotted Natalie seated at the far end of the bar, her feet propped on the barstool next to her.

"Hey, everything cool?" Natalie asked, slipping her feet off the barstool and pushing forward a mug of beer. "I had one of the guys buy them for us," she said in response to Dani's unasked question. She had let her wavy brown hair out of her braid from earlier, and dark eyeliner and bright red lipstick accentuated her sexy look.

Natalie, always the sly mastermind. She went out more often than Dani and knew how to talk people into getting what she wanted.

"No, everything isn't cool. I'm done with my dad." Dani sat on the barstool and took a long sip of her beer, grimacing as she plopped the mug onto the counter.

Natalie leaned on her elbows, tracing the rim of her mug. "You say that every week. Is it about ditching Ethan today? I told him your dad was a hard-ass, and he seemed to understand."

Dani's expression hardened. "Yes, but this time was the tipping point. He doesn't care about anyone but himself. Screw Syracuse and all of the scouts." She took another swig.

Natalie raised an eyebrow and quirked her red lips. "Damn, girl, I've never seen you act like this. I like it!"

Dani raised her mug in agreement. "Cheers to that."

The night dragged on in a blur for two more hours. Dani had a few more beers and danced to the DJ's music, getting lost in the high of her freedom and the buzz pulsing through her veins. She and Natalie lingered as the crowd gradually shrank, and it wasn't long before the bartenders eventually ushered them out for the night.

Dani shuffled out of the bar behind her friend and into the dense fog. It had thickened significantly since she left home.

Natalie paused on the sidewalk and pulled out her phone. "I'm gonna call you a Lyft. You had a lot to drink."

"No. If my dad sees his truck gone, I'm dead," Dani slurred. "I'm fine. I can walk straight, see?" She took a few relatively straight steps. "Besides, the roads are empty at this time of night."

Natalie eyed her skeptically, her eyebrows drawing down. "I really don't think you should…"

Dani ignored her and opened her dad's driver door. "I'm good, trust me."

*Failure after failure…* Her father's words echoed in her mind as she climbed into the truck, but she shook them away.

Before Natalie could respond, Dani tugged the door shut behind her and started the engine. She glanced at her phone and saw Jeremy had called twice and left her a text at midnight. It was now just past 2:00 a.m.

**Where are you? Call me.**

"Shit," she muttered.

So Jeremy had noticed she was gone. Had he told their dad? She didn't believe he would betray her, but maybe if he thought she was in danger…

Dani backed the truck out of the stall as Natalie stared at her with worried eyes.

"Stay safe!" she called through the window.

Dani gave an assuring smile as she pulled the truck around and turned onto the main street. The roads were empty as she drove onto the highway and exited down the long, winding dirt road that led to her house.

Her driving wasn't exceptional, but not bad with her buzz, if she credited herself. Natalie had worried over nothing.

She squinted through the blanket of fog, struggling to see the outline of the road. When she flicked the headlights to high beam, the forest pine trees leapt in front of her truck. Dani swerved sharply left, overcompensating—

*THUD. Thrum. Thrum.*

The pickup slammed into something on the side of the road, and Dani jammed on the brakes. Swinging the driver door open, she stumbled out of the truck. The front corner bumper's dent had collapsed further than its usual jagged position. Pulse escalating, she glanced around in the fog for what she had hit…

There. A light shone on the ground thirty feet behind her truck. Hurrying toward its source, she came upon a flashlight illuminating something in the grass several paces away. Her strained eyes adjusted to the brightness, following its beam—

She hadn't hit something. She had hit some*one.*

Her hand darted to her mouth as her stomach plummeted. *Oh, god, what have I done?*

*Failure after failure…*

A panicked breath escaped her trembling lips. *I wasn't driving that fast, was I?*

The crumpled person emitted a wheezing sound, and Dani crouched to see a huge spot of blood enlarging from the person's abdomen beneath a torn sweatshirt. It was a man, and now she was closer, she glimpsed a head of dirty-blond hair.

She had ploughed the truck into her brother.

"Oh my god, oh my god, OH MY GOD! Someone help!" she screamed to anyone who may have been close enough to hear her. The houses along this road were far apart, but she must have been close to home if Jeremy had ventured this far into the dark.

*He came searching for me by the forest… He probably didn't even see Dad's truck was gone because of the fog.*

*He didn't tell Dad I'd left.*

A rush of agony overwhelmed her as she fell to her knees in the damp grass and pressed her shaking hand to Jeremy's wound. It appeared that the sharp, curved dent in her dad's bumper had clipped Jeremy's midsection. Dani's stomach churned, and her mind spun in a dizzying frenzy as warm blood spilled out of him. It wasn't stopping. His breaths were strained, and he convulsed, spurting blood.

Her inebriated brain finally snapping to focus, she pulled out her phone with bloody hands and dialed.

"9-1-1," the operator answered. "What is your emergency?"

"My brother has been hit by a car on the eastbound Mammoth Road outside of Helena!" she wailed. "He's bleeding out!"

"Okay, honey. An ambulance will be there shortly, in about…fifteen minutes. In the meantime, try finding something to tie around the wound and cut off the blood circulation…"

The putrid smell of blood filled her nostrils as she shook off her jacket. It was too thick to tie around him. She tore off her plaid shirt and looped it around his midsection with shaking hands. There wasn't a good, narrow cut-off point—the blood kept coming and coming. The operator's advice was useless; didn't she know her brother needed a damn ambulance? Where was the ambulance!

Her hands blurred as she untied her shirt from his torso and pressed it against his open wound instead. It immediately soaked wet with blood.

*Failure after failure after failure…*

Dani saw the life draining from him with every breath, his eyes dimming in the beam of the flashlight. The ambulance would never get here in time—they were too far from town.

She grasped her brother's hand and peered into his eyes, weeping. "Jeremy, stay with me! Stay with me, goddammit!"

Jeremy looked up at her with his soft hazel eyes. "Dani," he gasped. "I'm…sorry…"

Her eyes squeezed shut to fight against her rising nausea. "No, no, no, no, Jeremy… Don't do this! Stay with me!" She bent her head next to his and whispered desperately, "If you stay, I promise I'll go to med school and…make you proud… I'll find a way to fix this! Just stay with me, that's all you need to do, and I promise, I promise I will…"

With one hand still on his chest, she reached down with the other to cling to Jeremy's arm. He was limp, his face draining of color with every passing second.

A second flashlight in the distance danced over the two of them, and she squinted against the brightness. As the source approached, she glimpsed the dim outline of her parents in their nightclothes, her screams probably having woken them from their sleep.

When the light illuminated the scene before her parents, her mom's hands covered her face, and she shrieked. Flashlight jerking left and right, Franc sprinted to where Dani was crouched over Jeremy, pressing her blood-soaked plaid shirt into his wound

"I d-don't know what else to do. The paramedics are on their way," she sobbed, snot and tears dripping down her face.

Franc Torres dropped to his knees next to her. His face contorted when he took in her hand pressing the blood-soaked plaid shirt into Jeremy's wound. Dani couldn't remember what color the shirt had been before; now, it was only a dark, messy red.

Sheer horror reflected in his brown eyes as Franc turned to her, his jaw dropping in disbelief. His hand replaced hers over Jeremy's wound. As his arm brushed against her, his gaze hardened.

"You smell of alcohol."

Dani cringed as his earlier words rang like a shotgun in her mind: *"You've failed time and time again to do the right thing. Failure after failure after failure… You never learn!"*

By the time the ambulance blared into view ten minutes later, Jeremy was barely breathing. The EMTs spilled out of the vehicle, sealed Jeremy's wound—now only trickling blood—and tied him onto a gurney.

A paramedic kneeled beside her and checked her pulse, then wrapped her arm in something. "Miss. Miss? Hello?"

Her heavy eyes were trained on Jeremy as they hoisted him into the ambulance and slapped a breathing mask onto his sweet, pale face. She could only watch helplessly as they stabbed him with needles and hooked him to a ventilator. He looked like the bloody victim of a horrific war scene.

"She has high blood pressure and smells of alcohol. It looks like a DUI…but we have to get the boy to the hospital. He has broken ribs and an open gash in his side. That may not be the extent of his injuries, though…"

Dani barely made out the paramedics' words as she squinted through her tears into the ambulance. *Why weren't they taking him to the hospital? Why were they still here?*

Her pale brother was a bloody, devastating mess. She had one final look at his limp figure before the paramedics jumped into the ambulance and slammed the doors behind them.

But the EMTs' efforts were in vain.

Jeremy died before he reached the hospital.

# *Forty-Four*

*May*

DANI CURLED ON HER BED, THE HORRIFIC IMAGES FROM HER nightmare still fresh in her mind. Her hands were clammy like they were the night she kneeled in the grass gripping Jeremy's limp arms. The dry, horrid smell of his blood filled her nostrils again, stirring the nausea in her stomach. When she closed her eyes, the wailing ambulance flooded her vision as it disappeared with her brother into a blanket of darkness…

A weight on the bed beside her jerked her back to reality.

"Tell me what happened." Carolyn's soft words permeated the air. "You weren't at his place long."

It took Dani a moment to gather the courage to roll over and face her roommate. "I told him," she choked, her voice hoarse from an hour of crying into the covers.

Carolyn's bright green eyes widened. "You did?"

"And he dumped me. He said he couldn't date a *murderer.*" Dani squeezed her eyes shut, stuffing her face into the pillows.

All the curiosity washed from Carolyn's voice, replaced with a caring tenderness. "I'm so sorry, Dani. You were so excited to be getting back together with him. Who knew he was such a jerk?"

Dani choked back the burning lump in her throat. When she spoke, her voice was surprisingly level, controlled. "He's not a jerk. He reacted like he should have. I was just stupid for thinking he'd judge me differently. As if I might deserve forgiveness. But I don't. Not for that. Not for anything."

Still, for some reason, a part of her felt betrayed by him; as if he was a different person than she imagined. If Tanner was as patient and consoling as she had thought, why had he so quickly pushed her away?

Carolyn rested a hand on her shoulder. Though it was a small gesture, it demonstrated a greater effort to push past any barriers than her parents had shown in the past three years.

"Dani, nobody should ever be okay with letting you feel like this regardless of what happened. If he were really a good guy, he would put aside his predispositions and love you for the amazing, strong woman you are."

Dani's words came out in a whisper as she blinked back the wetness behind her lids. "I don't even know what love is."

Her roommate pursed her lips and stroked Dani's hair. "Love is sometimes timid, but when you find it, it's so true and real and strong that you'll have no doubt about its validity."

Dani wrinkled her mouth. "How do you know so much about love? Have you…gotten together with Kyle?"

A nervous laugh escaped Carolyn's lips, and her face flushed red. "Uh, no, sadly. My dating game is so bad I'll probably remain single for the rest of my life. I just read a lot of romance books…" She scratched her frazzled head and turned back to Dani. "But Emma said she knew she was in love with Chase because her heart melted with his smile or something… I, personally, think that's a pretty lame algorithm—"

Dani sucked in a shallow breath. "I was so sure about Tanner. I felt so good with him. But he didn't even say it back. That he loved me."

Carolyn furrowed her brow. "Excuse my language, but Tanner seems to be nothing but a callous, booger-flicking asshole. It wouldn't have even mattered if he said he *did* love you—he judged you for an accident that has haunted you for three years instead of judging you for the person you've become, and that's not love. Your past doesn't define you."

"Yes, it does. Killing someone is kind of a big deal," Dani sputtered, swallowing the lump in her throat. "Tanner's not the only one who sees me as a monster; my parents have always seen me that way, and now I've finally accepted it too. I've been hiding from my past for so long because I didn't want to admit Jeremy's death was my fault. But it was. I deliberately made bad choices that night, and it wasn't just one small bad choice—it was a series of them. And those choices go back to the years leading up to that night. My dad was only trying to protect me from myself." She paused and curled into a ball beneath the covers, struggling to control her fragmented breaths. "I don't deserve any special, absolving treatment. It's about time you accepted me for the monster that I am too, Carolyn."

Carolyn expelled a defeated sigh and wrinkled her brow. "Well, you're wrong. You're not a monster, Dani. I just hope one day you can see the overwhelming good in yourself." She stood and pursed her lips, staring down at Dani with a gleam in her eye. "And you don't need a guy to prove it to you."

Dani tossed and turned to dreams of playing lacrosse with her brother. Jeremy's hazel eyes danced as he chased her in their family's back yard. Sprinting ahead into the forest, she looked back, but he was no longer there. She searched for him among the tangle of trees, the branches and undergrowth wrapping around her limbs, suffocating her as she crawled through the brush.

Then she found him. He was splashed in red, bleeding out as the trees strangled him, cutting off his circulation. She cried and clawed at her own restraints even as they crushed the air from her, and Jeremy's hazel eyes dimmed on his pale face. It was her fault for leading him into the forest, trapping them both. She screamed and screamed for help that would never come.

Dani jerked awake in a cold sweat, panting furiously. She glanced around her dimly lit bedroom, coiling under the covers. But everywhere she looked, she saw him: her lacrosse stick, her pre-med textbooks, that damn USC hat from the bookstore sitting on her closet shelf… Every USC logo in her room was a stabbing reminder of what she'd done.

He would never grow old and happy; never marry the love of his life. He'd never fly to California to cheer Dani on during her lacrosse matches. He'd never get to have children, explore the world, or see the west coast beaches.

Her throat squeezed tight, every breath impaling her. Her head dropped into her hands, and she clutched at the bed covers, fighting to hold back tears.

When she glanced at the mirror hanging by her closet, dark, cold pits stared back at her. The long dirty-blonde hair she once adored was an ugly, tangled mess. Her nails were claws on weak limbs. She bore the reflection her parents and Tanner and the world had always seen: a despicable, horrid piece of filth.

She needed something—*anything*—to keep her going other than the medication locked away in her drawer. She couldn't have come this far just to give up; to restart that robotic, ignorant life with her meds.

Dr. Turner's words from months ago echoed in her mind, offering a glimpse of light. *"My door is always open should you need anything."*

Dani rolled over and grabbed her phone from the bedside table, opening an email from Dr. Turner she had dismissed from yesterday:

*How are you doing, Miss Torres? You missed today's Zoom meeting. You are aware of the bio compound analysis due this week?*

She let out a long exhale. On top of a ton of papers due this week and next, she had finals coming up. Out of all her professors, Turner was the only one who had bothered to reach out to her like a high school teacher might. He seemed to really be rooting for her to get through medical school, though she still didn't understand why.

*Maybe he's your answer.*

Swallowing the lump in her throat, she emailed him back, asking to set up a Zoom meeting later that day.

After dinner, Dani sat at her desk and opened her laptop, clicking on the Zoom link Turner had sent her.

His dark, contemplative face appeared on the screen a minute later, his large arms folded over a desk. "Good evening, Miss Torres. It's good to see you." His warm smile took her by surprise.

"Hi, Dr. Turner. How are you?"

He leaned back in his chair, scratching his chin. "Not bad, not bad. I'm finally getting used to the online transition. But how are you doing?"

Her fingers twirled the pencil on her desk. "I'm so sorry for missing the past two classes, Dr. Turner. I…haven't been doing so well. With the whole pandemic thing."

"I'm sorry to hear that." He pushed his glasses up his nose. "I feel it's incredibly important during these times to check in with my students. Is there anything I can do to help?"

Dani stiffened, glancing down. "It's… I'm not sure…" She trailed off, fighting to keep her emotions under control. Taking a deep breath, she forced the words out. "Sometimes I just feel like…my mistakes hold me down."

She gripped the edge of her seat tightly as Dr. Turner studied her for a few silent seconds. Then he leaned forward and clasped his hands, his gaze lowering to the papers in front of him.

"A few years ago, my son Jessie wrote an article for the *LA Times*. He analyzed the most common trait among the most successful people in the world by interviewing many scholars, political leaders, and CEOs. One particularly common trait among them was that they were all ambitious, like yourself." He drew his attention back to the screen and flashed an inquisitive smile. "But the other most common trait among them was that they had all failed tremendously. They failed spectacularly, time and time again, but despite their peers' criticisms, despite the odds stacked against them, they continued fighting."

He paused to let that sink in. It was as if he had read her thoughts.

"But history doesn't remember people's failures, Dani. History only remembers their successes; their ability to overcome their failures."

Her eyelids stung as she realized the truth in his words.

She couldn't define herself by her failures. She had to suck it up and move on.

Rise above her failures.

"And one more thing," Turner said as he pushed his glasses back a second time. "Let's not forget the mantra of the school you chose to attend." He held up two fingers in USC's V-for-victory sign. "Fight on, Miss Torres."

Her mind grasped at a memory, and her brother's words surfaced from that day behind the giant lodgepole tree by the creek: *"Do what you want to do, study where you want to study. Lacrosse will help... You're smart, Dani. Really smart. Don't let your gift go to waste."*

She closed her eyes as her memory shifted, and she was crouching on her bed three years ago, finally somewhat stable after having cried her eyes dry for months. Her eyes grazed the twelve college offer letters sprawled in front of her. She had researched all of their medical programs, but one school in particular caught her eye. It had an exceptional med school *and* lacrosse team.

*"I wanted to go to California and see the beaches..."*

The University of Southern California. That was the college she would attend...

Dani lifted her head from her hands, scanning the pre-med books on her desk. Medical school was what she had come here for; what she had hoped would save her from that dark night, in a distant promise to Jeremy.

But maybe it wasn't just that promise that had kept her going, she realized now. Maybe it was the desire to prove to herself she didn't have to be defined by the bad decisions of her past.

Maybe, somewhere deep down, she had always believed she was capable of redemption.

*Fight on, Miss Torres.*

Dr. Turner's words of encouragement reverberated against her skull. Maybe there was something about USC's fighting spirit that had called to Jeremy. Wasn't that why she was here at USC too—to keep fighting despite her faults, despite her failures?

Jeremy wouldn't want her to keep crying about him. It wouldn't change anything; she couldn't bring him back. He'd want her to move on. To fight on.

But why was it so damn hard?

*May*

DANI LAY ON HER BED A FEW DAYS LATER IN FRONT OF HER CELL biology textbook, reading as much as she could in preparation for her finals next week. Dr. Turner's encouragement had helped push her past a steep roadblock and ground her in her goals once again. She just had to get through finals and finish preparing for her murder in the summer.

An icy chill crawled up Dani's spine, and she froze. *MCAT*. She just needed to finish preparing for her *MCAT* in the summer.

But that sinister voice whispered in the back of her brain. *"Murderer…"*

No. Dani's past failures didn't define her. It was her successes that mattered. She had to keep looking forward.

She bit her tongue and rolled over on her bed, staring at Channing

Tatum's taunting eyes on the opposite wall. "How do I get out of my damn head, Channing?" she asked. He stared back at her with his sexy smile, frozen in time.

She sighed and picked up her phone from the bed, scrolling through her messages. One of Dustin's texts caught her eye, dated a month ago. **Let me know if you need anything. I'll always be here if you need someone to talk to.**

A small piece of her warmed. She had been so broken that day she'd abandoned him at the hospital. *God, I'm sorry for responding so late to your texts, Dustin. I was such a shitshow.*

She found herself missing their thoughtful conversations, his crooked smile, and his sarcastic remarks. Had it really been a month since they'd seen each other at the protest?

How was he doing?

She shot him a quick text. **Hey, how are your shifts at the hospital going?** Hopefully, his work wasn't taking too much of a toll on him.

Lying back on her bed, she tossed her phone in the air and stared at Channing Tatum's taunting smile again. After waiting for five minutes to no avail, she crept downstairs and made herself a bowl of cereal before joining Carolyn on the couch. They sat through an episode of *Grey's Anatomy*, Dani glancing at her phone every now and then. But it was still blank.

It wasn't like him to not answer her texts. Even when he'd been busy at the hospital during his clerkships, he'd always texted her back during his breaks. Was he being overworked?

When the episode of *Grey's Anatomy* ended, she headed back upstairs to take a shower. She was at the bedroom door with a towel when her phone buzzed on the bed. Heart racing, she took two long strides across the room and swiped the device from her comforter.

It was her mom, wanting to Skype.

Dani flipped the phone back onto the bed with a long sigh before retreating to the bathroom.

After her shower, Dani passed the time by resuming her reading assignment. When she finished that, she returned her biology essay while keeping an eye on her phone, her lids feeling heavier with each word she typed…

*"Dani, where are you going?" Jeremy's worried voice carried behind*

*her as she trudged through the thick brush, the tall pine trees casting dark shadows around her.*

*"Away from Dad!" she yelled over her shoulder.*

*"I don't know about this—it's getting dark."*

*Dani scoffed and marched on. "Don't you want to see the beach? We're almost there!"*

*She glimpsed an incandescent light shimmering through the trees. The Pacific Ocean! I can see the sun's reflection! Dani sprinted forward, jumping over logs and skirting across a narrow creek in the direction of the shimmering light. Pushing aside branches, she broke into a clearing, and the light engulfed her.*

*Except it was not sunlight reflecting off the waves.*

*The light was from a truck's headlights. And in the grass, crumpled, was a man. She knelt in front of the person, shaking, and gazed upon dirty-blond—no, it was brown hair, and his eyes…they were blue.*

*"Where were you, Dani?" he wheezed, his face paling. "The virus… I can't breathe…"*

*"No! Dustin!" she screamed, laying her hands on his chest. When she pulled them back, they were soaked in blood—*

Dani jolted upright, panting, her heart hammering a hole in her chest. Her eyes darted around the room, latching onto the familiar Channing Tatum and lacrosse memorabilia hanging on the walls, the damp covers, the bedside table…

She was back in her apartment.

Dani sagged on her elbows, her limbs weak. Dustin had been the one dying in her dream, not Jeremy. She hadn't been able to save him from the coronavirus…

Her head fell in her hands, and she breathed deeply until her pounding heart lulled.

*God, what is happening to me. Am I that paranoid?*

She glanced at the clock: 9:20 a.m. She'd slept through the night? Her eyes found her phone on the bed next to her laptop, and she quickly picked it up.

Still no response.

Why hadn't he replied? Surely, he would have seen her text by now. He never went so much as a few hours without responding.

Her clammy fingers dialed his number. It went straight to voicemail.

A shaky breath whooshed out of her. **Call me.**

Now it seemed their positions had been flipped, and *he* wasn't the one returning her texts.

An idea popped into her head, and she pulled her laptop from her desk, opening a Google search. She clicked on the first link that took her to the *LA Times* website and scrolled through their list of editors and columnists.

There he was. Jessie Turner.

An email was listed next to his name, and she clicked on it, opening a new window.

"Hi, Jessie, it's Dani Torres, Dustin's friend from the protest last month…" she wrote. "He hasn't been answering his phone, and I'm curious if you've heard from him?"

She hoped he got her message and it wasn't filtered to some weird inbox. Five minutes later, an email pinged on her phone. She opened it and read the short reply:

*That's not good. He hasn't been answering my texts lately either, though he usually does whenever he gets home from work. Last I heard from him was a few weeks ago, and he seemed really stressed out. I know he and his family are going through a lot. I'd stop by his house, but I'm in Atlanta for a week. Maybe you can check on him?*

Below that was an address in Culver City.

A few hours later, an Uber dropped her off in front of a small blue house in a cute West Los Angeles neighborhood. The streets were eerily quiet like the rest of the city, and a chill crept up her spine as she pictured a zombie creeping around the house in an apocalyptic movie scene.

She raised an eyebrow at Dustin's Honda Accord parked alongside another car in the driveway. She'd taken a chance by coming here—it was more likely he was at work considering many LA hospitals were understaffed, nurses working overtime, according to the news.

She walked up to the front door and knocked. "Hello? Dustin, it's me, Dani!" Her usual bright voice sounded worried and distorted through her mask.

No answer. But his car was here.

She knocked again and waited but got the same silent response.

Conscious she might be acting like a creep, she meandered to the window and peered through as inconspicuously as she could. The blinds had been drawn slightly, and an empty living room stared back at her, no sign of life. She walked toward the side gate—

"Dani?"

She halted in her tracks and spun on her heel, spotting Dustin staring at her from the porch of the house next door. She brightened when she saw him, but her happiness dissipated as she scanned his disheveled state.

His brown hair had grown over the tips of his ears since she'd last seen him, and his normally clean-cut beard ran scraggly below his mask. He wore wrinkled sweats and a Nike T-shirt—all in all, not the look of the well-put-together physician she knew.

He stared at her with sullen, darkened eyes. "What the hell are you doing here? How'd you get my address?" His voice was hoarse.

Dani clasped her palms, shame flooding her cheeks. "I'm sorry for showing up out of the blue. I, uh…I wanted to talk to you, but you weren't replying to my texts. I was worried."

His expression softened, and he glanced off to the side. "Sorry. My phone has been off…" He rubbed his neck.

Dani took a few timid steps toward him. "What's been going on?"

He didn't answer, only shifted his gaze to the street.

"Is everything okay?" she asked softly.

"Dani, go home," he ushered sternly, but she didn't budge. He shook his head and put a hand on his hip. "You shouldn't be in contact with me," he added gruffly.

A woman's voice called from the house. "Are you going to keep chatting with her outside all day, Dustin? Invite the sweet girl in!"

Dustin turned toward the door from the porch. "It's a health risk, Bettie."

"You know that line doesn't work with me, Dustin. And she's just one person—I'm sure the risk is minimal."

Dani adjusted the fabric above her mouth. "I have my mask, and I haven't really been around people besides my roommates." *Well, except for Tanner.* She took another hesitant step in his direction. She couldn't leave now when something was clearly wrong. *Fight on, Miss Torres.*

"Jessie is worried about you too," she pleaded. "He's the one who gave me your address."

He scrunched his eyes at her, contemplating. After a moment, as if understanding he had no other option, he expelled a large breath. "Fine." His hand ran through his tousled brown hair. "Keep your mask on." He gestured for her to follow him inside the house.

The living room was small and tidy, the floral furniture and curtains adding a '60s fashion design. The wood paneling on the wall also seemed a bit outdated, but Dani supposed it complemented the furniture well.

Mel sat on the couch with a plate of Mexican food, chewing away. "I thought I recognized you walking outside," she mumbled through a mouthful.

"Hi, Mel. How are you?" Dani greeted with a smile before realizing Mel couldn't see her expression through the mask.

Mel's eyes dimmed. She lowered her head and gave a small shrug, contrasting the peppy little girl Dani remembered.

"This is my neighbor, Bettie," Dustin introduced, and Dani turned to see an old lady with curly white hair emerge from the kitchen. Her soft, friendly eyes beamed, and her bright pink lips stretched into a smile.

Lightning shot through Dani's nerves.

Dani knew her. She was the old lady from Uniqlo on Black Friday.

Dani nodded in acknowledgment of the woman, but it was a nod flushed with shame. *Does she remember me?*

"Hello there, honey. It's good to see Dustin with some company after all this time. Would you like some rice and beans?" Bettie asked. If she recognized Dani, she didn't show any sign.

"No, thank you, I just had lunch. But it smells delicious." Dani rubbed an arm and turned to Dustin, awkwardly waiting for him to do something.

He tilted his head. "Come on—let's go in here." Dustin led her to a back bedroom and shut the door behind her. She sat on the bed biting her lip as he walked to the far end and planted himself a fair distance away from her.

After what felt like an eternity, Dani asked, "Is there a reason you aren't at work?"

He scratched the scruff beneath his mask before meeting her eyes, his eyebrows drawn. "I was dismissed from work for a while."

Dani's eyebrows went up. "Why? Is everything okay?"

He looked away and shook his head, leaning forward on his knees. "No, it's not." He hesitated, and Dani's heart picked up pace.

What was going on?

He inhaled deeply. "My mom… She's sick with COVID. An ambulance picked her up a week ago."

Dani's eyes widened, her stomach dropping. "Oh my god, I'm so sorry." Her mind raced as she connected the dots of his withdrawal. What could she say? Dani had isolated herself in a similar manner, helplessly withdrawn, only a few weeks ago, yet she hadn't gotten through that too well. She did not have any valid consolation to offer him.

And his situation was different. Dani hadn't been able to handle a bit of pain from three years ago, while his mom was sick in a hospital in the middle of a pandemic, possibly fighting for her life, while his dad was in jail. How could she begin to relate—or offer comfort, for that matter?

After a minute of searching for the right words, she decided to remain silent and let Dustin speak when he was ready.

He stayed quiet a long time, his face drained of emotion. She had never seen him like this before. What had happened to his witty, optimistic attitude? She was supposed to be the one who was hopelessly depressed, not him.

And that depressed state was something she had earned; he hadn't. She deserved the gut-wrenching pain that lanced through her heart every time she thought of her brother. Dustin's mom getting sick was something completely out of his control.

Finally, he met her gaze, grim defeat washing through his ocean blue eyes. "They intubated her yesterday. Mel and I FaceTimed her right before, and she could barely lift her head to see us…" His next words were strained. "She is suffering, and there's nothing I can do." He punched the bed before crumpling, his head falling into his hands.

Dani swallowed, her fingers squeezing the bed cover. *He needs someone to care for him. He's broken, just like you were. And still are.*

She scooted closer to him and reached out a tentative hand. When she touched his arm, he flinched slightly.

"You should leave," he ordered, raising his head. "I've been exposed to sick patients."

"Don't worry about me," she said softly. "I'm staying with you."

## Forty-Six

*May*

DANI AWOKE THE NEXT MORNING TO THE SMELL OF FRYING bacon. She sat up on the floor in Dustin's spare sleeping bag and stretched her arms, glancing up at the guest bed Mel had been sleeping in.

The covers were in disarray, and the bed was vacant. Dustin's little sister sure was an early riser.

Dani squinted through tired eyes at the digital clock on the bedside table: 8:04 a.m. It was the earliest she had awoken since quarantine.

She yawned and stood in her checkered pajama bottoms and T-shirt, stretching her arms to the ceiling. She was thankful Bettie and the Mottleys had agreed to have her stay over while their mom six in the hospital. Dani's roommates had been skeptical when she returned to the apartment yesterday to grab a pack of clothes and school supplies, but they conceded in the end.

An elaborate breakfast display greeted Dani when she crossed the living room and entered the kitchen. Dustin had mentioned Bettie was an extremely generous old lady, and it certainly seemed so the longer Dani stayed at the house. Yet in spite of all that, Dani still wasn't sure if Bettie remembered her.

Mel was perched at the table in checkered pajama bottoms, already digging into a plate of half-eaten pancakes, bacon, and eggs. Her large brown eyes shone when Dani approached them. "About time, Dani! You'll never get breakfast at Bettie's house if you sleep in."

Dani's mouth quirked, and she draped her hands on the back of one of the table chairs. She watched Bettie fry bacon in a saucepan, fully dressed in jeans, a casual button-down shirt, and a flowery apron.

"She's right, you know. No food if you sleep in at this house," the old woman teased with a wink.

Why was Bettie being so nice to her after everything that had happened? She must not remember Dani.

"That's so nice of you," Dani replied, glancing around the kitchen. "I suppose Dustin isn't aware of the house rules?"

Bettie's pale blue eyes dipped slightly. "Oh, he knows."

Mel scoffed, stabbing her fork into some eggs. "Don't worry about him. He's been a downer lately."

Bettie brightened and turned back to the task at hand. "Come help yourself to a plate while the food's still hot!" She plucked some pieces of bacon off the frying pan and onto a dish with some tongs. "There's a stack of pancakes over here waiting to be devoured."

Dani smiled and picked up a clean plate from the table. "I admire your early-bird routine," she told Bettie as she piled two pancakes on her plate, followed by eggs and bacon. "I barely made it to my 9:00 a.m. classes on time."

Bettie waved her hand in dismissal as Dani skirted around her by the stove. "9:00 a.m.? Honey, I'm up at 6:00 a.m. every day. My old bones won't let me sleep any later. And you can't let all that sunlight go to waste!"

Dani's lips perked up as she sat herself across from Mel at the table. "You got me there."

Mel scooped up the last of her food and brought her plate to the sink. "Thank you for breakfast, Bettie. Do you mind if I watch some TV?"

Bettie smiled as she dipped beneath the counter and plucked some dish soap from the cabinet. "Of course not, dear."

Mel beamed and marched out of the kitchen to the living room.

Dani chewed for a silent moment as the question that had been bothering her all day yesterday crept to mind. She swallowed and set down her fork. "Bettie, can I ask you something?" She paused and glanced down before taking a deep breath. "Why'd you do it? On Black Friday?"

Bettie's head turned from where she was scrubbing Mel's dish at the sink. "Do what, dear?"

Dani bit her lip and answered quietly, "Tell the officer to…loosen the cuffs."

Bettie turned her head back to the sink and stacked the clean plate on the rack above the counter. She turned off the faucet and wiped her hands on a towel before joining Dani at the table.

"I had wondered if you found out I was the one who gave the police information about your friends."

Dani's jaw dropped. "You did what?"

Bettie smiled and folded her arms on the table, replying in a soft tone. "When I saw you come out in handcuffs, that couple running frantically away beforehand looked pretty suspicious, especially since the girl was with you earlier that day. I phoned in a description of the young man from the Gap and the girl, but I only remembered to do so a couple months later—my memory isn't the best anymore. Anyways, I hope those kids were dealt with accordingly."

Dani bit her lip. "Haley—the girl—told me Mitch was arrested a few months ago because he was on probation." She looked away from the old lady's piercing gaze. "Mitch…stole from the cop and then left in a hurry. I was sort of framed."

"I'm glad there is a bit of justice in this broken-down world." The old lady's pale blue eyes shimmered. "My answer to your question applies to both the loosening of the cuffs and the phoning in of the couple. I did it because something about you didn't strike me as criminal. You looked like someone who could use some kindness. And people in distress," she said with an upward glance as Dustin's disheveled figure came into view, "often find kindness is most present when it is least expected." She winked and stood, dusting her hands along her apron before turning to Dustin. "Good morning, sunshine! The day is only half over." She placed a hand on his chest before brushing past him into the living room.

"Good morning," he mumbled as Bettie planted herself in the chair by the front door.

His brown hair was tousled, and he was dressed in a pair of basketball shorts and a tank top. Dani bristled, her lips tugging upward at the sight of her mentor in such an informal, disheveled state.

When Dustin's hollow eyes slid toward her, his shoulders tensed. Dani wondered if he'd forgotten she stayed over.

Dani's cheeks lifted. "Morning, Dustin. There's still some pancakes and eggs if you want some, although I took the last of the bacon. Mel ate most of it though."

He snorted and entered the small kitchen. "Thanks." He picked up a plate from the table and walked it over to the stove, stacking it with the remaining pancakes and eggs. "Thank you, Bettie."

"You're welcome, honey," she responded from her chair, pulling a book into her lap.

He poured himself a glass of milk and sat opposite Dani in Mel's previous seat. His once bright blue eyes were strained and sullen.

"Sleep well?" Dani asked as she picked at her pancakes.

"Not really," he murmured, stuffing eggs into his mouth. "You?"

"I did."

It wasn't completely true. Bettie's guest bedroom floor wasn't the best bed, but it still beat the old sofa. Luckily, Mel had enthusiastically offered her bedroom floor as an alternative when she saw Dani struggling to get comfortable. She'd gushed all yesterday about Dani's staying over, driving Dustin up the wall.

Dustin poured syrup over his pancakes, not meeting her gaze. "That's good." Setting the syrup bottle down, he locked eyes with her and raised a skeptical eyebrow. "Guess the mask thing doesn't apply anymore?"

Dani bit her lip. "I...I'm sorry. I forgot."

"Dustin, don't be unreasonable, dear," Bettie tsked from the living room. "We are all breathing the same air, and we won't be acting like she's a toxic biohazard while she's here."

Dani glanced down, the few remaining bites of her pancakes

suddenly looking unappetizing. Dustin continued eating in silence, offering no other attempt to engage her in conversation. It was alarming to see him so…detached. Apathetic? She didn't know what to do.

She stood and walked to the sink, rinsing her plate before turning back to Dustin. "Do you want to go for a run with me?" She nodded to the golden retriever watching them curiously by Bettie's feet. "Max looks like he could use some fresh air." Dani wanted to say, *You* look like you could use some fresh air," but decided against it.

He tightened his lips. "Nah, I'm okay. Thanks though."

She looked to the side. "All right, but he really wants to run with *you*, not me."

"I'll go with you, Dani," Mel piped in from the sofa. "Dustin's being a jerk."

Dustin rolled his eyes as he raised a piece of bacon to his mouth.

Dani leaned on the counter, scratching her cheek. She shook away her disappointment and shot Mel a playful smile through the bar window. "You run?" She couldn't blame the nine-year-old for missing Dani's intent to get Dustin's mind off things.

"No, but I'll ride my bike. I just have to grab it from next door." She sprung off the couch.

Dani laughed. "Deal. I'll meet you outside after I change, all right?"

Mel nodded and Dani retreated to Mel's guest room to change into running shorts, a tank top, and Nike shoes. As she pulled her hair into a ponytail, her thoughts drifted to Dustin and strategies for how she could ease some of his pain. When she had closed herself off after her flashbacks, it had been Carolyn and Dr. Turner who had reached out to her, but it hadn't been without effort on their part.

She smoothed the hem of her tank top with a sigh. Maybe she would think of something during her run.

She exited into the living room, leashed Max, and led the excited, drooling golden retriever out the door just as Mel wheeled her bike onto the sidewalk.

Dani's mouth tugged into a smile at the sight of the bright blue helmet perched Mel's ponytail of long brown hair. The girl had changed into a flashy pair of black-and-white checkered shoes, complimenting her jeans and button-down T-shirt.

Mel's face shone brightly as she approached Dani and Max on

the sidewalk. "Mmm, do you want to take Max to a dog park? Dustin sometimes takes Max to this one place, though I'm not really sure where it is."

"No problem." Dani dug her phone out of her pocket and searched for the nearest dog park. It wasn't too far. "Got it!" She began jogging down the street, tugging Max along, as Mel kicked her bike into gear behind her.

"So how have things been going for you?" Dani asked as Mel pulled up beside her on the sidewalk. "I bet you're bummed you don't get to play softball, huh?"

"Yeah, I really miss it," Mel pouted with a dip of her chin.

Dani wrinkled her mouth. "I know the feeling. I miss playing lacrosse at USC. My team was doing really well—we were undefeated! I thought for sure we would make it all the way to the PAC-12 Championship."

"No way! That sucks," Mel exclaimed, her mouth pulling into a frown. "I really want to play softball in college. I'm pretty good at it."

Dani grinned. She couldn't help but wonder if that was what she sounded like when she was Mel's age. "I bet you are. Balancing sports with college is a lot of hard work, but it's super fun."

"Is it hard? Getting a sports scholarship." Her large brown eyes shone with curiosity.

Dani's mouth curved into a half-smile. "It definitely isn't easy. My dad made me practice every day, and I ended up missing out on hanging out with my friends and doing other fun things, but..." Her voice fizzled as her thoughts shifted to all the missed opportunities lacrosse had stolen from her.

What had she been about to say? If given the chance to do it all over again, she wouldn't want a lacrosse scholarship? She would want a different life free of the pressure to live up to her dad's high expectations?

Mel saved her from finishing her sentence. "When my dad came to visit, he made me practice softball with him too." Mel paused, and the silence was filled by Max's harsh panting and the clomp of Dani's tennis shoes. "I really miss him sometimes, but I'm trying to forget about him because he's a bad influence," she finished.

Dani glanced at Mel, her throat tightening. Dustin had only talked about his dad once, and it was a difficult topic for him at that.

The mention of their dad summoned an image of Franc Torres wagging his thick finger at Dani as she labored to and fro on the lacrosse field.

"I miss my mom too," Mel went on. "I keep thinking of the little things she'd do with us to make us laugh, and I miss her peanut butter cookies. I guess when people are gone, it makes you wish you had more time with them."

Dani looked away at a lone car passing down the street, swallowing against the burning lump in her throat. "You're right. It does make you wish you cherished those moments with them. I never valued family time growing up…and you can't really get that time back." She fought to keep her tone level.

Mel nodded softly. "I can tell Dustin isn't doing so good, but he keeps shutting me out. I just want him to know we're here for each other, through the good and bad."

Dani couldn't help but marvel at the strength that emitted from this little girl. Mel had needed to mature at a much quicker rate than the average child, having been raised without a permanent father in her life and her brother and mom working around the clock.

*"We're here for each other, through the good and bad."* Mel had only said a small thing, but as the words repeated in Dani's mind, it sent a wave of emotion through her limbs. She scratched her cheek before glancing back at the girl and offering a small smile.

The dog park was further than Dani thought, and when they finally arrived, she was glad to let Max loose and have a moment to relax on the grass. The withdrawals of not having lacrosse conditioning every day were taking its toll on her sore legs.

Dogs of every size and shape scurried around the wide park as owners kept their distance on the grass, the benches blocked off with yellow tape. Mel plopped cross-legged on the grass next to Dani as they watched Max frolic around the park chasing other dogs, free as a bird.

"Max looks like he's making some friends," Dani observed, leaning back on her hands as she watched the dog zip after a cocker spaniel.

Mel giggled, loose wasps of brown hair wafting out of her ponytail on the cool breeze. "Max is the best dog. He keeps me company when Dustin is moping around and Bettie is asleep." She tilted her head to the side. "Do you have any pets in your family?"

Dani stretched out her legs as she shook her head. "My mom always liked dogs, but my dad thought they were too much of a responsibility. They didn't agree on a lot of things."

Mel turned her head to the side and picked at a dandelion by her legs. "My parents always argued too. Mom didn't like it when Dad visited, and she yelled at him even when he tried to do nice things for me and Dustin."

Dani's gut clenched for the girl. Every small little thing seemed to circle back to the broken state of Mel's family, similar to Dani's own life. Dani dragged her palm across the grass, pursing her lips.

"I'm sorry they didn't get along. It's hard seeing your parents fight all the time."

Mel shrugged as she tore off a leaf from the dandelion. "That's just the way they are. I know Mom doesn't like him, so I'm glad Dad stayed away for most of the time." She ripped off another leaf, balled it tightly, and threw it a good distance away.

"Wow, you have an impressive softball throw!" Dani exclaimed with a grin, hoping to wipe away any sinking thoughts about Mel's grim situation.

It seemed to work; Mel's face was zapped of any melancholy. "That throw was nothing. You should see me at my games." Her mouth slanted as she folded her legs.

Dani couldn't help the smile that stole across her lips. "I bet you're a legend."

Mel's face shone brightly as she watched Max spring across the park. "Uh, I'm only the best player ever. Seriously." She rolled her eyes playfully, and they both erupted into laughter.

With every laugh and smile shared with the nine-year-old girl, Dani's mind drifted further away from all that had been worrying her.

By the time they arrived back at Bettie's house, it was almost 1:00 p.m. Dani wiped her sweaty brow as she entered the house with Max while Mel stowed her bike next door. Dani brightened when she spotted Dustin and Bettie lounging in the living room, staring at the TV. Bettie smiled warmly from her chair in the corner, while Dustin's smile from the couch was brief and half-hearted.

Dani grinned uncertainly as she unleashed Max, and he panted over to his bed in the corner and plopped down, winded. *I feel you, Max. Me too.* She stretched her aching calves and turned to Bettie.

"Have you already eaten?"

Bettie smoothed her hands along her stretchy brown pants. "Oh no, dear. I was just about to make some sandwiches."

Dani straightened, planting her hands on her hips. "Don't worry—I've got it! I'm happy to help out, especially after the wonderful breakfast you made." She turned to her mentor. "You want one too, Dustin?"

He shifted his knee and shook his head slowly, his gaze devoid of life. He had changed into a pair of jeans and a T-shirt, but his untrimmed beard and slumping arms were a sharp reminder of the dismal state he was still in.

She shrugged and headed to the kitchen, filling two glasses of water just as Mel waltzed in behind her. Dani handed her a glass, and they both chugged the water in one gulp, clinking their empty glasses on the table before sharing a smile.

"Are we gonna eat some lunch?" Mel asked as Dani began shuffling through the cupboards, grabbing paper plates and napkins.

"Yep. I'm making sandwiches." Dani opened the refrigerator and eyed the contents, contemplating different options before deciding on a simple PB&J. "Whew, the fridge feels so nice!" she exclaimed, fanning her sweaty face as she pulled out the jelly.

Mel lifted her shirt, wafting some air to her stomach. "It *is* pretty hot in here. I'm gonna eat outside." As soon as Dani handed her a plate, the girl skipped through the front door.

Dani carried three more sandwich plates out of the kitchen, handing one to Bettie, who accepted it with a grateful twinkle in her eye. She made her way over to Dustin and held a sandwich out to him expectantly.

He frowned at Dani's creation. "Really, I'm fine."

Her extended hand didn't budge. "Take it. I know you haven't eaten."

After a few seconds, his hard gaze loosened, and he took the plate. "Thank you," he murmured before taking a bite.

Dani gave a small smile and sat beside him on the couch with her own PB&J. She watched him eat silently, her finger tracing the seam of the couch cushion as she contemplated what to say. She swiveled her head toward the front door to double-check Mel was still outside before turning back to Dustin.

"Remember when we were in your car on the last day of the volunteer program, and you told me it doesn't hurt to hope despite all the bad shit?"

He snorted and whacked her generously crafted sandwich on the plate. "I just said that 'cause it seemed nice at the time. It was really bullshit."

It was the equivalent of tearing a knife through her gut.

She tried with great effort to brush his comment aside. *He's in pain. He doesn't know what he's talking about.* Her voice softened. "Your mom's gonna beat this, I know it."

He closed his eyes tightly, his teeth grazing his bottom lip.

*Fight on, Miss Torres.* Dani shifted on the couch and set her PB&J on the coffee table before turning back to him. "I think you were right. It doesn't hurt to stay positive. Your mom is young, healthy, and strong. If anyone can get through this, it's her."

Dustin swallowed and set his plate on the table next to hers, turmoil swallowing his features. "You don't know what it's like to see patients, day after day, come through the hospital looking like she did and come out in body bags. You haven't seen their faces, the number of nurses I've talked to who told me how many 'young and healthy' patients they had to see die before their eyes." He paused, his Adam's apple bouncing. His elbows planted on his knees, and he projected a dangerous gaze. "You know what the percentage of survival is for people who are put on ventilators?"

Dani stared back at him with a heavy heart, bracing the couch cushion tightly.

"Dustin, honey," Bettie cautioned from her recliner. Her worried eyes swiveled between the two of them as she straightened in her chair.

"Fifty percent! Fifty percent." His voice broke on the last word, and he brought a hand to his face, shielding his eyes. It was a few seconds before he lifted his head, his tone sharp. "So don't tell me how to act, dammit. My mom is dying, so do me a favor and don't sugarcoat it."

Dani grimaced as his words stabbed her. But the pain was nothing compared to the horror that jolted her body when she caught Mel's frozen figure standing just inside the front door.

Dustin followed Dani's gaze to Mel, and he stiffened.

Mel clenched a fist. "Why do you keep being so rude to Dani? She's only trying to help!"

The nine-year-old's defense took Dani completely off-guard. "It's okay, Mel," she soothed, trying to keep her hands from trembling.

"No, it's not okay!" Mel burrowed on, her heated eyes turning glassy. "All he's been doing is moping around while the rest of us try to be hopeful. It's not fair to Mom!"

Bettie stood from her chair and approached Mel, placing a hand on her shoulder.

Dustin scuffled a hand through his hair. "I'm done with this shit," he mumbled, standing from the couch. He disappeared down the hall, his barely-eaten sandwich staring daggers at Dani.

Dani looked over at Mel, her gut tightening with trepidation. Bettie smoothed back Mel's hair as the frustration drained from her large brown eyes. "He doesn't have the right to act like that. She's my mom too. He doesn't get to just…give up. It's not…" she faded out as Bettie pulled her into a tight hug.

As they embraced, Dani saw herself standing on the rim of a private family moment she had no business partaking in, let alone observing. She sucked in a deep breath, struggling against the guilt wrenching through her chest.

Staying here was a bad idea. She was just making things worse.

She stood, walked into Mel's room, and collected her things, bringing them to the living room.

Bettie looked up as she approached, her pale blue eyes widening. She released Mel and turned to face Dani. "Where are you going, dear? You just got here."

Dani shook her head, her eyes down. "I'm sorry, I can't stay."

"No!" Mel objected, stepping toward her in a panic. "Why?"

For the first time, Dani didn't know what to say to the nine-year-old. "I'm…not helping things."

"Dani, dear, you have helped tremendously. You'd better believe it!" Bettie's brows drew as she placed a gentle hand on Dani's arm.

"Dani, please stay. At least until tomorrow?" Mel reached for Dani's hand, and the gesture tugged at her heart. "Just one more night. Please." Her eyes were a mixture of hope and sorrow, and Dani couldn't help but feel her pain. The girl had been abandoned by so many—her dad, her mom, and now her brother. As much as Dani didn't want to involve herself with the Mottleys' family affairs, she didn't want to be just another person who abandoned the nine-year-old in her time of need.

Dustin may not have wanted Dani around, but Mel did. The least Dani could do was stay for one more night.

Dani expelled a small sigh and nodded. It was hard to argue with the sweet girl, especially after the fun day they'd spent together. "I'll stay the night, Mel. But I'm leaving in the morning."

Dani couldn't sleep. She shifted in the sleeping bag on the hard carpet by Mel's bed, staring at the ceiling.

Dustin's ominous ventilator statistic floated through her mind, eating at her.

He had been so broken earlier; so inaccessible. She tried to picture horrific scenes at the hospital and the faces of the sick patients he'd described. She knew he kept seeing his mom in their place, her arms stabbed with needles as she clung to life, her only tether to the world a breathing tube that was shoved mercilessly down her throat.

Just like Jeremy.

The image of Rachel's unconscious, sunken face morphed into her brother's, and Dani recalled the way he had looked, pale and lifeless, in the ICU unit. She had been so horrified, furious at the doctors who couldn't save him, before turning her rage back onto herself. *She* was the one who had stolen his life, not the doctors. It was all *her* fault. She had ruined everything…

Dani yanked herself back to the present. What the hell was her problem? This wasn't about *her;* it was about Dustin and Mel. Their mom was fighting for her life, hanging on by a thread, while Dani was here sulking in her own problems. It was disgusting.

She choked back a sob.

This virus, it wasn't a game. People old, young, weak, and strong were dying every day in the thousands. Lacrosse wasn't coming back. This wouldn't just blow over, and life wouldn't go back to normal as quickly as she had thought.

She rolled over and shifted her gaze to Mel's sleeping figure. She watched the rise and fall of her shoulders and smiled softly.

Dani had always wanted a sister, always wanted that girl-to-girl talk you couldn't get with a brother. She admired how strong the girl was, smiling and optimistic when her mom was in such a dire condition. Dani hoped she could be strong like Mel one day.

Suddenly, a small cry escaped Mel's lips, and her shoulders trembled.

Dani sat up and shrugged the sleeping bag off herself, watching Mel carefully. The girl squirmed under the covers, her cries coming more sporadically.

Dani crawled to her feet and eased herself behind Mel, wrapping her arms around her curled form. "Shh, it's okay, hon. It's okay."

Mel bristled against her, gasping as tears rolled down her cheeks. She rolled over and buried her head and arms into Dani's chest. The gesture chipped at Dani's heart as she remembered that whatever strength this girl possessed, she was carrying a burden far too large for anyone to carry, let alone someone her age.

"Don't go," Mel managed to whisper in between sobs, her fingers tightening around Dani's T-shirt. Was she having a nightmare about her mom? Or was she talking to Dani?

Dani stroked Mel's long brown hair, struggling to swallow as she studied her.

She saw a familiar frightened girl—someone alone, overlooked, and never good enough. Someone who just wanted to be loved and told that everything would be all right when things were going terribly, terribly wrong.

Dani kissed Mel's head and hugged her tight. She couldn't leave Mel tomorrow, not like this.

Not like this.

She brushed away the girl's tears and whispered, "I'm here. It's all right. Shh, it's all right. I'm staying."

## *Forty-Seven*

*May*

THE NEXT AFTERNOON, DANI KNOCKED ON DUSTIN'S DOOR after helping Mel with her homework. "Want to play a boardgame with Mel and me?" she asked with a hopeful smile. He had been tucked away in his room ever since yesterday afternoon when Dani had so graciously failed at consoling him. Maybe today he was feeling a bit better.

"No thanks," was his muffled response.

Dani caved and retreated down the hall to join Mel on the couch. She clearly still wasn't helping things.

*Calm down, Dani. Remember what he's going through.*

Mel scooped the dice into a cup and shook, shifting her gaze to Dani. "I told you, it's no use. He would only ruin our fun anyways." She rolled and perked upward on the cushions. "Full house! I'm totally gonna win this round." She peered over Dani's shoulder at the Yahtzee score sheet and flashed Dani a smile, but Dani's mind wasn't on the game.

Maybe it was time Dani heeded Bettie's words and put in a greater effort to show Dustin she was there for him. Although she may never be a good problem solver, maybe she could still attempt to be useful somehow. She should make more of an effort to get past his walls, to show him she still cared, even if he tried to push her away.

An hour later, Mel stuffed the game onto a bookshelf in the corner of the room and turned on an episode of SpongeBob. Dani fiddled with the drawstrings of her sweatshirt, contemplating how to get through to Dustin, as Mel snuggled beside her.

So far, nothing she'd tried had helped get him out of his head. She knew exactly how he felt, drowning in helplessness and fear, but she was still struggling with finding the antidote herself.

Then an idea popped into her head. He couldn't decline helping her with her studies, could he? He *was* her mentor after all.

"I think I'm gonna do my homework, okay?" she told Mel as she stood from the sofa.

Mel frowned before giving a small nod and returning her attention to the TV.

Taking a deep breath, Dani summoned the courage to walk down the hall to Dustin's room. She raised a fist to knock on his door again and stopped when she caught her reflection in the mirror on the adjacent wall.

She somehow didn't appear to be the same hollow creature she was not so long ago. Her posture was straighter, her cheeks had more color, and her dirty-blonde hair was combed neatly to her elbows. Her limbs didn't look as menacing or frail, her hazel eyes a little brighter.

She appeared to be a decent person for once; someone who was just trying to do some good for others.

Dani swallowed and rapped on his door.

"Yeah?" he answered.

She eased the door open and found him sitting at a desk by the door, his laptop propped open in front of him. He peered up at her beneath his dark lashes with weary eyes, his brown tousled hair falling loosely over his brows.

Dani bit her lip, palming the doorknob nervously. "Hey, would you mind looking over my biology essay? I just want to get your opin-ion before I turn it in this week for finals…"

He wrinkled his mouth and scratched the stubble on his chin. "Sure," he sighed.

It was a start.

"Great! I'll grab my things." She headed to Mel's room before he could change his mind. Snatching her laptop out of her backpack, she sauntered back to Dustin's room.

Upon entering, she nearly tripped over a pile of dirty laundry on the floor. Shoes, a small suitcase, and toiletries were scattered around the room. Despite being a visitor, he had managed to make a mess of things.

He crouched to the floor, attempting to tidy up. "Sorry about the mess," he muttered. "I'm usually pretty tidy."

"It's okay," she cooed, brushing her hair back with a small smile. "Thanks for doing this. I figured I could use your insight before I turn it in."

"No worries." He finished stuffing a few socks into his suitcase as she sat on his bed and opened her laptop, pulling up her essay.

"Here you go," she offered, holding her laptop out to him, and he took it and sat on the bed a few paces away from her. He read it over with tired eyes; he looked more drained than yesterday.

She bounced her knee as she waited for him to finish reading, the silence growing suffocating. Maybe she could lighten the mood and speak his language of cheesy jokes. She straightened, her mouth quirk-ing. "Hey, what grades do pirates get?"

A few seconds passed before he looked up at her in confusion. "What?"

"Pirates. What grades do they get?" she repeated.

He shrugged, disinterested. "I dunno. What?"

"High seas!" she laughed softly.

His lips perked ever so slightly. "That was…one lame-ass joke," he said, shaking his head.

She considered herself successful.

Dani nudged his arm, grinning. "It was one *fantastic* dad joke, and you know it. You laughed." She missed his playful bantering. Anything she could do to ease it back into him would be a win.

He shook his head again and glanced at her with the barest hint of that crooked smile she remembered. Dani couldn't tell if he regarded her as amusing or a nuisance.

She dropped her teasing demeanor and shifted closer to him, dipping lower onto the bed. "I'm sorry if I got on your nerves," she said softly. "It just tears me apart to see you so down. I wish I could do something to help."

He leaned slightly away from her, and she realized she'd forgotten multiple times now to keep the distancing rule in their house. She hadn't worn her mask for the past two days either. It was probably useless at this point anyway.

He eyed her curiously. "You're apologizing?"

Dani folded her hands and stared at the floor. "Yes. I…I get it if you don't want me around anymore."

He sighed and licked his lips as he set aside her laptop, his eyes softening. "Dani, I'm the one who should be sorry. You've been nothing but helpful, and I've only been a dick to you. Thank you for everything you've done. For entertaining Mel, for taking Max for a run, for making lunch yesterday…"

Dani played with her sweater sleeves, biting her lip. "I just hope you've cheered up a bit. But it seems my shitty jokes aren't working."

When she met his gaze, his smile was weak but genuine. He dropped his head and rubbed his eyes.

"Dammit, I'm really sorry, Dani. I know it's hard to see, but as messed up as I am right now…" He paused and dropped his hand before locking eyes with her again. "I appreciate you being here."

His piercing blue eyes studied her for a moment before turning away. "It's just…" He paused. "Every day, I think it's gonna be her last."

Dani's heart chipped as the life washed from his face. She had the strong urge to wrap her arms around his shoulders and pull him close, consume his pain and bring that crooked smile she adored back to his face.

*Tell him. Tell him what happened. It might be the only way to get through to him. He may open up more after knowing you've been down a similar dark road. The least you can do is let him know that whatever lies ahead, he doesn't have to face it alone.*

*But what if he turns away like Tanner did…?*

*Dammit, this isn't about you! Whatever happens, at least you tried to connect with him.*

Dani swallowed, her airway suffocatingly tight.

It was now or never.

"I can sort of relate. I know what it feels like…to lose someone," she said quietly. She bit her tongue and scratched her cheek. "Sorry, that's not what I meant. What I wanted to say is…I know what it feels like to be at your breaking point." Her breath was shaky as she inhaled. "I know what it feels like to have a weight of uncertainty and helplessness drag you down day after day."

Dustin tilted his head at her and drew his brows, concern etched into his gaze.

The haunting images from that night crept to the forefront of her mind, and along with them, the small, stabbing pain in her stomach. Her heart hammered inside her chest, so loud she wondered if he could hear it.

*His mom is fighting for her life. He's suffering. You can be strong for once in your life and get past this. For Dustin.*

*Fight on, Miss Torres.*

*Fight on.*

She swallowed again and tugged on her sweater sleeves. "My brother…"

Dustin folded a leg onto the bed and turned fully to face her.

"My brother, Jeremy, was…killed three years ago." She paused, and his attentive gaze dropped to the bed.

"Shit," Dustin whispered. He raked a hand through his hair. "I'm so sorry to hear that…" He rested a hand on her arm as she began to tremble. "It wasn't your fault."

Dani squeezed her eyes tight, trying to block out the blood soaking her hands, Jeremy's pale face staining her eyes, his pained wheezing reverberating in her ears. "But it *was* my fault," she squeaked.

She opened her eyes and read the disbelief in his stare.

"I doubt it," he consoled.

"You don't understand," she whispered.

He sat silently as she tugged her sweater sleeves further along her hands, finding her voice. Her words came out hoarse and frail. "I had been angry at my dad for a long time…and one day in high school, I snapped. I drove to a bar late that night while he slept, in his truck, without him knowing. I was underage…and I had at least four or five drinks. I was so stupid."

She paused to take another deep breath. Dustin's eyes never left hers as she went on.

"Then I drove home afterward. Like a damn psychopath. I knew what I was doing was wrong, but I didn't care. I was so…*furious* at my dad and didn't give a shit about anything else."

Dustin's face remained calm, focused, as he took in every word.

She took a moment to fight against the rising nausea and dug her fingers into the edge of the bed.

*Breathe. Just breathe.*

"I drove home, drunk…"

The swarm of emotions and dark memories oozed back to her consciousness.

*She squinted through the thick blanket of fog and saw the dark outline of the forest straight ahead. She flicked the headlights to high beam and saw she had drifted off the road, the trees in her direct line of driving.*

"It was really foggy that night… My brother had been looking for me in the dark, and I—"

*The pickup slammed into something on the side of the road, and Dani jammed on the brakes. She looked around in the fog for what she had hit—*

"I *hit* him with the truck. I…I killed him." Dani's voice broke. The sickening *thud, thrum, thrum* echoed in her mind, and she saw Jeremy as clearly as if he were right in front of her, bleeding out.

*The crumpled person emitted a wheezing sound. It was a man, and now she was closer, she could see that he had dirty-blond hair…*

"You don't have to go on. It's okay," Dustin soothed, shifting closer to rub a hand along her back.

She bit her tongue. What was she doing, spilling all of her trauma on Dustin?

"I'm sorry—this is s-supposed to be about you, not me," she whimpered. "I shouldn't have gone there. I'm *such* a shitty person." Her head fell into her hands as tears spilled down her face.

The bed shifted, and Dustin's arms were around her, engulfing her in his ocean-breeze cologne. Dani stiffened, shocked at his closeness, but when he squeezed her tighter, she collapsed against his chest.

"It's all right," he murmured through her hair.

"I-I'm sorry," she sputtered again. "I just…I wanted you to know I understand a bit of your pain and…f-fear of what lies ahead." Her voice cracked through her burning throat. "I'm s-sorry. I'm sorry."

"It's okay. Don't apologize." He stroked her long dirty-blonde locks as she began to shake in his arms.

With a lurch of her heart, she clung to him and didn't let go.

Dustin held her for what felt like hours, although it couldn't have been that long. He breathed in her pine tree scent and braced against the shaky rise and fall of her chest. After a while, her sobbing lulled, and she pulled back from him, sitting upright.

"I…I don't understand how you can be so…consoling to me," she choked.

He shot her a puzzled look. "Why do you say that?"

Her head shook, spilling her dirty-blonde hair across her face. "Never mind. It doesn't matter."

He rubbed his hand along her back. "What is it?"

She closed her eyes, and her next words rasped. "My own dad… won't even talk to me anymore. I see the blame and hatred in his face every time I look at him. Even my mom… All they see is that high-school girl who makes bad decision after bad decision. A criminal who brought shame to the family. But they're right."

Dustin pursed his lips, his heart breaking for her. "That's not the person I see."

She sucked in a deep breath. "I'm not so sure."

Suddenly, everything made sense. Her near tearing up on the way home from the volunteer program when she had told him criminals didn't deserve forgiveness. Her storming away from him at their last mentor session after telling him he didn't know her.

And was that why she blacked out at the protest and fled afterward? Did something trigger her trauma then?

He trailed a hand up to her shoulder and brushed her hair aside. She had endured so much suffering for so long—and he'd pushed her away during the past few days.

Nausea crept up his stomach. He hated himself for berating her lack of focus on her studies last fall; for lashing out at her when she'd tried to console him about his mom the previous day… He'd had no idea she was harboring these traumatic memories. They were still as raw for her now as if they had only happened yesterday.

And yet, though she had lost her brother, his mom was still alive. There was still hope, just like Dani had said. Just like Mel had said too.

As much as he feared losing his mom, he couldn't give up. While she was away, he needed to be useful, optimistic. He needed to be there for his sister. He had a responsibility to Mel and to himself.

He swallowed a burning lump in his throat as he realized he had broken his promise to look out for Mel, to be there for her when their dad wasn't. Dani was the one who had taken care of her, entertained and distracted her, when he'd been sulking like a damn coward in his room.

Dustin expelled a painful sigh and dropped his head. "I had no idea you were hiding so much pain all this time. God, I feel terrible for it."

Her eyelids fluttered closed. "Nobody should ever have to…go through the pain of losing a loved one," she whimpered.

He braced at her words, and a silent tear escaped his eye. He turned his head to wipe it away before he lost control completely.

Dani remained silent on the bed next to him, fidgeting with the sleeves of her sweatshirt and breathing shallowly. A barely audible whisper met his ears.

"Do you believe in God?"

He turned his head to meet her defeated gaze. "Hmm?"

Her eyes were glassy as she rearticulated her question with trembling lips. "Why does God let this happen? If He exists? Why does He let people suffer? Why does He let this pandemic and deaths and all these horrible problems happen if He can just make them all go away?"

Dustin furrowed his brow as he pondered her question, searching for a response. He hoped for her sake his answer was sufficient. "I'm the wrong person to ask, but… I believe God lets bad shit happen because…light shines brighter in the darkness. If there was light all the time, what would be the point? Maybe God allows evil and suffering so love and compassion can prevail." He paused, the powerful statement tasting foreign on his lips.

A glimmer of hope shone in Dani's hazel, puffy eyes, and he realized his honest words were the answer he had needed to hear too.

His brow wrinkled as he studied her broken features, reflecting on her actions the past few days. He felt as if he was seeing her for the first time. She didn't look like the wild, combative twenty-one-year-old girl he had made her out to be; she was much more sophisticated than that.

She had carried a horrendous burden for three years, yet had moved on through life, pursuing her goals of a lacrosse championship and med school.

And on top of that, she had put aside her own grievances to care for him and Mel.

He had judged her for all the wrong things.

He expelled a deep breath. He had to do something. God knew there were enough tough times ahead for Dani in med school and the hospital, even without the shadow of grief haunting her.

"Dani," he said softly, placing a tender hand on hers. She jostled at his touch, but he didn't pull away. "If there's anything I can do to help…" He rubbed his neck. "Have you taken any medication?"

She turned away and fidgeted with her sleeves again. "I did, for three years, but I stopped last summer." Dustin stiffened as she went on. "I felt like I was cheating my brother by blocking him out—blocking out his memory. I thought I could get past the meds on my own and remember him as a positive guide in my life, but I guess I was wrong." She closed her eyes as her lips trembled.

Dustin ran a hand through his hair, wracking his memory for anyone he might've known in pre-med who went off to therapeutics. One guy came to mind.

"An old buddy of mine specializes in therapeutics for PTSD. I can reach out to him for you?" he offered softly.

Fear washed over her hazel eyes, and she bit her lip. "I…haven't had positive therapist experiences in the past."

Dustin scratched his chin. "Michael's the best guy I know. He graduated top of his class. Plus, he's a super friendly dude. Maybe you should give it a shot?"

Dani averted her eyes. A strand of dirty-blonde hair fell into her face and stuck to her wet cheek.

His throat constricted as he continued. "I can't imagine what you've gone through, and I only want the best for you."

Her swollen eyes glazed over him, studying his features.

He took a deep breath and tensed his jaw. "Please, Dani, let me help. You've already done the hardest part by telling me about it. Please."

Dani closed her eyes again and inhaled a shaky breath. She swallowed before meeting his gaze. "Okay," she whispered.

# Forty-Eight

*May*

THE NEXT AFTERNOON, DANI SHUT HER LAPTOP WITH A SIGH OF relief after completing her first final exam in Mel's guest room. Online exams were definitely more convenient, and she could thank COVID for that.

She glanced at her smart watch: it was barely 1:00 p.m. She had finished the exam in under fifteen minutes—a new record! Only five more exams over the following few days…but until then, she could relax.

She shrugged into a tank top, spandex shorts, and running shoes and sauntered into the living room, gazing down at Dustin with a gleam in her eye. "Happy Cinco de Mayo!"

Dustin raised his head and arched his brows from where he sat sprawled on the couch. "You're done with your finals already?"

She shrugged and shifted her weight. "Guess I paid attention in my Zoom meetings and assignments." In fact, her eidetic memory had recalled the exact passage in each textbook where the answers were located.

He snorted. *"Or you didn't know any of the answers and flunked the exam, rendering my mentor assistance useless."*

Dani's lips tugged upward. "Guess we'll just have to see which one it is." She flexed her calf and placed her hands on her hips. "You want to go on a run with me?"

"Sounds like a plot to get me out of the house." He stretched to his feet and cracked a smile. "I'm in." His eyes shone as they raked her running attire. "Guess I'd better change."

Dani's lips tugged upward as he brushed past her down the hall to his room. She was in a good mood, all things considered, and it appeared Dustin was feeling somewhat better also.

He seemed to have a little spring in his step when he came out of his room a few minutes later, shirtless in black Nike shorts and running shoes. The sight of her mentor showing so much skin made Dani stiffen. She tried to hide the heat rushing to her cheeks with a tuck of her hair behind an ear.

His expression remained neutral as he passed Dani and leashed Max where the dog lay by the front door. When he led Max out of the house, she took a deep breath and trailed hesitantly behind him into the afternoon sun.

"Wanna take a long route?" he asked as she closed the door behind her.

She shrugged, tilting her head down to fix her ponytail. "You're the boss." When he turned away and stepped onto the sidewalk, her eyes darted along his upper body.

Even from behind, he looked ripped.

She ogled at his broad shoulders and firm biceps, her mouth twisting before she tugged her gaze away. *What the hell. Are you checking out your mentor?* Dani let out another long exhale as he broke into a jog down the pavement, and she hurried to fall in pace beside him.

Her feet pounded in a rhythm next to his, carrying her thoughts to the deep portions of her mind. Yesterday's confession played on rewind, her brain sorting through all the tears to make sense of what had happened.

It was supposed to be Dani who comforted Dustin yesterday afternoon, but somehow, it had been Dustin who comforted *her*. She had selfishly turned his grief into her own, yet he had let her weep in his arms and wiped away her tears without a second thought. And then he'd contacted Michael, his therapist friend, and set up sessions with Dani for next month.

Why was he so good to her? Even Tanner hadn't bothered to offer her help; to hold her after she'd revealed her deepest scars to him.

Dani inhaled the cool breeze that brushed her cheeks as they rounded the street corner. The exhausting weight that had pressed on her shoulders for years felt as if it was beginning to lift. She felt oddly relieved to be getting help this time despite her fears. Maybe it was because Dustin knew some of the pain she was going through, and she trusted his advice.

Was this what the healing process felt like?

*The cure cannot be worse than the problem itself,* the small voice whispered in the back of her head.

*But the cure isn't worse*, a dominant, wiser voice responded. *It never was.*

Dustin turned left when they reached the end of the vacant street, leading Max and Dani into downtown Culver City. The bright morning sun warmed Dani's legs, feeling great after the past months' winter chill. Although it was still early May, she could smell the fresh grass and salty ocean breeze that reminded her of summer.

Dani stole a glance in Dustin's direction. The planes of his face were relaxed, his breaths even and unlabored.

"It's nice to be able to run with someone who can actually keep up with me," she taunted. "Emma, my roommate, is fast, but she's dead after five minutes."

Dustin raised a skeptical eyebrow. "Who said *I'm* keeping up with *you?* Damn."

She whipped her long ponytail over her shoulder and squinted ahead. "I could totally beat you in a race to the end of the street."

He snorted loudly. "Yeah, right. You don't want to make a fool of yourself."

"All right, you're on. Let's do it." She perked her mouth at him.

"Nah, I don't think so," he objected, shaking his head.

"Why not? Afraid I'll kick your ass?"

He scowled. "Don't flatter yourself. It wouldn't be a fair run 'cause Max would slow me down." He turned his head, but not before a flicker of a smile escaped his lips. Her heart bristled in response.

Dani tuned in to their syncopated breaths and the rhythm of their footsteps before she noticed Dustin peeking a curious eye at her. "What?" she demanded.

"Why didn't you tell me about Peter?"

Dani's breath caught in her throat. Did Dustin know about her lacrosse suspension? She tried to hide the surprise in her response. "What about him?"

His curious stare morphed into a smug smile. "You got into a fight with him *before* the frat party. And he got you kicked off the lacrosse team afterward? I thought kicking his balls was the worst of your undergrad drama."

*Shit. He knew. Well, now it seems like a trivial secret to hide compared to the one I revealed yesterday.*

Dani wrinkled her mouth. "How did you hear about that?"

"I ran into him at the store a few months ago."

Her eyes widened. "You didn't tell me!" She punched his shoulder, and he chuckled.

A few seconds passed as she mulled over his question, her teeth grazing her bottom lip. *Why didn't I tell him? I told him about my arrest, didn't I? Was I really more embarrassed about almost losing my scholarship?*

"Uh…I guess I was just ashamed of getting nearly kicked off a team I worked my ass off for," she murmured.

A small laugh met her ears. "Well, you shouldn't feel ashamed— Peter's the one who should be. His big-ass ego couldn't handle being told 'no' by a girl. If it makes you feel any better, he only went out of his way to punish you 'cause he had a serious thing for you."

Dani threw back her head and guffawed. "He's just a huge dick who likes showing off. He mocked me in front of his friends for nearly passing out at practice. I'd *never* consider going out with someone like him. Blech." Her face scrunched in disgust as she remembered toying with Peter at the bowling alley in September.

Damn alcohol. She should have never obliged Haley.

Dustin switched the leash to his other hand as Max ran in between them, tugging him to his other side. "Well, he *is* a huge dick, but dudes usually are when they like someone."

She shrugged and lowered her eyes. Tanner's judgmental brown eyes seared into her memory, his rejection still an unsealed wound in her heart.

"I used to think I was someone capable of being liked, but it turns out I'm not really cut out for anyone," she answered with a swallow. Her dad's voice echoed in her mind: *You're not relationship material.*

Dustin's mouth popped open, his head swiveling in her direction. "Yes, you are cut out! You're beautiful, smart, *and* a badass lacrosse player. But none of that compares to your strength. You've fought through unimaginable trauma and summoned the courage to talk about it."

She bit her lip, not sure how to accept his stream of compliments—especially since Dustin was someone she'd never anticipated them coming from.

"Thanks," she muttered.

As they continued down past some closed restaurants, it took Dani a second to wrap her head around this new view of herself. Dani was well aware of her pretty features and had hidden behind them for years. But her frail emotions and dark past had always demonstrated weakness, not strength, which was why she had tried to keep that part of her locked away from the world.

She took a deep breath and wiped the sweat from her brow. When Dustin opened his mouth, she was quick to change the subject. "I should've told Winston about Peter from the start. I acted so stupid."

Dustin hesitated, staring at her as if her statement had caught him off-guard. Then he turned a reassuring smile to her. "Don't worry about Peter. Karma catches up to dicks like him sooner or later."

Dani's mouth quirked as she caught the twinkle in his eye.

They slowed to a stop when they reached a corner of a major intersection on Venice Boulevard. Dustin stepped in front of her to push the cross button—an almost laughable move considering how empty the street was.

Hidden behind him, Dani couldn't help but peek curiously in his direction. He had called her beautiful? Smart? Strong?

Her eyes followed the sweat trickling down Dustin's back as he pulled tan, muscular arms over his head and leaned over in a stretch.

He straightened, gazing out at the street, and her eyes were drawn to the soft dip of his cheekbones, his dark lashes, the light stubble trailing along his jaw…

When Dustin brushed aside his sweaty bangs and met her eye, she glanced away, her cheeks flushing a furious red.

"What's up?" he asked coolly with a twist of his lips.

"I…"—her mind rampantly searched for something to say—"was thinking about how happy Max is to get some fresh air." *Smooth, very smooth.*

Max barked and circled Dustin, tangling him in the leash.

"Dammit, Max," he muttered, and Dani laughed. Dustin unwound himself and held out the leash. "Here—you take him."

Dani took the leash, and when their hands brushed, a fiery current shot up her fingertips. She gasped and nearly dropped the leash, her heart hammering.

*Whoa, what is happening to me?*

In an instant, the vacant streets of Culver City melted away into a dimly lit sidewalk across from USC's campus…

*"Bro, you look like an Arctic bum." He tugged her hood over her eyes, and she giggled, pushing his arm away.*

*"Leave my freezing Arctic bum self alone!"*

*His low, throaty chuckle warmed her bones. Their sides brushed, and she sucked in a breath as tingles shot up her spine.* Whoa, what is happening to me?

*The remaining few blocks sent her pulse into a frenzy, and though she tried to concentrate on their small talk, she failed, her mind instead concentrating on the proximity of his body to hers…*

The scene morphed into a small dorm bedroom, sheets wrapped around Dani's legs as she lay underneath him.

*"No—get off." She tried to push him off her, but his hands seized her wrists and held her in place. Her heart seized in her chest as she found herself trapped underneath him…*

The bedroom vanished as Max tugged her off the curb into the crosswalk after Dustin, jolting her from her flashback.

Dustin raised an eyebrow as he slowed for her to sluggish feet to catch up to him across the street. "You good?" he asked.

"Um…yeah. Sorry." Dani swallowed as she fell back into pace beside him, trying to ignore the pounding through her head.

*Breathe. Just breathe.*

When Dustin's arm brushed hers, Dani shuddered away from him.

He shot her a worried look, his lips pressing tight. "Uh…how are things with Tanner? Peter mentioned…you two were together."

Dani stumbled, nearly colliding with Max before she clumsily recovered her footing. *Did my flinch somehow indicate I was thinking about Tanner? How much does Dustin know about us?* She averted her eyes from Dustin's curious gaze. "Uh, things are good," she answered with a brief grin.

His eyebrow arched, skepticism settling in his eyes before fading away an instant later. "I'm happy for you." He flashed a timid smile before turning his face to the street.

She pursed her lips and sighed, concentrating on the pound of their shoes on the pavement. She couldn't hide anything else from him. "Actually, we're not seeing each other anymore. Things got kind of ugly after I told him about…" She faded off as Tanner's judgmental expression and that darkening abyss swallowing her whole jostled her mind. "About my brother. He didn't take it too well, but I was an idiot for thinking he would react any differently." Her throat clenched tight.

Dustin's eyebrows drew, and his teeth grazed his bottom lip. Then his hard expression dissolved into a mixture of sympathy and…something else. Worry? Concern? Relief?

"I'm sorry to hear that," he surmised. "That's a horrible reason to end things, but I don't think you're an idiot for assuming he was a decent guy. He should've been more…understanding. It was a horrific accident, and you were traumatized."

"That's the same thing my roommate said…" Dani bit her lip and squeezed her eyes shut as Tanner's fiery brown eyes danced across her vision again. "Looking back…I guess things weren't as smooth as they could have been before that either."

Dustin's eyebrows arched again. "What do you mean?"

Her grip on Max's leash tightened as Dustin's concerned stare prickled her skin. "I…was afraid to move so fast in the relationship. It wasn't fair to him, so I get why he got angry. I just didn't expect him to be so…forceful."

Dustin's eyes widened, and he slowed to a stop, Dani following suit. He put his hands on his hips and wiped his brow, gritting his teeth.

Her pulse quickened as the silent moment weighed down on her shoulders like bricks. He probably didn't think she was so cut out for guys now. Would he take back the compliments he gave earlier?

Finally, Dustin looked down at her, his face a serious, hardened mask. "Did he ever…hurt you, physically?"

Dani swallowed again and focused on the wind brushing the leaves of the small fern tree beside them. "He…slapped me. One time."

When she scanned Dustin's face, the alarm in her mentor's eyes made Dani grimace. Her throat tightened as he clenched a fist and pursed his lips.

Dani rubbed an arm, her tongue rushing to her defense. "He only hit me because I tried to back out of sex. It wasn't the first time I cock-blocked him, so he got upset and hit me and held me down—" As soon as the words left her mouth, she regretted spilling the intimate moment.

"He did what?" Dustin hissed through gritted teeth.

She tucked a loose, sweaty hair behind her ear. "No, he didn't end up—it's fine, really—"

"Dani," he interrupted, his eyes swimming with contempt. "That's absolutely not fine. It sounds like assault, if not attempted rape."

She frowned, perplexed, and dropped her gaze to the sidewalk. "Rape? No… He apologized for hitting me—he didn't mean to hurt me… He was just upset—"

Dustin stepped close, and she caught a whiff of his ocean-breeze cologne. It was a while before Dani looked up and met his deep blue eyes, and she could see herself, small and frail, reflected in them. But his tone was soft, gentle.

"Regardless of what it was, Dani, if he hit you and tried to force anything on you…he's dangerous. If you weren't comfortable with anything at all, mentally or physically, it shouldn't have continued."

Dani's limbs locked as she considered the weight of Dustin's words. Had Tanner really tried to rape her? Her eidetic memory replayed the frightening scene in front of her, right where it left off.

*"No—get off." She tried to push him off her, but his hands seized her wrists and held her in place. Her heart seized in her chest as she found herself trapped underneath him.*

She closed her eyes as Tanner's lustful, frustrated gaze swam in her mind, and the sting of his slap throbbed against her cheek.

*The shock of his force froze her. Her throat constricted as sheer terror overtook her body.*

*"It's okay, I got you. Just relax. You wanted this, remember?" he murmured.*

*She hardly registered his words. Her body was immobile, lifeless. Her arms stopped flailing and fell limp, bolted next to her head by his hands.*

*He released her wrists. "There you go, babe. It's all right. Almost there." His hand trailed down to her panties again.*

*Her heart hammered against her chest as his hands dipped beneath them.* No, no, no, no. I'm not ready!

Dani opened her eyes, lurching herself away from that dark place and back to the present. Her voice shook as she focused on the leaf by Dustin's shoe. "It was my fault. I led him on and pulled away at the last second—"

"Bullshit. Look at me." He cupped her jaw and tilted her head so she had no choice but to stare her own horrors in the face. "You may blame yourself for a thousand other horrible things, but you can't blame yourself for this. You did nothing wrong. *Nothing.* That piece of shit should never have touched you. It's *not* your fault. You hear me?" His teeth dug into his bottom lip, and his hand trembled against her cheek. "That bastard can go to hell. He doesn't deserve you. He doesn't deserve *anyone.* He'll never hurt you again. I promise."

Dustin's consoling face morphed into Tanner's fearsome gaze. *"And I promise, I will never control you…or do anything to make you feel abandoned…"*

Dani squeezed her eyes tight. The last time she was vulnerable with a guy, she had been nearly raped, then pushed down a bottomless abyss of despair. How could she trust anyone with her scars? How could she trust herself?

She didn't notice the tear slipping down her cheek until Dustin brushed it away.

Dani's breath became labored as the weight of what had almost happened to her sunk in. A swirl of embarrassment, hurt, and shame flooded her bones.

How could she have been so stupid; so naïve? Had she been so blind, so foolish, to think what she had with Tanner was love? She never imagined Tanner could be so selfish, so *cruel,* but looking into Dustin's horrified eyes now, it was clear as day to her how wrong she had been.

And then it struck her like a punch to the gut how alike she and Haley were.

They had both been blind; so desperate for love they had searched for it in the darkest of places. Even after Tanner put Dani through both physical and emotional pain, she had crawled back to him like some psychopath. He had almost raped her!

As bits of that traumatic day realigned themselves in their head, Dani whimpered.

Dustin's call... He had indirectly saved her from potential rape. No, not potential. Rape. He had saved her from rape. If he hadn't called her that morning...

Drawing an arm to wipe her face, Dani sniffed and peered back at Dustin with newfound gratitude. She fought against the urge to fall to her knees and break down as he studied her with a compassionate gaze.

"You...y-you called me that morning, when Tanner almost..." It took her a few seconds to find her voice. "On the first day of the volunteer program. You called me r-right before he could—"

Before she could finish, Dustin pulled her into a hug, sweaty chest and all. She crumpled, dumbfounded, and was launched back to yesterday when he had hugged her after her confession.

*I was wrong. The last time I was vulnerable with a guy, I wasn't abandoned. Dustin had pulled me close, just like this.*

Dustin was *not* Tanner.

He couldn't be. He was infinitely better.

With a pained gasp, Dani reached her arms around him as her emotions boiled over. Max barked and trotted around them, tying them tighter together, and a small laugh escaped Dani through her tears.

Dustin broke away from her and held her cheek, ignoring Max. "I'm so sorry that happened to you. God, it rips me apart." He closed his eyes tightly for a moment before opening them again. "Maybe Michael can also help...with that. Or he can direct you to a woman therapist who can walk you through USC's HR department. When you're ready, of course."

Dani's eyes darted back and forth between each of his, and she nodded. Maybe it was time she stopped trying to tackle her problems by herself. Maybe she needed more help than she realized.

He lifted a hand to brush her hair back and kissed her head. He peered down at her, his tender blue eyes locking with hers. "You are worth so much more than you know. Never forget that."

She quivered at his words as she gazed into his face. His soft features emanated such sincerity she found it hard not to believe him. Her chest tightened. Dustin was a blazing campfire in a snowstorm, full of life and promise when he was near. He made her feel safe—safer and better cared for than she had ever believed she could be.

It was another minute before Dustin disentangled them from the leash and Dani regained her bearings, finally ready to run again. With every stride she took alongside Dustin, she felt like she was running away from a dark, lonely part of herself and toward a brighter, better beginning.

*May*

LATER THAT EVENING, DANI HUMMED TO HERSELF AS SHE COMBED her hair in the bathroom after her shower.

Her mind seemed clearer like it always did after extraneous exercise. She'd replayed her conversation with Dustin hundreds of times on their run back home and again when she was showering, and the more she'd thought about it, the more she despised herself for being so naïve with Tanner.

Dustin had been right. As soon as she'd been uncomfortable with anything, she should have discontinued their relationship—especially after Tanner had almost forced himself on her.

She pursed her lips at the mirror, and a defeated face stared back at her. How had she still made bad decisions up until now? She had been so ignorant of blaring, red flags; how could she ever trust herself?

*I had been frustrated at Haley for the exact same thing.* Dani's thoughts drifted to the lacrosse captain and her earlier realization of how similar they had been, and a sharp pang throbbed in her chest. Maybe… the reason Dani had been so conflicted over her friend was because… on some subconscious level, Haley reminded her of herself.

A shudder erupted down Dani's spine, but then Bettie's consoling words surfaced in response: *"You looked like someone who could use some kindness. And people in distress often find kindness is most present when it is least expected."*

She smoothed the hem of her long-sleeved shirt with a deep sigh and plucked her toiletry bag from the sink. *How could I have let her sulk so long? What the hell is wrong with me?*

Dani exited the bathroom and called behind her as she walked down the hall, "Shower's yours, Dustin."

His tenor voice responded from the living room, "Could have gone on another run in the hour you were in there."

She smirked to herself as she entered Mel's guest room and plopped her toiletry bag on the floor, but her smile dissipated when she spotted her phone laying on her folded sleeping bag. *Would she still forgive me?*

Dani sat cross-legged on the carpet and picked up her phone, a throb pounding in her ears as she scrolled through her favorite contacts list. The sight of Haley's dozens of unanswered texts from months ago made her stomach sink.

It was a long minute before Dani forced her fingers to type out a text: **Hey, I am so sorry for everything. Can we talk?** After reading it over, she pursed her lips and pressed send. She hoped that Haley could forgive her, but a part of her whispered that it had been too long, and Dani had sunk the knife too deep to cleanse the wound.

Her eyes drifted around the room, latching onto Mel's small blue backpack by the closet. A smile crept to her lips as she remembered the talk they had when they'd taken Max to the dog park. Mel always seemed to see the positive in things, and it had wounded Dani to see her hurt by the pessimistic words Dustin had said about their mom. She hoped Dustin could be more optimistic for his sister. If he'd known that Mel had cried herself to sleep that night—

A long buzz from her phone interrupted her thoughts. She glanced down and froze: Haley was calling.

Dani's pulse rocketed in her veins, and it was another few seconds before she summoned the courage and raised the phone to her ear with a deep breath. "Hey."

"Hey." The sound of her friend's voice after so many weeks was refreshing. *Friend? Does she still think of me that way after what I did?* "Is this a good time?" Haley asked, her usually loud, wild voice unusually tame and cautious.

"Yes. Listen—"

"No, don't apologize," Haley cut her off. "I'm sorry, Dani. I'm *so* sorry." A shaky breath expelled through the line, and Dani found her chest tightening.

"Mitch was a total dick," Haley continued. "I'm sorry it took me forever to realize that. When he was arrested he got so angry, and I wanted to blame you for ruining our relationship. But all this time alone from him really opened my eyes…" Her voice wavered. "He deserved to go to jail, and I never should have left you alone with those cops. I should have been the one arrested instead of you."

Dani traced a finger across the soft carpet, the expanding knot in her chest making it hard to think clearly.

"I deserved your shunning," Haley continued.

Dani shook her head. "No, Haley. You didn't." She shut her eyes and forced a sob back down her throat. "You only wanted to make him happy, and you didn't deserve my shunning because of that."

"I…" Haley hesitated. "I broke up with him last month. I wanted to tell you as soon as I did, but I thought you didn't care to talk to me anymore."

"Haley—"

"I shouldn't have gotten mad at you for telling the truth in court. I was so stupid—"

"Haley." Dani's voice was firm this time. "I never had the heart to rat you out. I couldn't. I didn't want to ruin your relationship."

Silence. Dani's fingers squeezed the smooth fabric of the sleeping bag, counting her breaths.

Finally, Haley spoke. "What? Why…did you do that? You're innocent!"

Dani shrugged. "It was just a dumb fine."

"That is… the most selfless thing I've ever heard of, Dani." The words struck Dani like a gavel to the heart, and she bit her lip to quell the emotion building in her throat.

The line was silent again for a few more seconds before Haley went on. "If you didn't… who did?"

Dani inhaled sharply. "It's a funny story… I hadn't known for the longest time, and I only found out a few days ago."

"Yeah…?" Haley waited patiently.

Dani contemplated the irony in revealing Bettie's identity as the person Haley and Dani had scoffed at in the Uniqlo store. She supposed it was a perfect example of bad karma, but maybe some lessons were better learned without excessive, unnecessary details.

She smiled. "Let's just say the person who did it was only trying to help someone in distress."

"Mmm, Bettie outdid herself again," Dani murmured as she chomped on Bettie's amazing chicken salad sandwich for dinner.

Dustin looked up from where he was sitting across from her on the porch and snorted as he lifted his own sandwich. "I thought we already established that the woman a godsend."

Dani wiped some dressing from her mouth. "Yeah, but I don't get tired of praising her." She grinned and gazed out across the street, capturing the fading sun's spill of pink and blue on the cute little houses. Her talk with Haley couldn't have gone any better, and it seemed as if another weight had been lifted off her shoulders. She realized she'd been carrying more burdens than she'd cared to admit, and it seemed every few hours she found a new leak that had contributed to the flooding of her emotions' shallow reservoirs.

But finding leaks was a good thing, because it meant the hole could be patched.

Dani turned back to Dustin and found it hard to look away from him. As he chewed, she studied the subtle dip of his shoulders, his cool gaze, the brown hair wet from his shower curling over his brows. Although she had only been at Bettie's house for three days, in that small amount of time, she felt as if she had grown to know and trust Dustin on a deeper level than she had with anyone else. He had seen her leaks and dents, and hadn't turned away.

It opened a gate to a new sort of freedom. A safe freedom.

"You know what's funny?" she asked before she could stop herself.

He raised a curious brow from where he sat in the chair opposite her. "What?" he asked through a bite of sandwich, crumbs falling onto his T-shirt and sweatpants.

She took a deep breath and busied her fingers with peeling the crust off her bread. "In the almost three years I've been in LA, I've only been to the beach once. And not even on the sand, just on Ocean Avenue overlooking the waves." Jeremy's golden, smiling face coalesced in front of her as his distant, hopeful words drifted through her ears: *"I wanted to go to California and see the beaches…"*

Dustin frowned as he wiped his mouth with his wrist. *"What? You're not a true Southern Californian if you don't go to the beach at least once a week."*

Dani grinned and looked down at her plate again. "It's mostly because…it reminds me of him. And it just makes me sad all over again because he never got to see it."

Dustin shifted in his chair, and she peered up at him, biting her lip. His eyes softened, his lips curving ever so slightly. "I'm sure he would have been happy to know you saw it for him."

She glanced out again at the darkening sky, and her brother's smirking, freckled face flashed in front of her.

Dustin's mellow tone broke the silence. "I'd like to hear more about him—if you're okay with it."

The innocent question pulled her attention back to him. His blue eyes shone as he inspected her face, his composure relaxed. He had shaved the excessive stubble snaking down his chin, and he looked more present and attentive than she had seen him in a long while.

She folded her legs and set down her plate on the bench beside her. She hadn't talked amicably about Jeremy since before his death. The thought of sharing his story raised a soreness in her throat, and she swallowed it back.

"You don't have to if you don't want to," Dustin said softly.

She tucked a damp hair behind her ear. "No, I…I want to." A timid smile stretched across her lips. "He…had a lot of my same features. Hazel eyes, tan skin, a messy mop of dirty-blond hair…" She smiled as a memory of Jeremy at her aunt's wedding surfaced. "He was the absolute *worst* dancer. He would do this ridiculous knee-shuffle that made me say I didn't know him when people asked who he was."

Dustin laughed and set his own plate aside, locking his fingers around his knee.

"And…he loved Bruno Mars and H.E.R. His favorite song was 'Best Part.' He'd gush all the time about H.E.R.'s vocals, and said his girlfriend beat him up for it." Dani's lip curled as her fingers traced the bench's slick wood. "He was a great teacher. He taught me everything about lacrosse—more than my dad. He also taught me a lot of guy things like hunting and skateboarding. And he was the first person I'd run to when the other girls bullied me at school, or when I needed help with homework."

She blinked back a tear and dropped her gaze to her converse. Why had she never talked about him? Was she so tied up in her shame she couldn't share the happy moments she'd had with him?

"I'm sorry," she sniffled with a small smile, glancing up.

Dustin leaned forward, his Adam's apple bouncing. "Don't worry about it. It sounds like he was a better brother to you than I've been to Mel."

Dani dipped her eyes and nodded, her breaths labored. "He…was the best brother. I think…Jeremy's passing was the reason I had such a love-hate relationship with lacrosse. All of my favorite memories were tied on that field with him, but thinking of him only brought back the guilt and shame—"

She cut off as the front door opened and Mel strutted out of the house, plopping down next to Dani on the bench. "What are you guys doing?" she asked with a playful smile.

Dani shifted next to her, wiping away her tears. "Just…talking about some happy memories." She looked at the girl's feet and noticed Mel wore the same white-and-black checkered shoes she had worn for the past few days. "Very cool shoes," she noted.

Mel's face lit up as she raised them off the ground. "I know! A girl on one of my favorite shows wears them, and I've wanted them ever since."

"Wow, I love it!" Dani glanced at Dustin, and he smirked.

Mel's smile dipped briefly when she met Dustin's eyes, and Dustin rubbed his neck. He turned back to Dani with a sly perk of his mouth.

"Bettie got them for her for Christmas at a Black Friday sale. She's only worn them, like, every day for the past four months."

Dani gasped as the memory came back to her, and Dustin wrinkled his brow. She scratched her cheek and nodded at Mel's feet. "I actually forgot to tell you I saw Bettie the day she bought those shoes. I didn't know her then, but we were at the same store!"

"Really?" Dustin raised an incredulous eyebrow and tilted his chin.

Dani glanced at her feet, heat rushing to her cheeks. "Yeah. She stood up to some douchebag in the line to get a discount for those shoes. And…she proved to be an incredibly generous woman that day in more ways than one."

Dustin's eyebrow hitched up in curiosity, but Dani only gave a look that said, "I'll tell you later."

He shook his head, a grin spreading. "That's Bettie. She's the best."

Mel swung her feet, her pudgy cheeks lifting as she admired her shoes. "Yep, if there was an award for coolest person, neighbor, and buffest lady in her eighties, they would all go to Bettie."

Their booming laughter echoed across the porch, attracting the attention of a man walking across the street.

"Freaking Mel," Dustin smiled, twisting in his seat as his phone pinged on the small table beside him. He picked it up and scanned the screen, his shoulders sagging.

"Shit—I mean, crap."

Mel wrinkled her nose as he shot her an apologetic look then turned back to his phone.

"A lot of Midwest states are beginning to open up right now, but the US curve barely started flattening," he muttered.

The lively atmosphere was sucked from the air with his statement. Dani dropped her eyes, knowing he was thinking about his mom.

"There will most likely be a second wave this summer or fall," he continued with a sigh.

Mel tightened her lips before focusing her large brown eyes on her brother. "Are you gonna go back to work?" she asked softly. The vulnerability in the girl's tone pierced Dani's heart.

Dustin leaned back in his chair, his teeth grazing his bottom lip. "I would go back to work, but my supervisor doesn't want me to return for a while. I couldn't focus since Mom went in."

Mel's eyes shimmered with relief, but it washed away a moment later.

Dani reached a tender hand around Mel and rubbed her back. "Your mom is gonna be okay," Dani whispered. "If she's anything like you two, she's a fighter."

Mel's eyes closed, a ragged breath escaping her.

Dustin watched his sister with a somber gaze for a few seconds, then stood up. "Wait here," he murmured to Dani. Slipping off the porch, he walked next door to his house and disappeared inside. He reemerged a minute later with an old steel guitar and reclaimed his seat on the porch.

Dustin turned to Mel as he rested the guitar's oak body on his knee. "You remember that song Dad sang to us years ago when we were feeling down?"

Mel's eyes softened, and she nodded.

"You play?" Dani asked with a perk of her mouth.

He shook his head as he plucked the strings and twisted the tuning pegs. "I took some music classes in high school but haven't really played since my dad's been gone. I wouldn't consider myself an expert, although the girls might disagree." He wiggled his eyebrows.

Dani snorted as a smile played on her lips. "I'm sure." *Of course he plays guitar. Basketball, med school, musical instruments... Is there anything he can't do?*

He strummed the guitar in an upbeat, cheery reggae pattern. Dani's skin prickled as her eyes followed the smooth glide of his fingers between the chords. Dustin licked his lips, smirking, and when his warm tenor voice met Dani's ears, a shiver shot up her spine. His words were quick and soothing over the strums:

"Don't you cry now, child, just
Look at all the rainbows in the
Sky, now, child, it's
Just a breeze away for you to

"Fly up there so,
Don't for-get to,
Smile now, child, you can smile now, child, you can
Smile now, hon-ey..."

Dani's breath caught as the music danced around her like a warm breeze. The lyrics conjured happy images from her childhood—ones with her and Jeremy laughing as they rode a roller coaster at the Helena fair; her mom smiling as Dani, Jeremy, and Franc surprised her on her birthday after work; Jeremy whistling from the sidelines during her middle-school lacrosse match; Jeremy slugging her playfully when she mocked his dance moves in their living room…

A hitch in Dustin's strums drew her eyes back to him, and her mind replayed all the times he had been there for her when he didn't have to be—driving across town amid his busy schedule to help her with her med school application; accompanying her to the nursing program at Dignity Health Hospital; showing up to her lacrosse match…

She peered at Mel. The girl's eyes were glassy as she whispered the lyrics along with her brother. When Dustin glanced up at his sister, his infectious, crooked smile crept across his lips.

"I can see you, child, now,
Running toward the finish line and
Soar-ing high, now,
Don't look down, just keep in mind that

"If your heart's true,
I know you'll bloom
Smile now, child, you can smile now, child, you can
Smile now, hon-ey…"

His strums slowed to a stop on a final resolving chord. "Something like that," he finished, resting his arm on the guitar body. "Sorry for the awful singing."

A wetness on Dani's cheeks made her bristle. She quickly wiped her face with her sleeve and smiled up at him. "That was amazing, Dustin."

His appreciative blue eyes met hers briefly before falling away and fixing on Mel. The nine-year-old slipped over to him, pushed the guitar away, and hugged her brother.

He stiffened for a moment before melting and wrapping his arms around her. "I'm sorry," he whispered.

"It's okay," Mel whispered back, squeezing him tighter. "We'll get through this together, remember?"

*May*

"Finished with junior year!" Dani shouted down the hallway a few days later, a wide smile stretching across her face as she stepped out of Mel's guest room.

Dustin's head poked out of his own guest room down the hall, his blue eyes shining. "Yeah? Thank God. Keeping quiet for twenty minutes at a time is *such* torture."

Dani laughed and turned away, shuffling into the living room as Mel and Bettie peered up at her from the couch.

"Congrats, honey!" Bettie exclaimed, setting aside the book she'd been reading.

Mel cuddled Dustin's iPad against her chest, her lips pursing. "You're so lucky you're done with school!"

Dani laughed and planted her hands on her hips. "Uh, I still have, like, five more years. What are you talking about?"

The nine-year-old rolled her large brown eyes, but her mouth tugged upward. "You know what I mean."

Dustin stepped into the living room beside Dani, folding his arms across his *Star Wars* shirt. "So…does this mean Dani's buying dinner?" His lips teased into a grin.

"Yes! I'm starving!" Mel shouted, throwing a fist in the air, and Dani giggled.

Dustin opened his mouth and closed it as a vibration hummed from his jeans pocket. He dug out his phone and glanced at the caller ID, and his face grew rigid.

A weight dropped in Dani's stomach as she read the trepidation in his eyes. He brought the phone to his ear and walked past the couch.

"This is Dustin Mottley."

Dani's eyes trailed him as he exited through the sliding glass door and into the evening sun, sucking the energy from the room with every step.

Bettie and Mel stared from the couch, peering through the glass after him, and Dani knew they were all thinking the same thing: it must be the hospital. Though Dustin had called the hospital every day to get a status report of his mom, *they* never called *him*.

A nauseating fear gripped her throat. *Oh, God. No, no, no, no… Not before Mother's Day.* The past few days had gone so well; Dustin and Mel had smiled more often and engaged in boardgames and movie-watching parties… Their high spirits couldn't be ruined now!

Dani couldn't read his expression from where he stood with his back turned in the back yard, and her throat constricted tighter with each passing second. After a few seconds, he covered his face, his phone hand dropping to his side.

Dani's heart shattered.

She dashed through the glass door and across the lawn toward him. She laid a consoling hand on his shoulder, and he turned, tears streaming down his face. Dani's gut plunged, and it felt as if the earth was swallowing her whole, taking her back to that dark place.

Except this time, Dustin was being swallowed along with her.

"They're taking her off the ventilator," he whispered, his Adam's apple bouncing as he swallowed. "She's doing better. She did it."

Dani's eyes widened, a sob bursting through her mouth as her mind struggled to comprehend Dustin's words. Then, in a sudden rush, the earth spit her back up from its depths into glorious, fresh air. She threw her arms around Dustin's neck, shuddering against him. He squeezed her tightly, his warm embrace shoving away all the sinking fears that had permeated Bettie's house for the past week and a half.

"Oh my god, Dustin," she cried into his chest. "Thank God, thank God…"

Mel stepped through the slider door in an instant, brows drawn and eyes awash with fear as she paused by the doorway. "What is it?" she asked quietly as Bettie appeared behind her looking just as worried.

Dani pulled away from Dustin to wipe her cheeks, realizing their tears may have sent the wrong message.

Dustin's broken voice drifted across the back yard. "Mom is doing better. She can come home in a few days."

Like a switch, Mel's face wiped clear of any melancholy, and she bolted into her brother's arms, weeping uncontrollably against his stomach. Bettie trailed quickly across the grass after her, the old woman's pale blue eyes shining as she smoothed her button-down shirt. The old woman smiled at Dani and gathered her and the Mottley siblings into a large hug, joining in the happy tears.

Dani trembled with joy as she stood there, tangled in a bundle of smiles and sobs. She had wanted more than anything for Dustin and Mel to see their mom again, recovered and healthy, because she knew how horrible the alternative was and didn't think she would be strong enough to see them endure what she went through.

But that grim possibility was no more.

Hope had prevailed after all.

On Mother's Day two days later, Dustin drove Mel and Dani to Olympia Medical Center. After much arguing with Bettie, he had finally convinced the old lady to stay home due to the high health risk for her age.

He pulled into the parking lot and scowled at the small media crowd gathered outside the hospital with balloons and cameras.

"Shit," he muttered as he drove past the entrance and down the lot. He'd forgotten the hospital staff would be performing a special goodbye ceremony for Rachel and a few media reps would be attending.

But that didn't look like a few.

They hadn't even considered his thoughts on the spectacle. He just wanted to meet his mom again without a damn camera being shoved up their asses. Couldn't the media respect the fact his mom had nearly died? Was a private family moment too much to ask?

Once he had parked, Mel and Dani masked up and walked beside him toward the small crowd of chatting media reps. They had all dressed semi-formal for the special moment. Dustin wore a collared shirt and jeans, Mel a silk shirt and tights, and Dani a long-sleeved purple blouse and dark jeans.

Dani had gone out of her way to pick up the blouse and stud earrings from her apartment for the occasion though Dustin assured her it wasn't a big deal. The gesture warmed his heart. He stole a glance at her from where he walked beside her, and his breath caught at her beauty. She had added a touch of mascara to her curly lashes, which brought out the shimmer in her hazel eyes and iridescent smile.

She was gorgeous. How did she ever end up with such a piece of shit like Tanner?

His teeth gritted at the thought of Dani's ex, and the physical and emotional pain Tanner had wrought upon her.

And yet, Tanner wasn't far different from Derek Mottley, whose similar actions had pained so many people.

The comparison triggered a new, electrifying current of hatred and disgust for his dad, and a surge of regret for daring to suggest to Dani that monsters like his dad were capable of redemption.

Dustin was temporarily torn from his bubbling pool of motions when a photographer skirted in front of him. "Are you guys the family?" the lanky guy asked, his fingers twitching toward his camera.

Dani stepped to the side as Dustin pulled Mel close, not answering the photographer. His sister's shoulders were tense; he knew she was anxious to see their mom, and this damn crowd of oglers wasn't helping the situation.

"Dustin!" Dr. Leopold brushed the photographer aside, his white physician's coat sweeping behind him. His bright green eyes twinkled above his N-95 mask. "I am so happy for you."

Dustin adjusted his own mask and pursed his lips. "Thank you, Doctor."

Appearing behind him a second later was Lila, her eyes shining. She wore her scrubs, her hair pulled back in the usual bun behind her mask and face shield. Dustin's throat tightened as she clasped her hands behind her back and beamed up at him through her glasses.

"Hi, Dustin. I'm so glad your mom is doing better. I worried about your family for the past two weeks."

He shifted his feet and curled his lip. "Thanks, Lila."

His head dipped toward Mel. "This is my sister, Mel." He turned his head, searching for Dani, and found her waiting patiently a few paces away. He waved a hand, and she clutched her purse tightly to her, grasping an elbow before stepping forward hesitantly. Dustin turned back to Lila. "And this is Dani, my…" *Med school mentee? Lila would think it weird I brought a mentee to such a personal event.*

"Nice to meet you both," Lila greeted before he could finish. She reached a hand underneath her face shield and pushed her glasses up her nose, nodding at the two girls before him.

Mel didn't so much as blink, but Dani nodded back. "Nice to meet you too," Dani responded. "You probably can't tell, but I'm smiling underneath my mask."

Lila laughed, and the tension in Dustin's chest loosened. When she relaxed, she stepped toward him, digging in her pocket, and pulled out a small square envelope. Her thumbs traced the edges as she eyed it for a few long seconds. "I'm not so sure you would find value in this…" she murmured so only he could hear.

Dustin's brow narrowed. "Don't be ridiculous," he scowled.

Her eyes shimmered, and she extended the envelope to him. He took it, noting his name written in her elegant font on the front.

"You didn't have to do this, but thank you."

Her cheeks lifted behind her mask. "It doesn't have anything other than…well-wishes." She stepped back, and he tucked the envelope in his back pocket. Dustin was sure whatever she had written was above and beyond anything he deserved, but he appreciated the gesture all the same.

Another media rep stepped around Leopold and Lila, pointing at Dustin and Mel. "Those two are the family." The two photographers hiked up their cameras and snapped away at the Mottley siblings, the clicks of their cameras attracting the attention of the other media reps.

Dustin squeezed his sister's shoulders as a frenzy of media reps soon surrounded them, brushing aside his medical colleagues. The reps paid little notice to social distancing, pushing past colleagues to snatch a good picture of the stranded siblings.

A sharp, familiar voice broke through the buzz of excitement from behind. "Damn, give them some room!"

Dustin swiveled his head, and Jessie's tall figure appeared above the flashing cameras. He weaved through the crowd, waving his arms, and a few media reps shot him irritated looks before dispersing.

Jessie halted a few paces away from Dustin, his hands on his hips. He looked sharp in his blue blazer and jeans, and a blue mask with an *LA Times* logo covered his dark face. "Dustin…" He paused, his brown eyes squinting. "Man, I'm so happy for you… When I found out it was your mom, I nearly lost it. Sorry about the crowd. I tried to vouch for you at the *Times*, but they sent at least three or four guys."

Dustin's chest tightened. "It's okay, man. Thanks. It means a lot." He glanced down and brought a hand to his eyes, rubbing them. Mel clasped her hands around his waist and buried her face in his stomach.

He clutched her against him as a rising cheer echoed throughout the hospital entrance. Mel broke away from him, and they both looked toward the large glass double doors, propped open wide in preparation for a parade of nurses. The photographers snapped their heads up and darted forward, cameras at the ready.

There she was.

Dustin's heart skipped a beat as Rachel Mottley appeared in a wheelchair pushed by a nurse down the hallway. A flock of clapping doctors and nurses trailed her, the joyous applause making his eyes water.

As his mom came closer, Dustin studied her face, and his stomach dropped. She had lost an alarming amount of weight. Her pale cheeks were sunken, and wisps of brown hair flew messily behind the mask tucked over her mouth. Her thin arms hung limp on her thighs, a bouquet of flowers draped across her lap.

Despite her frail state, however, a fire burned in her eyes.

He sucked in a deep breath. She had suffered alone in a hospital bed for weeks, prodded and stabbed with needles as they stuffed a tube down her throat.

And now she was being greeted by a circus.

As soon as their mom cleared the entryway, Mel dashed out of Dustin's grip and ran toward her, weaving through the spectators.

Dustin forced his stiff legs into motion and hurried behind his sister, feeling as if he were in a dream.

Rachel's gaze latched onto them, and her defeated face scrunched with emotion. Her arms opened wide, and Mel and Dustin fell into them in a sweeping hug. A ripple of applause rose around them, and the cameras flashed furiously, but it all fell away as time slowed to stop.

It was just Dustin, Mel, and their mom.

Rachel Mottley was alive, here, in the flesh. A part of Dustin had feared this day would never come, yet here it was.

He couldn't believe it.

He breathed her in, careful not to crush her weak state as he sobbed into the crook of her neck. Mel buried her head into Rachel's chest, her tears soaking their mom's shirt.

Rachel brushed back Mel's hair and kissed her forehead. Her voice came out breathy and weak. "I've missed you two so much. I love you."

Dustin didn't know how much time had passed when he finally pulled away and crouched beside Mel. Rachel locked her glassy brown eyes with theirs.

"A day didn't go by when I didn't worry about you two. My heart is full."

Mel glanced down, wet strands of hair enveloping her puffy eyes. "Mom," she whispered.

"Yes, baby?" Rachel cupped her cheek and brushed away a tear.

Mel's brow drew tight. "Please don't ever leave us again."

Rachel's eyes fluttered close, a shaky exhale escaping her lips before she locked eyes with her daughter. "I'll do my best to make sure that doesn't happen again. Not until I'm an old lady and have seen you both grow up to be beautiful, successful adults." She reached a hand to Dustin and stroked the bangs spilling across his brows. "Your hair has gotten longer. You usually gel your bangs back, but I like it down." Her cheeks lifted, and he smiled in return.

"God, I missed you, Mom." He choked back a sob before she pulled them both into another tight hug.

After a long minute, they broke away, and Rachel turned to address the hospital staff. Her voice was hoarse as she placed a shaking hand on her chest.

"Thank you all so, so much... I will never be able to repay what

you have done for me. I won't ever know why I was so fortunate…
when so many others cannot say the same."

The onlookers broke into more applause, and the surrounding sniffles
and eye-wipes were too much for Dustin. He covered his face just as a
hand caressed his arm.

Rachel's tear-stained brown eyes peered into his. "Let's get out of here.
I've had enough for one day." She scanned the crowd. "Is Bettie not here?"

Dustin shook his head. "She wanted to be, but I made her stay
home."

Instead of disappointment at her neighbor's absence, relief swept
Rachel's features. "I'm glad that old woman finally listened for once."

Dustin's lip curled before he remembered Dani. He whirled, his eyes
scanning the ogling photographers, nurses, and physicians.

Where was she?

"What is it, Dustin?"

He turned to face his mom, licking his lips. "There's someone who
came with us. My mentee, actually. She has…" He paused and rubbed
his neck. "She has done more for Mel and me than anyone could have
asked for while you were gone."

Dani's heart leapt in her throat as Dustin and Mel rushed through the
crowd and into their mother's waiting arms. Applause rose around them,
and if there were any dry eyes before, now there were none.

Dani fixated on the embracing family, the photographers eternaliz-
ing the precious moment with their cameras. She had dreaded for days
now that Dustin and his sister would never get to see their mom again,
but here they were, their prayers answered. She failed to suppress her
shoulders from shaking in joy for the Mottleys.

And yet despite Dani's tears and wave of relief, a dangerous twinge
of jealousy piqued at the sight of them all together, reunited at last. What
the hell was wrong with her? She wiped her eyes and tried to ignore the
poke in her reservoir of dark emotions.

When they finally released each other, Mrs. Mottley beamed at her
children, her eyes a well of happiness. She held Mel's cheek and exchanged
a few quiet words with them before hugging them again, and that nagging
poke in Dani's stomach sharpened into a stab.

Unable to watch their private moment, Dani turned away, her fingers digging into her purse strap. Their reunion was too precious, too sweet.

Too unrelatable.

After a few minutes, the applause died down, and a breathy, hoarse voice broke the silence. Dani turned to see Mrs. Mottley addressing the crowd, a pale hand shaking on her chest.

"I won't ever know why I was so fortunate…when so many others cannot say the same."

The onlookers erupted into bittersweet applause once more. Tears trailed silently down Dani's cheeks as she watched the Mottleys win over the crowd, and she wasn't sure if they were tears of joy for the family or tears for her own self-pity.

"I'm so happy for them," said a soft voice beside her. Dani turned to see the nurse, Lila, staring glassy-eyed at the Mottleys. She was about the same height as Dani with kind brown eyes, a slender neck, and a timid posture. Even with Lila's face shield, mask, and glasses, Dani could tell the nurse was a beautiful woman. The tender way she handed Dustin the envelope had made Dani wonder if Lila was fond of him.

The young nurse pushed her glasses up her nose and dipped a shoulder. "I'm glad you've been able to care for him."

Dani cocked an eyebrow, wrinkling her mouth in confusion. *Why would she assume I've been with him every day?*

*Oh.*

She shook her head, her cheeks heating, and curled a loose hair behind an ear. "Dustin and I—we're not…" The very thought made Dani's heart bristle. They were still just friends, right?

Lila gave a small laugh. She folded her small arms, her long lashes flitting back toward the Mottleys. There was something about the way she stared at Dustin that made Dani's chest cave.

"It was so hard to see him broken at work since his mom became sick. I can't imagine what he went through."

Dani's eyes widened. "He worked even while his mom was sick?" she managed, a lump blocking her throat.

Lila nodded. "Yes, and he continued to do so when she was hospitalized. He didn't tell us right away that his mom was taken in, but it was evident he was out of it, robotic, depressed. When our supervisor told him to take some time off, Dustin refused to leave at first."

She lifted her glasses and wiped her eyes with her sleeve. "He said he couldn't sit at home and sulk when the hospital needed all the help they could get. He said his mom had never given up, so he couldn't either."

Dani clutched at her sides as the river of emotion flowed harder. Dustin was the most selfless person she had ever met. Even when he was deep in grief, he had put others before himself. How dare she turn everything inward on herself in the face of Dustin's actions?

She wanted to slip away in that moment, hating herself for daring to feel sorry for herself when she should have nothing but rejoice for Dustin and his family.

"Dani!" Dustin's voice broke through the bustling crowd. She glanced up to see him wheeling his mom in Dani's direction, Mel walking stoically beside them. When Dani turned to excuse herself from Lila, the nurse was nowhere to be found.

She wiped her eyes and sniffed away any remaining sobs as the Mottleys approached. Their faces were wet but otherwise glowing.

*Stop being so pathetic. Celebrate with them.*

Dustin pulled his mom to a stop in front of Dani. Mrs. Mottley looked malnourished; her cheekbones were pale and limbs thin, and dark bags hung under her eyes. Dani's heart sank as the image resurfaced of Rachel coiling in pain on a hospital bed, attached to IVs and a breathing tube.

"Mom, this is my friend, Dani," Dustin introduced with the hint of a smile.

Mrs. Mottley's eyes twinkled, and she stretched out her hand. Dani hesitated, unsure of the health risk to a recently recovered COVID patient.

"Honey, you don't have to worry about COVID with me," Rachel ushered.

Dani swallowed before obliging and shaking her hand. The woman's grip was weak. "It's so nice to meet you, Mrs. Mottley. You are such an incredible, strong, inspiring woman." She clasped her hands and smiled.

Mrs. Mottley's cracked lips spread wide. "You can call me Rachel." She waved a hand dismissively. "And please. Lying helpless, hooked up to a ventilator? The health-care workers deserve all the praise. And so do you." When Dani gave her a confused look, she went on. "Dustin told me how you've helped him, Bettie, and Mel around the house since I've been gone. Thank you so much, from the bottom of a mother's heart."

Dani's cheeks flushed, and she shifted her feet, her words catching in her throat. Her gaze focused on the lingering photographers who were snapping photos of the four of them from a distance. She didn't belong here in their family moment, in the photos of their happy memory.

"Dani, short for Danice? Danielle?" Rachel asked, pulling Dani's attention back down to her.

"Danica," she corrected with a scratch of her cheek.

Warmth spread in Rachel's brown eyes. "Danica. What a pretty name."

Dani returned the best smile she could manage. "Thank you, but I've always hated it."

"Just like Melody," Rachel chuckled.

Mel's lower lip protruded, and they all laughed. The tension in Dani's shoulders eased slightly at the sight of seeing Dustin and Mel so bright.

"Well, you are more than welcome to come back to the house for a little celebration in thanks," Rachel offered.

Dani took a deep breath. She had more than overstayed her welcome with the Mottleys at this point, but Rachel's offer warmed her heart all the same.

She bit her lip before her mouth stretched into a grateful smile. "That...would be amazing."

*May*

DUSTIN FLIPPED THE STEAKS ON THE BARBECUE AND FANNED the smoke away from his face, feeling more elated than he had in a long time.

It was odd being back home after having spent over two weeks at Bettie's. When he'd entered his house last week to grab his guitar, the place had felt desolate and reeked of the horrible memory of the EMTs whisking away his weak mom. Now, as the smoking steak excited his taste buds and laughter reached his ears from the living room, the house seemed vibrant once again.

"Mmm, smells good!" Mel licked her lips from the sliding door of their back yard, her pudgy face brightening in the fading sunlight.

He lowered the spatula and shot her a teasing look. "Aren't you supposed to be setting the dinner table instead of bothering me?"

"Already set. And Bettie and Dani finished the salad. We're just waiting on you, slow poke."

He smirked and pressed the spatula against the searing steaks. "All right. It'll be another five minutes or so."

She grinned, spinning on her heel and leaving him alone in the back yard.

Dustin switched off the burners and propane and piled the cooked meat onto a tray beside the barbecue. Then he wiped his hands on his apron before walking the tray into the house.

Dani and Mel had set up a folding table in the living room to accommodate the many dishes. He set the tray of steaks next to a salad and Bettie's mouthwatering homemade mashed potatoes, gravy, and deviled eggs. The old woman had also whipped up a blueberry pie for dessert—Rachel's favorite.

Their meal would not have been as extravagant, or as cheery, without Bettie.

"That's the last of the food. Shall we dig in?" Rachel offered from the end of the table. She had been seated during all of the meal prep, too weak to so much as stand for ten minutes.

"Yes!" Mel chirped, dropping into a chair in between Bettie and her mom.

Dustin headed to the kitchen to wash up and nearly crashed into Dani as she rounded the bar with several glasses of tea in her arms.

"Oh, sorry!" she blurted, stepping back awkwardly.

He smiled and took the glasses from her, setting them on the kitchen table. "Here, let me do that. You've been working all day."

A small grin crept from her lips. "So have you…but thank you."

Dustin was aware of her eyes on him as he discarded his apron in a drawer and washed his hands. She stepped forward and leaned on the counter beside him, pulling her long, dirty-blonde ponytail over a shoulder. "How are you feeling? With all this going on, I mean."

He dried his hands on a towel and turned to face her, licking his lips. "It all kind of feels surreal, but in a good way, you know? Like a movie."

Dani nodded and brushed a strand of hair behind an ear. "I'm so happy for you, Dustin." She took a hesitant step toward him and gazed up at him with timid hazel eyes. "I…just wanted you to know that."

His mouth slanted. "Thank you."

She bit her lip and played with the ends of her blouse sleeves. "Um…I—"

"Come on, you two! The food is getting cold!" called Bettie from the living room.

Dustin's lips teased into a smile, and he brushed past Dani to collect the glasses from the table. "Guess that's our cue."

She smiled as she gathered the remaining two glasses sitting on the counter and followed him out of the kitchen. They set the drinks in front of each plate and took their seats across the table from Bettie, Mel, and Rachel.

"Dustin, this steak is delicious. Thank you!" Rachel exclaimed, covering her mouth as she chewed. Her plate had a light serving of steak and salad; the doctor had cautioned her to eat smaller portions as her strength returned.

Dani grinned as she loaded her plate with deviled eggs and mashed potatoes. "As soon as he heard the news you'd be coming home, he drove to five different grocery stores to find a steak for your 'welcome home' dinner."

Rachel's eyes widened. "You did?"

Dustin's mouth quirked as he added a slab of steak to his plate. "Honestly, I would have been happy with cereal for dinner, but I wanted it to be perfect for you."

Rachel's eyes softened. "Aww, thank you." She leaned forward, her lips perking. "Careful, Dustin—you haven't shown this much sentiment since you cleaned your room in an effort to woo your middle-school crush."

"Thanks, Mom." Dustin scowled, his cheeks heating, and they all laughed.

Bettie smiled as she squeezed a bottle of dressing over her salad. "Noah had a parade of girlfriends himself, although I don't know what ladies saw in him. He was such an idiot…"

Dustin's attention drifted to Dani beside him, who was struggling to skewer a piece of steak with her fork. "Is the steak cooked good enough?" he asked.

"Hmm?" She looked up from her plate, startled. "Oh, yeah." She gave him a reassuring smile, then her mouth pulled into a smirk. "You got some barbecue sauce on your shirt."

He followed her stare to the splotch on his chest and frowned. "Well, damn. There goes my only collared shirt."

Dani choked on her tea and set the glass down, covering her mouth. "You only have *one* collared shirt? How the hell did you make it this far?"

"Just kidding." He winked as he sliced off another bite of steak. "I have two collared shirts."

She shot him a sly grin, that familiar dimple denting her left cheek. "Two collared shirts. The key to success."

The corner of Dustin's mouth pulled up, and he studied her light freckles and vibrant eyes as she dug into Bettie's mashed potatoes. Only a week ago, her bright face had been soaked in tears as she re-opened the deep wounds of her past.

But she had done it for him. To express that she understood some of his pain.

A tiny knot formed in his chest. He hoped she was doing better.

When a wisp of her hair fell out of her ponytail and grazed her plate, he itched to brush it behind her ear. She glanced up, catching him staring, and her lips tugged up. "What?" she asked.

He pursed his lips. "I'm just…happy you're here with us."

The amusement in her eyes faded for an instant before she gazed back at him with a mixture of softness and something else he couldn't comprehend. "Me too," she whispered with a small smile. They locked eyes with a deep intensity for a long moment, and the knot in Dustin's chest unraveled a bit.

Bettie clapped her hands suddenly, turning his head. "I think it's time for dessert! Mel, be a dear and collect the dirty plates, will you, please?"

Mel stood from her seat with a grin and began clearing the table.

"How is your family doing, Dani?" Rachel asked as Bettie retrieved the homemade blueberry pie from the kitchen and started to cut it up.

Dani smiled. "They're doing good. Helena wasn't hit too hard by the virus."

"I'm sorry, Helena…?"

"Oh—Helena, Montana. Sorry." She looked up as Bettie handed her a slice of pie. "Thank you," she told the old woman.

"What do they do for a living?" Bettie asked, setting a slice in front of Dustin.

Dani curled a loose strand of hair behind her ear. "They own their own tile business, started with some money they inherited from my mom's parents after they passed away."

Rachel twirled her fork in the air. "Inheritances are always a huge help. My parents' savings helped me out during med school. But I'm still paying off loans. Crazy, huh?" She set down her fork and wiped ranch dressing off her lips with a napkin. "Do you have any siblings? My brother would throw a hissy fit if we were held captive during this crisis at your age."

Dustin sucked in a breath as Dani hesitated. *The poor girl can't catch a break from her past.* She looked down at her pie, her eyes softening.

"I...I don't have any siblings," she responded, and he sensed the struggle in her voice.

Rachel and Bettie exchanged a quick glance.

"But did you know she's an amazing athlete?" Dustin interjected, leaning forward on his elbows with a wide grin. "Full-ride lacrosse scholarship to SC."

Dani peered up at him, a gleam in her eye.

"Is that so?" Rachel's eyebrows shot up. "I always wished I knew how to play lacrosse. Maybe Mel and I can try to catch one of your games after this is all over?"

A smile tugged at Dani's lips as she dug a fork into her pie. "I would love that."

"What about my softball games, Mom! You barely went to any of them," Mel whined.

Rachel waved a hand. "What are you complaining about? I went to all your games that I could. Plus, you were on a slump, so let me know when you start hitting again, and I'll make it back out there." She winked at her daughter.

Dustin leaned over to Dani and muttered under his breath, "Sometimes I just drop her off at her games and chill at Starbucks, then tell her I saw the whole thing. Works every time."

Mel glared at her brother from across the table. "Stop talking about me!"

They all laughed, and Mel rolled her eyes, chomping the next few bites of her pie in silence.

Rachel smiled at Dani. "Hon, thank you again for joining us to-night, and for everything you've done to help with Bettie and my kids."

Dani blushed and covered her mouth stuffed with pie. "My

pleasure." Her gaze dropped, and she shoved her crust along her plate with her fork. "I'm…sure Dustin and Mel are sick of me by now. I'll be out of your way as soon as dinner is over."

Rachel's pale face sank, and she placed a hand on her chest. "My dear, you stay as long as you like. You're practically family at this point."

Dani beamed. "Thank you for the kind words. You've all been so welcoming…" Her head dipped, and she studied her slice of pie.

Mel's large brown eyes pleaded with Dani. "Please stay, Dani! Mom could use your help while she recovers." A wide smile broke across Mel's face. "You can stay in my room again!"

Dustin scowled at his mom and sister. "Stop pressuring her. She's been here a week already. I'm sure she wants to go home."

A smile teased Dani's mouth. "It's okay." She bit her lip, glancing at Rachel. "Mel's right—I'm sure your mom could use the extra help. I'll stay a little longer."

Mel and Rachel brightened, and Dustin couldn't help but feel a sense of relief.

Dani would stay.

He stiffened as his phone hummed in his pocket. Straightening, he slipped it out and glanced at the caller ID: Dad's Jail.

His heart skipped a beat. *Shit. Not now.*

Then a brief lance of pain shot through his chest; Dustin had forgotten to call his dad's attorney to tell him Rachel had been released from the hospital. It was the least he could have done after breaking the news to Derek she'd been sick a few weeks ago.

His eyes darted to his mom, and she raised her eyebrows in response.

"Who is it?" Dani asked, peering over his shoulder at his phone. She stiffened when she read the screen.

Dustin ran his hand through his hair. "Dammit. Uh, I've gotta take this."

Dani placed a consoling hand on his arm and nodded. Then she stood and gestured to his sister. "Hey, Mel, why don't you show me that game on Dustin's iPad you were telling me about?"

"Ooh, yes!" Mel abandoned her half-eaten pie and danced over to her bedroom. Dani followed less animatedly and shut the door behind her.

Bettie stood up as well, gathering up the finished plates. "I'll start cleaning the dishes. Don't worry about it," she said, stifling Rachel's silent protest.

When Bettie retreated to the kitchen, Rachel nodded toward the backyard. Dustin preceded her, answering the call on what must've been the final ring and putting it on speaker.

The jail operator spiel's monotonous voice drifted through the line as he opened the sliding door and walked across the darkened grass, triggering the backyard motion sensor light.

When the spiel finally ended, Dustin answered hesitantly, "Dad?"

Derek's rusty voice cut through the line. "Dustin! Hey, how's it going?" Dustin pictured his dad's handsome, clean-shaven face with brown hair combed over his blue eyes. He had a tall, athletic figure that still drew the eyes of women at his age, but Dustin wasn't sure if he still looked the same after nearly a year in jail. Dustin hadn't bothered to visit him in the time since, too ashamed and conflicted with Derek to want to see his father's face.

The sound of muffled footsteps behind him made Dustin look up to see Rachel seating herself at the wooden table beside the barbecue, listening intently. "I'm good," he breathed into the phone. "How are you doing? How is the jail coping with the virus?" He started pacing, holding out the phone so both he and his mom could hear.

"I'm doin' all right," Derek replied with a deep sigh. "The virus just gave us a good scare—I heard a couple hundred were released early after some inmates tested positive, but our place was one of the luckier ones. We've been tryin' to pass the time with some slow-pitch. I gotta tell ya, Mel would kick half these guys' asses. I cracked up just thinkin' what she would say if she saw some of the guys play." His rough chuckle drifted through the line.

Dustin stopped pacing, and his grip on the phone tightened. His voice came out low and ominous. "Don't talk about her. You abandoned Mel the moment you touched that woman."

"I...I know, Dustin. I messed up." Any trace of humor from Derek's voice had vanished. "I, uh… My whole reason for calling is...I just wanted to apologize. I'm so sorry for...for everything I put you and Mel and Rachel through in the past years. I've been such a goddamn fool, and I'm ashamed it's taken this long for me to admit I haven't been the father you all deserve."

Dustin couldn't believe his ears. He had longed for a deep, sincere apology from his dad for months, but the words Derek offered now fell pathetically flat.

It was because of people like him that Dani suffered. It was because of people's quickness to forgive that allowed predators like Derek to meander carelessly on with their lives, preying on women and shattering livelihoods because they knew they'd always be forgiven in the end. And as a result, women like Dani paid the price, their trust and capacity to love permanently damaged because of one man's single, shameful and selfish action.

How dare Derek even *attempt* to apologize. Did he really believe he could repair all the damage he'd wreaked with just a few aimless words?

Dustin gritted his teeth, unable to quell the fury seeping through him. "Bullshit, Dad. You're telling me you're rotting in a jail cell just because you *messed up?* Because you just made another dumb mistake we can all brush off after some time? I don't even know what the hell to say to you. Never mind the atrocious crime you committed; you threw away our family. Maybe a part of me still wanted to believe you were a good guy after all these years, but after what you did, I'm embarrassed to call you my dad. It's pretty clear you have no damn intention to be better."

The silence in the air hung like a calm before the storm.

"Listen, Dustin—"

"No, you listen to me!" Dustin couldn't keep his hands from shaking. Rachel stepped forward and rested a hand on his shoulder, but he shook it off. "You *destroyed* our family, Dad. Mel barely saw you from the start, but now she'll grow up without even a damn *separated* father. And when mom got COVID, Mel didn't have a single parent to turn to! I gave you chance after chance, even when Mom tried to keep you away. Just because you didn't get to stay with us, it didn't mean you could go screw yourself up and pretend like it wouldn't affect us. Your stupid *mistake* didn't just destroy you and the woman you assaulted—it destroyed *us.*" He took a few deep breaths as Rachel stared at him with pained eyes.

An agonizing minute passed before Derek spoke, his voice frail. "I know, Dustin." Another long silence followed, and Dustin thought he heard a sob. "I'd understand if you and Mel and Rachel never forgive me. I just wanted you to know…I'll still always love you, no matter what you think of me." His voice trembled with his next words. "I deserve your hatred and every dirty, shitty insult you can think of. I deserve to rot in this cell forever because of what I did to this family. You're completely right. I was given chance after chance to prove myself, and I failed every single damn time. Truth is, I've still felt guilty all these years for failing Rachel and you kids, and last summer I just lost it. I'd been sober for seven straight years until then. I missed having a woman in my life, and knew what would happen if I drank, but I did it anyway. *I did it anyway.* I was so stupid. I can never forgive myself, and I don't expect you to. Your mother did the right thing by leaving." He paused, taking a deep breath. "I know my words mean nothing to you, but I'll say them anyway. I'm so, so sorry. I mean that from the bottom of my heart, Dustin. As black as it is."

Derek's apology ripped through Dustin's chest, rocking him back on his heels. His grip on the phone loosened, the fist at his side unclenched.

For as long as Dustin had known him, Derek had spewed apologies that didn't hold water, pledging he was a better man. He'd argued his cheating on Rachel had happened years ago and blamed it on the alcohol, claiming he'd given up drinking for good after that night.

Dustin had expected more excuses and empty promises from Derek now, but something about his apology this time took Dustin back to the day Dani had confessed her past to him, her hands shaking as tears streamed out of her puffy eyelids. "*I was so stupid... I drove home afterward. Like a damn psychopath. I knew what I was doing was wrong, but I didn't care. I was so...furious at my dad and didn't give a shit about anything else.*"

Then the backyard faded and Dustin was back in his car, riding home with Dani from the hospital volunteer program so many months ago. Her strained voice echoed in his ears: "*So the liars and the thieves and criminals should just be given chance after chance? Because somewhere deep down, they're good people? Where do you draw the line?*"

Dustin pinched his nose, fighting tears as a burn crawled up his throat. Maybe a deeper part of him had always believed everyone deserved forgiveness, but he never really understood what that meant until Dani. She had made mistakes that altered her life forever, and continued to be haunted by the demons of her past to this day. And yet, she'd fought against her demons, kept marching forward, and put others before herself.

If he had learned anything from Dani, it was this: There was no road too far gone from the main path. People who had ventured down the darkest of trenches, including his dad, were still capable of redemption—if they recognized their faults and truly wanted to be better.

And the apology he'd just heard from his dad sounded like someone who'd finally accepted his wrongs.

"Dad…" Dustin's voice came out weak, the authority from minutes ago having dissipated. "I accept your apology."

The deep, uneven exhale trickling through the phone was a stark contrast to Rachel's sharp inhale on Dustin's left. "Thank you, Dus," Derek murmured, using a nickname Dustin hadn't heard in years. "I didn't expect you to say that."

Dustin heaved a long breath, tilting his head up to stare at the moon's bright beam seeping through the night sky. "But don't think this ends here. You have a long way to go to repair the relationships you ruined, and you can be sure no woman will ever trust you again."

A heavy, deafening silence hung in the air before Derek's raspy voice broke it. "I know." Another agonizing, silent moment passed. "Uh, your mom there? I saw on the television they had a whole ceremony at the hospital for her."

Dustin licked his lips, lost for words. He glanced at his mom, and she shook her head. She had stopped talking to Derek years ago, when they first separated. Dustin wasn't convinced his mom would as easily forgive Derek—especially now, after his sexual assault record. But he couldn't blame her. Hopefully, she would come to forgive Derek on her own time.

"She…can't talk right now," Dustin answered softly.

A long sigh expelled through the line. Derek knew Rachel was avoiding him, and there was a small part of Dustin that pitied his dad. Maybe after all the fear and pain of wondering if Rachel would live or die, Derek deserved to hear her voice.

"Okay, just…just tell her that I love her, and…I'm sorry for everything and always will be. This whole thing of being in jail and feeling so goddamn *helpless* to you kids… And then when you told me she was on the tube… I didn't think I'd get the chance to tell her. I know she doesn't deserve me or what I did to her, but just tell her that I love her and thank God she made it out because…"

Rachel closed her eyes and bit her lip, holding back tears. Dustin turned his head away from the sight. *Just talk to him, Mom. Maybe it will give you a bit of closure.*

The line stayed silent, and when Rachel whimpered, Derek went on with a strained tone. "I know you're there, Rachel, so I'll just say it. There isn't a day that goes by that I don't think you were the best thing that ever happened to Dustin and Mel. You've always been the best mother to them, a better parent than I could ever be. Being locked away might not change me or fix what I've done, but I'll be damned if it kept me from telling you how grateful I am for you. I was afraid I… wouldn't be able to tell you that."

When he paused, Rachel took the phone from Dustin with trembling hands.

"Derek? I… Thank you for…" She trailed off, her voice hitching.

"You don't have to say a damn thing, Rachel. I'll happily live out the rest of my life behind bars knowing you heard what I said."

**May**

DANI LAY ON MEL'S BED FIDGETING WITH HER BLOUSE SLEEVES while Mel played through Candy Crush on Dustin's iPad. She peeked through the blinds to see Dustin pacing with a clenched fist, his mom sitting stoic on a bench beside the barbecue. Although Dustin's words were obscured, the hurt in his voice was palpable.

It was alarming to see Dustin so vexed as he talked with his dad. The one time her mentor had mentioned his father, his eyes swam with melancholy and anguish. Maybe his grief from the past week stemmed deeper than she realized.

Dani leaned back on the bed and closed her eyes, trying to block out his pained voice. She knew what it was like to feel abandoned by your father; to be wounded so deep by him, it was as if he didn't care at all about you. It brought back the gut-wrenching memories she'd had arguing with Franc nearly every night over the dinner table. Maybe it was better he didn't speak to her anymore.

Her mind drifted back to tonight's dinner, when she'd locked eyes with Dustin in that frozen moment in time; in that small instant, she'd forgotten about her brother's absence and her quarrels with her family. She'd been entirely absorbed in the present, free of past burdens. Looking back, she wished she could have corked that happy, peaceful moment in a bottle to save for a rainy day.

Because happiness never lasted long for her.

Dani swallowed a lump in her throat and rolled to face Mel, who was still viciously hooked on her game. "Did you pass level 46 yet?" she asked.

A small snort drifted from the girl, her big brown eyes never leaving the screen. "I passed that level twenty minutes ago."

Dani chuckled and shifted on the covers, glancing around the nine-year-old's room. A scrap board of sports teams and pictures hung on the wall next to the window, similar to Dani's, except it referenced softball instead of lacrosse. A cute framed picture of Mel beaming in her uniform with a large trophy hung by the closet, and the light blue walls were decorated with butterflies, music notes, and glow-in-the-dark stars.

"I like your room," Dani noted, smiling at her surroundings.

Mel dropped the iPad onto her lap. "My room was pink at first. I repainted it blue with my mom, and she painted the flowers and music notes on the wall."

Dani redirected her attention to the meticulous brush strokes lining the walls. "Oh, wow. Your mom's really talented."

Before Mel could respond, a knock sounded on the door, turning their heads. Dustin's brown-haired head poked through, and he gave a small smile when his eyes glazed over Dani curled up on the bed at Mel's feet.

Dani's heart bristled. The tension from earlier had drained from his face, and his posture was relaxed.

He was okay.

Mel scowled at her brother. "Uh, what happened to knocking and waiting for an answer? I didn't say to come in!"

"You're still playing Candy Crush?" he asked, ignoring her accusation.

"Yeah, why?"

He narrowed his eyes. "You're such a boob. Did you let Dani play? It's kind of rude to play in front of her."

Dani laughed and sat up straight, swinging her legs over the bed's edge. "I'm really bad at it. Mel was just showing me how much of a pro she is."

Dustin rolled his eyes and opened the door further. "Uh-huh, I'm sure." He nodded toward the hallway. "Want a break from the boob?"

Mel rolled onto her stomach, chucking a pillow at him.

He caught it and tossed it back at her with a laugh. "That your best throw, softball player?"

Mel's lips tightened into a thin smile. "Not even close."

Dani stood and stepped in between them, laughing, even as a part of her ached for her brother. "You guys are adorable." She rested a hand on Dustin's arm and lowered her voice. "You're good?"

His broad shoulders lifted in a deep sigh. "Yeah… My mom's still talking to him though."

Dani raised a curious eyebrow. From what she had gathered from Mel, Rachel had always been at odds with her husband and made it a point to avoid him at all costs. Hopefully, that was a sign things were going well…or really bad.

"Oh…" Dani rubbed her arm. She was more than curious to hear about his talk. "Well, can you show me your room? I haven't seen it yet!" She smiled and gave a small nod in Mel's direction.

His inquisitive gaze lingered on Dani for a long second, making her skin tingle. Then he nodded and waved a hand, stepping through the bedroom door.

Dani followed him across the hall, the clink of silverware and rush of running water from the kitchen indicating Bettie was still busy with cleaning up. Dani bit her lip. She had forgotten to offer to clean the dishes! The old woman worked too much for her old age.

Dustin opened his door and strode inside, piling up some documents on his desk while Dani absorbed the living space of her mentor.

A few movie posters hung on the wall above his bed: *Fast and Furious 5, 6,* and *7, The Dark Knight, The Hurt Locker*… Her gaze drifted to the bookshelf squeezed in between his desk and bed. It was stacked with novels, biographies, textbooks, fiction—were those Nicholas Sparks books? She shuffled through the bindings and spotted a familiar set of dark covers: The *Twilight* series.

Dani's mouth stretched into a wide grin as she beamed up at him. "Oh my God, you love teen romance?"

He turned from his desk to face her, his cheeks blanching tomato red. A smile crept across his lips as he leaned against his desk. "Kind of a guilty pleasure of mine, but yeah."

She tsked and folded her arms. "Are you Team Edward or Team Jacob?"

Dustin snorted. "Team Edward all the way."

Dani's jaw dropped. "Are you serious? Jacob is *way* hotter!"

He laughed and stepped around her to sit on the bed. "You got me there, but Jacob is shit. Only cares about himself."

Dani rolled her eyes. "Sure, but hotness wins in this case." She scanned the variety of literature lining his bookcase. "I didn't know you were such an avid reader." A small scoff escaped her lips. "Well, you're already an athlete, musician, and med extraordinaire—what did I expect?"

"I told you, I'm the master of pretty much everything. You didn't believe me?" He wiggled his brows.

"You are such a dick, you know that?" Dani tossed her hair over a shoulder, her mouth slanting upward.

A low chuckle met her ears. "I'll take that as a compliment."

Dani scoffed and turned, leveling her gaze with the top of the bookshelf. A frame displayed a younger version of him and Jessie playing basketball; hidden behind it was a smaller photo of Dustin and an older man with Dustin's same tousled brown hair and piercing blue eyes. Finally, on the end stood a larger portrait of Dustin, Mel, and their mom laughing as they hugged one another.

A grin spread across her face knowing the three of them were reunited happily once again. But her smile dissipated an instant later as that seed of jealousy crept up her throat. Jeremy would never be able to join his family in a "welcome home" dinner; he'd never be able to share in their laughter and attend any of Dani's future lacrosse matches like Rachel; he'd never be able to grow old, marry, and see the Pacific ocean...

*Stop it, dammit! Stop making everything about you! Can't you just be happy for Dustin and his family without thinking about that? You're more than your failures, remember?*

But seeing the Mottleys sharing laughs over the dinner table had reawakened the painful memories of her past. It was hard to be fully present when her heart constantly longed for her brother, and if it hadn't been for Dustin's reassuring smile in that one moment, Dani wouldn't have been able to shake away her selfish thoughts.

Dani tried to swallow, but when she caught sight of Lila's small envelope buried between two books, the lump in her throat wedged tighter. Had he read it yet? Lila had seemed hesitant to give it to him—was it something personal? Regardless, perhaps Lila was…someone who could fully share in Dustin's happiness.

Dani took a deep breath and turned to face him, and the sanctity of his cool blue eyes dropped a brick in her stomach. She grasped her elbow, searching his face. "Dustin, I…" The words dissolved on her tongue as a flash of red and gold behind him caught her attention. A long banner with elegantly laced edges hung by his window, the words "USC's Men's Basketball—2015 MVP" engraved in huge block letters.

Dani's eyebrows shot up. "You were MVP?"

A grin spilled across his face as he shuffled to the bed and sat. "Eh, no big deal. It really should've gone to Jessie."

She rolled her eyes devilishly. "Har, har. Dustin, that's *incredible*. It *is* a big deal, and you know it."

His mouth curved. "Thanks. It means a lot coming from a star athlete such as yourself." She couldn't tell if he was making a jab or being sincere. Regardless, her heart brimmed with respect for Dustin. *She* wouldn't have been able to keep such a prestigious title quiet; she'd had the audacity to boast to him about her own MVP status—for a pathetic high school league.

Dani bit her tongue hard before meeting his eyes. "Why didn't you go pro?"

He sighed and ran a hand through his brown hair. "Basketball is cool, but my heart is in medicine." His gaze shifted to the banner behind Dani, and his Adam's apple bobbed. "Although, looking back, the payout would have been nice with all the bills we have now…"

Dani scratched her cheek. "I think…I get what you mean. About weighing your happiness against the easy, safer route."

"Yeah?" He tilted his head in curiosity.

She expelled a deep sigh and came to sit next to him on the bed. "I've always liked science, but my dad never gave me the opportunity to focus on anything other than lacrosse." Her fingers crept up to tuck a stray hair behind her ear. "Jeremy was the one who convinced me to look into med schools. He did everything my dad wanted him to regarding getting a full-ride to Syracuse on a lacrosse scholarship but realized too late it wasn't what *he* wanted. And…" Her voice hitched, and her eyes lowered to the carpet. "I guess…my studies in med school—it's to make Jeremy proud, not my dad."

A hint of a smile stretched across his lips. "I think Jeremy would be more than proud to know you're doing what makes you happy, regardless of what anyone else thinks."

Dani dipped her head and smoothed the thin hem of her blouse. "I hope so."

His tone softened. "How is your family coping with…that, if you don't mind my asking?"

She wrinkled her mouth. "We…don't talk about what happened. It's too dark of a time. My dad has never forgiven me for what I did, and I don't blame him. I have a better relationship with my mom, but not by much. We always end up fighting."

Dustin inhaled sharply. "I get it. Since my dad got arrested this past summer, I didn't talk to him either. But after our call, I realized… it definitely helps to talk about the difficult stuff. Sometimes, the things we think of as weaknesses ultimately make us stronger."

"It went well, huh?" She folded her legs and looked up, fixing a hopeful gaze on him.

His eyes shifted to the floor. "Actually, yes. He apologized for tearing our family apart, and…I wasn't expecting him to talk the way he just did. It's like I saw a different side of him. I don't know if it was because of his fear of my mom dying, or because jail time brought him a come-to-Jesus moment… but he sounded genuinely…changed." His chest rose as he took a deep breath.

Dani felt a strong, irresistable urge to caress him, and before she could stop herself, her hand crept its way to the back of his neck. She weaved her fingers through his short brown hair and was surprised by how soft it was. He seemed to relax, leaning into her touch, and tingles cascaded up Dani's arm.

Dustin pursed his lips. "Of course, my dad's apology can't ever fix what happened…but it brought me some peace of mind, knowing he acknowledges the pain he caused."

An image of Franc flashed through Dani's mind at his words. She pulled back her hand and sat up straight, a ripple of guilt trickling through her. She swallowed and nodded to the side, remembering the photo she had browsed earlier. "Is that him over on your bookcase?"

He glanced at the small picture and pursed his lips. "Yeah. I forgot about that." He offered a weak smile.

"Are you okay?" Dani asked softly.

This time his smile was genuine. "Yeah, I'm okay. Actually, since my mom came home, I haven't been happier."

Jeremy's pale, motionless body surfaced in Dani's mind, the EMTs connecting the breathing tube and other useless machinery to him as they hoisted him into the ambulance. Dani's fingers squeezed the bed covers, and she shook away the image.

There it was again. How could she be so selfish, *still?* Even after all this time wishing Dustin and Mel well and celebrating their mom's return, Dani was still pitying herself? Why had she come here in the first place if she couldn't be happy for them?

*Because you found solace in sharing grief with them. And now their mom has returned, you envy them because they can rejoice over something you never can.*

She bit her lip, forcing away the sinister thoughts. No. That was despicable. Dustin didn't deserve that. He'd already had so much going on in his life that had only been exacerbated by his mom's hospitalization. His parents' separation had left him and his sister with not only financial troubles but emotional turmoil as well. Add the fear for his mom's life on top of that, and it was too much for any one person to handle.

She would never, *ever* wish harm on Dustin.

Dustin rested his elbows on his knees and looked up at her beneath his dark lashes. "On a lighter note, Bettie told me what happened to you. At the billiards place."

Dani grimaced. *That was a lighter note?* "So you know I wasn't lying. About getting arrested." She sank into his bed and curled her hair around her index finger.

He wrinkled his brow. "No. Bettie told me you said you didn't steal anything and it was your friend's boyfriend who did it."

Her eyes raked him curiously, searching his expression. She expected to see revulsion for not telling the whole truth at their mentor meeting months ago, but all she saw was a flash of contentment in his eyes.

"I knew you were innocent." He gave a small smile. "But why'd you act like you did it? I would have easily believed you if you'd said you were innocent."

Dani tugged on her blouse sleeves. "I'm not completely innocent. I resisted arrest and cursed at the officer."

He scowled. "Don't give me that."

She glanced down at her hands and sighed. "I acted like I was guilty because…I guess I wanted to see your reaction—to see if you would judge me. And when you said I wasn't a criminal, it struck a chord, because I had done something infinitely worse than steal a stupid bill. I *am* a criminal, and I deserve to be treated as such."

Dustin combed his bangs out of his face before locking his eyes with hers. "You know what rekindled my hope through all this? Through my mom's illness and my dad's absence and all this pandemic shit? You know what inspired me to forgive my dad?"

She arched an eyebrow. "What?"

His lips curved upward. "You."

Dani cocked her head, baffled.

His eyes never wavered, staring intently at her. "Hearing your story, about all the pain you went through, and then seeing you here, offering support to me and Mel… It was humbling. If you could do all that, how the hell could I not be hopeful? You made me believe goodness would always come through in this shitty world." His blue eyes twinkled beneath his dark lashes. "So tell me, how can someone so compassionate and strong like you deserve anything less than admiration? From me or your parents or anyone?"

Her teeth dug into her bottom lip as a slow, searing burn crawled up her throat.

She wished she had an answer.

*May*

DANI SAT ALONE THE NEXT AFTERNOON AT DUSTIN'S DESK, HER foot bouncing rapidly as she waited for her parents' faces to appear on her laptop. She had made an effort to look nice, having combed her long hair, applied a touch of mascara to her lashes, and shrugged on a V-cut shirt, cardigan, and jeans. It felt odd to be even slightly dressed up for her parents, but perhaps such an effort was long overdue.

This was it. This was the thing she had avoided for three years; the thing that always threatened to reignite the flame beneath those awful memories, those dark feelings of guilt, anger, hatred, self-pity… Yet this was the very thing Dustin had convinced her would set her free during yesterday's talk.

She hoped.

She bit her tongue and concentrated on Dustin's consoling words: *"It helps to talk about things. Sometimes, the things we think of as weaknesses ultimately make us stronger…"* Thinking back through the past few days, she realized the truth in his statement. Being vulnerable with him and talking about Jeremy and her past had not destroyed her; it had strengthened her. And after seeing Dustin's sense of closure after his difficult conversation with his parents, a seed of hope had sprouted in Dani's core.

He was proof that she would be okay.

And even if her parents didn't forgive her…well, at least she would be free of a burden she had held onto for so long.

Her heartbeat hammered through her throat as her laptop screen went dark and a buffer wheel spun. She tightened her grip on the edge of the chair.

*Fight on, Miss Torres.*

*Fight on.*

A moment later, her parents' taut faces appeared, their living room couch visible behind them. In the months since she'd last Skyped them, her dad's dark hair had grown scraggly over his ears, his mustache sprouted into a thick beard along his jaw. Her mom's normally shoulder-length blonde hair had lengthened to her back, and her cheeks looked a tad more withered.

"Hi, Dani. How are you doing?" Angelina asked, always the one to initiate conversation. She wore a long-sleeved sequin shirt that brought out her hazel eyes as she squinted at the camera. "That doesn't look like your apartment… Where are you?"

"I'm doing fine, just been staying with Dustin for the past week." When her mom raised an eyebrow, Dani quickly tacked on, "His mom has been sick in the hospital, so I've been trying to offer some support."

Worry etched into Angelina's eyebrows, and she lowered her gaze. "I'm sorry to hear that. It's nice of you to be helping out."

"Yeah…" Dani scratched her cheek and rested her chin on her fist. "How have you been doing since we last talked?"

Her parents exchanged a hesitant glance. Angelina turned back to the screen and smiled. "Things have been all right for the most part. The tile business has been slower, but it's hanging in there." She folded her hands. "We've missed you, honey."

Dani blinked slowly, her throat suddenly dry. "I've missed you too." She took a deep breath and rubbed her arm. "Listen…I wanted to apologize for how I've been behaving lately."

The hard lines in Angelina's face loosened, but her Frank's expression remained neutral, unreadable.

Dani swallowed. "I actually haven't been taking my medication since last summer."

Worry washed over Angelina's hazel eyes. "Honey, why? Your flashbacks…"

Dani sucked in another deep breath. "I lied to you when I said I didn't have any flashbacks. I have had multiple episodes." She curled her hair behind an ear. "I stopped taking the meds because…I didn't want to hide behind the meds like a coward. I wanted to live my life without a crutch to wash away the pain I thought I deserved."

Her mom's shoulders sagged, and her voice came out pained. "Oh, honey. I'm so sorry you went through that."

"It's okay. I'm actually doing better now. The point is… I realized I was off the meds for the wrong reasons…" Dani paused, and her next words trembled. "I…I really miss him, Mom." She looked down at the desk. "And…I've been tired of keeping him locked away. All this time, I've been so afraid of his memory. We've all been. But…that doesn't mean we can just forget him. He deserves to be remembered. To be celebrated." Her voice held firm now. "I want to live in remembrance of him and make him proud. I want to live as he would have wanted me to, instead of worrying about everything he's missing. I want to be able to tell his story to keep his memory alive. And you should too. I—*we*— have been living…ashamed, frightened of what the memories would bring back, and look what that fear has done to our family."

Angelina's head drooped, and tears swam in her eyes. "Dani, honey, that is our fault. You're right. We were so worried for you and afraid of bringing back all of that pain. We didn't know what to do. You suffered so much in those months after he died, and we couldn't bear to see you hurt like that again."

"I felt…like you hated me," Dani whispered, choking on tears. "I believed it for so long, I started to hate myself. I felt so guilty…"

Angelina shared a pained look with Franc. "Oh, Dani. We are so terribly sorry. I'm so, so sorry." Her voice broke, and tears spilled down her strained face.

After a few heart-wrenching moments, Dani broke the silence. "Dad?"

Franc looked up and locked eyes with her through the webcam. His brown eyes looked tired, burdened, and dark folds sagged under them. He looked older and more frail than she had ever seen him.

"I just wanted to let you know that…I'm so sorry for being angry with you all these years. I know you wanted me to go to Syracuse, but USC is where I belong, and…med school is why I'm here, not lacrosse. I'm here for *my* goals, *my* ambitions, even if they don't align with yours."

Franc leaned forward and linked his large hands above his knees. He stayed silent for a long minute, his mustache twitching. A flash of him lashing out and jabbing a thick finger in her direction stampeded through her mind. That fear in the pit of her stomach and the pain of that traumatic night resurfaced for a brief second.

*Failure after failure… You never learn!* She swallowed a lump in her throat.

"Danica, don't apologize." His deep, husky voice was somber. It was a stark contrast to the authoritative growl ingrained in her memory for years. His dark eyes searched the floor. "I'm the one who should be apologizing. I was wrong to push you so hard in high school. I never told you this, but…growing up, I didn't play lacrosse just to get into college. It ended up being my way of…exerting my emotions. Training on the field and winning games gave me a sense of control that compensated for things in life I couldn't control. And then when you came along and opposed my rigorous lacrosse training… You were right that I took my anger out on you because I couldn't get over my mother's death." He paused and looked away. "When she got sick…lacrosse was my lifeline; my way of proving to myself I was not completely useless."

The turmoil in Dani's stomach subsided, replaced with a wave of deep sorrow for her father. Franc Torres never talked about his mom; he had only said she suffered a slow and painful death from leukemia. She had died right before he attended college.

Angelina ran her hand through her husband's hair consolingly before he continued. "That night when Jeremy died, it felt like it had happened all over again, and this time, it was my fault. It was my fault for pushing you so hard—for tearing our family apart."

Hot tears blurred Dani's vision. "I thought all this time…you were angry with me for what I did. For stealing your truck and…acting so *stupid* and immaturely, and causing something so *horrible*…" She paused to steady her shaking voice. "When Mom said you left during the lacrosse match on TV at the bar…I thought you couldn't stand to watch me."

He shook his head. "Of course not. When I watched you play at the bar—whenever I watch you play a match—I just remember how you and Jeremy would play lacrosse together in the backyard, laughing and having fun. And then I remembered how I changed that, pushing you and pushing you to train, and you never had that same smile you had when you played with Jeremy. When you ran off drinking, and then Jeremy was killed, I blamed myself for all of it. My withdrawal from you had nothing to do with what you'd done."

Dani sniffed back a sob but couldn't stop the two silent tears that trickled down her cheeks. "Dad…I…"

He wiped his eyes and went on. "What happened on that night was *my fault*. It's all my doing. Please understand that."

Dani grimaced at his words, and her fingers squeezed the edge of Dustin's chair. All this time, she'd been afraid her dad hated her for her deadly mistakes, but he blamed *himself?* It came as a shock that her dad had suffered with guilt in a similar way to Dani all these years, and a tremor of guilt shot up her spine. She hadn't once thought he could be in as much pain, and never bothered to repair their relationship.

Dustin's words from so many months ago rang in her mind. *"Sometimes, given enough time, people do change."* For so long, she'd wanted her dad to change, to love her and accept her, despite her flaws. But it had been an excuse she'd fallen back on to cover for her own mistakes. *She'd* been running away from change, running away from her shame. But there couldn't be change without forgiveness, and there couldn't be forgiveness without acceptance of the past.

"Dad, no, you're wrong," Dani forced. She had to swallow back another sob before she could get out her next words. "We've both made bad choices, but it's because of what *I* did that Jeremy is gone."

She paused and let out a shaky breath, and her dad folded his hands uncomfortably over his knees. When she closed her eyes, it was Dr. Turner's words that came to mind: *"History doesn't remember people's failures, Dani. History only remembers their successes; their ability to overcome their failures."*

The professor's statement ignited a compelling truth from her lips. "But…the poor choices of our past don't have to hold us down. We can always move forward, to try and be better. Dark times exist so…so light can shine through." Her eyes opened and focused on her dad's strained brown ones. "Maybe we can still give Jeremy's memory justice, Dad. It's not too late. Maybe…maybe his death can serve a bigger purpose."

"How?" Franc uttered in a barely audible tone. The vulnerability in his voice sent a ripple of pain through Dani's core.

She inhaled deeply to compose herself, staring between her mom and dad's dilapidated expressions. "It can start by fixing our relationship."

Franc's eyes softened, and his gaze fell to the floor. "Yes. Of course it can." After a moment he looked back up, his face drawn with agony. "Jeremy would want that."

And then, at long last, the stern, impulsive father she had known all her life broke down and wept with three year's worth of emotion. Her mom hugged him as he sagged on the couch, crying into his hands.

The only thing Dani could do was watch them through her own tear-stained eyes, yearning to be sitting there next to them, hundreds of miles away.

*May*

"My tongue is on fire!" Mel exclaimed with a scrunch of her face, dropping her wing on her plate. "Dustin, you know I don't like spicy wings."

Dani shot a sly smile across the kitchen table from where she sat beside Rachel. "Yeah, Dustin, I thought you were going to get Olive Garden. Way to take others' food preferences into consideration."

After the roller coaster of highs and lows in the past forty-eight hours, Dani and Dustin had been too exhausted to cook dinner, so KFC had seemed the most convenient option.

At least to Dustin.

He scoffed, circling a wing in front of his mouth. "Well, *sorry.* Most places had lines out the door. Next time, you guys can drive across town and grab whatever food you like. But since you didn't, suck up your first world problems, my valued guests."

Dani snickered, her sparkling hazel eyes locking with his. His lips tugged upward as he licked his fingers and wiped them on a napkin. Dani's face had been brighter since her talk with her parents earlier that day, and Dustin's heart warmed to see her so happy.

"How are you feeling, Mrs. Mottley?" Dani asked, fishing another wing out of the bucket between them.

Rachel clasped her hands on the table, eyeing her scarcely touched wings. "A bit weak still, but better than yesterday."

Dani wiped the buffalo sauce from her lips with a napkin and grinned. "I'm glad you're doing better."

Dustin watched his mom as she took small bites of her wing. There was a little more life to her movements, a tad more color to her cheeks. Perhaps the long conversation with Derek yesterday had also contributed to her health. She hadn't needed to sit all day and was eating more, which was a big improvement in the past twenty-four hours.

He picked the remaining crust off the bone on his plate. Although he hadn't voiced it out loud, he was concerned about the possible long-term effects of COVID for his mom. Reports had come in from the news about many people suffering from shortness of breath and other difficulties after recovering. He only hoped his mom would be fortunate enough to return to the healthy life she knew before she was sick.

Dani brushed the hair away from her face. "I just want to thank you again for your generous hospitality and offering for me to stay here despite all that's been going on."

Rachel beamed. "Of course, dear. I'm so glad we got to know one another. If it weren't for this pandemic, I'm not sure we would have met. It proves good things can come out of a crisis, no matter how small."

Dani offered a brief smile before her gaze lowered to her plate. "That is true. I just wish Dustin got to walk in his graduation ceremony."

Dustin stood, taking his and Mel's empty plate. "Eh, it's all good because I ended up graduating earlier. Also, I got a job out of it, so I don't have to worry about the residency for this summer." He brought the ceramic plates over to the sink and began washing them, then dried them and set them on the drying rack on the countertop.

"When are you going back to work anyways?" Mel asked, swinging her leg from her chair.

Dustin folded his arms and leaned back against the countertop. "Yesterday, I emailed my supervisor that I'd be back on Monday."

Dani's eyebrows shot up. "So soon?"

He shrugged. "Mom's not going back in the immediate future, so someone has to pay the bills. Plus, there's still an international crisis going on, and I can't just sit by."

"Yes, you can," Mel muttered as she rocked forward. "You don't have to always prove you're man of the house."

Dustin tightened his lips, focusing on his sister's sullen brown eyes. "Maybe a little more appreciation for the man of the house's hard-earned paychecks you'll be surviving off?"

Mel dipped her head. "Whatever." She sauntered to her room, shutting herself inside.

He turned a raised eyebrow at his mom. "What's her problem?"

But it was Dani who answered. "I think she's just upset you're leaving again after she finally got to spend so much time with you."

Dustin unfolded his arms and rubbed his neck. Had his sister been that lonely? "Shit. Well, it's not as if I really have a choice."

Dani shifted in her seat, her gaze drifting up to him. "Don't they have some sort of paid leave? Mrs. Mottley barely came home—you should be spending more time with her, don't you think?" She bit her lip and glanced down. "Especially since you'll be putting yourself back at risk. Your family doesn't want to isolate themselves from you so soon."

The pleading in her eyes chipped at his heart. He sucked in a deep breath and shook his head. "I wish it was that easy. I'm too new. I don't get paid shit for time off."

Dani's gaze tore from his. Her voice was soft. "That's not fair to you."

He bristled as she stood from the table and collected her and Rachel's plates.

"Well, since you're working, I'm especially glad to be helping out a little longer." She walked the dirty dishes to the sink beside Dustin. "Besides, I'm sure my roommates are loving the extra bathroom time."

Dustin smirked, gripping the counter behind him as he watched her scrub the dishes clean. "See, dudes don't ever fight over the bathroom. Life is so much simpler for us."

Dani rolled her eyes. "Mm-hmm. That's why dudes are messy, disgusting creatures."

He muttered so his mom couldn't hear, "And girls are annoying, overdramatic nuisances."

Her cheeks flushed, and a smile played on his lips.

He was excited to see her reaction after he busted Harrison and his dad for the cheating scandal. He didn't think Dani had seen the documents on his desk a few days ago…

Once Dani finished drying the dishes, oblivious to Dustin's plotting, she danced out of the kitchen. "Thank you for the dinner suggestion, Mrs. Mottley!" she piped as she headed to Mel's bedroom where she had slept the night before. IThen, as if having an afterthought, she added, "Oh, and thanks for picking up the food, Dustin." She shot him a smug grin before slipping inside his sister's room.

Dustin smiled, shaking his head and turning from the counter. Classic Dani.

"She still calls me 'Mrs. Mottley,'" Rachel laughed quietly, folding her hands on the table. "You know that girl is a gem, right?"

He searched the seriousness in her eyes. "Of course she is."

"She has been…incredibly generous to stay here with you two. And the way she plays with Melody and helps her with her homework… I've only known her for two days, but Dani has already stolen my heart."

He turned and leaned forward on the counter, staring down the hallway where Dani had disappeared a moment ago. His thoughts drifted back to the moment they'd locked gazes at the dinner table two nights ago; the moment when everything seemed perfectly in place. She had come into his family life so quickly and unexpectedly, he'd had a hard time wrapping his head around the fact that she'd been his mentee—still was his mentee. But there was something different about her now. Something modest, intriguing, and pure… Or maybe it had been there all along and he had just been blind to it before, too consumed by his own damn personal matters.

Then, with a guilty jab to his gut, he remembered Lila's letter. He'd stowed it in his bookcase as soon as he got home from the hospital yesterday. But if he was perfectly honest with himself, he hadn't been eager to read it with Dani around. It just didn't seem right.

Rachel's words carried across the kitchen from behind him. "She reminds me of how I was at a young age—full of smiles and optimism."

Dustin inhaled a deep breath, his fingers clenching the counter. If his mom had seen Dani last week, he didn't think Rachel would classify her as "full of smiles and optimism." However, he supposed it was appropriate to note that Dani *had* been a shining ray of sunshine in the past two days. Just the thought of her radiant, teasing smile with the small dimple denting her left cheek sent a flurry of warmth through him.

"Except Dani is smart and knows what's good for her, while I was gullible and stupid," Rachel added under her breath.

Dustin peered over his shoulder to see his mom gazing into the distance, lost in thought.

She gave a small smile and rose from the table, stepping in his direction. "When I met Derek, I followed him around like a puppy dog, eager to capture the attention of this successful businessman, and then yearning to please him once I did. I was so in love with him, I brushed aside red flags like his irregular drinking habits, his ogling of other women... I thought marriage and having kids would improve things, and it did for a while. Everything was great until after Mel was born."

Dustin bit his lip. He'd heard this story before.

Rachel brought a hand to her forehead, and her brow wrinkled as she closed her eyes. "Derek was my first love. My only love. When he cheated, he shattered me, Dustin. He tore out my heart and crushed it into a million irreparable pieces. I never believed I could love again. The fact that he finally seemed to realize the full weight of what he'd done and apologized for cheating, committing assault, and ruining our family... It doesn't change the disgust I have toward him, but it does give me a bit of closure, at least."

Dustin closed the distance between them and rubbed her back as her voice broke. "That man, damn him! I wanted him to know you and Mel would always be my priority. Our family had no place for a faithless bastard like him." She looked up at Dustin, her large brown eyes a swirl of agony. "I'm so sorry you two never had a proper dad... That's the worst part through all of this. Knowing that I failed my kids."

When the tears broke loose, Dustin pulled her into a hug. She sank her head into his neck, trembling, and Dustin's gut clenched. "You didn't fail us, Mom. You did the right thing. You've always been my biggest inspiration." He rubbed her back as her tears soaked his shirt, and his heart grew heavy. Had he never before told his mom how much of an inspiration she'd been to him? What the hell kind of a son was he?

It was a long minute before Rachel spoke again, her voice cracking. "I've only wished for you two kids to experience the fully requited, wholehearted love I missed out on, and I pray you don't make the same mistakes I did."

She pulled away and stared at him with bright, teary eyes. Her hand cupped his jaw, and she brushed a thumb along his cheek. "My reason for saying all this is because it's written all over your face."

Dustin's breath hitched as he watched the tension in Rachel's cheeks ease. A nurturing softness spread across her eyes, the kind of look a mother gives when she sees her newborn child for the first time.

"You love her," she finished.

*May*

DANI SAT BETWEEN THE TWO SIBLINGS ON THE COUCH AS *ENCHANTED*—Mel's choice, of course—played on Amazon Prime later that night. She smiled to herself as Mel's head slowly dipped and settled on her lap only half way into the movie. Reaching over her with the remote, Dani turned down the volume and stroked Mel's hair while she slept.

It had been an exhausting and emotional forty-eight hours for everyone, not least of all, Mel. Dani could only conclude that such steep highs and lows in a short time interval weren't good for the nine-year-old's health, but regardless, Mel had proven to be an unfazed, optimistic bundle of joy. The girl had been quick to organize a movie-watching party as soon as Dustin returned from the kitchen with his mom, although Rachel passed on the invitation in favor of an early dismissal to bed.

Dani's gaze drifted down from the movie and landed on Mel, tuning into the girl's soft, shallow breathing and memorizing her angelic face. Mel had always made the effort to liven up the atmosphere in those few dark days when Rachel was sick, and she was the one who had convinced Dani to stay after she nearly left.

Would Dani have been here, present in this moment after the crazy turn of events, without her?

As Dani sat there with Dustin to her left and Mel curled on her lap, a sense of weightlessness filled her. Did she dare to think it was…happiness?

Her parents had forgiven her. She had shared her story with Dustin and felt stronger for it. People she barely knew a week ago had accepted her as family. And Dustin had set her up with a therapist.

For once in her life, she was content, even if her brother wasn't there by her side.

Dustin scooted closer, bending his head down to peek at Mel. "She asleep?" he asked with an amused look.

"Yep, she's out," Dani whispered, grinning as Mel's soft snores reached her ears.

Dustin sat back, his arm grazing hers, and goose bumps rose on Dani's skin. She caught a whiff of his ocean-breeze scent, and her heart raced.

"She adores you, you know," he said softly.

Dani gazed at Mel's pudgy cheeks and brushed the hair out of her face. "You'd better watch out before I adopt her."

He snorted. "You can take her—she's a pain in my ass."

Dani smirked at him and scratched her cheek.

"You scratch your cheek a lot," he noted with a lopsided smile.

"What—", her hand darted back to her face. "Oh." She lowered her hand, flushing, and he laughed softly. "I didn't realize… I guess it's a nervous tic." She averted her eyes as her lip curled. *Does he pay attention to me that much?*

When she looked his way, a hint of amusement flickered across his face. She wrinkled her mouth, trying to ignore the loud pulse in her ears. "Well, you rub your neck a lot." Her hand reached to her cheek again. "Dammit!"

His lips perked. "What's making you nervous?"

*You.* She swallowed as his blue eyes seized hers, releasing butterflies in her chest.

And along with the butterflies came the image of Tanner's fiery stare, the terrorizing memory of her locked limbs as she lay trapped beneath him, and her esteem spiraling downward into that dark, endless abyss…

*No, no, no. This is different. This is Dustin.*

She dragged her eyes away and focused on Mel again, heartbeat racing. Whether it was from trepidation or excitement, she wasn't sure. She racked her mind for a quick escape. "I…guess a lot of things have been making me nervous—anxious—lately. These past few months have been crazy."

Dustin's tone turned somber. "I'm sorry you couldn't finish your lacrosse season. In some parallel universe, you'd be celebrating with your team after winning the PAC-12."

She hesitated before meeting his eyes again. "I'm not sorry."

He raised an eyebrow.

"I've been thinking about this whole pandemic, and…" She paused, trying to summon the right words. "Regardless of how much I missed out on this year, it led to me being here. I'm in a different, better place mentally than I was months ago." Her hand crept up and twisted a lock of her hair. "There's this philosopher, Alan Watts, who came up with the 'backward law,' which says, 'The idea that the more you pursue feeling better all the time, the less satisfied you become, as pursuing something only reinforces the fact that you lack it in the first place.'"

Dustin arched a brow. "Yeah?"

She nodded. "For the past three years, I was so messed up, because I wanted so many things. I wanted my brother to grow old by my side, I wanted my parents to forgive me, I wanted to win a lacrosse championship, I wanted to get into med school… But the pandemic put a mirror in my face and made me realize the things I don't have only make what I do have that much better. It's kind of like what you said about the light shining through the darkness."

A smile played on his lips. "You remembered that?"

She tilted her head. "Actually, your exact words were, 'Light shines brighter in the darkness. If there was light all the time, what would be the point? Maybe God allows evil and suffering so love and compassion can prevail.'"

Dustin chuckled softly. "Damn, I'm impressed."

"Eidetic memory." She grinned, tapping her temple.

"Really?" He sat back and gave an amused scowl. "I can't believe you never told me! Is that how you recited all that biology stuff at the volunteer program?"

Dani shrugged as she twirled her hair. "Yeah…"

He shook his head, smirking. "That's incredible. I always wondered what it'd be like to have a near-perfect memory. I'd never forget where I put my keys or have to worry about studying…which, now that I think about it, what's your excuse for not getting perfect scores on all of your exams?"

Her lips tightened. "I guess… my brain constantly sorts through all my retained info, so it's hard for me to focus. And having an eidetic memory seems great when you want to watch an episode of *Jeopardy*, but honestly, it does more bad than good." She paused, her right hand drifting down to smooth a wrinkle out of Mel's shirt. "My brother's death… When I stopped taking the meds, I couldn't shake the horrific details of that one night. It's haunted me ever since." For the first time, her voice came out stable at the mention of her brother.

Dustin shifted on the couch and ran a hand through his hair. "Trauma already heightens people's memories of incidents, so I can't even imagine what you've gone through." He sighed. "Were you…okay during the pandemic?"

She closed her eyes. "The pandemic made it worse. Quarantining made me alone with my thoughts twenty-four-seven." Her hand fell to the couch cushion and squeezed the fabric. "But as crazy as it sounds, I'm grateful for the pandemic." She turned back to the small girl in her lap and focused on her soft breathing. "The coronavirus may have thrown our lives into chaos, but there were a lot of good things that came out of it—at least for me. It forced me to focus on the things that mattered, like family, friends…" She met his gaze, and her pulse throbbed louder in her ears. She twisted her lock of hair again. "And it led me to you."

He pursed his lips, and she drowned in the depth of his eyes. They were so blue. So *ocean* blue. The beach seemed to have been calling her for a long time now.

Dustin reached out and tucked the hair she had been twisting behind her ear. His soft fingers traced down to the back of her neck, shooting tingles up her spine—and then he pulled away as Mel stirred on Dani's knee.

"Is the movie over yet?" the girl asked groggily, rubbing her eyes.

Dustin leaned back with a lopsided smile, seemingly unaware that his close presence was sending Dani's body into overdrive. "It just ended," he answered coolly, though the movie was probably only half over.

"Great. I'm out," Mel muttered below half-closed lids, not even taking note of the characters talking on screen. "See you guys in the morning." She trudged around the couch and into her bedroom.

As Mel closed the door, Dani giggled and turned back to Dustin. "You are such a *liar*," she mocked, punching him in the shoulder.

He returned a cunning smile. "She wasn't watching it anyways. She hates princess movies, remember? She only suggested it because you said you're a fan of Anne Hathaway."

A warmth spread in Dani's chest, and she glanced down at the floor, her lips tugging upward. "Your sister…is such a joy." Her grin dissolved as quickly as it had come, however, as the image of Mel's tiny sobbing figure curled in Dani's arms flashed through her mind.

She bit her lip and dragged her shoe across the carpet. "When I saw what you two went through…it made me realize how lucky I am—how nobody in my family is sick, how I have enough money for basic things in a broken economy, how I had a damn *list* of schools to choose from with full-rides…" She trailed off, realizing she was venting. She probably sounded like some dumb middle-school kid.

Her head dipped, and she rubbed her eyes. "God, I've been so stupid. I've been so ignorant about my privileges… I've been such a selfish ball of shit."

Dustin stared at her blankly as if disappointed she was so late in understanding these things. "Even with your privileged, selfish ball of shit…"

She grimaced at her own words. They sounded harsh coming from his mouth.

"You're amazing, Danica," he finished, holding her gaze with a warm smile.

She stared at him, dubious. He knew she hated her full name, but this time, coming from him, it sounded different.

It sounded…beautiful.

She searched Dustin's cool blue eyes, trying to understand this guy who had upturned everything she thought she knew about herself. He hadn't shied away from her scars, from her ugly past, like Tanner. Dustin had nothing but support and encouragement for her, making her feel like she was worth something and had so much to offer. He consistently put others before himself, caring for his family and working tirelessly for his patients at the hospital. She admired his passion for med school, the way he was quick with a laugh, the way he sacrificed his own needs and put his mom and sister first…

Dani wasn't the amazing one; it was *Dustin*.

And as she lost herself in the guy before her, studying the curl of hair above his dark lashes, the curve of his crooked smile, and the handsome trim along his jaw, a realization hit her square in the chest. It was a realization so true and real and strong that when it came to her, she had no doubts about its validity.

She was in love with Dustin Mottley.

She tried to swallow and found her throat dry. Her fingers squeezed the seam of the couch again as her pulse pounded through her veins.

Somehow, the space between them had gotten smaller, and when Dani inhaled, Dustin's ocean-breeze cologne washed over her. Her eyes latched onto the curving tease of his mouth, and when he cupped her chin, her breath caught in her throat. He drew closer until finally, his lips melded with hers.

Electricity shot through her body, inflaming every last inch of her. Her toes curled as her heart somersaulted in her chest, and her brain dissolved to a mess of useless fuzz…and then suddenly, whether ten minutes had passed or just a few seconds, he pulled away.

When he studied her face, she wasn't sure what he saw, but whatever it was brought out his crooked, infectious smile.

She sat there, breathless and dumbfounded, as a million thoughts swam in her head.

*What just happened? Did we just…kiss?*

*He likes me too! He wants me!*

*He wants me?*

And then the sinister voice she thought she'd locked away crept beneath her conscious. *How could he want you? You just admitted you were far from amazing. He doesn't know what he wants. You'll never be good enough for him.*

But hadn't she changed? Wasn't she a better person than she had been eight months ago?

*No. You're still a selfish ball of shit. He doesn't deserve you. You still can't put others before yourself.*

*You wish Jeremy could be in Rachel's place.*

The thought dropped like a brick in her stomach. Franc Torres's heated glare flashed in front of her eyes—a memory she'd thought she'd banished after resolving things with her parents earlier that afternoon. *"You're not relationship material."*

Dustin leaned slowly back toward her—

*If I really love him, I can't do this to him.*

"No…" she whispered. She forced herself to turn away.

His weight shifted on the couch, and a soft intake of breath met her ears. With an immense summon of courage, she faced him, shame coating her insides. The confusion in his blue eyes and the bob of his Adam's apple sent a lance of pain through her heart.

He sat back after a long moment, chagrin washing over his features. "I'm sorry." His dark lashes flitted as he rubbed his neck. "I thought… Never mind."

Dani shook her head, biting her lip. "No, no. I'm the one who should be sorry."

His eyes raked hers in consternation. "What are you talking about?"

"I…I've been here too long." She stood and turned, but he clasped her hand, holding her in place.

His brow furrowed as he looked up at her in confusion. "Wait—I don't understand."

She closed her eyes and pulled her hand away. "I'm sorry. I shouldn't be with you like this. It's wrong. I'm not—I can't…"

The confusion in his eyes was misplaced by something akin to understanding. He stood and brushed the hair from her face, peering down at her with a consoling gaze. "It's okay, Dani. There isn't anything wrong—"

"Yes, there is, Dustin!" Her words cut through him, but she continued even as his chest rose. "I'm not good for you."

His lips tightened. "Don't think like that. Your past doesn't change how I feel about you—"

"No, you still don't get it!" Her tone wavered as a burn crawled up her throat. His words of affirmation were only making this twice as excruciating. She took a deep breath to steady herself even as a fissure ripped through her core. "I'm a mess. I've always been a damn mess." She swallowed and lowered her gaze. "Since your mom came home, I've been jealous of you. At the dinner table the other night, I kept seeing my brother's face instead. I'm still selfish, after all this time, and I can't fully share in your happiness."

He scanned her face, pity rising in his gaze. "Dani..." He ran a hand through his hair. "I didn't realize. I'm so sorry..."

Her eyes watered, and she clenched her hands into fists at her sides. "That's the problem—stop feeling sorry for me! You should be happy for your mom, and all I'm doing is getting in the way. Don't you see how toxic I am? Maybe some people change, like you said, but I haven't changed from that stupid, broken girl from three years ago. You're better off with someone strong like Lila. She really cares for you."

She tried to step around him, but he grabbed her shoulders, halting her exit. Her body froze in a terrifying moment of déjà vu, and she stared up at Dustin's intense gaze as an icy chill crawled up her spine.

Dustin's eyes softened, and his hands immediately dropped from her shoulders. "I—sorry. I didn't mean to grab you like that." She relaxed slightly, and he took a hesitant step closer. "Dani. Your brother's passing has left a deep, terrible wound, and I can never blame you for the repercussions of that. I want to help you through it." He raised a hand to her face and traced a thumb along her cheek. "And how can you say you're toxic when you helped Mel and—"

"Dammit, Dustin! I can't stay here!" She struggled to keep her voice at a nighttime level as the burn in her throat seared a hole through her neck. As much as she wanted to believe Dustin was right and succumb to his caress, he truly didn't understand. Her demons belonged to her, and her only. It was the only way she could protect him. "Stop trying to be a damn saint who forgives me all the time and sees me as some perfect angel! I'm no good. For you or for anyone!" She shoved his hands away and skirted around him to enter Mel's room, fighting tears.

"Dani, you're wrong." His voice was strained as he followed her to the bedroom door. "Don't do this," he pleaded softly.

Even after she'd exposed the bitterness in her heart, he still turned a blind eye.

He was too perfect.

With a heavy heart, she ignored him and quietly folded the sleeping bag at the foot of Mel's bed, taking caution not to wake the sleeping nine-year-old. After collecting her duffle bag and backpack, she crept toward Dustin and turned to give one last longing look at his sister.

Mel's precious form curled under the covers facing the window, soft snores drifting from her. Leaving the girl would wound Dani deeply, but it was better that Dani be out of her life. Dani's heart sunk as she tore her eyes from Mel's sleeping figure and brushed past Dustin.

"Dani, wait."

She only turned when she reached the front door, meeting his defeated gaze with a resolute iron stare.

He took a hesitant step and paused by the coffee table, looking as if she'd punched him in the gut. "I, uh…" Dustin ran a hand through his hair before locking eyes with her. "I'm sorry for kissing you." He shoved his hands in his jean pockets, his face a grim mask of defeat. "I understand if you want to leave. But maybe we can just…go back to the way things were before? As friends?"

His words shot like lightning through Dani's stomach. She gripped the doorknob with trembling fingers. "I think it's better if you stayed away from me," she whispered as a hot tear trailed down her cheek. "I'm sorry." Dustin's pained blue eyes branded her memory as she pulled open the door and swung it behind her.

The final click of the door ripped her heart clean of her chest.

*May*

"How are you and Chase?" Carolyn asked Emma, twirling her fork in spaghetti. "Seems like you haven't talked about him in a while."

Dani shifted in her seat across the table, her thoughts returning to the guy she'd abandoned three nights ago, and she looked up at her roommate. Emma's hand darted to her earlobe and back down. The hoop earrings she had worn nearly every day since December were no longer there. She pursed her lips, her gaze dropping to her plate. "Mmm, we haven't been talking. It's kind of complicated. Our fight when he came over was only a small piece of it."

Chase and Emma, not seeing each other? Dani had thought them to be an iconic couple.

Emma played with the bracelets on her wrist and frowned. "I'm really upset because he was the perfect guy. He spoiled me, complimented me all the time, and took us out to all these fancy dinners. But things got kind of ugly when I didn't agree with some of the people he hung out with. Those guys from that dumb frat acted so irresponsibly and started having a bad influence on him…"

Dani poked at a meatball as Emma went on explaining her love life to Carolyn, trying to ignore the throbbing hole in her own heart.

"This is why I prefer to eat dinner alone," Alisha muttered on her right.

"Hmm?" Dani looked up from her plate. "Oh, yeah. I think I'm finally starting to relate."

Alisha smirked, but the tease dropped from her shadowed eyes when she caught Dani's stoic expression. "What's up with you? You've been out of it for the past few days."

Dani wrinkled her nose. "Is it that obvious?"

Alisha's loud snort made Dani cringe. "Yes. You're all gloomy and shit." She folded her arms on the table and scratched her elbows. "I thought you said Dustin's mom came home from the hospital and everything was good?"

Dani nudged the meatball around her half-eaten spaghetti. "Yeah. His mom is doing great. I'm just…dealing with some small personal stuff."

"You suck at honesty, but whatever." Alisha's brow twitched as she turned her gaze back to her food.

Dani sighed and lowered her fork. She didn't think she'd be able to talk about Dustin without breaking down.

Emma's voice carried across the table, interrupting Dani's thoughts. "Anyway, long story short, I still love him because I know he only wants what is best for me. He's just struggling with some life choices right now. His friends and family led him to experience things differently than I have."

Carolyn covered her mouth as she chewed. "So you forgive him for yelling at you? And breaking your heart?"

Emma's brown eyes shone brightly, a warmth spreading across her features. "Yes, I forgive him—even if he doesn't know it yet. And I want to help him work through his struggles. When he's ready, *if* he's ready to try again, I'll be waiting for him."

Dani tore her gaze from Emma. Some people were meant to have happy endings, but Dani wasn't one of them.

That damn burn began creeping up her throat again.

She placed her napkin on her plate and stood. "Thanks for dinner, Emma. I think I'm gonna save the rest of this for tomorrow. Just not super hungry."

Emma looked up at Dani skeptically. "Um, sure, no problem! I did make a ton of food..."

After stowing her spaghetti in Tupperware and rinsing her plate, Dani shuffled past the kitchen table. Alisha shot her a curious stare before Dani rounded the corner and trudged up the stairs to her room. She sank on her bed and pulled out her MCAT prep guide, flipping to a bookmarked page. Studying was moot, though, as her mind flooded with thoughts of Dustin like it had done for the past three nights since she came home.

Didn't Dustin understand that her leaving was for the best? Or was he heartbroken and waiting patiently for her to mend their severed relationship like Emma was with Chase?

She wondered what he was doing right now. He was supposed to start work again this week, so maybe he was just coming home from the hospital. Or maybe he was going on a late-night stroll with Lila.

Her teeth dug into her lips, stinging her. Lila was best for him. She would make him happy.

And what about Mel? Dani imagined a scene of the girl waking up only to find Dani had left without saying goodbye. What kind of a big sister was she?

*No, no. Stop thinking about them! No good will come of it. They're better off without you. You did the right thing. Leaving them was for the best.*

Her leaving hadn't completely spared Dustin though, because she had thrown his heart in the trash, wounding him all the same.

Dani rubbed her watering eyes. Even when she tried to do the right thing, she always hurt people in the end.

Her head sank on her arms as images of all the people she'd hurt surfaced behind her eyelids. Noemi's bewildered face when Dani had so naïvely asked her about anime, her dad's emotionless stare when she'd berated him three years ago for not getting over his mother's death, Jeremy's helpless eyes as he'd choked on his final breaths...

And now Dustin.

Dani didn't deserve him. He and Mel would have been better off if she never went over to his house to begin with. She had gotten too close to them, too absorbed in their family life. Too comfortable in their shared grief.

And yet through all the muck and grime coating her conscience, a glimmer of light had flickered to life in her heart. Maybe there was one good thing to take away from all of this, despite everything: she had felt it.

Love.

Even if she would never be good enough for Dustin and his family, at least she loved and had felt love in return, if only for an instant. She could be content knowing she'd seen that small piece of beauty in her world as she moved on with her life and tried to forget about Dustin.

Yet as hard as she tried to shove him out of her thoughts, she couldn't. She missed the little things with him, before all of this had happened. She missed talking to him about med school, missed his jabs about her lack of focus, his venting about his little sister, even his pathetic womanizer jokes.

It couldn't be bad for her to miss those things, could it? The things they'd done as friends? He was still her mentor, wasn't he? Shouldn't they at least be amicable?

She dragged her phone out of her pocket and scrolled through the message he'd sent, dated as soon as she'd left his house three days ago:

**Dani, I'm sorry for making you feel uncomfortable in any way, and that includes any pressure you felt to stay and help with my Mom. The last thing I wanted was to put you in a position you didn't want to be. Can you talk?**

Her fingers hovered over the keypad for what must have been the hundredth time.

*Stop it. You already told yourself he's better off without you. Texting will only make things worse.*

But didn't he at least deserve a response? She warred with herself for another minute before sucking in a breath and typing, **I'm sorry, Dustin, but I think it's better if we keep our distance.**

She scanned what she'd written and bit her lip. It would be a knockout punch to his already wounded feelings, and he didn't need that.

She deleted the message and set her phone down. Her mind wracked for something else to say. *It'd make sense to check in on his mom though, wouldn't it?* She picked up her phone and typed, **Hi Dustin. I'm sorry for the late response. How is your mom doing?**

Wow, such a pathetic approach. Did she really think avoiding the topic would make anything better?

Her thumb punched "delete" faster than she could blink.

She shouldn't be talking to him, wasting his time, just because she missed him. She didn't deserve any sense of closure. It was she who ruined everything; this was all her fault.

*Dammit, just apologize and talk to him! You shoved a knife into his chest, remember?*

Her fingers flitted across the screen. **I'm sorry for yelling at you. Please forgive me for my dumb, overblown emotions. I just needed some space.**

She read it and cringed. She had left him for a good reason, and this response would only open up the door for him to convince her to be friends again. But there was no way they could be friends without Dani making him feel guilty about his mom.

Just as she was about to throw her phone into the closet, it vibrated in the call pattern. She straightened, her heart catching in her throat, but it wasn't his name that flashed on the caller ID.

"Hey, Mom," she answered, pressing her phone to her ear and sinking into the pillows.

"Danica." It was her father's deep, husky voice.

Her grip on the phone loosened, and her breathing became shallow. "Dad?"

"I borrowed your mom's phone because, uh, I realize you got a new number this year, and I never found out what it was…"

Dani's throat went dry. She hadn't bothered to give him her new number when she'd upgraded to the new plan in September. She hadn't worried about it because he hadn't called her in three years. Still, that fact didn't warrant her not giving her number to him.

"How are…things going?" he continued, breaking the awkward silence.

Dani tried to imagine the calm, consoling face she remembered from her Skype call with him earlier that week. It wasn't without difficulty. "I'm…good. How are you doing?"

Franc cleared his throat, and she heard a bird chirping in the background. He was probably outside on the back porch, in the usual place he went to gather his thoughts.

"I'm doing all right. Your mother and I have been taking more precautions and staying home, so it's been a bit quiet around here." He paused, and there was a scuffle of shoes on a hard surface. "I just wanted to...uh...check in with you. I know it's only been a few days since we last talked, but..."

Dani sucked in a deep breath, her eyes dancing across the lacrosse scrap board on the wall closest to her bed. "It's...nice of you to call." She hadn't talked to her dad amicably in years, and now she was finally doing so, she found herself lost for words. What could she talk about? Her boring quarantine life? Her roommates? Everything she hadn't told him about in the past three years?

"How is Dustin's mom doing?" Franc asked, breaking her from her thoughts. "Is she...still in the hospital?"

Dani bit her lip. Dustin was the last person she wanted to talk about. "Um...yeah. His mom recovered and came home, actually. They had a huge ceremony for her at the hospital and everything."

"Oh, that's great! Tell her we have been praying for her and are glad to hear she's doing better." Franc and Angelina didn't know the Mottleys, only that Dustin was her med school mentor. It was nice to hear Dani's parents had included them in their prayers all the same.

But since when did her parents pray and isolate at home? Maybe Helena was being hit harder by COVID in the past few weeks.

"Uh...I'm actually back at my apartment again. But I'll let Mrs. Mottley know." She twirled a strand of hair as the empty promise stung her tongue. "So...has Helena been doing all right with COVID?"

Franc sighed. "We've had an uptick in cases, although it hasn't been as bad as Los Angeles. The husband of one of your mother's old high-school friends caught it, however, and he passed." He paused, taking a deep breath, and Dani's heart sank in her chest. "Maggie and your mom only corresponded a few times in recent years," Franc continued, "but it's a striking blow regardless. From what I hear, Maggie and her children are distraught. Samuel was only fifty-three. They had all been going out to gatherings downtown like we did a few times, so it was a real wake-up call to your mother and me."

Dani hugged her legs through her jeans, her eyes fluttering closed. "That's so sad. The family must be heartbroken."

"Yes." Her dad hesitated, letting the second drag out between them. "Danica, I know I haven't been the best father to you, and these past few days have really got me thinking how I can…mend our relationship. I know I'll never be able to make up for lost time, but I'm hoping we can chat once or twice a week like this. You know, just casually. I want to hear more about your hobbies and friends. Would that be okay?"

It took Dani a minute to comprehend Franc's request. She had been more than content with the resolve their Skype call had provided a few weeks ago, but now her dad wanted to chat with her weekly? About her life? The statement was so uncalled for, she found herself lost for words. But then a smile crept to her lips. Her dad wanted to be in her life again. She would get to know him, and he her, as a father and daughter should.

"We can do monthly if weekly is too much—"

"Dad," Dani interrupted, and he waited patiently on the other end of the line. "That would be great. And how about every few days? It's not like I have anything else going on."

A deep, raspy chuckle met her ears. "That's true. Sure, we can do that. You'll have to tell me all about your trips to find toilet paper."

Dani laughed, and the sound felt so good coming from her lips it wrangled all the tension from her body she had bottled up about Dustin. "Toilet paper, the hottest commodity of 2020!"

He chuckled again, lifting Dani's spirits even higher. "Looking forward to it. I'll call you tomorrow," he promised.

"Sounds good."

"I love you, Danica."

Those four words unleashed a tsunami in Dani's core, and her lips lifted with an elation she hadn't felt in years. "I love you too, Dad."

When the line cut out, her eyes welled up, and she fell back onto the pillows.

Before she could process what had happened, however, a quiet knock sounded on the door.

"Dani?" It was Carolyn.

"Yeah?" Dani whimpered.

The door opened and Carolyn's bright red head stuck into the room, her green eyes brimmed with caution. "Everything okay? You didn't really eat much."

Dani wiped her eyes before sitting up and offering a smile. "Yeah. I'm good."

Carolyn's brows shot up. "You sure?" When Dani gave a pathetic nod, Carolyn entered the room, shutting the door behind her, and shuffled across the room to sink beside her on the bed. It was becoming a familiar scene.

Carolyn gazed at the floor, scratching a freckled arm. "Does your crying have anything to do with Dustin? You haven't mentioned him much since you came home."

"He's fine." Dani bit her lip and closed her eyes. "I don't really want to talk about him right now. I'm sorry."

"Oh." Carolyn let a few silent seconds pass between them. "I didn't mean to bother you. If you wanted some time alone…"

Dani shook her head. "No, it's okay. He wasn't the reason why I was crying… My dad called a few minutes ago."

Carolyn's eyes widened with fear. "Is everything okay?"

"Yes. More than okay, actually," Dani responded with a reassuring smile. "He was just checking in with me. He wants to…work on our relationship."

"Dani, that's great!" Carolyn squeezed Dani's shoulder. "That's huge!"

Dani's lips tilted upward as the tears began to build again. "I know."

Carolyn was right. The fact that her dad had called her *was* huge. It promised the start of a new chapter in her life. One that had always seemed too distant and improbable to ever reach.

*Remember what Alan Watts said,* she reprimanded herself sharply. *I already have everything I need right in front of me.*

*Fifty-Seven*

*May*

After Dustin dismissed another patient, Leopold sauntered up to him and folded his large hands behind his back, his green eyes shining through his mask and face shield. "How are you doing, Dustin? I can't believe it's already been two weeks since you've been back!"

Dustin grinned as he sprayed the counter with disinfectant and wiped a towel along the surface. "I'm doing great. Thanks for checking."

"Glad to hear it. If you need any more time off to care for your mom, just let me know. We can manage with the new influx of transfers."

Dustin set aside the towel and swapped his gloves for a new pair. "She's doing a lot better, actually. She has most of her strength back and may start up again in a few weeks."

Rachel had been enjoying the time at home with Mel, and he was glad she was finally able to rest. It seemed all too soon that she'd be joining the workforce again, and a part of Dustin coiled at the thought of her risking her health a second time. There were several patients in the past few days who had previously recovered from COVID, only to learn that they were showing the same symptoms again. New data revealed catching the virus once did not automatically make you immune to the virus in the future.

Leopold cocked his head. "Oh, really? That woman is amazing, truly."

"I know."

The doctor unlocked his hands from behind his back, smoothing the folds of his long PPE. "Oh, I just remembered! I found something left behind at one of the stations the other day, but it's been a week and nobody has claimed it. I figured you might like to have it, as a reminder of the hope you inspire." He walked over to one of the portable bins below the computer and reached inside, pulling out a silver chain. "I don't know if you care for jewelry," he chortled as he placed the pendant in Dustin's palm. "But guys wear necklaces, right?"

The necklace bore the medical symbol of the Rod of Asclepius; a snake encircling a rod. Dustin vaguely recalled the significance in Greek mythology: the son of Apollo, Asclepius, had barely survived at birth. His miraculous healing powers led him to study the art of medicine and cure every illness and injury, thus becoming the god of medicine. The snake's ability to shed its skin was supposed to represent healing.

"Uh, thank you," Dustin murmured with a smile.

A flicker of amusement crossed Leopold's green eyes. "Of course. I figured, with all that's going on, it's a nice reminder of the good work we do. Even as something as mundane as screening, we touch and heal many lives."

Dustin bit his lip, and was thankful his mask obscured his reaction. The idea that someone as broken as him had healed anyone was laughable.

Leopold smoothed the front of his gown again. "Well, let me know if you need anything. You can go ahead and take a quick break. You've earned it."

"Oh…thank you." After tucking the tiny necklace into his pocket beneath his PPE, Dustin smiled and retreated down the aisle past his busy coworkers, his back and legs aching from standing for four straight hours. The surge of tests hadn't eased in the three weeks he'd been on leave. It appeared cases were beginning to rise again as states loosened restrictions.

As he walked through the tent flap at the end of the aisle, Lila's slim figure caught his eye. He paused and watched her insert a swab into an older woman's nose, offering consoling comments as the patient grimaced and squeezed her eyes.

She had been avoiding him ever since he came back to work. Every time he tried to strike up a conversation with her, she politely smiled and engaged in brief, awkward small talk before dismissing herself to her duties. He supposed it was a proper response after he had so rudely pushed her away when she'd tried to console him weeks ago. And she wasn't ignoring him in a vengeful sort of way—she was still courteous and kind as always.

He tugged his eyes away and ducked under the flap, seeking one of the break chairs stowed behind the tent. His temples throbbed as he pried off his facemask and plopped into the seat, letting out a long exhale. He stretched out his leg into the pocket of sunlight that crept around the tent just as Lila appeared from around the corner, downing a cup of water. Dustin froze, his breath stilling in his lungs.

"Lila," he greeted.

Her eyebrows rose behind her glasses as she lowered her cup, and she turned a surprised face to him. "Oh, hi, Dustin. How is your shift going?"

"Same as every other damn day. You?"

She swirled her cup, laughing softly. "Same." It was odd seeing her entire face without her mask. It was a good look for her.

She pursed her pink lips, turning her head to the side. "I didn't know you were on break too. I can give you your space—"

"No, it's fine." He narrowed his brow. "I…wanted to talk to you. I read your letter." He'd only read it yesterday after work. He'd put off reading the letter ever since Dani had left nearly two weeks ago, but Lila didn't need to know that.

Her brown eyes looked up hesitantly at him. "Yeah?"

Dustin rubbed his neck and stared at the grass beneath his feet. "It was very heartfelt and kind. Thank you. I didn't know you felt that way… It just meant a lot." He raised his head and offered a warm smile.

She pursed her lips again. "You're welcome. I worried the letter was too…forward. I'm sorry."

The corner of his mouth tilted up. "It wasn't."

Lila glanced at the chair a few paces away before slowly walking over to sit across from him. She grasped her water cup tightly with both hands on her lap, averting her gaze. "I'm sorry for avoiding you. I was embarrassed for…violating health and safety protocol and making you feel uncomfortable. It was wrong."

Dustin licked his lips, thinking back to that day he had fled out of the tent and Lila had come to his aid. She had always cared for him, and if he'd had any doubts about how she currently felt, her letter had washed them away.

When he said nothing, she went on. "And then when I met her… I felt even more stupid for what I did. I never would have touched you like that had I known you already had someone."

He raised an eyebrow, jaw tensing. "Dani?"

A smile played on Lila's lips. "She's really beautiful. I'm glad she was there to care for you while your mom was hospitalized."

A weight dropped in Dustin's stomach. He didn't want to think about Dani right now. It was too painful.

"Dani and I…we're not together." The words left a bitter taste in his mouth. "We're…" Were they even friends still? She'd said they should stay away from each other, but he hadn't been sure she actually meant it. So far, though, she'd stayed true to her word; she hadn't texted him back since she left two weeks ago.

A scorching burn crept up his throat. "Dani and I aren't really talking right now."

Lila gaped at him. "Oh… I'm so sorry." Her eyes fell to the grass, and she took another sip of her water.

He sighed, reaching up to tug at the elastic band on his face shield. "It's fine. But we were never together to begin with, anyway."

Lila dropped her gaze, murmuring, "I thought she was just being modest…"

Dustin cocked his head. "What?"

"Oh, never mind." She pursed her lips before locking shimmering eyes with his. "If you ever…want to talk about it…"

He took a deep breath. After all the turmoil he'd been through in the past month, he couldn't deny the fact that his heart desperately wanted to latch onto something—or someone—who could help him make sense of things. Someone who could share in the happiness of his mom coming home; in the daily frustrations of anti-maskers; in the unexpected solace of his dad's apology.

He studied Lila's hopeful features: her gorgeous brown eyes, the smooth contours of her cheekbones, the promise in her kind smile. Here was a girl who cared deeply for him, and had expressed her yearning for his happiness time and time again.

Just like someone else.

He gritted his teeth, shaking his head. "I think I need some time to…collect myself."

Her lips pressed and she raised a shoulder. "Of course. I didn't mean to imply anything. I just meant—as friends—"

"But…" He stood, his lips teasing upward as he met her chagrined gaze. "It would be nice to have someone to talk to. Maybe I'll reach out to you soon."

She rose to her feet also, and the hesitant smile that stretched across her lips warmed his heart. "I would love that," she said with a tilt of her head.

Dustin parked his car in the driveway after his usual long ride home, his eyes heavy with fatigue. He blinked at the setting sun's blinding glare as he trudged through the side gate to the back yard.

A neon mesh of orange and purple shone through a streak of clouds across the sky. Such a priceless sight made him choke up, his mind replaying everything that had turned his world upside down this past year: missing a proper graduation ceremony, landing a job amid a pandemic, combatting COVID on the frontline, hearing his dad's heartfelt apology, crying endlessly about his mom, and Dani…

He closed his eyes briefly and shoved the agonizing thought of her away. Adjusting his mask, he walked toward the hose by the small garden his mom hadn't tamed in a while. The few flowers that had managed to not be choked by the overgrown weeds withered in the dying sun.

He undressed to his boxers and wrapped himself in a towel he'd left by the barbecue before slipping off his boxers as well. After hosing down his scrubs for two minutes, he carried them through the back door into the garage to start a load of laundry, It was only right before he tossed his damp scrubs into the washing machine that he remembered to take the Rod of Asclepius necklace out of the pocket. He sighed and clutched the pendant in his palm, then grabbed a new mask from a cupboard and trudged through the kitchen.

His mom sat with Mel snuggled against her shoulder on the couch, the news blaring on the television. They both looked up when he entered the living room, pausing a good six feet away.

Mel scrunched her face in disgust. "Yuck. Hurry up and put some clothes on."

Dustin ignored her, his gaze latching onto the television. Four different cities stretched across the screen, painted by a familiar scene from the past few nights: An angry crowd of protestors marched the streets with fists raised in the Black Power salute; smoke swirled the bright sky from flaming cars; and glass from broken shop windows littered the pavement.

"It feels like the damn world is ending," he murmured.

Rachel pursed her lips. "I know." She had gained a bit more weight and color in her cheeks in the two weeks she'd been home.

It had been four days since a video surfaced of George Floyd, a Black civilian from Minneapolis, being choked to death by a police officer's knee on his neck. Peaceful as well as violent protesters were organizing across the nation, demanding justice for him and the countless other Black people who had died at the hands of officers. The movement was gaining international attention as well, calling for an end to the systemic racial injustices that had persevered in countries for hundreds of years.

Dustin tore his eyes away from the screen. "I should join Jessie on the march he's helping to organize."

His mom's expression dimmed as she focused on the television. "People shouldn't be out in crowds, though. The hospitals are already being overwhelmed with COVID right now as it is; there is no reason to cause a rise in cases and hospitalizations." Rachel frowned. "And many of these protestors are vandalizing and stealing what small business owners have worked so hard to build! There's a better, safer way to protest. Like Martin Luther King." She swung a leg over her knee and shook her head at the television, which showed a group of men and women looting items from a Target duplex.

Dustin exhaled, his breath coming back hot on his face under his mask. "I hate to break it to you, but for all the messages of love and peace he shared, MLK was still killed. And while I condemn the looting and violence, most of the Black Lives Matter protests have been peaceful. Its core message is to advocate equality for Blacks, but it seems that their message for basic human rights is constantly ignored in all this political shit. " He turned back to face the flaming, chaotic streets displayed on the television and shook his head. "Peaceful protests have been going on forever, Mom, but they've all been criticized and brushed aside. What do you call Colin Kaepernick's kneel during the anthem? What about Beyoncé's Super Bowl performance? What about Rosa Parks' sitting in the front of the bus? Opposers of Black civil rights always want to focus on the 'inappropriateness' of the protest and draw attention away from the call for justice. And then when violence does occur, opportunists and the media jump on it, using it as an excuse to condemn the entire movement."

Jessie had told him countless stories when they were in school: the time a security guard followed him around the grocery store; multiple occasions when random guys on the subway had called him the n-word; the atrocious racial slurs Jessie had gotten on Instagram for dating a white girl…

The list went on.

Rachel tightened her lips as she turned to face him. "I agree that the few cases of police brutality and racism is devastating. The cops who murdered George Floyd deserve to be punished. But my concern is that Blacks aren't the only people who are suffering right now. Small business owners, health-care workers, low-income families… Many people have lost loved ones in this pandemic and had their lives uprooted. Protesters need to take others' lives into consideration before gathering in crowds and escalating already harsh tensions due to COVID."

Dustin's fist clenched tight around the necklace, the Rod's point digging painfully into his fingers. He took a step forward, his voice rising. "Mom, Blacks are already being disproportionately affected by the virus. More of them have died from COVID because of poor socioeconomic factors, and a lot of them are essential workers. So when Black deaths by police officers—the very people who are supposed to be protecting them—keep happening on top of that, how can Blacks not take to the streets? You think they should just sit idly by? They're being killed disproportionately on multiple fronts! Nothing has been done to protect them!" His nostrils flared as his eyes scrunched in a furious glare at Rachel. "Why the hell are people so blind!"

Both Mel and his mom stared at him with palpable hurt, and the whiplash of his own words stabbed him. "I'm sorry. I didn't mean to lash out," he said in a softer tone, relaxing his clenched fist.

His mom had been on the edge of life and death merely weeks ago, and he was treating her like this? He was only contributing to the country's already incredibly hostile political divisions.

It must have been his exhaustion. Rachel's very presence here was a miracle. He owed it to her to be thankful for her and every other little gift for the rest of his life, but he hadn't even been able to do that for two weeks.

He walked past them to his room to avoid any further comments, raising a hand to rub his neck. His hand paused. Shit, he *did* rub his neck a lot, like she said. *Dammit, stop thinking about her.*

But as he stepped in front of Mel's open door, the blue sleeping bag caught his eye, and the gaping hole in his chest he'd been trying to ignore throbbed. The sleeping bag was neatly folded at the foot of the bed where she had slept, untouched since she'd left nearly two weeks ago.

He hadn't realized how used he had been to seeing her every day. She was someone he could talk to and just spend time with when he got tired of Mel's incessant whining. And she had made him appreciate the little things in life.

*Shit.* He couldn't keep denying how much he missed her. Even Mel and his mom seemed to miss her.

Maybe that was why his emotions were so unhinged.

He hadn't forgotten the time Dani had marched him over to the cornhole board at the Village and made him step away from all his stresses and concerns, just to make him have a little fun. She had shoved away all the pressing matters worrying him and focused on the moment. She was good at finding ways to get people out of their heads, concerned more about funny things such as losing a cornhole match or getting shoved by a lacrosse competitor.

He gritted his teeth. Things had been going so great in the week she'd visited, and then he'd scared her away.

And she had taken his heart with her.

But that moment when they had kissed had felt so perfect. He didn't know how strong his feelings were for her until just then. Maybe it had started after their conversation in his car on the way home from volunteering at Dignity Health Hospital, when he felt comfortable enough with her to tell her about his dad. Or when Harrison and his basketball friend talked shit on her, triggering some defensive instinct inside him. Or when he saw her caring for his little sister when his own grief held him down.

Dustin shut his bedroom door behind him and peeled off his mask before chucking the silver necklace onto his bed.

How could Dani see goodness in everything, including a devastating pandemic, but not see the good in herself? She was wrong. She *had* been able to share in his happiness for his mom. She'd rushed into Dustin's arms when he'd gotten the phone call saying his mom would be taken off the ventilator. She'd lit up at the chance to prep Rachel's "welcome home" dinner and wanted to help out more around the house while his mom recovered.

Sometimes, he wanted to grab Dani by the shoulders and shake away her insecurities, but he couldn't blame her for her troubled conscience. The girl had been through so much she couldn't tell right from wrong, left from right, good from bad.

It would probably be best if he hadn't kissed her. Dani wasn't ready for a relationship. Her brother—the pain was still too raw for her. Dustin had too easily forgotten about the trauma that had swallowed her alive for three years, crippling her sense of self-worth. And seeing Rachel come home must've—

*No.* He shook his head and clawed a hand through his hair. He shouldn't have to worry about Dani's feelings every time he thought about his mom. Rachel was a living, breathing miracle, and every minute he spent with her was a minute that deserved to be rejoiced.

*That's exactly why Dani left. She didn't want me to worry about her when I should be happy for my mom.*

He swallowed and rubbed his burning eyelids.

PTSD was an expertise beyond his field—hopefully, Michael would be able to give Dani the help she needed in a few weeks. God knew if she would ever be able to move beyond her past, but if anyone could do it, it was Dani.

Pulling a clean towel from his closet, he went down the hall to the bathroom and showered. He stood for a long time under the showerhead, the steaming water easing his troubled mind and washing his sordid thoughts away.

Afterward, he trudged back to his room and shrugged on a black tank top with Lakers pajama bottoms.

Glancing down at his bottoms, his heart sank. It seemed like forever since Kobe had died in January. His death had seemed like the tragedy of the year at the time, but little did they know… Dustin supposed it was a good thing Kobe didn't have to live through all of the madness and hatred that would come to possess the world in the months following his death.

But then again…2020 was the year everyone had been forced to take a minute to recognize all of the world's evils. The pandemic had revealed a lot of bad things, but Dani was right: it had revealed a lot of good things too. If Dustin looked hard enough, he could find beauty in the chaos, such as his graduation and immediate job recruital; his mom's survival; his dad's belated albeit sincere apology for years of failing as a father.

He missed having those deep conversations with Dani about his parents, the virus, about Alan Watson or whatever the hell his name was. Why couldn't they just talk like they used to? Even if it was just as friends? It was driving him insane.

He slumped in the chair at his desk and pulled out the huge manila envelope containing the documents he had completed since she'd left, ready to be mailed. He stared at the envelope for a minute before picking up his phone and scrolling through Jessie's messages. His thumb paused on the awkward photo of him and Dani at the hospital protest.

The photo had been funny to stare at once, but Dustin looked at the memory now with nostalgia. He smiled at her posture, her accusatory eyes and folded arms, while Dustin's amused self shrugged helplessly beside her. Her mask obscured most of her face, but it didn't block out the humor in her soft hazel eyes. Those vibrant eyes that had shed so many tears since the week and a half she'd visited.

This was the girl who had trembled violently and clung to him the day she told him about her brother. The same girl who had rushed to embrace him when he shared the news his mom would be taken off the ventilator.

Gritting his teeth, he scrolled through his message list and paused when he spotted her name. He rapped his fingers on the desk, contemplating if he should try again.

*Shit. Just give it up. It's probably better this way. It's not meant to be.*

Maybe Dani was the wrong person to talk to. Though he couldn't deny his lingering feelings for her, her whirlwind of emotions and circles of self-doubt left him helplessly frustrated. He'd expressed time and time again that he would support her through anything, but if she didn't want him around, there was nothing more he could do.

Sighing, he set down the phone on his desk and rolled onto his bed, staring at the ceiling. His eyes roamed over to the bookshelf and paused on the tiny square envelope sticking out. He sat up and pried it out from between *Grapes of Wrath* and *Jane Goodall: My Life with the Chimpanzees*. The letter crinkled as he pulled it from the envelope, worn on the edges from how many times he'd read it. Lila's writing was long and elegant, a stark contrast to Dani's small, messy font he remembered from her notebooks during their mentor sessions.

He read the letter for what must have been the hundredth time, Lila's bright face drifting to the forefront of his mind. Her tear stains blotched out some of the letters in places, but he'd read it enough times to decipher the words.

*Dustin,*

*I apologize in advance if I start crying all over this letter, but please know that I'm writing this with complete joy in my heart for you and your family. I've been praying for your mom every day since you left work, and I'm so happy you all get to reunite again. After so much heartbreak this year, it truly is a blessing.*

*I've always admired your strength and humility, and the fact you've been such an incredible role model for your younger sister amid your dad's absence is inspiring. You gave me hope when I was transferred to your station because I was really struggling during these dark times, and seeing your familiar face brought a sense of comfort. I'm sorry if I never showed you enough appreciation before. You were always there for me, so I will always be here for you should you ever need me, whether it's as a friend, acquaintance, support system, something more...anything.*

*Yours always,*
*Lila*

His lip curled as the conversation with Lila from earlier that day replayed in his mind. He read the letter twice more, but it was the same phrases that stuck out to him each time: *"You gave me hope...You were always there for me, so I will always be here for you...Friend, acquaintance...something more...anything."*

His eyes traveled to the necklace he'd chucked earlier, coiled in a sorry heap on the bed covers.

After a minute of contemplation, he set the letter on the bed and plucked his phone from the desk. His finger scrolled through his contacts, stopping on Lila's name as his pulse rocketed through his veins. Finally, with a deep, heavy exhale, he dialed her number.

Fifty-Eight

*May*

“OH MY GOSH, THE PROTESTORS NEED TO STOP vandalizing!” Carolyn exclaimed from the couch as she munched through a bag of pretzels.

The four of them sat scrunched on the cushions, staring at the news. Protestors had been flooding Minneapolis and other cities across the country, demanding police reform and justice for George Floyd. Los Angeles was one of the many cities placed on curfew in an attempt to isolate the looters and vandalizers from the peaceful protestors.

Alisha threw up her hands. “The protestors who are actually a part of the movement aren’t the ones vandalizing! But why is the looting and vandalism always the main focus? Seems like people are more worried about damn material things than the death of an unarmed Black man at the hands of an officer.”

Dani folded her arms and glanced at Emma to her right. The Salvadoran wrinkled her mouth as the other two roommates brawled at the far end of the couch. The arguing had become a familiar scene after dinner for the past four days since George Floyd had been murdered.

Carolyn narrowed her eyes at Alisha. "Burning the city down only destroys people's livelihoods and divides people further. Plus, they're calling to defund the police and painting them to be murderers! My uncle is a cop—I wouldn't want him to go out and defend the city against these crazy people."

Alisha brushed her dark curls out of her face, laughing. "That mindset is the exact kind of racist shit society wants you to see. Blacks are labeled as dangerous thugs and consistently blamed for crime and violence when most of them are good, decent people. And the whole 'defund the police' thing is supposed to concentrate funding to social resources, 'cause most of the time, police presences only escalate things. Something is clearly wrong when Blacks are more likely to die at the hands of a cop than any other race."

Carolyn lifted a pretzel to her mouth and paused. "Cops have a hard job! They have to make life or death decisions in the span of a few seconds. And crime is statistically higher in Black communities, so it makes sense that they have a higher death rate by cops, as sad as it is."

Dani gripped her sides as the memory of the Black Friday cop flashed in front of her eyes.

*The guy with the thick build called Dom kept his angry eyes trained on Dani. "This girl's trouble, I can tell." He gestured with his open hand again. "Hand it over unless you want to be arrested."*

*"You're insane." She wrenched her hand away and bolted past him, but the third guy grabbed her. Dom stomped over, twisted her arms back, and slapped a pair of handcuffs on her.*

*"Dom," the second guy warned again with a frown. "This is a bit much."*

Dani wondered how many times Dom got away with arresting people unnecessarily, and how many times his sidekick officer was encouraged not to say anything.

Alisha rolled her eyes at Carolyn. "But look at how many cops killed unarmed Blacks for unjustified reasons and *weren't held account-able?* Breonna Taylor, Ahmaud Arbery, Eric Garner, Michael Brown...

That's straight-up systemic racism." She folded her arms. "If it weren't for the tear-gassing war zone right now, I'd be out there protesting too."

Emma piped in, leaning over Dani. "It really isn't safe to be protesting at any time of the day, really, considering the coronavirus is still at large."

Dani rubbed her temples. After witnessing firsthand what COVID was capable of, she also wasn't keen on mass gatherings spreading the disease. "I agree with Emma."

Emma smiled smugly and straightened, folding her hands on her butterfly pajama pants.

"But I also agree with Alisha," Dani murmured, thinking back to Warren's argument. "There is a problem with racism in our country, and not all cops are being held accountable for their actions. A cop murdered someone on video in cold blood and didn't even get fired or put into custody *until* people protested. If that isn't enraging enough to make people gather in the streets during a pandemic, I don't know what is."

That drew a sharp scowl from Carolyn. "Gah, not you too!"

"Oh, stop whining," Alisha hissed, lounging back in the cushions. "It's about time Dani disagreed with you for once."

Dani's lips quirked as she caught Alisha's eye. It was definitely odd to be in agreement with her; just a few months ago, she would have laughed at the absurdity. "Oh, stop," she shot at Alisha, but couldn't suppress the small smile from her lips.

Though Alisha's gaze stayed fixed on the television, a small grin flicked across her mouth.

Carolyn scratched her frizzy head. "I just don't see why there's so much backlash at the officers. A few bad ones don't mean they're all bad."

Alisha snorted, her brown eyes narrowing. "Same goes for the Black Lives Matter protestors. Just because a few have been violent doesn't mean they all get to be labeled as thugs and looters. Most have been protesting peacefully. How do you not see the double standard?"

"But the founders of BLM were Marxist! That means the entire organization was based on an aggressive, anti-capitalist principle!"

"Come *on*," Alisha growled. "You're gonna shoot down the entire movement for *that* weak argument? The movement's entire purpose is to fight for racial equality, and most of the protestors aren't even Marxist. Besides, there are a limited number of extremists in every movement if there are that many people involved!"

Dani let out a sharp exhale. "You're both right, okay?" she half-shouted over the bickering roommates. Alisha and Carolyn turned surprised faces to her, their quarrel momentarily halted. "Though there are extremists on both sides," Dani continued in a level tone, "the vast majority of them are good, decent people who just want their voices heard. Yes, cops have to make life and death choices in a matter of seconds, but Blacks are unfairly targeted. And yes, the law enforcement system needs to be reevaluated, but it doesn't mean we should completely defund the police. We need cops to protect everyone equally in a way that doesn't call for escalating calm situations."

Before Alisha could respond, Dani reached for the remote on the coffee table and changed the channel to a sitcom. "Let's watch something other than politics. I'm tired of everyone fighting all the time. Can't we just get along like the boring, useless roommates we used to be?"

"You're, right. Sorry," Carolyn apologized with a chagrined look. She stood, stretching her hands to the ceiling. "You guys do what you want. All this arguing wore me out." She clipped the bag of pretzels and picked it up, trekking to the kitchen.

Dani raised a hand to scratch her cheek and stopped. *Damn tic!* She shoved away the thought of the guy who had pointed it out to her.

When Carolyn was hidden behind the bar, Dani turned to Alisha. "You shouldn't have been so hard on her. You know she means well."

Alisha shrugged, flipping her long curls over a shoulder. "Fighting for equality is never butterflies and rainbows, Dani. Change begins when light-skinned people like you and me call their other light-skinned friends out for their oppressive comments."

Emma sighed and rose from the couch. "I'm worn out from all this political talk too. I'll see you guys in the morning." She sauntered out of the room and disappeared up the stairs behind Carolyn.

Alisha shook her head, fixing her gaze on the TV as an episode of *The Big Bang Theory* wrapped up. "And that, my friends, is America in a nutshell. Ignorance and apathy at their finest. At the cost of people's lives."

A small wave of guilt crept into Dani's gut. She'd been apathetic about politics for most of her life, irritated with the back and forth and the hotheadedness of it all. How many people had she turned a blind eye to when she didn't vote; when she handed the power back to the oppressors?

Alisha was right. It was everyone's civic duty to be involved, to voice his or her concerns, and stand up for something. People were out on the streets dying, being discriminated against, being denied basic living necessities regardless of how hard they worked for them… There were more important things to worry about in life than your own personal problems.

It was the exact kind of thing *he* would have said, with the way he put others before himself.

Dani forced the thought away. She had managed to avoid thinking about him for two weeks now—she wasn't about to dive down that rabbit hole again. The wound in her heart had slowly begun to heal with the help of her roommates' friendly bantering and her dad's talks every few days.

*IfBut if it hadn't been for his encouragement, you wouldn't have even apologized to your parents in the first place.*

Dani grimaced as a pang lanced through her chest. Why was that damn voice suddenly coming back? She snapped her attention back to the television and tried to follow the episode of *The Big Bang Theory*, but when Leonard made a joke and Penny kissed him, the strong foundation Dani thought she'd had beneath her feet began to crumble away. She bit her tongue to suppress the searing burn creeping up her throat.

*God, as hard as I try to deny it, I still miss him.*

"What is it?" Alisha asked, cocking her head.

"Nothing," Dani murmured, turning her head away to wipe her wet eyes.

"Doesn't look like 'nothing,'" Alisha noted, drawing her brows.

Dani sniffed and bit her lip before meeting her roommate's eyes. "Can I ask you something?"

Alisha swung her legs onto the couch and folded them cross-legged, facing Dani. "Yeah, what's up?"

Dani's finger traced along the seam of the cushion. "Have you ever… loved someone even though you tried hard not to? Because being with them would bring more pain than happiness?"

Alisha's face turned beet red, her gaze lowering. A moment later, she wrinkled her mouth and laid an elbow on the back of the couch. "Why? Is this about Tanner? He definitely brought you more pain than happiness. You two were the most toxic couple I'd ever heard of."

Dani gripped the edge of the couch cushion tightly at the mention of her ex, her heart sinking. "Well, thanks. And why do you say that?"

Alisha flicked her eyes to the TV. "Carolyn said he was a jerk to you. And it was obvious you two weren't working out. After a month of dating, you barely hung out with him or mentioned him at all, and then came home crying that one night after you were so happy he'd asked you to come over."

Dani cringed. Hearing Alisha so effortlessly assess Dani's piece-of-shit ex-boyfriend made Dani feel like even more of an idiot. Alisha hadn't even met the guy, yet she'd summed Tanner up perfectly.

Had everyone seen right through him except Dani? The image of his sexy smile, dark bangs, and beautiful brown eyes morphed into the dangerous, heated face she'd stared up at as he pinned her to his bed. Even after he'd hit her and almost raped her, she'd begged for his love.

That *was* a toxic relationship. Dustin had expressed as much to her early on.

Dustin. Her mouth went dry at the thought of him.

She sighed and squeezed her phone on her lap. "You're right. What Tanner and I had was…horrible in retrospect. But…he's not who I'm talking about." She lifted her head and met Alisha's searching brown eyes. "It's…about Dustin."

Alisha stiffened, and Dani looked away, a bit surprised and embarrassed at her own confession. Yet as afraid as she was about recalling her painful swirl of feelings toward Dustin, there was a sense of relief in unbottling the truth that had eaten her away for the past few days.

After a few silent seconds, her roommate said softly, "Does he know how you feel?"

Dani closed her eyes, raking her nails on the ridge of her phone case. "Yes. No. I'm not sure. We got pretty close in the week I stayed at his house, and I think we were both aware that something was different between us." She tucked a hair behind her ear. "He was the one who leaned in and kissed me, but I—"

"Wait."

Dani opened her eyes and turned to Alisha.

Her roommate tilted her head, perking her lips. "You two kissed?"

Dani glanced down and squeezed her phone again. "Yeah, I…" She dropped her head into her hands and rubbed her temple. "I'm so stupid. It shouldn't have happened."

Alisha shook her head, her curls falling over her eyes. "No, no,

I'm sorry. I didn't mean to sound like an ass… I actually think it's really cute he kissed you."

Dani lifted her head, drawing her brows at Alisha. "Really?"

Alisha shrugged, her eyes softening. "Yeah. You seemed to care for him when you said you would stay with him while his mom was in the hospital. And I thought it was sweet you came home that one time to grab a blouse and earrings for his mom's hospital release." She twisted a strand of hair, her eyes tracing it up and down. "Why are you so conflicted by the kiss anyway? Is it 'cause he's your mentor?"

Dani shook her head. "It's because…" She weighed telling Alisha about her brother's death. She'd talked about Jeremy more in the past month to Dustin and her parents than she had in the past three years. Perhaps she was ready to share her story with others as well.

Still, maybe that was a story for a different day. Not here, not now, when her emotions were scrambling to make sense of the past few weeks.

She pursed her lips as her brain wracked for an answer to Alisha's simple question. "I'm conflicted because Dustin has been amazingly kind to me, but I haven't reciprocated his kindness."

Alisha arched a dark eyebrow. "Uh, being there for him while his mom was sick didn't show him kindness?"

Dani scratched her cheek. "It's…more complicated than that. I… haven't gotten over some things in my past, and it wasn't fair for him to deal with that when he should only be happy for his mom. That's why I left. I couldn't put him through that."

Alisha snorted, blowing the curls from her face. "If he's half the guy Tanner was, he'd understand and have patience. Nobody's perfect, Dani. Everyone has different struggles in life. It's just a matter of adapting and trying to understand them."

Dani inhaled shakily, a lump forming in her throat. Dustin was infinitely more times the man Tanner was. Even after she'd revealed her jealousy and shoved him away, he'd fought for her.

His warm tenor voice rang through Dani's mind. *"Sometimes, given enough time, people do change… Even with your privileged, self-absorbed ball of shit, you're amazing, Danica."*

She rubbed her burning eyes and swallowed the lump in her throat. "I just wanted him to be happy."

Alisha drew her brows and cocked her head. "Despite whatever stuff you're worried about, did you ever think *you* might make him happy?"

Something tugged on Dani's heartstrings as she drank in Alisha's words. Her breaths strained against the pounding ache in her chest.

She couldn't be good for him, could she? Hadn't she done the right thing by distancing herself from him?

*Maybe Alisha's right; maybe distancing myself hurt him more than helped him. He kissed me, and then I pushed him away and yelled at him for it. I ghosted him and ruined our friendship.*

Dani bit her lip hard as the agonizing burn in her chest from a few weeks ago returned. "I...I don't know. Even if I did make him happy, he shouldn't have to worry about my problems. I have to fix myself before I can be with anyone, and I don't even know if that's possible."

Alisha's lip twitched as she scratched the skin showing through the hole in her ripped jeans. "But you don't have to fix all your problems by yourself, and you shouldn't. That's what a partner is good for."

"Dustin has enough on his plate to deal with. I'm not just gonna dump all of my stuff on him."

Alisha smiled—a genuine, full smile—and leaned on her elbow, boring her dark brown eyes into Dani's. "Of course partners aren't there for you to *dump* all your problems onto. What I mean is, you help carry each other's weight when it's too much for one person. He supports you, and you support him too. You fight through shit *together.*"

The way Alisha explained it made Dani feel like a kindergartner being taught about relationships for the first time, although there was no hint of condescension in Alisha's tone this time.

Alisha licked her lip and gazed down at the couch, her tone softening. "And even without a partner, you always have your friends and family to support you too. I know you feel like your burdens are yours alone to carry, but trying to deal with them by yourself is a losing battle. Believe me, I know. When my mom got sick and went to the hospital, I felt so ashamed and guilty for having yelled at her right before, but Noemi was there to pull my head out of the gutter." She looked up, connecting a soft gaze with Dani. "Get it now? There's no reason you need to push people away and do everything alone."

Dani squeezed her eyes shut as memories of heated arguments

with Carolyn, Emma, and Alisha swam through her head. She had pushed them all away when her guilt about her past threatened to tear her apart, yet her roommates had stayed by her side through it all.

Her parents… They'd put up with her temper tantrums and bi-polarity for years, to the point where Dani had almost completely shut them out.

And Dustin. He had been there all along. Even after she had pushed him away, he had wanted to help her fight through her PTSD.

He had fought for her when she couldn't fight for herself.

Dani shuddered and closed her eyes. For the past year, she had focused her time and energy in people like Tanner and Haley who dis-tracted her from her problems and made her feel good about herself.

All while shoving away the friends who tried to help her overcome her fears.

She choked on a sob, curling into herself on the cushions. She didn't even register that Alisha was watching her breakdown.

Why couldn't she ever make the right decision? Would Dustin even forgive her now, after she tore out his heart and didn't bother to text him, even as a friend? He might have moved on already. But she owed it to him to try to fix things. Even if she didn't deserve closure, he did.

She dug her phone out of her pocket, her heart hammering in her ears as she typed out a text two weeks too late. She read it to herself and patched it up two different times before deciding it was decent enough: **Hi Dustin. I'm so sorry for the late response. I should have responded sooner. Are you still up for talking? Maybe we can meet at our usual spot at the Village sometime next week when you're off work.**

She sucked in a breath and pressed send, then laid her phone on her lap and tried to focus on *The Big Bang Theory* while she waited for his reply. Alisha paid her no mind as she gripped the edge of the couch cushion, the stretching minutes driving a hole deeper in her chest. Had he already moved on from her? Had he seen her text and scoffed, thinking an apology from her now was far too late?

When her phone vibrated on her lap fifteen minutes later, her heart skipped a beat. She lifted the device, trepidation surging through her veins, and read his text: **Dani! So good to hear from you. I'm ac-tually off work tomorrow. You free? Maybe you can swing by my place before we go to the Village. I know Mel would want to see you.**

She couldn't suppress the sudden sob escaping her, and her crippled heart fluttered to life in her chest. His lighthearted response threatened to shove all of her bottled emotions from the past two weeks over the edge.

Her fingers danced over the keypad, then hesitated. As quickly as excitement had raided her senses, it was washed away by terror in the next moment. He wanted to meet her *tomorrow?* She didn't even have an apology worked out… Would she have the courage to meet him face-to-face after purposely avoiding him for so long?

Before she could respond, however, another text from him slid into view: **I missed you. I should have told you earlier that I'll always be here for you. As a friend, mentor…whatever you need.**

Dani clamped her eyes shut, a small smile creeping to her lips as a tear leaked from her eyelid. *I've missed you too, Dustin. More than you can even know.*

*Fifty-Nine*

*May*

As soon as Mel's curious face peered from around the door, she lit up like the sun. "Dani! What are you doing here?" Without warning, she launched herself into Dani's arms, jostling the purse on her shoulder.

Dani's voice came out muffled through her mask. "Mel! It's so good to see you!" She squeezed Mel tightly, brushing the girl's long brown hair and reveling in her warmth. After a long minute, Dani pulled back and scanned Mel's features, admiring her bright round cheeks, her long dark lashes, and thin curved lips. She wore a softball "Outlaws" T-shirt and blue tights.

Dani smiled. Mel was as perfect as she remembered. She was glad Dustin had suggested Dani meet him at his place so she could see the nine-year-old again.

She adjusted the mask on her face as her eyes drifted around the vacant living room. "Dustin didn't tell you I was coming?" Dani glanced around the living room hoping to see his face, but the room was empty.

"No. He doesn't tell me anything. He's in his room, probably still sleeping," Mel answered with a smirk. "He sometimes sleeps till 2:00 on his days off—it's pretty pathetic. One sec." She pranced to his door down the hall and pounded. "Dustin, get up! You have a visitor!" Mel walked back to the living room, a smile stretching ear-to-ear as she beamed up at Dani.

Then his tall, groggy figure appeared around the corner, making Dani's heart skip a beat. His tousled brown hair stuck up above his dark eyebrows. A black tank top hugged his muscular upper half, complemented by purple Lakers pajamas. He froze when he saw her, his eyes widening.

"Dani."

She cracked a smile and arched an eyebrow. "Still sleeping, huh? It's 12:30! Were you planning on ditching me?" Her heart raced as he took a moment to react. She hoped they could ease back into their humor without too much trouble.

When that curved, infectious smile crept onto his face, relief flooded her. "Ah, sorry! I totally forgot you'd be coming. I crashed hard last night—long shift again." He ran a hand through his messy hair as he raked her figure, his lips quirking. "Give me a second to clean up."

As soon as he disappeared down the hallway, Mel stepped in front of Dani. She shoved her hands on her hips and batted her long lashes furiously. "Why did you leave us? You didn't even say goodbye!"

Dani closed her eyes briefly as the painful memory of that night two weeks ago washed over her. Dustin's somber face and Mel's peaceful, sleeping figure danced in her mind, rekindling the sinking feeling in her gut.

She swallowed, shoving away the memory. Bending, she brushed Mel's hair behind her ear. "I am so, *so* sorry for leaving so suddenly, Mel. I messed up."

Mel's nose scrunched, but her hands remained on her hips. "You didn't answer my question."

A chuckle escaped Dani as she straightened. "I know." She sighed and scratched her cheek, then scowled. *Dammit. Ever since he pointed it out, I realize it every time!*

Dani focused her attention back on the girl waiting patiently in front of her. "It's just…I didn't want to…" She bit her lip as she struggled for words.

Rachel Mottley's emergence from the hallway saved Dani from an explanation. "Dani! I thought I heard a familiar voice!" She crossed the living room in three huge strides and swept Dani into her arms. So much love from Mel and her mom tugged at Dani's heart, and she squeezed Rachel a little harder than she intended. Finally, Rachel pulled away and braced Dani's shoulders, raking her up and down with joyful eyes. "It's so good to see you!"

Dani met her gaze with equal optimism. "Same to you! You look great!" Rachel appeared years healthier than she had two weeks ago. The smooth planes of her face had more color, her posture was straighter, and her grip on Dani's shoulders felt strong.

Rachel's face lit up before Mel stepped in between them, stifling any opportunity for her mom to respond. Mel peered up at Dani with her large brown eyes.

"Did you come to help out again? Dustin's been back at work."

Rachel brushed back Mel's hair, her mouth teasing upward. "Shush, Mel. She's had enough of this place!"

Mel's head fell, and Dani chuckled. "No, I loved staying here! But today, I just came to visit. Dustin and I are actually going to hang out by USC."

Movement in the hallway caught her eye. She gave a shy smile as Dustin approached, dressed in a red USC shirt and jeans, his hair combed neatly with the bangs gelled back to their usual state. A mask covered the crooked smile she adored.

Her spirits dipped when her mind settled on the last time the two of them had been in this same exact spot. *I was standing right here by the door as he approached, asking if we could still be friends.*

*And I shot him down.*

She bit her lip. He was probably thinking the exact same thing, reliving her pushing him away.

"Need to be rescued?" he teased with a quirk of his head.

*Just act normal.* Dani scowled. "I don't need to be *rescued* from an angel like Mel." She returned her gaze to Mel and her mom. "It was so great to see the both of you. I'd love to catch up soon!" *Assuming I mend things with Dustin, that is…*

She turned to leave, but a tug on her arm stopped her in her tracks.

Dani pivoted just as Mel swarmed her with another fierce hug, nearly toppling her over.

She squeezed her eyes shut and hugged Mel tightly, her throat constricting. Mel clung to her longer than Dani anticipated, brewing a burn behind her eyelids. The girl had been abandoned by her dad, her mom during her illness, and then Dani. She deserved better. She deserved to know she would be loved and cared for no matter what happened in this cruel world.

Dani planted a kiss on Mel's head, drowning in the blunt fact Dustin's heart wasn't the only one she broke that night.

*Lord, keep me away from innocent, beautiful people. I can't bear to hurt any more of them.*

With one last squeeze, Dani pulled away from Mel. A sharp twist in her gut left a feigned smile on her face before she passed Dustin through the doorway.

When she grazed his arm and caught a whiff of his ocean-breeze cologne, a waterfall of tingles cascaded down her skin. She sucked in a breath and tried to tamper her body's response to him. *Dammit! Pull yourself together!*

Dustin shut the front door behind them and walked beside her down the path to the driveway. "I'm sorry for waking up late. I was dead yesterday. Long shift again…" He looked up as a silver Volkswagen pulled up to the driveway next door.

Out stepped Bettie in a button-down sweater and jeans, looking vibrant as ever with her curly white hair and bright pink lipstick. She beamed at the two of them as she walked around to the trunk of her car and pulled out two thick grocery bags. "Hi, Dustin. And Dani! So good to see you."

Dani waved back, smiling widely. "Hi, Bettie. Nice to see you too!"

Dustin wasn't as happy as her, apparently. "Why didn't you let me shop for you?" he called with a low growl. "We had a deal."

Bettie waved a hand as she shut her trunk. "I didn't want to bother you on your days off since you started working again. And you know very well I can take care of myself."

Dustin expelled a heavy sigh. "I love her, but she can be so damn incorrigible," he muttered under his breath as Bettie slammed the trunk shut and rounded her car.

"I was beginning to wonder when you'd show up again," she

reprimanded Dani with an arch of her brow. "Mel has been a whiny fit ever since you left, and Dustin too."

Dani's cheeks heated. "I know. It's been too long. But I'm glad I got to see you!"

Bettie grinned as she continued up the drive. "I'm just teasing. You come on by any time you like, and I'll whip up some of those tacos everyone likes." She winked before offering a final wave and heading up the porch, disappearing inside the house.

"I do miss her tacos," Dani giggled, turning to Dustin.

He snorted. "She loves you, you know. She'll do anything to bait you over to her place again. Problem is, we can't take risks by meeting her inside anymore, especially now that I'm back at work." He opened the passenger door of his car and held out a hand to usher her inside. "After you."

The small gesture warmed her heart.

"Thank you." She smiled softly and slid into the seat. He closed her door and climbed into the driver's seat a few seconds later, starting the engine.

"Going to Dulce again? Your favorite place?" he asked as he looked over his shoulder to back the car out of the driveway.

"We don't have to go there. You hate it, remember?"

He chuckled. "Nah. It's not really that bad." His fingers played with the radio dial while he pulled onto Venice Boulevard and headed to the freeway.

Dani took a deep breath, her thumb fiddling with the zipper of her purse. "So…how have you been? How is work?"

He shrugged and glanced at a couple walking their dog along the sidewalk. "I've been good. Work has been taxing lately, but my supervisor said in a few weeks, I can start helping out with non-ICUs."

Dani's eyes widened. "Oh, that's good to hear!" She hoped she didn't sound overly perky.

Her gaze meandered through the window. A trail of clouds streaked the bright blue sky underneath a beating sun. She was grateful she had worn shorts; it looked like it was going to be a hot day.

"How about you?" he asked casually, flicking his blue eyes to hers.

God, it seemed they were starting all over again, like two people who just met. Why couldn't they just skip to the part where they joked and teased like the friends they used to be?

After the heated words she had stabbed him with two weeks ago, starting again as friends was more than she could ask for. She would be content with whatever he was comfortable with.

Having him with her was enough.

*Remember, this is your damn fault. Deal with it. Fix it.*

She shook away her thoughts and lifted a shoulder. "I've been doing okay. Pretty bored, mostly. And my roommates are getting on my nerves with their bickering… Who knew people could become more annoying after three months of being cooped up with them twenty-four-seven?"

He smirked as he fiddled with the radio dial. "Well, shit. Never would have guessed."

Dani snickered and raked her hair back into a ponytail.

That was the last of their friendly banter though, as the next few minutes passed in silence save for the buzz of pop tunes on the radio. Dani stared out the window as they pulled onto the 10 freeway, the road still mostly empty. The streets had appeared to be busier in the months since they first went on lockdown, but the amount of open road on one of Hollywood's busiest freeways was still an odd sight. Her finger traced the fabric on his car door as the stretching minutes ticked like a time bomb in her ears. Dustin probably felt the same discomfort and was wondering when she would bring up the part where she'd shoved him away and left his house in pathetic fashion.

She had to fix this.

Dani glanced down at her Converse. When had her knee started bouncing?

"Listen," she said softly. *Baby steps; don't push him.* She forced her knee to still and took a deep breath. "Um, I wanted to—"

"It's okay. Don't worry about it." She glanced at him, surprised, and his lips pursed. "It's my bad. I'm sorry about the kiss. I shouldn't have put you on the spot like that. It was…bad timing with everything." He gritted his teeth.

Dani's chest constricted a bit tighter as Dustin exited the freeway. *He already apologized so many times already. Why is he making it seem as if it was all his fault, and I did nothing wrong?*

She dug her nails into her purse strap, trying to summon the words to contest him, but he smiled back at her, his eyes shining. "Let's just forget it and have fun today, okay?" he finished. "Like old times, before the pandemic apocalypse."

Dani sucked in a breath, nodding, and the pain in her chest lulled a bit. Things would be okay between them. Like old times.

But...did he not want to talk about it because he thought she didn't return his feelings? Should she tell him how she felt?

Dani bit her lip. No. That ship had sailed. Better to not mess things up between them again.

After a while, Dustin eased the car to a stop and parallel-parked on Hoover St. in front of the Village. Shutting the car door behind her, Dani glanced over to USC's north gate. A handful of student protestors stood with their "open up" signs in the same spot by the gate she had seen them last time.

"What's up?" Dustin asked, shutting his door and joining her on the curb.

She turned to face him and swallowed. "It's just...I used to think the same way those protestors did, but after my roommate's mom got sick...and seeing what you and so many health-care workers go through...and your mom..." She trailed off and busied herself by threading her hair into a ponytail.

Dustin glanced down at the pavement. "I get it," he said softly. "I'm still living in a sort of daze myself. Everything has been so crazy lately, I haven't fully been able to process that my mom had COVID, or all these historic Black Lives Matter protests..." He gestured and began walking into the Village.

Dani inhaled a sharp breath as she willed her legs into pace beside him. "I'm embarrassed to say I never fully understood people of color's persistent frustration until recently. The words 'all men are created equal' don't yet apply to everyone while significant racial disparities exist." She swallowed as her brother's freckled, smiling face surfaced in her mind. For years, she'd deliberately pushed aside Jeremy's memory for her own selfish, prideful interests. "Ultimately..." she continued softly, "ongoing racism is really a testament to the fact that we can never fully move forward until we reckon with the past."

They rounded the corner, and Cafe Dulce came into view. The tables by the fountain where Dani and Dustin had met for their mentor sessions were blocked with yellow tape.

A wave of nostalgia crept over her as she reflected on a world where she and Dustin had been laughing about her lacrosse scuffle in her first home match that year. A safe, happy world where

Dani worried about trivial things such as lacrosse and boys and parties…

And yet it was an ugly, ignorant world compared to the one Dani was in now.

Dustin shoved his hands in his jean pockets. "I know what you mean. Although I believed racism still largely existed, I didn't really see it for my own eyes until I met Jessie. People acted differently around him in public. Like, they would give him suspicious looks and clutch their children or valuables closer. And he told me a bunch of crazy stories… Anyway, he's been organizing BLM marches in downtown for the next few weekends." He bit his lip. "I've come to accept that I will never fully understand the Black perspective, just as I will never fully understand the female perspective. It's insane that abuse still gets pushed under the rug today, even in 2020. Especially if it's from people in power—Olympic doctors, presidents, film producers, police…" He sighed and looked away, his bangs riffling in the light breeze. "Even dads."

The sting of Tanner's slap bubbled to Dani's cheek as well as the jolt of fear that shot up her spine when her limbs went limp, succumbing to Tanner's firm grip. A sinking feeling crept into the pit of her stomach.

Dustin let a few heavy seconds tick by as they approached the door to Cafe Dulce. "But even though I will never fully comprehend the depth of what some of those victims go through,"—he glanced up at her, his eyes softening—"I can at least offer support where it's needed."

Dani's lips hinted a smile as he pulled open the door for her. He was still the compassionate, driven guy she remembered, and her heart ached a little more for him.

It was humbling to hear him talk about urgent societal problems when he had gone through so much himself in the past year. But of course he would dismiss his own stresses. Dustin had always put others before himself, regardless of what he dealt with personally.

Maybe she could be like him one day.

When Dustin brushed past her to pay for their drinks, Dani's eyebrows shot up. "No, you don't! I can get my own."

He waved a hand and pulled out his wallet. "Don't worry about it. And, uh…six feet please?"

Dani's lip curled as he shooed her toward the end of the counter.

She folded her arms and sighed, watching him share a friendly grin with the cashier.

Why did he continue to do nice things for Dani? Why did he so easily forgive her? *Alisha was right. He cares too much about me. He refuses to let me push him away.*

Dani forced back a whimper and dug her fingers into her sides.

He tapped his card on the reader, then meandered to join her by the end of the counter. "You okay?" he asked, tucking his wallet into his back pocket.

She gave a small nod and turned away, staring at the cafe's empty tables. In truth, she wasn't sure if she was okay. Since her talk with Alisha, the guilt had piled on, and Dustin's cool, gentle attitude only made it worse. Her mind replayed the scene from two weeks ago, his shattered expression scarring her memory when she closed the door and fled as if his kiss was domestic abuse. She wondered if he was replaying her harsh rejection just as much as she was, and the thought drove a dagger deeper into her chest.

"For Dustin?" the barista called.

Dustin smiled at the girl behind the counter and grabbed their drinks, then turned to Dani and inclined his head toward the door. "Guess we have to walk with them." He handed her an iced caramel Frappuccino, her favorite, usual drink.

Dani glanced at the seating area. The tables and chairs were blocked off just like the ones outside. She followed him through the door and meandered beside him along the sidewalk, slipping off her mask to take a refreshing sip of coffee.

"Mel was really upset that you left," Dustin teased as he pulled his mask below his chin. "You're like her big sister."

She tried to ignore the wound in her chest as they walked past the fountain square. His words were another sharp reminder of the hearts she had broken that night two weeks ago.

"She's too precious," Dani murmured, concentrating on the concrete path ahead of them.

Dustin scoffed and took a sip of his coffee. "I thought you were going to adopt her to take her off my ass. What's up with that?"

She shrugged, twisting her straw. Mel's frustrated expression from earlier surfaced in Dani's head. Her cute, round face had glared up at Dani, her hands planted on her small hips.

Dani turned her head to hide the emotion brewing behind her eyes. Would she continue to ruin and repair relationships for the rest of her life?

Could she truly ever be better?

The pressure behind her lids built, blurring her vision. She halted on the pavement as her legs began to tremble.

"What's wrong?" Dustin stopped beside her, worry washing across his face.

"Dustin," she choked through shallow breaths, "I am so, *so* sorry. For everything. For making you feel like shit and leaving, for ghosting you for two weeks, for my stupid random mood swings—"

He stepped close and squeezed her shoulder. "It's okay," he consoled with a half-smile.

"No, it's *not*. Please stop saying that." She gasped as an irrepressible wave of emotion washed over her. She fell to a squat, her drink slipping from her grasp and spilling into a mess of whipped cream and coffee on the pavement beside her.

Dustin dropped to a crouch and set his coffee aside before pulling her into his arms. "Dani," he whispered into her hair.

She tried to stop the tears from falling, and failed. Where was that strength she'd found a few weeks ago when she talked to her parents about living life for Jeremy? The resolve and sense of happiness she'd had when she admitted to Dustin she was grateful for so many things? Why did it feel as if her scars had reopened and she was drowning in her stupid, selfish past all over again?

But Dustin just held her like he had before, showing no signs that her sobbing deterred him.

Dani reached a shaky hand to wipe her swollen eyelids. "God, how are you not tired of this by now? I'm always crying."

He licked his lips. "I try to put things into perspective." He leaned back and searched her face, melancholy swirling in his cool blue eyes. "I was the same way when my mom got sick. Fear and anxiety blocked everything else out. I wasn't aware of the things in front of me—the things that should've made me happy." He traced a thumb along her cheek, wiping away a lone tear that leaked from her wet lashes.

Dani looked down as the dull patter of a passing stranger's footsteps faded down the sidewalk. "I-I wish I hadn't been so cruel to you," she whispered. "Anger has always been my defense mechanism. It keeps me from feeling guilty about all my mistakes."

His dark lashes dipped. "Trauma…can be a complicated, life-altering phenomenon. Healing doesn't happen overnight—but I believe you'll get better with time."

"How can you be so sure?" Her voice came out weak through her dry throat. "It's no good if I keep making the same mistakes over and over. I keep hurting people, like your dad did."

He stiffened, and she cursed herself for daring to bring his dad into this. But there was no hint of malice in Dustin's tone when he spoke. "No, it's not the same thing. My dad knew damn well he would hurt people when he did what he did, but *you* never meant to hurt anyone. We've all made bad choices; it's only human. The difference is that your mistakes happened to have far worse consequences than you intended, and it tears me up to see you still suffering from those scars."

Dani looked away from his piercing gaze, closing her eyes as her breath rasped against the burn in her throat.

"I know this has been anything but easy," he went on, "but I know you'll get through this because you're the most stubborn, badass, driven girl I know."

She opened her eyes and took a deep breath. "Stubborn, yeah. And there's hot-tempered, weak, ignorant, self-centered…"

His jaw tensed, and something like a low growl crept from his throat. "You should stop putting yourself down all the time."

Her eyes fell to the pavement, shame squirming through her stomach, but he lifted her chin to fix her gaze back on his.

"My point is, you're a *good* person, Dani. That fact outshines all the other crap. Believe it, because if you don't, I will drill it into your head for as long as it takes until you do. You're a lot more deserving of love than you give yourself credit for." He paused and studied her with unwavering, ocean blue eyes. "Dammit. Just once, I wish you could see yourself the way I see you."

Why was he so confident in her? She had proven herself to be a helpless, weak person time and time again, but for some reason, Dustin didn't think so.

Dustin glanced down and reached into his front pocket. "So… I actually was meaning to give this to you today."

When he undangled a silver chain with the Rod of Asclepius,

Dani's eyes widened. "What for?" Her gaze traced the Emergency Medical Service's symbol; a silver snake entwining a staff with cunning elegance.

"It reminded me of you." He smiled and rubbed the snake with his thumb. "My supervisor found it and gave it to me, but I felt as if I didn't do anything to earn a symbol of hope and healing—"

"Yes, you have," she objected. *You gave me hope,* she wanted to say, but the words wouldn't come out.

His lips tilted up as he rotated the Rod in his fingers. "Regardless… I couldn't think of any better promise of hope and healing than you, Dani." He lifted her hand and draped the necklace into her palm. "For the longest time I had wondered why a snake—a cold, menacing reptile—was the symbol of medicine. But the snake symbolizes rebirth." His lip curled. "Whatever you're afraid of from your past, Dani… it only makes you stronger in the end."

She squeezed the pendant and shut her eyes again, trying to see herself through his perspective to understand what he meant. The past few weeks with him replayed in her mind like a film, and in nearly every moment spent with him, she was a crying mess. But maybe she was looking at it all wrong… She recalled Dustin's disheveled, broken appearance in the first days she had spent with him, and then his smile when he'd locked eyes with her at the first dinner home with his mom, when he said he was glad Dani was with them. She remembered their conversation in his room after he'd talked with his dad on the phone, when he proclaimed Dani was the reason he'd rediscovered hope.

As much as Dani had wanted to separate herself from her past, Dustin saw her past as a source of strength; something that made her cherish people closer to heart. Maybe her past *had* made her stronger.

And then, searching deeper, she saw the person Dustin had seen all along: a young, passionate girl who had blossomed into something beautiful. She was far from perfect; she was rash, selfish, incorrigible, troubled by scars and self-doubt, and so many other things. Yet despite all of her flaws, she had persevered. In the past few months alone, she had opened herself up to growth as a volunteer, a daughter, and a caregiver. Although she had a long way to go with her own self-esteem, she had begun to accept her past and wanted more than anything to rise above it and be better. Amidst everything, she had strived for healing, even now.

*That* person could be forgiven.

*That* person was capable of being loved.

And in turn, that person could love others, because her love would be worth something. It would be strong, true, and whole.

Dani opened her eyes as this new sense of understanding washed over her. She drew the pendant around her neck, bristling as the cold silver nestled against her skin. When she clasped the hook and glanced down at the symbol, it felt right, like a beacon of hope shining from her chest. Something to remind her of all the trials she had endured, and the promise of what lay ahead.

"Thank you," she whispered. "It's perfect." She met Dustin's patient, calm gaze, and beamed. His mouth teased into a lazy smile, and he stood, offering her a hand. When she took it, he drew her upward and steadied her with soft palms on her sides, stealing her breath. He gazed at her tenderly, his hands trailing down to rest on her hips.

Butterflies flapped to life in her stomach, followed by a reignited longing within her chest.

Now was the moment to tell him. But as soon as she opened her mouth, his hands dropped from her hips, and he quickly stepped away.

His eyes fell as he scratched the stubble on his chin. "Sorry, I shouldn't …" He trailed off, but she didn't miss the sharpness in his tone.

Dani's heart cracked, and she cursed herself for it. *Of course he doesn't feel the same way. He just wants to be friends. What the hell am I trying to pull, anyway? A damn pity rose from* The Bachelor?

*Maybe he had already moved on with Lila.*

A sharp sting penetrated Dani's chest as an image of the pretty nurse surfaced. *What does it matter, anyway? It isn't my place.* Whatever he'd decided, she told herself, she had faith it was for both of their best interests. The only thing that mattered was that she had apologized, and he had understood and forgiven her.

This is what she had wanted—for things to go back to normal between them.

As friends.

Dustin glanced at the mess of whipped cream and coffee Dani had spilled beside them and smiled weakly. "Want to grab some ice cream? I can't stand this heat."

Dani wiped the last of her tears with the back of her hand,

a redemptive, small light flickering to life in her chest. "I hate ice cream," she replied sourly.

He wrinkled his mouth and rubbed his neck. "Uh, smoothie?"

She elbowed him in the gut, a smile crawling effortlessly to her lips. "What is wrong with you? Of course I like ice cream!"

*May*

Dustin and Dani meandered around the Village's small perimeter, racing to eat their Baked Bear ice cream before it melted as the hot sun dipped lower in the sky.

"I was thinking about the lame-ass dad joke you mentioned a while back, and I thought of a better one," Dustin said in between each spoonful of rocky road ice cream.

"Uh-huh?" Dani baited, licking her spoon clean of cookie dough.

"What is brown and sticky?" he prompted.

Dani wrinkled her mouth, pretending to ponder the familiar joke. "A stick?"

The amusement dropped from his eyes, and his lip curled into a frown. "Shit," he murmured before wolfing down another spoonful of ice cream. "I need to get some new jokes."

She came to a halt and burst out laughing. Her hand darted to her stomach as she dropped to a squat.

"What's so funny?" He gaped down at her. "You heard the joke already."

She wiped the tears from her eyes. "Oh my god, I applaud you. You are the *king* of jokes. You're so good, you make jokes without even meaning to."

His confused expression didn't budge. "I don't get it."

Dani shook her head, smiling. "You just answered your own joke. You said *shit.*" Realization dawned on his face, and she giggled. She stood, taking a deep breath to relax her giddiness. "Damn, you almost made me drop my ice cream."

"Now *that* would have been funny," he snorted, licking his fingers.

She rolled her eyes. "What, my coffee spilling everywhere wasn't enough for you?" A grin spilled across her face as she bit into another liquid chunk of ice cream, reveling in his crooked smile.

Dustin was back in her life. Things were as they had been before—comfortable and fun. His presence filled the small void in her chest she'd tried to ignore for two weeks. More importantly, he appeared happy. That small detail lifted Dani's spirits more than anything.

It was enough.

She smiled as they rounded the corner across from USC's north gate entrance. "Thank you for buying me ice cream *and* coffee. I'm still upset you didn't let me pay for something."

His chuckle was a warm, welcoming sound to Dani's ears. "Next time, I'll be sure to make you buy me something super expensive to make up for it."

She raised a dubious eyebrow as she finished off her ice cream. "*Next* time, I expect you to not wake up so late. Why are you still working so much? Can't they handle giving time off to someone who nearly lost his mom?" She blanched as soon as the words were out of her mouth. "I'm sorry—I didn't mean..." The pandemic was taking a terrible toll on all health-care workers, and she knew Dustin didn't want to elevate his family's situation above his coworker's own sacrifices and anxieties.

And of course the last thing he wanted to talk about was his mom's near-death experience.

Dani's eyes squeezed shut. *Stupid, stupid!*

Dustin didn't react to her comment as he ate the last of his own ice cream. He glanced at her empty cup and grinned. "Well, shit. We finished those fast." He collected her cup with his and tossed both pieces of trash in a can by the curb before stepping back in pace beside her.

Dani rubbed her arm as they continued down Hoover St. "Thank you."

His eyes danced as they approached his small Honda Accord. He pulled open the passenger door and flashed a slanted smile before tugging his mask over his face. She returned a grin before also affixing her mask and slipping inside the car.

As she fumbled with her seatbelt, Dustin hopped into the driver's seat and started the engine. "I'm glad we got to hang out," he noted with a gleam in his eye. "And it's a win-win when you get ice cream on a hot day."

"Look at that—I accomplished something in my three months of quarantine," Dani responded with a quirk of her mouth. He glanced at her amusedly as he pulled out onto the street and headed down the two short blocks to her apartment.

Dani tapped her fingers on the armrest as Miley Cyrus's "Party in the U.S.A." blared on his radio. She reached over to turn up the volume.

"What is this trash?" he scowled.

"How dare you!" she laughed, punching his arm. "This was my jam in high school! You know, all the cool kids listened to this song."

His eyes twinkled. "Ah, so you're saying I wasn't cool then?"

She turned the dial louder, reveling in the bass vibrations thumping through her seat. "What's that? I can't hear you over this dope song!"

He shook his head as Dani strummed an air guitar and rocked back and forth in her seat. Somehow, Dustin's mere presence gave her such liberation. He made all of her worries and problems from the past few weeks—months—vanish, and he didn't even know it. And when he smirked and mocked her dance moves with a roll of his eyes, she fell a little harder in love with him.

Love. There it was again.

*No.* She willed the feelings away as he pulled the car up to her driveway. Her heart wouldn't get in the way of their relationship. It wasn't fair to him.

She could learn to love him as a friend, nothing more.

"I'll walk you out," Dustin said as he turned off the engine.

Her lips tugged upward, and she exited the car and swung her purse over her shoulder. She walked a few steps up the driveway and turned to face him, tugging her mask away and stuffing it in her pocket so he could read her full expression. She clasped her palms. "Thanks for putting up with my horrible dance moves. And I'm sorry I flooded your car with Miley Cyrus's 'trash' music."

He snorted and unhooked his mask as well to reveal a lopsided smile. "Thank you for putting up with my shitty jokes." He tossed back his head, moaning. "Damn! I'm good. *Shitty.*"

She smiled and rolled her eyes, letting him soak in his lame joke points. After a long moment, she curled her lip and shifted her weight. "I had a lot of fun today. Seriously. Thank you." Her voice dipped. "Thank you for helping me through my dramatic episodes. And not just for today." She rubbed her arm and let out a deep breath. "You put up with me every time I broke down—at the hospital protest, at your house, today… You've always been there for me."

Compassion flooded his features, and he studied her with the same tender look he gave her in front of Wahlburgers. "Of course. You're worth it, Dani. Every single time." His eyes shone with a brightness so candid, it stripped away any prior fears she had of him ever abandoning her.

She stared at him a moment longer before smiling and turning to head up the driveway.

"Dani…I need to tell you…"

His voice halted her in her tracks, and she pivoted back to face him. Any further time spent with him only made it harder to leave, but she treasured every minute, nevertheless.

He shoved his hands into his pockets, his gaze falling to the sidewalk. A warm breeze rippled his T-shirt against his chest, blowing a few of his bangs across his face as his eyes seized hers. "Coming into today, I hoped we could ease back into what we had before—as friends—considering all the crazy shit that's happened, and considering your concerns about your past." He raked a hand through his tousled brown hair. "But after today… Being with you made me realize that my feelings for you are a hell of a lot stronger than what I thought." He licked his lips and tilted his head, sighing. "I know we've both been through our own highs and lows, but everything I went through was better with you. I just thought you should know."

He paused, trying to read Dani's expression, although she wasn't even sure what was on her face. Her brain took a long moment to fully digest his words, but when it did, her heart itched for him, sprouting wings in her chest.

He hadn't pulled away from her earlier for a lack of feelings for her; he just thought he was doing what was best.

Her hand crept up of its own accord to squeeze the silver pendant against her chest. She *did* make Dustin happy after all this time.

And not just as a friend.

"But what really matters is what *you're* comfortable with," he quickly continued. "Tell me to piss off, and I'll do so. You've dealt with so much already, and I don't want to make things worse. I just had to get this off my chest." He bit his bottom lip with a pained look. The gesture was so innocent and heart-wrenching, Dani nearly crumbled.

She inhaled deeply as her heart somersaulted. A wave of emotion propelled her forward, and she closed the gap between them in two long strides. Hand darting to his cheek, she kissed him—*finally* kissed him—with all the longing she'd stowed away for the past month.

His soft lips melted into hers, and he kissed her back with a passion that rivaled her own. His hands wound around to the small of her back, drawing her against him, and she gasped at the perfect feel of his body pressed with hers.

Her core burst with electricity just like it did the first time—only this time, she didn't hold anything back. She dragged both her hands through his hair and folded them around his neck, her body arching into him of its own accord. When his arms tightened around her, her heart fluttered like a drunken bird in her chest.

How had she been so fortunate to stumble across this amazing guy? And how was it that he wanted *her*, even after all this time? Was she really that lucky?

Dustin's hand crept to her jaw, and he deepened the kiss. His lips slowed to a delicate rhythm while his fingertips caressed her cheek; he touched her as if she were the most precious, fragile thing in the world. If any shred of doubt lingered in her mind about how he felt, he erased all suspicions with that kiss.

Finally, she drew back and clasped both his hands, pulling them down between them. When she summoned the courage to speak, her voice trembled. "I should have told you sooner, but I've had feelings for you for a while, too, Dustin." She glanced down, squeezing his palms. "I...I realize I'm probably confusing you a lot right now. I have been so confusing and messed up for as long as I can remember...but I just wanted you to know that despite everything, there's one thing I'm not confused about, and that's you."

She lifted her gaze and memorized his face, taking in the perfect curve of his cheeks and the clean trim of stubble along his jawline. Her eyes crept up to his long, dark lashes and then the brown bangs gelled up messily above his forehead. Finally, she met his eyes—the piercing blue eyes that had seen the best of her through all of this.

"When you kissed me that first time," she recollected, "it was so amazing, so perfect, it made me question everything. It terrified me. I was so afraid of yielding to my feelings because I didn't believe you could deserve someone like me." She swallowed a lump down her throat. "You are so perfect and good to me..." His mouth curved upward as she stumbled for words, and her heart skipped a beat. "You're always so understanding and tolerate my crazy emotions, and you always light up my day with the lamest, funniest jokes. You make me want to be a better person, to believe in myself and see all the things that make me beautiful, and—"

Dustin kissed her forehead, saving her from her pitiful words of affirmation. "Come here," he murmured as he pulled her into a hug, and the sound of his heart beating powerfully through his chest warmed her bones.

Maybe he knew it, maybe he didn't, but that embrace meant the world to her. It was another confirmation of the truth she had failed to see so many times: she was worthy of love, she was valued, and she was wanted.

She was good enough.

He pulled back and bowed his head against hers, tracing the backs of her hands with his thumbs. "You are adorable. And gorgeous. And you make my damn heart flip inside out."

Tears rushed to Dani's eyes, and her legs weakened. Could this really be happening?

He brushed a wisp of her hair behind an ear and held her gaze, the heat in his eyes prickling her skin. "Understand this, Dani. I'm yours—regardless of what you think I deserve." He ran gentle hands down her sides, sending a waterfall of shivers down her spine. "I appreciate that your reason for leaving was because you only wanted what was best for me, but you never considered the reasons why you should stay." He smiled and wove his fingers through hers. "You inspire me. You make me laugh. You give me hope. You make me feel vulnerable, happy, and lucky to be alive. Nobody else has ever made me feel that way."

Dani stifled a sob, but couldn't help the name that squeaked from her lips. "Lila…"

Dustin's smile faded, and he slid a hand up to her cheek. "Is an amazing friend who will find a great guy one day," he finished. "Don't worry about her. She only reaffirmed what I wanted this whole time." His crooked smile crept back to his lips. "It's only been you, Dani. It's always been you."

Dani's lips trembled at his words. Did she really mean that much to him, even after everything she had put him through? She wanted to break down and cry; to kiss him and hold him in her arms and try to express just how grateful she was for him.

She slid a hand along his chest and clutched his shirt. "I feel like such an asshole, Dustin. I'm sorry for being so frustrating. I'd been lost for so long, I didn't know what was best for anyone anymore." Her voice strained with emotion. "I'm sorry for losing my sanity."

He chuckled, and then his eyes lit up. "Come with me."

Dani didn't have a chance to object as he took her arm and dragged her, almost playfully, back to his car and ushered her inside. He ran around to the other side and hopped in.

She raised a curious eyebrow even as a giddiness stirred within her. Was this how Chase had felt when he looked at Emma? This excited, adventurous adrenaline pulsing through her veins?

"What are you doing?" she asked.

He grinned amusedly. "You're so full of questions. But if you must know, I'm teaching you how to retain your sanity." He gave a mischievous smile as the memory of their cornhole game danced in Dani's mind.

A memory, she now realized, that suggested the first moments she'd started to fall in love.

# Sixty-One

*May*

A FEW HOURS LATER, DUSTIN PULLED ALONG THE CURB OF OCEAN Avenue beside the scenic boardwalk that led down to the famous Santa Monica Pier. He parked at a meter in the shade cast by the tall palm trees lining the sidewalk, blocking out the fading sun.

Dani shot him a sideways glance with her bright hazel eyes. "What are we doing here? I thought you were taking me home after our Chipotle trip."

He could have talked to her over bowls of Chipotle in his car all day. He would never get tired of watching her teasing smile and listening to her witty banter. More importantly, it was amazing to finally talk to her without being afraid of hiding his feelings—as an exuberant guy who knew she felt the same way.

But that hadn't been the goal of this trip.

He grinned and opened his door. "You'll see. Follow me."

She hesitated before exiting the car after him and stepping onto the curb. He felt her eyes tickling his back as he paid the meter up until the expiration time. When he turned to face her, she was holding an elbow and biting her lip, and for an instant, he worried he had made a mistake in bringing her here.

*No—she can do this. She needs to do this.*

He crossed the patch of grass that led to the boardwalk and began walking toward the ramp that led down to the beach, Dani in tow. It was late in the day, and the sun dipped closer to the horizon, partially obscured by the slim bundle of clouds that drifted in front of it.

It thankfully wasn't as hot here by the beach, the salty ocean breeze providing a nice chilling contrast to the blazing heat they'd felt at the Village. Dustin silently cursed himself for wearing jeans. At least Dani was smart and had worn a cute button-up T-shirt and shorts.

He reveled at her golden skin glinting in the sunlight as she fell into pace beside him. She peered over the boardwalk railing to gaze at the ocean below, and her face glowed with something akin to longing or nostalgia.

Dustin's lip curled briefly at her reaction, relief washing over him. A part of him worried she would get caught up in the bad memories of her brother, but she needed to be reminded of the good memories too.

She needed to know light shone brighter in the darkness.

He said nothing as they walked side by side down the empty ramp, arms brushing slightly. When they approached the beach, Dani watched him take off his socks and shoes before he trekked forward, feeling the warm sand slip through his toes. He turned back to see her hesitating on the sidewalk. After a moment, she did the same, following him over the sand.

The orange rays of dying sun fell over a few surfers and sunbathers on what would normally be a packed beach for a summer evening. With Los Angeles' social distancing rules, the pier was off limits, but people were still permitted to use the beach as long as they stayed six feet apart and wore a mask when in close proximity to others.

Dustin slowed as they approached the small hill before sand and water intersected, Dani taking the lead now. She dropped her socks and shoes on the hill and trudged down into the wet sand, the waves lapping up to her calves. Dustin placed his socks and shoes beside hers, rolled up his jean legs, and sauntered through the waves next to her, the cold water soaking his shins.

His gaze fixed on her as she stared out into the ocean with shimmering hazel eyes, hands hanging motionless at her sides, the silver Rod of Asclepius glistening brightly on her chest. The light wind carried wisps of dirty-blonde hair out of her ponytail, and if he were an artist he would seize the moment to draw her breathtaking sight.

Then her hand crept up to clasp the snake-entwined staff hanging from her neck, and he wondered what she was thinking.

He exhaled and followed her line of sight along the horizon, a swirl of purple and orange now spilling out over the clouds in a perfect, encapsulating sunset. It was the most beautiful painting of colors he'd ever seen.

"Dustin." She touched his arm. He looked at her and caught the wetness on her cheeks. "I…" she whispered, choking up. "Thank you."

He faced her completely and dug into his pocket, searching. Had he brought it? Yes, he had! He pulled out his AirPods and then his phone from his other pocket.

"I want you to hear something."

She raised an eyebrow but didn't question him, taking one earphone from his outstretched hand as he put the other one in his ear. After scrolling through Spotify for a few seconds, he found one of the songs her brother liked and pressed play.

Soft acoustic guitar-plucking filled his ear, followed shortly by H.E.R.'s elegant voice drifting over the chord changes. He watched Dani closely, and when recognition spilled across her face a few seconds later, she closed her eyes, and the corner of her mouth eased upward.

He put his hands around her waist and pulled her close. Bringing a hand to her cheek, he bowed her head against his. She sighed as she swayed with him to the soothing music, and Dustin was overcome by a peaceful bliss, unperturbed by the splashing of cold waves against his legs. He marveled at how the song's lyrics and the melody's smooth rise and fall articulated perfectly how he felt for her.

As he stood there in a swarm of emotions for her, the pain of the past few months piled high in his chest: the turmoil of his mom's illness, the frustration with his dad, the worry about providing for his family, and the toll of twelve-hour shifts… Dani wasn't the only one who'd needed healing. He had been drowning for a long time too. But he might not have made it out without her.

His eyes welled with tears, and his hands began to tremble at Dani's sides. God, was he crying?

When he lowered his head to wipe his eyes, Dani combed his hair, drawing his gaze to hers. Her hazel eyes swirled with compassion and understanding, stopping time for a bittersweet moment, and then she brought her lips to his. She kissed him slowly, easing away all his fears, pain, and worries from the past year. In her tender touch lived a similar recognition of grief, pain and longing for her brother, but along with that, a sense of comfort, happiness, and peace; an assurance that good would always come through in the end.

During H.E.R.'s vocal postlude, he pulled back and whispered, "Out of everything in this crazy damn planet, you're the best part, Danica Torres."

Her sweet smile lit up the darkening sky. "Not compared to you."

The raging rush of love he felt for her overwhelmed the music in his ear, the roar of the waves, and anything else on his mind.

Reaching up with both hands, he undid her ponytail and wound his fingers through her long, luscious hair. The wind enveloped him in her pine tree scent—a scent that made him think of expansive forests and all things green and wild.

He cradled her face and kissed her again as a larger wave splashed against their calves. She shrieked, curling her shivering body into him. With a smirk he reached down to her thighs and hoisted her out of the water, and she locked both her legs around his waist.

"I'm freezing," she whispered with an innocent smile.

He clutched her tighter, studying the brightness in her eyes. He wanted more—to tighten this blossoming, magnetic pull between them. He wanted to show her just how much she meant to him; that she was defined by more than just her scars.

Turning through the shallow waves, he carried her over to the small hill where their shoes had been tossed aside. Laying her gently in the sand, he pried his AirPods from their ears and stuffed them in his pocket before taking care to memorize her perfect figure poised beneath him. She leaned back and gazed up at him, her hazel eyes glowing iridescent in the fading sunlight. He reveled at the sun-kissed skin of her athletic legs, the slim curve of her hips, and the perfect dimple in her left cheek. He traced a finger along her smooth skin and smiled as goosebumps trailed his touch—from her thighs to her sides, her arms, her shoulder, her cheek.

"You're so beautiful," he murmured, peering into her radiating face. "Never forget that."

The corner of her mouth tugged upward. "I've heard those words before, but you have been the only one to ever make me feel that way."

He lowered his head and sealed her words with a kiss.

As he lay there caressing her, he knew he would do anything for her. For this girl, Danica Torres, who had so brazenly stolen his heart and given him hope in the darkest of days.

"Dustin," Dani breathed as his mouth trailed to her neck. The feel of his warm lips on her skin sent a shiver down her spine, and she dug her nails into his damp shirt. Her heart pounded so hard she thought it might burst free of her chest. Nothing had ever felt so good in her life.

"Stop," she exhaled, and he froze. She gently pushed him off her, rolling him until his back was against the sand. "My turn."

The alarm in his eyes faded as she leaned on an elbow and gazed down at him.

He had done so much for her this past year, been so patient with her as she pushed him away time and time again. The least she could do was reciprocate the way she felt for him.

She ran her palm under his shirt, along his washboard stomach. He brought a hand up to stroke her cheek, but she brushed it away. "No," she rejected. "Let me."

His fists retracted to his sides as she kissed every inch of his skin, from his arms to his shoulders, his navel, his neck, his cheeks, his nose. When she finally lowered her mouth to his, his lips responded with fire.

Any restraint Dustin still retained failed, and he pulled her down tight against him. Their lips never broke as he tangled his hands in her hair and rubbed her scalp.

The electricity flooding through Dani obliterated all rationale. She was drunk on Dustin. He made her forget where she was, how she had gotten there, and even her own name. She wanted him—all of him— and a crazy thought sprouted in her head. She didn't even care that they were on the beach. It was practically dark, and the beach was probably near vacant now.

She shimmied her hips against him, and his lips paused. "I want you to touch me," she whispered. Her hand clasped around his and dragged it to the top of her jean shorts, but he pulled away.

She bit her lip, her mind racing. "We could go to my place. I can kick my roommates out." Such an idea sounded ludicrous even to her own ears, but she hadn't been able to tame the rush of emotion that forced the words out of her mouth.

"No," he responded softly, albeit firmly.

Dani shrank back, hurt prickling her skin. "Don't you want me?"

He chuckled, and the rise and fall of his chest beneath her made her breath catch. "More than you even know."

Dani wrinkled her brow, confusion settling even as his affirmation jostled the butterflies in her stomach again. He stroked her cheek, and Dani's disappointment faded almost as quickly as it had come, washed away by tingles where his fingers touched.

"We have time," he finished. "I'm not gonna rush any precious moment with you."

Dani bristled, awestruck at his response. How did he have such self-control? She was offering herself to him, and he was telling her they should wait?

Yet, as puzzled as she was, she couldn't help but admire him even more for his restraint. She had never known a guy like Dustin before.

And yet here he was; a guy who had consistently proven just how much more he cared about her than she cared for herself.

Dani sat between Dustin's legs with her back against his chest, his chin on her shoulder, as they watched the last light fade from the pink and purple sky. Grains of sand had uncomfortably found their way into hidden places on Dani's body, but she didn't care.

Today had been the best day of her life. It didn't matter to her that she'd broken down at the Village earlier, because afterward, it seemed her soul was wiped clean and she was being given a second chance.

She felt whole again, valued, happy.

No—more than happy. She was exuberant.

Of course, somehow, Dustin had known exactly what she needed. He had taken her to the place that reminded her most of her brother, and his overwhelming act of care for her warmed her heart. Dustin recognized her pain and continued to remind her of the same mantra she had told her parents: Jeremy was alive in her.

*It's funny how everything about Dustin always pointed to the ocean, the very thing Jeremy always wanted to see.*

*And now we're here.*

Everything seemed more beautiful now—the ocean, the fading sunset, the feel of the sand between her toes. Even the palm trees, the deserted pier, and the cargo ships in the distance seemed to smile at her. It was as if they knew she would end up here, and were waiting for her this whole time.

Because maybe… maybe everything had all been part of a master plan—Dani's trauma; the pandemic; meeting Dustin—all of it.

Would she have gone to USC and pursued med school if her brother hadn't passed away? Would she have been as compelled to come to Dustin's house had she not gone through a similar, lonely withdrawal herself? Would he have opened up to her had she not exposed the trials of losing her brother? Would she have improved the relationship with her parents otherwise?

Whatever the answer, she did know this: nothing could have happened in a more beautiful way. Maybe everything—as harsh and cruel and unforgiving as the world was—had happened for a reason.

Maybe she had to lose everything to find herself.

"You know that 'Danica' means 'morning star?'" Dustin asked from behind, pulling her from her thoughts.

Dani dragged her fingers through the sand, her mouth tilting up. "Yeah. It never made sense to me. You can't even see stars in the morning, anyway."

"Uh, what about the sun?"

She turned so he could see her eye-roll. "Uh-huh, I'm *totally* a dazzling ball of sunshine." She fluttered her eyelashes.

The warm breath of his soft laughter tickled her neck. "Okay fine. What if it has a different meaning? Like, you never really think about looking for the stars during daylight, but they're there, regardless."

"So what you're saying is that my name means 'hidden gem with a purpose though no one can ever see it.' How inspiring," she smirked as she faced forward again.

He snorted. "Yeah, it *is* kinda lame. 'Morning star' sounds too dainty for you, anyway. You're more like a 'morning pain in the *ass*.'"

She turned and punched him in the chest, then laughed as he threw his arms around her and buried his lips against her neck. She squirmed in his grip, giggling, and he finally released her with an amused chuckle.

When he leaned back on his palms, Dani rested her head against his shoulder, breathing deeply with a permanent smile etched across her lips.

"Speaking of stars," he murmured, "there is one pretty cool constellation that just happens to be visible at this time of day in the summer."

"Yeah?" she asked, tilting her head up to stare at the flickering specks of light scattered across the darkening sky.

"Ophiucus—'The Serpent Bearer.'" He lifted a hand and traced a diamond-shaped figure above them, connecting a few of the brightest stars.

Dani clutched the silver snake resting against her chest, imagining the mythical god Asclepius holding a thick snake in the pattern Dustin had drawn. She'd seen the image before in one of her pre-med classes.

"I like 'serpent bearer' over 'morning star,'" Dustin murmured, trailing his fingers up her bare arm. "It has a heroic, badass sound to it."

Dani closed her eyes, breathing in the cool night air as goosebumps rose from where Dustin's hand caressed. She listened to the push and pull of the waves, the rustle of the palm trees high on the cliff behind them, and tthe steady thump of Dustin's heart beating against her back.

It was all perfect.

"Dustin," she said quietly, turning her head to the side.

"Hmm?" He stroked back her hair and wound it around to her opposite shoulder.

She bit her lip. She wanted to tell him so badly, but after the last time she said the words, everything had spiraled catastrophically out of control and left her heart shattered.

But when she turned her head fully and met the sanctuary of his deep, ocean blue eyes, all doubts and fear vanished.

"I love you," she said with a conviction so strong that the words scorched through every limb in her body.

He held her gaze with an unreadable stare as her proclamation hung between them—those three words that had caused her so much turmoil for as long as she could remember.

Then he leaned forward, sliding a soft palm across her cheek, and that crooked smile crept across his lips. "I love you too, Danica."

They were the five most beautiful words Dani had heard in her life.

Dustin brushed away a tear that had escaped her eyelid and pressed his lips to hers, pulling her tight against him.

Everything disappeared into oblivion: the darkened beach, the lapping of the waves, the crunch of sand in irritating places all over her body, Los Angeles, and the world.

But this time, it wasn't because of a blackout from fear, grief, self-doubt, guilt, shame, or trauma.

It was because of love.

When the sun finally dipped below the horizon and the last streams of orange and purple faded from the sky on that perfect day, Dani cuddled into Dustin, and he wrapped his arms snugly around her.

And for once, as the darkness settled, she didn't tremble in fear.

*Sixty-Two*

***Epilogue***
***One year later***

Taylor intercepted the ball from one of Oregon's attackers and sprinted down Soni McAlister field, her long strides outpacing the other girl's short legs as the wind whipped her ponytail.

The crowd roared as Dani raced ahead to the opposite corner of the field. The bleachers were packed with vaccinated fans sporting a mix of red, gold, green, and yellow. After a year of quarantining, it was exhilarating to see people gathered in crowds again; to feel the rush of lacrosse adrenaline pounding through her veins.

The fans' cheers and whoops escalated as Taylor chucked the ball over a midfielder's head to Haley who snagged it midair. When Haley approached midfield, a girl stick-checked her aggressively, but she held onto the ball and swerved around the defender.

"4–3, 4–3 blitz!" she shouted in her commanding captain's voice as she scanned the field ahead.

A few yards away, Zoey raised her stick eagerly, and she caught Haley's pass in a smooth grab. The Trojan players on this side of the field outnumbered Oregon's defenders, but in seconds, their advantage would be gone; an Oregon midfielder was sprinting to help her fellow defenders.

Dani trekked in an anxious circle near the goal before a tall girl with long arms came into her path. Dani sidestepped her, but the defender spun around and blocked her open route to the goal. The other team had kept a close guard on Dani since the start of the game, and rightly so—she had been an unstoppable force for the Trojans this spring, on a course to break her all-time record for both goals and assists in a single season. It appeared Oregon's coach had caught onto Dani's backdoor route, which explained why the tall girl remained locked on her instead of defending Zoey when she approached.

Dani could only shake her head in exasperation as Zoey's pace slowed. Zoey's eyes widened when Dani didn't dart to the goal, and she swerved around, abandoning the play.

"Zoey, here!" Haley shouted from the top of the crease, but too late. The Oregon midfielder caught up to Zoey from behind and whacked her stick, knocking the ball out of bounds.

The referee blew the whistle, and the crowd jeered. Dani cursed and clenched her fists. Oregon had been leading the whole game, and the Trojans were down 8–9. They had just missed a golden opportunity to score, but the tall defender had ruined their play.

A buzzer's blare signaled the end of the third quarter.

"Dammit, Zoey. I had it!" Haley barked as the team gathered by Winston on the sideline.

Zoey tugged off her face guard and bit her lip. "Sorry—I was waiting for Dani, but she was blocked, so I didn't know what to do."

Winston's thick eyebrows narrowed as her voice rose to a yell over the fans' raucous chanting. "Don't worry about it, girls." She turned to Dani. "Torres, you need to figure out a way past 28. That was a perfect chance for us to score!"

Dani tugged off her face guard and clutched it to her side. "I'm trying, but Long Arms keeps pinning me in the corner. We need a different play."

"How about J-14?" Arianna piped in.

Dani fixed hopeful eyes on her teammate. J-14 was named after a trick play Jeremy had invented in college. When the team had finally reassembled for fall training at the beginning of the school year, Dani was proud to introduce the play to Winston and credit her late brother. Within a day of trying out the new play, the team had decided to rename it "J-14" in his honor—"J" for Jeremy, and his number "14," which was also Dani's number, now.

Winston glanced at Arianna and smiled in agreement at her proposition. "We'll run that the next time they have a one-on-one matchup."

The girls nodded, and Haley placed a tender hand on Dani's shoulder. "He's got your back even now," she whispered.

Dani covered the captain's hand with her own as an appreciative smile warmed her cheeks. She was grateful their friendship had renewed last year. Forgiving her friend, Dani realized, had been one of the small steps on the road to forgiving her*self*.

"As for now," Winston continued, "Jenson, sub for Martinez. Let's have the other same nine on the field." She gave a single loud clap. "All right, girls—one, two, three…"

"Fight on!" they whooped before dispersing.

They still had a few minutes to hydrate before the final quarter started. As Dani turned toward the bench to grab some water, Arianna stepped next to her. "Guess you're glad you don't have to worry about Peter suspending you anymore, huh?"

Dani froze in front of the team's water barrel. "What?"

Arianna raised an eyebrow. "You didn't hear the news?"

Dani shook her head, frowning as she set her face guard on the bench. She grabbed a paper cup off a cart and filled it with water from the barrel.

The goalie's voice lowered. "It came out that Peter's dad was one of the parents involved in the huge USC admission cheating scandal. He was bribing the athletic director."

Dani's eyes flew wide as she downed her water. She remembered the tall, bald athletic director she had met that fall day one year ago. She had disliked him ever since he made her write that stupid apology letter to Peter.

"What! That's insane."

Arianna nodded, grabbing her own water cup and filling it. "Yeah.

The investigation is still pending, but Peter's degree isn't gonna look so hot anymore. A frat guy spilled to me that the school looked deeper into his dad's contacts with the athletic director, and it looks like Peter's admission on a rowing scholarship may also have been compromised."

A wide, dirty smile stretched across Dani's face. *Finally, the justice that kid deserves.*

Arianna's lips quirked as she leaned forward. "There's a rumor going around that Dustin may have somehow helped the investigation against Peter's dad. Did he not say anything to you?" Dani shook her head. Arianna stole a glance behind Dani to the bleachers and smirked. "You should ask him," she finished before turning away.

Dani pivoted to face where Dustin was sitting in the front row. Her tall, handsome, blue-eyed boyfriend was chatting happily with his mom, who in her bright red tank top appeared healthier and livelier than Dani remembered her from a year ago. Scrunched between them sat Mel in her dirty softball uniform, peering around the electric scenery with her big brown eyes.

Dani sucked in a breath as her heart flipped in her chest. Just for Dani, Dustin had allowed Emma to paint his cheeks in red and gold with the numbers one and four. He donned a "USC Women's Lacrosse" shirt, and between his knees lay one of those damn cardboard cutouts her roommates had made of her face.

He had requested the day off work for the semi-final PAC-12 game the moment Dani had told him her team would be advancing to the next round. He had even convinced Jessie and Dr. Turner to come to her match, and the father and son sat chatting animatedly in USC shirts on Dustin's opposite side.

Dani's breath quickened, and she fought a burn behind her eyelids. Even after almost breaking his heart last year and everything else she had put him through, he was still her biggest fan.

When he looked up and caught her eye, he flashed his crooked, attractive smile and winked. Her cheeks gushed a furious red, and she returned a bright smile with a wave.

Carolyn whistled loudly a few paces away, next to Rachel, brandishing another huge cutout of Dani's face. "Yeah, Dani!" she shouted. On her left, Alisha sat cheery-faced next to Noemi, the happiest Dani had seen Alisha in a long time. Emma was planted beside them with her arm hooked through Chase's, the couple having made up when Chase reconciled with her last summer, confessing his agreement with Emma's opposition to his fraternity. They looked absolutely smitten.

And finally, beaming proudly next to her roommates, were her parents. Franc Torres sat in his quiet, game-focused state, his eyes scrunched in focus while Angelina clapped and whistled loudly on his left. Both of them sported red and gold shirts with the number 14.

"Let's go, Dani!" Angelina shouted, waving when she noticed Dani glancing over.

Dani's heart tugged at the sight of them seeing her once again in her happy place. She blinked back a tear and curved her mouth upward.

It was then she realized lacrosse had been the only thing to gather all the people she cared about together in one place. And after the months-long quarantine last year, new friends and old ones had assembled to cheer her on at her favorite sport.

The only face missing now was Bettie's. Dani's smile faded as a sinking pain lanced through her limbs. The loss of the bright, spirited woman had left a deep hole in Dani's chest.

A week after Bettie's stolen trip to the grocery store last summer, Bettie's vibrant health had rapidly deteriorated. She passed away in the hospital the day after she'd been admitted on a sunny afternoon in August, while Dani and the Mottleys gathered in solemnity. They counted it a blessing that the old woman hadn't suffered for too long, yet that knowledge did not make the tears any less painful.

Dani glanced at the dazzling blue sky and closed her eyes, breathing in the cool spring air and shutting out the electric buzz surrounding her. She clutched the silver necklace draped snugly across her chest; in the past year, she had found herself clinging to it as a source of strength. Now, as she looked out across the field, she knew Heaven had one more angel looking down on her lacrosse match today. Since the kind woman's passing, Dani had kept a promise in Bettie's honor: She would try her best to find beauty and hope in the small things and always offer a helping hand like Bettie had.

"Dani, hurry up!" Haley's shout drew Dani back to the bustle and hoots of the crowd. Bettie's smiling face faded from view as Dani tugged on her face guard and trotted over to her huddled team.

Haley gave orders as soon as Dani joined them. "All right, Lisa, you take 33, Victoria, 12, and I'll take 62 when we're pressing."

The girls nodded, and the referee whistled, calling for one player for each team to start the fourth quarter in a face-off. The buzz of the crowd grew into a roar as the Trojans took the field.

When the referee blew the whistle, the match resumed with immediate aggression from both teams. The winner of the match would go on to the PAC-12 championship, and the Trojans hadn't come all this way to lose after a spectacular season.

Several times when the Trojans gained possession, Oregon trapped them in a press and recovered the ball, firing shot after shot at Arianna. Luckily, she held firm and blocked each one.

"Stop running down the sides! Pickett can't block all day!" Winston shouted over the roar of the crowd. Dani knew Winston was anxious for the Ducks to switch to a one-on-one matchup so USC could run their trick play, but Oregon maintained a zone defense play after play.

Dani scooped up the ball after another one of Arianna's fantastic blocks. "Haley, go left!" she shouted, but the team's captain was already running downfield. Dani flung the ball over an attacker's head, avoiding the press, and watched it arc with precision into Haley's outstretched stick. Oregon's attackers spun and raced to catch up with Haley, but she was too fast. Haley passed to Hannah who was running alongside her, and Hannah tossed the ball back as a defender blocked her path. Haley took a long, sweeping strike and whipped the ball above the goalie's head to even the score at 9 all.

After a timeout by Oregon, Isabel faced off with a small girl, bodychecking her as they circled the ball. When Isabel scooped up the ball, Long Arms hustled to where Dani stood by the sideline. Across the field, the other Oregon players followed suit, matching with each of the Trojans as USC took the offensive.

Oregon had switched to one-on-one.

Dani shot a glance at Haley, and the captain nodded. "J-14!" Haley shouted while running ahead of Isabel to the left corner. All of the Trojan attackers and midfielders moved to the edge of the field, drawing the defenders outward and leaving a promising lane for Isabel to drive to the crease.

"Watch 5!" Long Arms shouted across to the teammate guarding Haley.

Isabel trotted forward at the same time Haley sprinted behind the goal in a wide arc toward Dani. The defenders swiveled their heads left and right, bouncing on their toes. One of them broke away from Zoey to step in Isabel's path, so Isabel flung the ball to Zoey.

"Watch 5, watch 5!" Long Arms kept warning as Haley neared Dani, outrunning her defender. Zoey darted forward with the ball as Haley rounded Dani.

"Shit!" Long Arms yelled. She moved from Dani to block Haley, opening the lane for Dani. Zoey was already flinging the ball as Dani launched forward. The other defenders poised to block Zoey's shot, but her aim wasn't at the goal. The defenders' eyes widened as the ball arced perfectly into the small gap where Dani was headed.

*This is for you, Jeremy and Bettie.* Dani took a tremendous leap and whacked the ball from the air into the bottom corner of the goal.

The crowd went wild.

Dani was barely able to register her go-ahead goal before a pair of arms wrapped themselves around her. It was Haley.

"You damn prodigy! You killed it!" she yelled over the roar of the fans and her cheering teammates.

Dani turned and hugged her friend. "I couldn't have done it without you." They squeezed each other tightly before the other girls swarmed them.

When the final horn blared a minute later, there was another deafening roar of the crowd. Dani threw her stick and face guard into the air, whooping as she ran and leaped onto the dog pile covering Winston. Cameras flashed and streamers shot into the air, raining around them in a magnificent display of red and gold.

"We're going to the championship!"

"Oh my god!"

"We did it!"

Dani crawled off her teammates and shared hugs with every girl and coach, even Winston, as they cried and smiled and laughed.

But there was one person she wanted most to see.

Before anyone else could congratulate her, Dani's eyes darted across the crowded field. Amid the jubilant sea of chaotic fans, she saw him. He was smiling proudly and racing through the crowd toward her. Dani pivoted around a family and sprinted to him, leaping into Dustin's arms. He swung her around with a joyful laugh, and it brought her such happiness she thought her heart would burst.

When he set her down, he lowered his head to hers. "I knew you would win it. You never fail to amaze me."

She kissed him as he pulled her tighter, and nothing felt so good in all the world.

"You were awesome!" exclaimed a familiar little girl's voice, and Dani turned from Dustin to see Mel beaming up at her. Dani's breath caught as the ten-year-old closed the gap between them and hugged her tightly. "I want to be as cool as you someday."

Dani laughed and leaned down to kiss her head. "But I want to be as cool as *you* someday! Do me a favor and never change, Mel."

Mel giggled and pulled away.

Rachel came into view behind her daughter and placed an arm on Mel's shoulder, smiling down at her. "She hit a homerun today."

Dani's jaw dropped. "Wow, that's awesome, Mel! Look at you. Coaches are gonna be fighting over you in a few years. I'm your biggest fan. Just let me know where and when you're playing college ball, and I'll be there."

Mel's round, pink cheeks lifted as Dani rubbed her head.

Dani looked up as her roommates approached, along with the Turners. Alisha stepped forward with a slanted smile, hand-in-hand with Noemi. The two of them looked adorable; they wore matching USC T-shirts and red and gold fingernail polish. Dani knew the bright sparkly polish was Noemi's doing. Ever since the two of them came out last year, Alisha seemed to wear brighter colors and smiled more often. Dani couldn't have been happier for her roommate.

"Can you stop being such a show-off?" Alisha teased. "You're only, like, the most talked-about lacrosse player in California."

Dani laughed. She *was* all over USC's sports page, and her scoring stats this season had led her to be one of the top twenty women's lacrosse scorers in the nation. She might have glorified in it a year ago, but she didn't care about it now.

Warren came up behind Alisha, his face drawn in disappointment. "Damn, Dani. Did I miss the cursing you promised, or…"

Dani's jaw dropped. "Warren! You came? I didn't see you!"

He laughed. "Hell, yeah, I came! I told you I would, didn't I?" He shot an accusatory glare at Noemi and Alisha. "These butts didn't save me a seat."

Noemi shrunk into herself, but Alisha rolled her eyes. "We told you the stands fill up fast, and you got here like five minutes after the game started," she grunted.

"Whatever, man," Warren snorted, turning back to Dani as she giggled. "But I didn't know you were such a freakin' beast on the lacrosse field!"

Carolyn nodded, her green eyes dancing. "Dani's awesome!"

"Yeah, she's great!" Emma beamed.

"The best!" Chase agreed.

"She's the *shit*, man!" Jessie slapped her on the shoulder.

Dani gave a nonchalant shrug but couldn't help the smile tugging on her lips. All of her friends' enthusiasm made her ecstatic.

Dr. Turner peered down at her from his tall figure, his friendly eyes dancing. "Great game, Dani! And congrats again on getting accepted to Keck!"

Dani clasped her hands. "Thank you!" Turner had been one of the first people aside from Dustin and her parents she had told about her med school acceptance. "I couldn't have done it without your support." She turned to Dustin, remembering all of their mentor sessions. "Or yours," she added. Her boyfriend had jumped in joy and taken her out to a nice dinner when she'd told him the news in person.

Dustin tugged her against him. "You'd be useless without me."

She whacked his arm and tried to squirm away, but he held her in place and kissed her. She fought for a few seconds before giving up and losing herself in the softness of his lips.

"I hate you and your damn charm," she whispered after he pulled away.

His warm chuckle sent a shiver up her neck. "I can't help my charm when I'm around you. It just sneaks out."

She snorted, and Dr. Turner chuckled behind them. "I'm guessing I made a good mentor recommendation," he noted, and the others laughed softly.

Dani's cheeks heated, and Dustin took the opportunity to swoop in for a showy, sloppy kiss, embarrassing her further. "I'm gonna kill you," she murmured against his mouth.

"Mmm, that's my girl," he purred.

Then she remembered what Arianna had mentioned earlier. She pulled away from him, frowning. "Hey, what do you know about Peter Harrison's dad being investigated?"

He gave an innocent shrug, and she narrowed her eyes, tugging a hand to her hip. His fingers trailed up her back. "I may have done some things. Guess you could call it an early birthday present for you." He ran a hand through his upright bangs. "Remember when I said I ran into Peter at the store last spring? He was dumb enough to spill the beans about his dad trying to get some superstar lacrosse girl kicked off the team."

She gasped. "What?"

A smirk spilled across his face. "Long story short, it ended with me solving things in 'Danica Torres Fashion'—kicking his ass. And not just with a written report. I actually physically kicked his ass."

Dani's jaw dropped, and Dustin's smile spread wider. He pinched her cheek, making her flush.

"Danica."

The low, familiar voice made her bristle against Dustin. She turned away from her boyfriend to see Franc approaching alongside her mom. They had been the last of her support group to join the circle of smiles. In all the excitement, she had almost forgotten they were there; perhaps a cold part of her had learned to shut out the thought of her parents whenever she had reason to celebrate something. The realization sent a jolt of guilt up her spine.

Dani searched her dad's neutral face. His dark mustache twitched beneath the hard ridges of his cheekbones as his dark brown eyes absorbed her. Then his lips pulled upward as he held out his arms, and Dani fell into them. Her mom joined the hug, and the warmth emanating between them seemed to fill a void in Dani's life.

"I am so, *so* damn proud of you, Dani," her dad whispered as they embraced, his voice hitching.

Dani crumbled against him. For all the good an eidetic memory was, she couldn't remember the last time her dad had called her by her preferred name. He probably never had.

"And not just for lacrosse," he went on. He pulled back and met her eyes, and she saw that they were brimming with tears. He smoothed back her sweaty hair. "I'm proud of you for getting into med school, for reporting to HR, and for being the best you that *you* wanted to be. You've kept Jeremy's memory alive in you. *Te quiero mucho.*"

Then Dani's heart did burst. She didn't care that everyone was watching an intimate moment; she pulled her dad back into her arms as the tears spilled down her cheeks. "He is alive in all of us. I love you too, Dad. Love you, Mom."

Angelina leaned close and kissed Dani's forehead, wiping away her daughter's tears. "No matter what happens, we love you, Dani. Always have and always will."

When Dani squeezed her eyes closed, she saw Jeremy's bright face grinning ear-to-ear, his dirty-blond hair and tan, freckled cheeks as clear as if he were standing right in front of her. His hazel eyes twinkled as he watched Dani hug her parents, surrounded by her family, friends and teammates while they celebrated the Trojans' long-awaited entry into the PAC-12 lacrosse championship.

Opening her eyes, she took in all of the happy faces surrounding her and realized everyone who had helped her through the past three years was there now with her—minus two, but it was enough.

Dani's eyes were glassy as she beamed back at her mom and dad, Dustin, her roommates, Warren, Jessie, Dr. Turner, Mel, and Rachel. She was beyond thankful for all of them and their support.

The past year had been anything but easy; after undergoing counseling, she had summoned the courage to report the sickening details of Tanner's assault to USC's human resources department. It turned out that Dani's case against Tanner was one on a long, alarming list of rising sexual assault allegations within USC.

And then there had been PTSD therapy. She'd come to an agreement with Michael, her therapist, about a treatment plan that was free of medication, but his process of identifying triggers had summoned flashbacks and left her shaken. Many times, she had thrashed in her bed and awoken in a cold sweat from the familiar, vivid nightmares about Jeremy's blood-drenched, crippled form.

But the good dreams came too. Dreams about Dustin kissing her at the beach; dreams about Jeremy's radiant smile shining from the audience at her med school graduation; dreams about paving the way for women in the medical field; dreams about red and orange sunsets with her family wrapped tightly in her arms…

And *those* were the dreams worth living for.

# Notes

Dear Reader,

Thank you for taking the time to travel with me along this long, emotional journey. This book covered many heavy topics including racism, social injustice, sexual abuse, and PTSD, and it was not easy to write about these difficult subjects. I understand these topics may have been uncomfortable for some readers, but ultimately, avoiding them would have served an injustice to the year 2020. Moreover, I feel these topics are better understood in a story where they are unexpected, as life often presents heavy material in a similar, unexpected way.

With that said, I touched on these subjects to emphasize that every voice matters, and every person deserves to have their story told. Though I tried to offer a variety of perspectives to help paint a clearer picture of some of these issues, this book is a far way from serving these topics justice. And so, the conversations about race, sexual abuse, and trauma do not end with this book.

As Dani has learned, the path forward is not easy, but we cannot begin to move forward until we reckon with and learn from the past, as well as one another. If we can all open ourselves up to different perspectives, then hopefully this book will have achieved a good purpose.

To begin, I've listed some additional resources below:

**Sexual abuse resources:**

National Sexual Abuse hotline: 1-800-656-4673

www.rainn.org

www.ncbi.nlm.nih.gov

**POC resources:**

www.centerracialjustice.org

www.cinemalatteproductions.com
(production company started by one of my USC friends!)

teens.artsconnection.org

*The Souls of Black Folk*, by W.E.B. du Bois

*13ᵗʰ* (Netflix documentary)

*Throughline* (NPR podcast)

# Acknowledgments

Okay, deep breath. WOW. I cannot believe the crazy chain of events that unfolded over the past year that allowed me to write this book! (This story began as a sort of weekly short story writing activity back during March 2020, but little did I know how much it would expand!) Let me start by saying that as a first-time author (as a film composer, I don't have much business writing books), I had no idea what I was doing (and still don't) and was as excited and awed about the book-writing process as a little child. That being said, I am amazed by the sheer number of people it takes to publish a single book, and I will be forever grateful to every single person who has contributed in some way. There are quite a few people, so bear with me!

First and foremost, I have to thank my brother, Garrett, and my mom and dad for putting up with my hundreds of hours of isolation in my bedroom hunched over my laptop. Thanks for being *moderately* patient and allowing me the time I needed to sculpt this book into a decent piece of… art? Hope? Trash? Yes. Whether this book entertains people or makes readers want to chuck it against a wall, thanks mom and dad.

Thank you to one of my best high school friends and one of the brightest scholars I know, Melissa Morgan. She left me scrupulous notes on every chapter, providing feedback on everything from racism and social injustice to character quirks and med school facts. She should seriously go on *Jeopardy* 'cause she would put those fools to shame with her smarts.

Thanks to my best college friend and fellow USC composer Sonia Coronado Cuesta who gave tremendous feedback, told me how terrible my Spanish translations were, and provided invaluable commentary on the book's social issues. She is also one of the most hard-working, hilarious people I know with whom I've swapped many stories over a glass of wine. Or two. Or three.

Thank you to Jaimie Pangan and Yifan Lin, two of my super talented USC composer friends who offered insightful perspectives of racism in the United States. They both indulged me in lengthy discussions about their experiences, which led to improved character development and backstories.

Thank you to Ruth Amos, the awesome author I consulted for strategies on tackling the self-publishing industry. She answered every one of my long, logistical questions, and finished her responses with a laugh and a huge smile.

My editor, Sarah Collingwood, deserves a HUGE, very special thank you. She went above and beyond what I could ever expect from an editor, and was incredibly patient and kind with my poor writing skills. She offered so much wisdom about little, often unnoticed writing techniques that enhanced my story tenfold. My book never would have been what it is without her expert storytelling advice and profound insight on some of the heavier topics. I'm amazed at the speed with which she read through my story, provided lengthy, detailed comments, and still managed to correct my grammar! I will forever be indebted to you, Sarah!

Thank you to my proofreader, Bryony Leah, who was always quick to respond with her emails, offered friendly words of encouragement, and was an absolute pleasure to work with. She read through my story with record speed and was still able to help with formatting my manuscript, correct my syntax, write invaluable comments with linked sources, and add hundreds of commas!

Thank you to my formatter, Stacey Blake who was prompt, patient, and made my book interior so pretty! I have no idea how you did it and have such a deep appreciation for the meticulous work you do.

Thank you to my book cover artist and good friend, Hylton Mayne, who blew me away with his artistry when I met him at the Disney College program a few years ago. In addition to cover designing, he is also a gifted interior designer and spends his off-time making COVID masks. More importantly, Hylton has always been a deeply thoughtful, humble intellectual who has a knack for capturing the heart and minds of anyone he comes across. Lastly, he provided riveting feedback on the subject of race and its impact on socioeconomic disparities between POCs and their white counterparts.

And finally, thank you to my readers who have stuck with Dani and Dustin's journey to the very end, even when many of you might have been bummed to find out you were reading about the sordid events of 2020. Especially health-care workers. You are the true inspiration for this book! I wish this story was a source of hope for you and anyone else affected by those difficult times. On that note, trauma and sexual abuse are very serious matters, and should anyone need professional help I have provided additional resources on the "Notes" page.

Lastly, if you're still reading this, Malala Yousafzai and Michelle Obama are my heroes, and everyone should try to be like them ☺

# About the Author

**Kara Ford** is a music-making, Disney-loving, puzzle-solving fantasy nerd who can often be found floating on a boat with her head stuck in a book. Kara was always a swirling vortex of bizarre creativity; creating board games, recording homemade videos, composing music, and writing stories were a few of the things that drove her family up the wall. One day she heard Thomas Newman's magical score for *Finding Nemo*, and thus her career in the film scoring industry began…

Kara graduated with a film scoring degree from Berklee College of Music and later a master's degree in Screen Scoring from the University of Southern California (Fight on!). Since then Kara has produced music and recorded piano for shows such as NBC's *The Good Place*, Fox's *Almost Family*, Nickelodeon's *Tiny Christmas*, and Amazon's *Homecoming*. She is grateful to have worked alongside many of Los Angeles's fabulously talented, Grammy-winning musicians (and to have snuck a photo or two with Thomas Newman).

Wait… So how did this book happen? Kara thinks it had something to do with a combination of her passion for storytelling, some inspiration from health-care workers, and a lot of free time during the 2020 quarantine era.

Currently, Kara lives in Southern California where she conducts the Huntington Beach Concert Band and produces music for film and TV. And of course, she always has time for reading, writing, wakeboarding, and other shenanigans.

Connect with Kara at www.karafordmusic.com.